THE SISTERS

NADINE MATHESON

Spectrum Books

First published in Great Britain by Spectrum Books 2015
Copyright © Nadine Matheson 2015

The right of Nadine Matheson to be identified as the Author of the Work has been asserted by her in accordance with the Copyright, Designs and Patents Act 1988.

ALL RIGHTS RESERVED

No part of this publication may be reproduced, stored in a retrieval system, or transmitted, in any form or by any means without the express written permission of Spectrum Books nor be otherwise circulated in any form of binding or cover other than that in which it is published and without a similar condition being imposed on the subsequent purchaser.

All characters in this publication are fictitious and any resemblance to real persons, living or dead is purely coincidental.

www.nadinematheson.com
www.spectrumbooks.co.uk

To my mum and dad
Much love, always x

"If you don't understand how a woman could both love her sister dearly and want to wring her neck at the same time, then you were probably an only child."

Linda Sunshine

ONE

'I'M AFRAID that the prognosis isn't good. It has come back.'

Richard sat back in the chair and finally exhaled the breath that he'd been holding since he'd stepped through the revolving doors of the hospital twenty minutes earlier. It was a different room to the one he'd been in five years ago. That room had been windowless, with a lopsided reprint of Monet's water lilies hanging on a wall that had been wiped clean too many times. The room he was now sitting in was bright with a large window behind Dr. Marcus' head. On the windowsill there sat a pale pink orchid. Someone must have given it to him, thought Richard. Maybe his wife or his daughter. He shifted uncomfortably in his seat.

'Is it my prostate again? I haven't experienced any of the symptoms that I had last time. I mean, I haven't been feeling great but…'

'No. Your prostate is fine,' Dr. Marcus said. 'But your blood tests results have produced the CA19-9 markers that we'd expect to see for pancreatic cancer.'

Richard nodded his head as if he understood but he didn't know what a CA19-9 marker meant. He wasn't even sure what his pancreas did.

'The scans show a mass on your pancreas, but thankfully your liver seems clear.' Richard stared ahead at the pale pink orchid.

'I suppose I better cancel my trial at Chelsea next week,' he finally said.

'Chelsea? I always had you down as an Arsenal man.'

'I am. But Chelsea would pay me more.'

Dr. Marcus laughed. 'If you watched the match over the weekend you might change your mind.'

'The less said about that the better. I was thinking of calling up Wenger and having a word. So what happens now? I mean, how bad is it? Do I need to get a refund on my season ticket?'

Dr. Marcus shook his head. 'First, we need to book you in for a laparoscopy and take a biopsy just to be absolutely sure and to confirm the stage of the cancer. Considering that it hasn't spread to your other organs I suspect that we're dealing with stage two cancer.'

'And then?'

'We'll discuss your options; chemotherapy and maybe surgery. But I want you to understand that this isn't the same as before. We caught the prostate cancer early but pancreatic cancer is different. It's aggressive.'

'So am I dying? I mean technically we're all dying but am I actually dying?'

'Richard, you know that I can't predict exactly what's going to happen to you but if your cancer is advanced, as I suspect it is, then…' Dr. Marcus hesitated. '…there's an 18% chance that you'll still be alive in 12 months. And only a 4% chance that you'll still be alive 5 years after being diagnosed.'

Richard had woken up that morning optimistic that Dr. Marcus would give him the all clear. Instead he left the hospital with confirmation that he was carrying a cancerous growth. Eight months ago he'd retired from his job as an engineer for British Airways. Five months ago his wife, Felicia, had changed his diet and he'd started walking the dog twice a day. This wasn't supposed to happen. Cancer had not been part of his retirement plans. Maybe if he returned to the hospital Dr. Marcus would tell him that there'd been a mistake – that his results had been mixed up with someone else's.

'Fliss. Where are you?' Richard threw his keys into the bowl on the sideboard table, ignoring the unopened post.

'I'm in the guest room. The other one,' Felicia shouted out.

Richard took off his shoes and walked up the newly carpeted stairs to the third floor determined not to stop and look at the family pictures on the wall. The guest room, the other one, was the converted attic that used to belong to his youngest daughter, Emma. Emma always used to joke about installing a stair lift and as he reached the top step, slightly out of breath, he started to think that perhaps it wasn't such a bad idea.

'How can you call it a guest room when it's still got Em's stuff in it?' Richard said as he walked into the room and sat on the double bed that had been stripped and had piles of neatly folded clothes on top of it.

'Stop being so pedantic,' Felicia said as she closed a box and sealed it with brown tape. 'I can't believe that the girl has so many books. She has three copies of Great Expectations. Why would she need three?' She moved past Richard and sat next to him on the bed. 'She should be giving all of this away to charity. I have no idea where she's going to find room in that tiny flat of hers. So tell me. How did it go?'

Richard swallowed. His throat suddenly felt dry and he looked away, unable to look his wife in the eyes.

'What happened? What did they say?' She said it in the tone of voice that she usually reserved for her students who knew the answer but weren't confident about speaking it out loud in case they were wrong.

'Richard,' Felicia said again, more sternly.

'I'm sorry sweetheart. I'm so sorry.'

It seemed the most natural place to be. Sitting at the same kitchen table where they'd made all of their plans. The back door had been left open allowing a gentle breeze to flow into the bright, sun streaked room. It would have been perfect if the news hadn't been so dire. Even the dog had sensed something was wrong and was sitting quietly under the kitchen table, close to Richards's feet. Felicia sat with her right hand under her chin and her left hand on top of Richard's. The tea that she had made them both had long gone cold.

'I thought you'd beaten it. I prayed that you'd beaten it. I was only telling Mary this morning that once you got the all clear we should celebrate. Throw a party or something.'

'A wake is a party,' Richard replied.

'This is not funny.'

'I'm sorry.'

'And stop saying that you're sorry,' Felicia said as her eyes began to fill with tears.

'Fliss. Please don't cry. Come on love.'

'It's just so unfair. I wasn't expecting this. You've only just retired. I'm retiring next year. We've been making plans, Richard, and now this…'

'We can still make plans. They'll just be with co-op funeral-care.'

'Oh for crying out loud.'

He got up, taking the two cups of tea with him and pouring them down the sink. 'Well at least I got to see the last episode of Breaking Bad,' Richard said as he opened the fridge and took out a bottle of Chablis.

'Oh my God. Look nuh! Enough of your jokes.' Despite the fact that she'd lived in London since the age of 12, her Grenadian accent still had a way of escaping from the recesses of her subconscious when she was upset.

'Ok. I'll stop. No more jokes.' He handed her a large glass of wine, which she took without telling him that she thought alcohol was not the answer, and took a large sip.

'Twelve months,' Felicia said as she placed the glass down.

'18% survive for another 12 months and four percent make it to five years.'

'It's hardly any time at all.' Felicia said as she wiped away the tear that had fallen down her cheek. 'No time at all.'

TWO

WHILE RICHARD and Felicia sat at their kitchen table in Greenwich, their eldest daughter, Lucinda, stood in her kitchen, in New York City with a bank statement in her hand.

'As I've already explained to you, I'm not asking for a loan. What I'm asking for is for you to extend my overdraft until the end of the month.'

'Mrs. Morgan, I'm afraid that facility isn't available to you.'

'It's not Mrs. Morgan,' Lucinda said through gritted teeth. 'It's Ms. LeSoeur. How many times do I have to tell you?'

'I'm sorry Ms. LeSoeur but that facility is not available to you.' Lucinda silently counted to ten to stop herself from screaming down the phone. This was the third call that she'd made to HSBC that week. It was hardly her fault that her ex-husband had been late with the alimony cheques for the past two months.

'Ma'am if you were to manage your accounts satisfactorily for at least six months then perhaps…' Lucinda didn't let the so-called relationship manager finish as she ended the call. She wished she had an old-fashioned rotary phone so she could slam it down dramatically. *Manage her accounts satisfactorily.* What did that even mean? Money was deposited into her account and she spent it. For the fifth time that morning she called her ex-husband no longer surprised that it went straight to voicemail.

'Where's my money Paul? How do you expect me to feed your children? You cannot put fresh air in a pot to boil. Call me back.' Lucinda sat down at the breakfast bar unsure of what to do with herself. It was far too early to start drinking. The twins were at school, her best friend was at work and she couldn't afford to *do lunch.* She wasn't used to this lifestyle. Living from alimony cheque to alimony cheque was a life that belonged to someone else.

Her marriage to Paul, one of New York's most successful music producers, had ended in divorce after 12 years. There had been so-called friends who had told her that she was being foolish to go knocking on a divorce lawyer's doors but Lucinda had her pride. There was no way she could have continued to share her life with Paul after she caught him with his latest signing, Alanna De Costa, doing her vocal exercises with Paul's penis in her mouth.

Lucinda picked up a pen and smoothed out the pages of her bank statement onto the kitchen counter. The monthly alimony cheques were $18,500. The monthly mortgage payments were $10,220. On food and clothes she guessed she was spending roughly $5,000 per month. The car payments on the Land Rover Evoque were $1200 per month. Logic told her that there was no way that she should have been calling the bank and begging for an overdraft. The landline in the hallway began to ring but she knew it was probably creditors so she ignored it. A few seconds later her mobile began to ring but she ignored that also. However, after feeling sick to her stomach after going through her bank statement again, she thought that maybe, just maybe Paul had seen the light and decided to call. When she saw the +44 on her screen, the dialling code for the UK, she knew it was unlikely that Paul had emigrated to England and was phoning to let her know that the cheque was in the post. It wasn't a number she recognised and the last thing she was going to do was call back a number she didn't recognise, especially if it meant she had to pay international call rates.

Jessica breathed a sigh of relief when after six rings the phone went straight to voicemail.

'Did you speak to her?' Felicia asked.

'No. There was no answer,' Jessica said as she walked into the kitchen regretting that today of all days she'd found herself in the area and had decided to just pop in. The second that she'd walked into the house she'd known that something was wrong. It was too quiet. Whether it was music being played or the TV being on, her childhood home had always been noisy. To find her parents sitting at the kitchen table barely talking, instantly told her that something was wrong.

'Well, did you leave her a message?'

'Mum, what sort of message did you expect me to leave? Hi sis. I know that we haven't spoken to each other for five years but I just thought you'd like to know that Dad has probably got about 12 months to live.'

'When you put it like that, it's not the greatest message in the world,' Richard said as he emptied the bottle of Chablis into his glass.

'Your father does not have 12 months to live,' Felicia said defiantly. 'That's just the opinion of one man. Nothing is definitive.'

'Then why are you both sitting here getting pissed at two in the afternoon?' Jessica replied as she finally sat down at the table with her parents. 'Sorry. I'm sorry. I didn't mean to say that.'

'Why aren't you at work?' Richard asked, in a poor effort to change the subject.

'I had to see a client. He doesn't live far from here, so I thought...' Jessica's voice trailed off. 'So what exactly did the doctor say?'

'That the markers were there for pancreatic cancer but that they needed to book me in for a laparoscopy and get a biopsy.'

'So mum's right. Nothing is definitive. There's no need for me or anyone else to be calling Lucinda and telling her anything.'

'Your sister has a right to know what's going on.'

'But dad, I don't understand the point of telling her. I mean when's the last time that she called you just to say hello.'

'That doesn't mean she should be left in the dark,' Richard said firmly. Felicia left the table, taking the empty wine bottle and glasses with her. She didn't want to admit out loud that Jessica might have a point. There used to be a time where Lucinda would call every week. She'd mainly speak to her dad, but it'd been months since the last call.

'I'm going to have to go back to work. I don't think you should be saying anything to anyone until we know for sure.'

'We'll see,' Richard replied. 'Don't work too hard.'

Jessica got up and kissed his forehead. 'And you will do as you're told. I love you.' Jessica left her parents still sitting at the kitchen table and let out a deep breath as she closed the front door behind her. She checked her phone to make sure Lucinda hadn't returned the missed call. She would have been more than content to never speak to her sister again as she deleted Lucinda's number from her list of contacts.

'Did we do something wrong?' Felicia asked as she followed Richard into the garden, twisting the single gold band on her ring finger with her thumb. Richard looked down at his feet and noticed that Ares, the dog, had followed him outside and was looking at him expectedly. He picked up the scruffy tennis ball that was nestled amongst the rosebush and threw it across the garden. 'You didn't answer my question,' Felicia said as she stood next to him. 'Did we do something wrong with the girls?'

Richard sighed as he took the ball from Ares and threw it again. 'No, we didn't do anything wrong. We did the best that we could.'

'I know, it's just that Lucinda lives halfway across the world and she never visits.'

'She visited when I was…' Richard was hesitant to say the word. 'She visited last time.'

'That was just coincidence. She didn't visit because you were ill.'

'She still visited.'

'You're always so defensive of her,' Felicia said. 'She doesn't always do the right thing.'

'When does anyone always do the right thing?' said Richard. 'Look, this thing is happening to me. It's in my body. It's mine. It has nothing to do with you or the girls. It has nothing to do with how we chose to raise them or the fact that two of our daughters don't talk to each other, or that our baby Ems is still…' Richard's voice broke. Felicia put her arm around her husband's waist and allowed him to squeeze her into him. She could hear his heart beating through his chest.

'Sometimes I think we got it wrong. That we should never have encouraged them.'

Richard shook his head. 'But Fliss, we didn't encourage them. We never pushed them to become…I don't know. Can you imagine what would have happened to them if we had encouraged them?'

THREE

'AS YOUR best friend I'm more than entitled to tell you that you're infuriating. Have you been living in a bubble for the past 10 years?' Harrie asked as she took the wine glass from Lucinda.

'I'm not living in a bubble. I'm just not obsessed with social bloody media. If it's not on Twitter then its Facebook. If it's not Facebook, then it's quickergram'

'Instagram.'

'Whatever.'

'Lou, honey. Paul is flat broke. He has no money. Nothing. Not a penny,' said Harrie.

'I don't accept that. Paul cannot be broke. He would have told me,' Lucinda said as she poured the remainder of the Shiraz into her own glass and walked out onto the terrace. She took a deep inhale of the warm air, which was scented with the perfume of oriental lilies, and tried to slow down the racing thoughts in her head.

'Lou, Paul has no money. He has filed chapter 11. It's all over Twitter. It was on E! News for crying out loud. How many times do I have to keep telling you to sign up to Twitter?'

'Just because it's on Twitter doesn't make it true,' said Lucinda.

'Stop being a fool,' Harrie said sharply. After being friends for 15 years, Harrie had more than earned her right to speak to Lucinda in this way without fear of retribution or social exclusion.

'See it for yourself, Lou,' Harrie said as she handed her the phone. Lucinda reluctantly took the phone. There was no way that Paul could be bankrupt. He had produced superstars. He had made millions. He had children and responsibilities. As Lucinda scrolled through the Twitter updates and opened the link to the bankruptcy order she had to accept that it was true. As flimsy as it was, her house of cards had fallen.

'How can he owe the IRS $25 million Harrie?' Lucinda asked. 'How the hell does that happen to someone like him? How?' Harrie kicked off her sandals and sat cross-legged on the sun lounger. With the benefit of hindsight Lucinda now wished that she'd followed in Harrie's footsteps. Her husband, John, was a baseball player who knew that he only had about another five years left before he got benched, and when Harrie developed nodules on her vocal cords they both realised that they needed a back-up plan. John had retired early and was now a sports correspondent for ESPN and Harrie was now a respected realtor to New York City's social elite.

'What can I say? Shit happens,' Harrie said.

'Seriously, Harrie is that the best you can do?'

'What is it that your mom says? He was stretching where his hand couldn't reach.'

'God, that's exactly what she'd say. I just don't get it. I don't understand how this could happen to him. To us,' Lucinda said, shaking her head.

'He was living beyond his means. Hell, they all do it. When was the last time that you spoke to him?'

'About three weeks ago but I wasn't too bothered because the twins were still in touch with him until he went incommunicado about a week ago. It was his weekend to have the twins but he cancelled and since then nothing.'

'You've got your own money though. It's not as if you were relying on him to…Oh Lou. Please don't tell me.' Lucinda didn't reply as she took a gulp of wine and looked everywhere instead of meeting her best friend's eyes. 'Lou, you do have your own money don't you?'

'I've been such a fool. I let Paul pay for everything. Even after we got divorced I just let him carry on.'

'Lou, you can't not have anything. That's just…I don't even know what it is. That isn't like you.'

'Harrie I haven't worked since I got here. I mean I made the album and it sold but it wasn't great. Then I just…I just stopped. All I know how to do is sing and I stopped doing that.'

'Oh Lou,' Harrie said softly.

'Don't say it. You don't have to say it,' Lucinda said as she put her glass down and put her head in her hands. Her fingers getting caught in her thick black curls.

'You must have savings,' Harrie said hopefully but Lucinda

shook her head. Harrie sat back on the lounger and said nothing. The only sound was of music coming from the open window of Lucinda's daughter's bedroom.

'You're just going to have to go back to music,' Harrie said once Lucinda had lifted her head.

'That's a ridiculous idea.'

'Why? Lou, you're a singer. Music is what you do. You were meant to be a star.'

Lucinda laughed bitterly. 'Funny. That's exactly the same thing Paul said to me when he first met me: "you were meant to be a star, angel. You don't need your sisters. They need you." What a load of bollocks.'

'So you're saying no?'

'I've tried and we both know how that worked out.'

'But, Lou you said it yourself. All you know how to do is sing.'

'I'm too old.'

'Please. You're 43, not dead. You're just scared of the hard work and the Lucinda that I know never used to be scared of hard work.'

'Yeah, well this Lucinda can't compete with 20-year-olds dancing in their knickers and shaking their arses on MTV. I can't compete. No one wants me, for fucks sake, even my own husband didn't want to work with me. I doubt that I could even get a job singing on Sesame Street.'

'Oh stop feeling sorry for yourself. Things aren't that bad. At least you've got a roof over your head.' Lucinda didn't say a word as she got up and walked back into the house. A few minutes later she returned with a letter in her hand and handed it to Harrie. There were now no more secrets.

'He remortgaged the house a year before we got divorced,' Lucinda said. 'I didn't think anything of it and he'd been making the repayments but now we're behind, well I'm behind two months.'

'Sell the house and go home,' Harrie said as she handed the letter back to Lucinda.

'What? I can't sell this house. It's my home and it's my children's home.'

'Lucinda I'm your friend and I'm telling you that you can't afford to live here. You can't keep up with this lifestyle. Sell the house.'

'And go where?'

'Go back to London…'

'London! You must be out of your mind. I can't just up and leave.'

'Why not? You did it before.'

'That was different. For starters, I was single and I didn't have two children. What sort of life would I be giving them if I just upped and left?'

'What life will you be giving them if you stayed? Life has got to be a lot easier for you over there and at least you have your family.'

'Family? That's a joke. I can't go back, Harrie. What will they think? God, I can see Jessica's face right now.'

'Who gives a shit what they think? What's worse? Going home to family and giving yourself the opportunity to start again or staying here broke and being ridiculed by these people that we call friends? You know what they're like. They'll pounce on you. Vivienne has already called me twice wanting to know if I'd spoken to you because she was *concerned*.'

'Concerned my arse. Vivienne makes Cruella De Ville look like a spokesperson for Peta,' said Lucinda.

Harrie suddenly got up and began to walk down the terrace stairs and into the garden. The sound of laughter and the smoke from a dying barbeque drifted over from Lucinda's neighbours garden. Neighbours that Lucinda had never spoken to.

'The market isn't great but it's getting better,' Harrie said as Lucinda followed her. Both of them walked in the grass in their bare feet.

'What are you talking about?'

'Last month I sold a house down the street for $3.8 million and that house had been remodelled.'

'Harrie, this house is worth at least $5 million.'

'Honey, you will not get $5 million. The market is getting better but it's not that good. Hell, even I'm not that good.'

Lucinda said nothing as she began to consider her dwindling options and then surprised herself with how quickly her brain started working towards an escape plan.

'The car is leased. I could just hand that back over.'

'How much did Paul remortgage the house for?'

'I'm not sure. Two and a half, maybe three million. I'm such an idiot. I didn't even ask why. I just signed the bloody paperwork.' Lucinda stopped walking and sat down on the grass.

Harrie sat down next to her friend and put an arm around her. What she really wanted to do was shake her. She'd seen it happen to women before, including her own mother. They relinquished financial responsibility and settled into their roles not giving a second thought about what they'd do if they were ever left on their own.

'Lou, let me sell this house and go home. I won't even take a commission. What do you call that at home, mate's rates?'

Lucinda laughed at Harrie's feeble attempt at a cockney accent. She could never get it right, no matter how many times she'd taught her.

'I can't ask you to do that. It's your job.'

'You're not asking me. I'm telling you that I'm not taking a commission. Look, if I sell it for 3 and a half that means you can leave here with at least 500 grand in your hands and you've still got the house in London, right? I don't remember you ever saying that you'd sold it.'

'It's in Notting Hill but it's being rented out.'

'That's good news, Lou. At least you've got some money coming in.'

'Harrie, I don't even notice when it comes into my account. I just spend it.'

'Jesus Christ, Lou. You just spend it. What's wrong with you?'

'Harrie, in all seriousness, when you're married to a multi-millionaire you don't really notice the small change anymore and you can't sit there and tell me that's not true.' Harrie didn't reply.

'Well, at least you have somewhere to go when you return home,' Harrie said.

'If I decide to go back home,' Lucinda said stubbornly.

'Half a million dollars is only about three hundred grand in pounds. That's hardly anything.'

'Lou, three hundred grand is better than a kick in the teeth or the alternative. Do you really want to lose your home to the bank and be homeless on the streets? Believe me, it's not so easy to walk these streets when you're wearing five inch Louboutins and dragging a Louis Vuitton luggage set behind you.'

FOUR

JESSICA COULDN'T sleep, which was why she found herself downstairs in the living room watching Moonstruck for the hundredth time at two o'clock in the morning. Her husband, Andrew, hadn't noticed that she wasn't in bed because he still hadn't made it home himself. The last time she'd seen him was when he left the house on Friday morning and shouted over his shoulder that he may be out with clients tonight. To anyone else, the words *"out with clients"* meant dinner or a few drinks but Jessica knew that Andrew was either entertaining in a member's only strip club or in the casino spending her money.

When the closing credits began to roll Jessica realised that the film had finished but she hadn't actually watched any of it. She picked up the remote control and surfed through the channels. She usually avoided the music channels but she pressed the blue button by mistake, which automatically went to her daughter, Lena's, favourite channels. Her stomach flipped when she saw herself, Lucinda and Beatrice on VH1. The video was of footage recorded over twenty years ago and the memories came flooding back.

'Mum, look how young you looked,' Lena said, as she leaned over the back of the sofa.

'Youth is wasted on the young,' Jessica said as she subtly placed the wine glass in her hand behind a cushion.

'Oscar Wilde didn't have 24 hour music channels. Otherwise he'd have been saying something completely different.'

'I doubt that very much.'

'Do you want one?' Lena held a shortbread biscuit under her mum's nose. Jessica shook her head and moved across the sofa to make room for her daughter, who snuggled into her as if the sofa was made for one instead of four.

'You should be in bed, not stuffing your face with biscuits.'

'I was reading and then I got hungry. Anyway it's Friday night, well Saturday morning actually, and I have no place to be,' Lena said as she stuffed another biscuit into her mouth. 'How old were you in that video?'

'Nineteen. Your auntie Bea was seventeen and… Lucinda was twenty.'

'*You electrify me. Lightening flowing through me. I just can't help myself.* I really don't think Auntie Bea should have been singing such explicit lyrics at her age,' Lena said as she began to sing along.

'Our lyrics were hardly explicit, thank you very much,' Jessica said. She was used to hearing Lena singing around the house but hearing her now, singing along to their song, scared her. Nevertheless, she knew the fear was unfounded because Lena had no interest whatsoever in a musical career. Jessica could remember Lena refusing to sit her grade three piano exam despite her dad's insistence, and her violin was still in its case gathering dust in the basement. Her aspirations were to be a journalist or to work in publishing, which was absolutely fine with her. She wanted her daughter as far removed from the music business as humanly possible.

'Even though this video is older than me, it's still good. I don't know why you all stopped. When I told Mr. Hart, my new English teacher that you used to be in Euterpe I thought he was going to drop dead with a heart attack. He went all gooey eyed and said "I loved them."'

'Why were you talking about us in English class?'

Lena rolled her eyes in a way that only the women in her family were able to do. 'Jackson Phillips has a big mouth and found one of your videos on YouTube.'

'It was Lucinda's idea to end it. She wanted to go solo,' Jessica said as she turned the TV off before the video had finished.

'It's that same old story. Like Diana Ross and the Supremes, Beyoncé and Destiny's Child, Geri Halliwell and the Spice Girls, Nicole whatshername and the Pussycat Dolls?' Lena said dramatically.

'How do you go from The Supremes to the Pussycat dolls? Anyway, it's all irrelevant. We were never going to be as big as The Supremes or Destiny's Child for that matter.'

'But mum, you could have been.'

Lena's words rang in Jessica's head as she lay in bed, squeezing her eyes shut, forcing sleep to come. It unnerved her how quickly the anger still overwhelmed her when she allowed herself to think about how callously Lucinda had ended their careers. Jessica liked to think that she'd moved on but deep down inside, it still hurt.

A few hours later, Jessica awoke to the sound of the front door slamming shut. Pilot, the six-month-old puppy started barking, equally disgusted at being woken up so early. The dawn light was starting to seep in from the shutters and she could hear the call of the morning birds. She closed her eyes and turned her back when Andrew came into the bedroom and started taking off his clothes. Jessica felt the bed sink as he lay down and she fought the urge to cough as the smell of sweat, cigar smoke and whiskey emanated from his body. As he rolled over and moved closer to Jessica, there was no escaping the smell of perfume that didn't belong to her.

'Are you awake?' Andrew asked as he began to push the sheets down Jessica's body. He shuffled towards her until she could feel his erection pushing against the back of her thigh. She moved towards the edge of the bed without answering.

'What are you doing? Come here,' Andrew said as he put his arm around her waist and pulled her towards him.

'You can't come in here at four in the morning and expect to have me,' Jessica said as she pulled the sheets back up her body.

'Come on,' Andrew said as he pulled her towards him again and buried his face into her neck, scratching her skin with his stubble. Jessica turned towards him. It was better to let him get on with it. She didn't have the strength to argue with him or, considering he'd probably been with someone else, ask him to wear a condom. She lay there with his weight on top of her and felt sick. Thankfully all of the alcohol he'd consumed meant he didn't last that long and after ten minutes she felt him go limp, pull himself out and roll back to his side of the bed. Jessica got up and went to the ensuite bathroom. She felt unsatisfied both physically and emotionally.

It was times like this that she felt her life was a joke but people openly envied her life and had told her so after she spoke at the Allure magazine Rising Women event the month before. She'd been applauded for being a successful businesswoman, mother and wife, for having it all, yet here she was standing in the bathroom, trying to bring herself to orgasm with the jet setting on the shower. So much for having it all.

FIVE

'BEA, WATCHING you breast feeding is not doing any wonders for my hangover.'

'What are you talking about? You can't even see my...' Beatrice said as she saw the top of her left breast displayed in bright Technicolor on Skype. 'I don't know what you're complaining about. Breastfeeding is perfectly natural. Anyway, you've seen me naked. In fact you've seen me give birth.'

'Don't remind me,' Lucinda said as she took a sip of tea. She didn't see Beatrice's husband Jake walk into the kitchen and promptly turn around again when he saw which sister his wife was talking to.

'So, how are things?' Beatrice asked as she adjusted her top and propped baby Sam up on her lap.

'Aw, look at him. He's such a beautiful baby. I can't wait to meet him.'

'He was a beautiful baby until he woke up at three o'clock this morning and refused to go back to sleep. Hold on a minute. What time is it over there?' Beatrice asked as she looked at the clock on the oven. 'Lou, it must be nearly four in the morning. What on earth are you still doing up?'

'I couldn't sleep.'

'You're always the same when you've been knocking back the Shiraz. You can't handle your drink. You look like shit.'

'You don't look so great yourself sunshine.'

'I've got a three month old and two children under six. What's your excuse?'

'I think I'm still drunk,' Lucinda said as she sighed heavily. 'Anyway, I've got some news that I wanted to share. I thought I might as well tell you now. Strike whilst the iron's hot and all that crap. I'm coming home.'

'You're doing what?'

'I said that I'm coming home. We're coming home.'

'Why? What are you coming back for? A holiday? You're not coming back for good are you?'

'God, so many questions. No, Bea. This isn't a holiday.'

Beatrice leaned in closer to the iPad but it was no use. She'd never been able to read her older sister. There was no way of knowing what was going on behind those eyes of hers.

'New York hasn't been good to me, Bea.' Lucinda said solemnly. Beatrice sat back. She wasn't used to hearing such words from Lucinda. She was the strong one. The impulsive one.

'How do the twins feel about this?' Beatrice asked. 'They're teenagers. They may not want to leave. Coming here for a few weeks on holiday is one thing, but living here…'

'Don't you want us to come back?' Lucinda asked.

'Lou. Don't be silly…I miss you every day. I just don't understand why all of a sudden, after seventeen years, you want to come back here.'

'It'll be good for the kids to be around their family.'

'When do you plan on coming back?' Beatrice asked, ignoring Jake who'd hesitantly wandered back into the kitchen and then ran to the coffee machine.

'As soon as the house is sold, but who knows how long that'll be with the market as it is. I also need to find somewhere to live.'

'Well, you could stay…' Beatrice stopped talking as Jake began frantically waving his hands and mouthing repeatedly, 'No, no, no.'

'Tell Jake to calm down,' Lucinda said laughing. 'I can see his reflection. I wouldn't do that to you. You've got a full house as it is.'

'Mum and dad have loads of room, even more now that Emma has moved out.'

'For God's sake, Bea, we're not a charity case. Anyway, I couldn't possibly go back to living with mum. Not again. I'll just to have rent somewhere until I get back into my own house. I'm not broke.'

Beatrice didn't get a chance to respond as the screen froze and then turned blue.

'Polite as always,' Jake said as he sat next to his wife and placed a cup of coffee in front of her.

'You're so rude,' said Beatrice as she handed a sleeping Sam to his dad and gratefully picked up the cup of coffee.

'How was I supposed to know that she could see me?' Jake said. He let out a loud yawn and wondered if the kitchen worktop would be a comfortable place to rest his head. 'I'm knackered. I don't remember Theo and Issy keeping us up like this.'

'I think that we've blocked it out. Either that or we're still in shock.'

'All I'm asking for is one Sunday morning where we can sleep in, read the papers, have breakfast in bed, then have a nice lunch and go back to bed.'

'You're living in a fantasy land.'

'It's not much to ask for.'

'Maybe in twenty years time, Spidey. I think the best we can hope for is one hours snooze now that this one has dropped off. I'm so glad that dad took the twins yesterday,' Beatrice said as she found herself yawning with an intense desire to return to bed.

'Can you believe that an hour's kip is more appealing than a quickie with you right now?'

'Is there something wrong with the fact that I'm not even offended by that?'

'Nope,' Jake said as he stood up. 'So, Lou is coming over. How long for?'

'Apparently for good,' Beatrice said as she registered the confused look on her husband's face and nodded. She couldn't quite believe it either.

'Nanna I'd like a puppy. Lena has a puppy. Do you think I can get one for my birthday?' Issy said as she sat on the grass with Ares' head on her lap. Felicia watched her granddaughter and felt a stab of sadness at the thought that Richard may never see Issy grow into a young woman. When they first became grandparents it'd scared Richard and Felicia how their very presence made them question their own mortality. How it was entirely possible that they would never see them get married and have children of their own, but to think that Richard may not even live to see his oldest grandchild go to university sent a sharp pain through her heart. It didn't surprise her one bit when Richard had returned home with the twins yesterday afternoon.

'You'll have to ask your mum and dad about that one.'

'Mum and dad will say no but I think it'll be good to have a pet. I can be responsible.' Felicia laughed at the precociousness of Issy as she sat there on the grass, still wearing her Disney princess outfit whilst Richard was on the other side of the garden standing in a goal marked out by the apple tree and a bag of compost, as Theo took another penalty kick. Felicia swallowed hard and blinked back the tears when it occurred to her that Richard might not even see the twin's next birthday.

Richard and Felicia had argued, in hushed voices, at six in the morning, whilst the twins had been asleep in their mother's old bedroom. Felicia had hissed angrily that there was no need to tell the family anything, to worry them unnecessarily until they were sure. Richard said no. It was his body. His disease and he'd be the one who'd decide when and how he'd share it. She said that telling them whilst he carved the Sunday roast was not the time.

'I'm back,' Emma shouted as she shut the front door behind her. Issy, who'd been tasked with checking that the cutlery was clean, ran out of the kitchen at the sound of her Aunt Emma's voice.

'Hello munchkin,' Emma said as she picked up her niece and kissed her on the nose. 'How are you?'

'I'm good. How's your new house and when can I stay over?'

'Well it's actually a flat and it's lovely. You can stay over whenever you like?'

'How about tomorrow?'

'I think you've got school tomorrow, plus I may have to unpack a few more boxes first.'

'More like all of the boxes,' Beatrice said as Emma walked into the kitchen. 'How's it going?'

'Sis, there's so much stuff that I don't know where to put it all.' Emma put her niece down and gave her sister a hug. 'I feel like I haven't seen you all for ages.'

'You haven't. Where have you been hiding?'

'Why don't you ask Jess? She's got me working like a…'

'Watch your mouth,' Jessica said as she handed Emma a glass of wine.

'You wouldn't be out of place in a Victorian workhouse,' Emma said as she took the glass of wine, sipped some, and handed it back. 'That's awful. Where's mum?'

'Upstairs with dad,' Jessica replied as she sat down and opened another bottle of wine so that she wouldn't have to look her younger sister in the eye.

'God, you don't think that they're…'

'Emma, don't be disgusting. Issy is right there,' Beatrice said as she reached out and covered her daughter's ears.

'They're only in their sixties, not dead. Why wouldn't they want to have some afternoon delights?'

'What's an afternoon delight?' Issy asked.

'Never mind. Go and get your dad,' Beatrice said as she ushered her daughter out of the door. 'I really shouldn't, I'm breast feeding,' she said as Jessica handed her a glass of wine.

'Still? Why? He can practically hold the bottle himself,' said Jessica.

'Funny, that's what Lou said this morning.'

'Oh, she's alive is she?' Emma said sarcastically. 'How is she?'

'She's ok, I think,' Beatrice said, not quite sure if she should be the one to spread the great news.

'You think?' Emma asked, instinctively picking up that Beatrice was hiding something. 'What's going on with her?'

'Well, she said that...' Suddenly, Sam's wails rang sharply from the baby monitor on the table. 'I should go and see to him,' Beatrice said as she got up and left the room.

'I wonder what that was all about?' Emma said as she took Beatrice's place at the table.

'I have no idea,' said Jessica.

An hour later the kitchen table was filled with laughter and a hundred different conversations. Andrew's absence had been noted and accepted but that didn't usually stop Jessica from being the most boisterous one at the table. For her, quiet and sullen was unusual.

'Are you alright, sis?' Emma asked as she handed Jessica a bowl of apple crumble and custard.

'I'm fine. Just a bit tired,' Jessica replied. 'Lena and I were up late watching a film.'

'And watching VH1,' Lena said with a smirk on her face as she stuffed her face with apple crumble.

Beatrice groaned. 'Oh God, don't tell me.'

Lena nodded her head, unable to resist the effort not to talk with her mouth full. 'And there you all were, singing and dancing away.'

'Those videos are so embarrassing. I don't know why they still play them.'

'Because you're part of pop culture. I even caught one of the guys at work playing it on YouTube the other day,' said Jake.

'Bloody YouTube,' Jessica muttered under her breath. 'Maybe I can sue them for copyright infringement.'

'Copyright infringement?' Richard said. 'Why would you want to…you know what never mind.'

'Dad, you wouldn't be saying that if you were the one all over the Internet. What video was it?' Beatrice asked. Even though pop stardom had never been her dream, she was still proud of what she'd achieved. She had, after all, lived every teenage girl's dreams.

'Electrify,' Lena said.

'Oh God.'

'Aunt Bea, it was a good video. You, mum and auntie Lou should have a reunion.'

'That's never going to happen,' Emma snorted. 'Pigs will fly before Princess Lucinda comes out of her ivory tower to grace the stage with her presence.'

'Right, what's going on?' Emma asked once Lena had left the kitchen to take her younger cousins into the living room to watch television. She knew that her instincts were right when she saw her parents exchange a nervous glance.

'Jess has hardly said a word all afternoon and you and dad are just being weird.'

'Can you pass the wine please?' Jessica said to Jake. Jake did what he was told. He'd learnt a very long time ago that when a LeSoeur drama was about to begin that it was best to sit back and say as little as possible.

'Oh my God, you're getting divorced aren't you? Either that or you're about to tell us that you've spent all our inheritance money,' Emma said.

'Don't be so ridiculous,' Felicia said as she got up and closed the kitchen door. 'But there is something.'

Beatrice stared at Jessica, who was sitting opposite her, aware that she didn't seem to be on high alert like the others. She looked like she'd already given up.

Richard, for some reason, decided that he should stand up. He pushed back his chair, stood up and said, 'It has come back. The cancer is back.' He then sat back down.

Jake spoke first. 'Shit.'

'What do you mean, it's back? You've been in remission for five years. It can't come back,' said Emma.

'Technically, it's not back. It's in a different place now, so I suppose that it's a new cancer.'

'Dad, I can't believe that you're making jokes. Why do you always make jokes?' Beatrice said.

'Where is it?' asked Jake.

'My pancreas.'

'Well you've beaten it before. You'll beat it again.' At that point, as tears began to fall down Jessica's face, Emma and Beatrice came to the same realisation.

'You already knew?' Beatrice said to Jessica.

'It wasn't for me to…' said Jessica.

Emma began to shout. 'You already knew and we're only finding out now. How long have you known?'

'Keep your voice down, Emma,' Felicia snapped. 'We only found out last week.'

'A week. What's wrong with you?'

'Emma. Stop. We didn't plan it this way.'

'I can't believe this. Nothing's changed. You're still keeping secrets.'

'Well, I take it that Lucinda doesn't know?' Beatrice said. 'What were you planning to do? Send her a press release.'

'I tried to call her actually,' Jessica said, feeling the need to defend herself. 'But no, she doesn't know.'

'You tried to call her? What happened? Did you fall and bang your head?' Emma said before storming out of the kitchen.

'Mum was standing over me. I didn't have much choice.'

'Well, you can tell her yourself when you see her. She's coming home,' Beatrice said as she chased after Emma.

Felicia winced at the sound of the front door being slammed.

'Well, I think that went rather well. Another glass Jake?' Richard said as he picked up the bottle of wine.

'I think that we'll need something stronger,' Jake said as he looked across at Jessica who was staring at him as though his wife had just announced that the anti-Christ had been invited to dinner.

SIX

'WHAT WE'RE you thinking? What possessed you to tell them?'

'You didn't say it was supposed to be a secret,' Beatrice replied as she stood in front of a mirror and rubbed serum into her face. She massaged, as instructed, the bags under her eyes and willed her ashy, almond toned skin to glow. The morning had been frantic. Jake had forgotten to set his alarm clock and Sam had slept longer than usual, which had meant they'd all overslept and the twins had been late for school. Beatrice almost didn't recognise herself. Her hair was pulled into a rough ponytail and she could see her grey streak trying to push through. She had no idea when she'd last been to the hairdressers.

'Are you still there?' asked Lucinda. If she'd been the one paying for this call she'd have put the phone down ages ago.

'Yes, I'm still here. Look, I'm sorry. It just came out.'

'It just came out? How? Don't tell me, mum asked you to pass the potatoes and you replied *oh by the way, Lou is moving back home.*'

'It was apple crumble actually.'

'Oh for fuck's sake.'

'And custard. I'd have preferred ice-cream myself.'

'Beatrice!' Lucinda shouted as she slumped back into her own bed.

'What do you want me to say? I'm sorry. It came out. I didn't know mum was going to call you.'

'It's our mother. What did you think she was going to do? She called me at three o'clock in the morning. Who does that? The least you could have done was warn me.'

'What else did she have to say?' Beatrice asked. She had no intention of telling Lucinda the news about their father. It wasn't her news to give.

'Not much really. Wanted to know why I was moving back, why she was the last to know, why I didn't tell her myself.'

'Hmmm, that's the pot calling the kettle black,' Beatrice said under her breath.

'What did you say?'

'Oh nothing. So what did you say to her?'

'I told her to call me back at a sensible time. Honestly, the woman does my head in.'

'She's just concerned. You have to admit that it's all a bit out of the blue.'

Beatrice threw the phone and herself onto the bed and stared up at the ceiling. There was a large crack, which Jake had promised that he'd get his mate to look at. That was almost a year ago. She looked at that crack and thought that it summed up the effect that Lucinda's return was going to have when she finally turned up at the arrivals gate. If she was forced to admit it she was looking forward to her big sister coming home. She'd forgotten how isolating it was being at home. Yes, she was on maternity leave and it was important to be at home with her child during these early months; but the reality of the situation was that once the twins were at school, Jake had gone to work and the baby was down, it was just her. Well, her and Jeremy Kyle, Loose Women and the Real Housewives. She was lonely. The few friends she had were busy with work and so were her own sisters. Maybe, just maybe this would be a good time for Lucinda to come home. At least then she wouldn't have to be alone.

Emma hadn't slept well at all. After she'd calmed down, she stayed for as long as she could, in the vain hope that her dad would tell her there had been a mistake. It was almost midnight when her mum had kicked her out of the house. Emma had given up on getting any decent sleep and had found herself opening up the doors to the agency at 6.30am. The only other person in the office was the stationery deliveryman who was currently unloading boxes in the reception area. Not for the first time, Emma wondered why Jessica had even bothered to start the agency in the first place. If it'd been her, Emma would have followed Lucinda's lead and gone solo or carried on as a duet with Beatrice. It wasn't as if they didn't have the talent to do it and the record companies had thrown money at them after Lucinda left, but Jessica, out of pride and stubbornness had refused.

'What are you doing here so early?' Jessica said as she walked in an hour later and stopped at the kitchen balancing a large box of croissants and an assortment of pastries in her hands, whilst her blue Celine bag hung from the crook of her arm. Emma put down her cup of coffee and took the box from her sister.

'I had a crappy night. I kept thinking about Dad and then about Lou and all of the things I have to sort out in the flat.'

'I'm sorry I didn't tell you,' Jessica said as she sat down.

'It's done now. That's not to say that I'm not still pissed about it.'

'I don't blame you. If it makes you feel better, I only found out by accident. It wasn't as though I was the first person they called.'

'Have you spoken to Lou yet?' Emma asked.

'I've absolutely no intention of speaking to her.'

'But she's going to know that something is up. I mean when's the last time that she's had a missed call from you.'

'She doesn't have my number so she wouldn't be any the wiser. Anyway, Bea can deal with her.'

'I wonder why she's suddenly upping sticks and coming back here?' Emma said as she picked at a cinnamon and pecan whirl. 'She hasn't been back here for ages.'

'Lucinda only ever thinks about herself. She's a selfish cow and I promise you that whatever her reason for coming here, it's for her own benefit.'

'Even so…'

'Ems, our priority at this time is Dad. Not Lucinda. In fact

I'm going to make some calls this morning and try and get him an appointment with a private consultant. I'm not accepting what's happening to him. Not with those rubbish odds.'

'Good because I'm not doing this on my own. Not like last time.' Emma had been living at home when their father was first diagnosed with cancer. She'd driven him to his chemo sessions and sat with him whilst he received his treatment. She'd also been with him when he'd spend his days either being sick or sitting in the garden playing chess. But that was five years ago. She wasn't sure if she had the strength to go through it all again. Not after everything that she had been through.

* * * *

'If I was you, I'd accept the offer,' Harrie said.

'But they're only offering $3.4million, Harrie. It's like I'm paying them to take my house. It's daylight fucking robbery.'

'Lou, use your head. A cash buyer doesn't come along every day. So you lose a hundred grand. So what? Just take the money and run.'

Lucinda was sitting in her best friend's office, resisting the urge to run out screaming. Instead, she opened up her Smythson organiser and looked at her calculations. $3.4 million. After taxes, credit card debts, mortgage repayments, and converting dollars into sterling she'd be left with just over £200,000. Her stomach turned in response. To most people £200,000 would be a godsend and it'd relieve them of their troubles. But she wasn't most people and £200,000 wasn't enough for her. She couldn't survive on that and the thought terrified her. She'd already spent her morning on the other side of the city being ripped off as she sold her collection of watches and jewellery. She felt humiliated even though she'd always been told by her grandmother that *gold was money* and would always help you if you were stuck. The owner of the jewellers had told her that she'd be surprised who had been in his shop over the last few years. That didn't make her feel any better, and she'd felt even worse when she'd made arrangements to withdraw money from the twins' college fund. Even though she kept telling herself that they wouldn't have a future if she didn't make these hard decisions, it still sickened her.

'Fine, I'll take the offer,' Lucinda said. As she sat back in the leather armchair, she didn't wipe away the tears that began to fall down her face.

'Oh honey, don't cry,' Harrie said as she grabbed a handful of tissues from the box on her desk and handed them to Lucinda. 'I don't want you to go, Lou. I'm going to miss you like crazy but I wouldn't be a true friend if I told you to stay.'

* * * *

'Are you out of your mind?'

'Oi, watch your mouth,' Lucinda said sharply.

'Watch my mouth?' Katelyn said matching her mother's south London accent perfectly. 'You make a decision that affects me and then you tell me to watch my mouth. You're so selfish. Tell her Reece.' Her twin brother didn't say a word as he sat chewing his food staring straight ahead. 'I don't want to move. What about my friends? What about my life? You're ruining my life,' Katelyn said as she gave her brother a dirty look.

'I'm ruining your life?' Lucinda couldn't help the laughter that escaped from her mouth as the memory of saying the same thing to her own mum, more than once, hit her. Lucinda didn't try and stop her daughter as she stormed out of the kitchen and ran to her bedroom. The sound of Katelyn's bedroom door slamming shut reverberated around the house.

'That's a bit dramatic,' Reece said as he spooned another serving of lasagne onto his plate.

'Don't you have anything to say?' Reece and Katelyn were twins but were complete opposites on the personality spectrum. Katelyn had the fiery and stubborn temperament of her mother and her aunt Jessica, whilst Reece was calm and measured but with the calculating qualities of his father.

'I know that dad is bankrupt. In fact everyone knows. You could have just told us. You didn't have to keep it a secret.'

'You haven't had any problems, have you? I mean at school.'

Reece shook his head. 'Mackenzie Fuller's dad was made bankrupt last Christmas. He lost all his money in a ponzi scheme. Cameron's parents filed for bankruptcy last month.'

'How do you know all this?'

'People talk and Twitter. Too many people trying to live large, mom. What's that thing that grandpa says? Oh yeah, champagne lifestyle with lemonade money,' Reece said as he chuckled to himself.

'We weren't trying to live large. Your dad just made a few

mistakes. Look, there's nothing wrong with a fresh start. A move will be good for us.'

'But mom, we can have a fresh start in New York. We don't have to leave the country.'

'Baby. I wish we could but it can't work.'

'It can't work for you but what about me and Katie?' Reece said.

There were times when Lucinda wondered when exactly her son had morphed from a 14-year-old boy into a 40-year-old man.

'Reece, believe me. I've thought of everything that I could do but it's not going to happen.'

'You could get a job.'

Lucinda stared at her son and was starting to wish that he'd just thrown a tantrum like his sister instead of asking sensible questions. The thought of being part of someone's payroll sent a shiver down her spine. She hadn't been technically employed since 1990 and that had just been a part-time job in Our Price. Other than holding a microphone and being able to hit a high E, what skills did she have? God, she'd been such a fool.

'Look, I'll make a deal with you,' Lucinda said. 'We'll give it six months and if it doesn't work then we'll come home.'

'But what are you going to do for six months?' Reece asked as he picked up the last piece of garlic bread and pushed it into his mouth. Lucinda's mouth kicked into gear before her brain did.

'I'm going to make an album. I've already started talking to a really amazing producer and your aunt Jessica has started looking at other projects for me.'

Reece slowly chewed his garlic bread as he watched his mother. Even though Jessica kept in touch with her niece and nephew he couldn't remember the last time that his mum had spoken to his aunt.

'Auntie Jess is going to help you?'

'Of course she is. Why wouldn't she? We're sisters.'

SEVEN

'DON'T GET me wrong, you've never been much of a looker but you don't look ill,' Stephen said as he took a sip of his pint.

'Shut up,' Richard replied. It was late afternoon and they almost had the Greenwich Tavern to themselves now that the lunch crowd had returned to work and the tourists had left to continue getting lost. 'How's the book going?' Richard asked.

'Slowly, badly. It's crap. I might burn it.'

'If it's crap then I don't want to be in it.'

'Oh that's a shame because you're the main character. So go on. Tell me. How's Fliss taking it?' Stephen asked.

'Badly. She wants a second opinion but I know that it's in there.'

'But it couldn't hurt mate. I mean, they could have made a mistake. Look at Dominic?'

'Who?'

'You know Dominic. He used to work at *The Guardian* with me. Looked like Scrooge McDuck.'

'Oh him. I remember him. Didn't he leave his wife for a

man?'

'A 25-year-old no less. He had testicular cancer and was told it was terminal. He was given six months and that was eight years ago.'

'So you're telling me that I'm going to live for another eight years and then I'm going to declare my undying love for you.'

'Well, I've always loved your eyes,' Stephen said. They both laughed. It was hard to believe that these were two men in their sixties as they sat there sniggering like a pair of schoolboys. They'd been friends for nearly 50 years and had first met in a school playground in Queens Park.

Richard was 15-years-old and had just arrived from Grenada. Despite wearing a woolly coat and a thick school scarf that concealed half his face he stood shivering at the back of the playground. Whilst he tried to figure out how he was going to convince his parents to put him on the first plane back to Grenada he noticed that a gang of sixth form boys were determined to beat the shit out of a mouthy Irish 15-year-old boy. Richard had stepped in and had spent the rest of the week in detention with Stephen. They'd been best friends ever since and were now brother-in-laws after Stephen had finally, after years of relentlessly pursuing her, married Richard's twin sister, Rachel.

'In case you're wondering,' Stephen said, 'I haven't said anything to Rachel. I didn't want to tell her over the phone. But saying that I'm surprised she doesn't know already; considering your twin telepathy.'

'Let her enjoy her holiday. You can tell her when she gets

back.'

'I hardly call a yoga retreat a holiday. How boring is that? Anyway, are you sure you don't want to tell her yourself?'

'What's the point? If I tell her she'll only end up having a go at you for not telling her earlier.' Stephen nodded and downed half of his pint in one go. To this day, Richard had never met anyone who could drink a pint quicker than Stephen.

'You should have gone with her,' Richard said with a grin on his face. 'A bit of chanting, downward facing dog and green tea would have done wonders for you.'

'Shut up. Are you sure that you're feeling ok?' Stephen said as he noticed that Richard seemed to struggling with his pint and had only managed to drink a third of it. Richard sighed and his shoulders slumped.

'I feel tired. I don't have much of an appetite but other than that I feel fine. I don't feel as though I've got an expiration date over my head.'

'What are you doing?' said Richard when he noticed that Stephen had stopped listening and was tapping away on his phone.

'Looking up the pancreas on Wikipedia. I ain't got a clue what it does.'

'Ask Fliss, she'll tell you. By the time I'm in the ground she'll be an expert.'

The men left the pub without Richard finishing his pint. They walked through the park. It was another exceptionally hot day. It briefly occurred to Richard that he might not see the end of the summer as they walked past couples, families and groups of friends spread out on the grass enjoying the heat wave.

'To my beloved husband Edward. Who loved to sit here and watch the birds,' Stephen read out the dedication on a brass plaque on the bench. 'Watch the birds, my arse? I bet you any money that her beloved Edward wasn't sitting here watching the pigeons,' Stephen said as he pointed at a couple of girls dressed in identical uniforms of denim shorts and camisoles, watching a group of boys playing football.

'I'm worried about the girls. Not those girls but my girls,' Richard said.

Stephen knew that the relationship between his nieces was strained and it saddened him. He was as close to them as their own father and had joined Felicia as the voices of descent when Lucinda had excitedly told them on a Sunday afternoon that she planned to go into the music business. At the time, Stephen had been the Arts Editor for *The Guardian* and had been to more than his fair share of showbiz parties. He was reluctant for his nieces to be exposed to the harsh realities of the music world, even worse be exploited professionally and physically.

'How did they take it?'

'You know what they're like, Emma and Jessica are just like their mum; determined to find a cure, get a second opinion. Bea has been calling every other day to make sure that I'm ok.'

'And Lou?'

'Nothing.'

'That's not like her.'

'Well to be fair, I haven't told her.'

'You can't do that, Rick. Just because she's living in New York doesn't mean…'

'I was going to tell her. I tried to call her on Friday, well Jessica tried.'

'Jessica?'

'Don't get too excited. They didn't speak but according to Bea, Lou is coming back. For good.'

'Lou is coming back? Why?'

'I don't know all the details. Bea mentioned it on Sunday and Fliss spoke to her this morning but from the sounds of things I don't think it was much of a conversation. And then Fliss got pissed at me when I told her not to tell Lou about…about the cancer. Anyway, the most important thing is that she's coming home. I'll be able to spend time with her, Katelyn and Reece.'

'You hope. Remember they're teenagers. I love Lucinda as if she's my own and technically as her godfather I'm supposed to look after her when you finally kick the bucket.'

'She's 43. I don't know how she's going to feel moving in with you and you tell her that it's past her bedtime. Look, all I've got left is hope, Steve. Who knows how long I really have left? All I really want is for the girls to sort themselves out. They're sisters but they're so disjointed. God alone knows why Lou and Jessica haven't spoken for years. Emma and Lou have no relationship to speak off, and Bea just tries to keep the peace. I want them to sort it out. They don't have to be the best of friends but they need to forgive each other and move on. I want them to remember that they're sisters. Life is too short.'

'Are you avoiding me?' Lucinda said as she walked into the garden with her iPad and sat down on the grass. It was the only part of her three-storey town house, which did not look like a bombsite. She had to decide between spending what little money she had on shipping her family's belongings over to London or paying for a removal company to pack for her. So she'd decided to do it herself and was regretting every minute of it, which was why she felt she deserved to have a large vodka and tonic at 12.30 in the afternoon.

'Why would you think that I'm avoiding you?' said Beatrice as she slumped into the armchair. She shifted herself as she pulled out one of Sam's toys from behind her back.

'You haven't picked up my Skype calls, you've ignored my texts…'

'Lou, I…'

'You haven't replied to my emails.'

'Lou, I haven't been avoiding you,' Beatrice lied.

'I can tell when you're lying, little sister,' Lucinda said as she leaned into the camera, causing the screen to be filled with her large brown eyes.

'I've just had a lot on. It's not easy you know, with the twins and the baby.'

'Get a nanny. That's what they're there for.' Beatrice felt herself bristling.

'Why would I want a nanny? And what would I do? Watch her whilst she looks after my children. I'm more than capable Lou.'

'It was just a suggestion. You don't have to bite my head off. Anyway, you'll be going back to work soon.'

'Lou, this is England. We don't have to go back to work as soon as we push the baby out. I've got a few months to go yet. You never know, I may even take the whole year out.'

'Yeah right. You wouldn't last five minutes. Look Bea, I have a list of things that I need you to do for me. I should have all of my stuff packed up by the end of the week.'

'Don't you have people to do that for you?'

'Of course I have people.' The lie ran smoothly from Lucinda's mouth. 'They're just having a break. Anyway, I'm going to send you an email right now.'

'Lou, I really don't think that I'm going to have the time to…'

'Well, if you really don't want to help me, I can always ask dad. He hasn't got anything else to do now that he's retired. In fact I'll give him a call.'

'No, don't do that,' Beatrice said as she almost jumped out of her seat.

'Why not?' Beatrice didn't say, because dad has cancer, he may not have long to live and no one has told you yet, and she bit the inside of her cheek to stop herself from speaking.

'Have you frozen? Bea?'

'No. I'm here. Look, mum has got dad doing a hundred and one things at the moment, so send me the email and I'll do it.'

'Thank you sis, you're a star. I've got to go. Love you.'

She never ceased to amaze her and Beatrice wasn't at all shocked with the speed at which Lucinda was moving. Lucinda was a force to be reckoned with when she was determined to get things done. In the space of a month she'd sold her house, enrolled the twins in a private school, and found a house to rent in London as her own home was still occupied by tenants. When Beatrice read Lucinda's email, the reality of what was happening hit home. Lucinda really was coming home.

EIGHT

'ARE YOU sure you don't want to leave Sam with me?' Jake asked as he tried to put a clean t-shirt on Sam, who was vigorously wriggling around in a determined effort not to be fully clothed whilst his mum stood in front of the floor length mirror critically watching her image. 'God, I look awful,' Beatrice groaned as she leaned closer into the mirror and pulled the skin back on her face.

'You look fine.'

'Fine? Is that the best you could come up with?'

'No, of course not. You're beautiful,' Jake said shaking his head, already knowing that he couldn't win no matter what he said.

'Beautiful? Have you seen me lately? I smell of eau de toilette baby sick and I'm still wearing maternity jeans. Beautiful, my arse.'

'Yes. Done it,' Jake said as he successfully got Sam into his t-shirt, lifted him up and smelt him. 'You never answered me, are you sure you don't want to leave him with me? I don't mind.'

'No it's fine. I'll take him. Lou doesn't land until 11am and you've got your meeting at 2pm. The last thing you want is to be stuck if the flight is delayed or I'm stuck in traffic. You know what it's like driving back from Heathrow.'

'If you're sure.'

'Of course I'm sure. You've worked too hard. Opportunities like this don't come along every day and Lou would kill me if she knew.'

'Yeah, she would,' Jake said with a grin. Even though Lucinda was being a pain in the arse at the moment, his sister-in-law had always been supportive and had encouraged him to set up on his own. *"What's the point of life if you're not prepared to take a risk?"* That's the last thing she'd said to him when he and Beatrice had gone to New York for his cousin's wedding two years ago. Jake was a comic book artist who'd spent the last three years developing his own graphic novel series and was now in talks to develop the novels into an animated series. He'd rather be spending the time with his children or working instead of dealing with the stress of having a series in development and sitting through endless meetings. Watching Jake with their youngest son, Beatrice thought back to how different her life had been before she met him. She was only 23 when Lucinda had unceremoniously broken up the group and was still struggling to come to terms with the fact that she hadn't seen it coming. She'd always thought that she and Lucinda were close; that they were all close. The break up shouldn't have even bothered her because she never wanted to be in the group in the first place. When Lucinda and Jessica were singing into hairbrushes with a towel wrapped around their head and devotedly practicing their dance moves in front of Top of the Pops on a Thursday night she'd been sitting behind the sofa reading The Color Purple for the one hundredth time. She'd read incessantly and fancied herself as the next Alice Walker or Jane Austen, not Madonna. Whilst she was upstairs in the bedroom she shared with Emma, studying Pride and Prejudice for A-Level English, she could hear Lucinda, Jessica and their friend Charmaine, practicing downstairs. Lucinda and Jessica's voices would float smoothly through the house and Beatrice would catch herself singing along, instinctively knowing that Charmaine's low and gravelly voice simply did not fit. Lucinda knew this too and didn't bat an eyelid when Charmaine decided to meet her boyfriend instead of turning up to the studio on a rainy Saturday afternoon in March to record a demo.

'Lulu, how many times have I told you? I don't want to be in your band,' Beatrice said as she walked up the stairs into her bedroom, closely followed by Lucinda and Jessica. She sat down at her desk and swivelled her chair round so that her back was to her sisters.

'I'm not asking you to be in the band, I just want you to sing backup on the demo tape.'

'I have exams. I don't have time to sing backup.'

'They're just mocks. They don't count,' Lucinda said as she sat down on Emma's bed with the bright pink Barbie duvet cover.

'Of course they count. Just because you don't care about having an education doesn't mean...'

'For God's sake, I'm not asking you to give up school and start

singing in pubs, I'm just asking you to do us a favour.'

'Where's Charmaine? I thought that she was your backup.' Lucinda rolled her eyes and gave a "you talk to her" look to Jessica.

'She's dumped us for her boyfriend. So, we're stuck,' Jessica said. 'Bea, we wouldn't ask you if we wasn't desperate. You know how hard Lulu has been working. She's worked her arse off in order to save enough money to hire the studio. If we don't go now, then she'll lose all of that money. Please will you come? Please,' Jessica said as she put her arms around Beatrice.

'Come on Bea, we're sisters. Please. Just this once,' Lucinda said.

'I don't know your songs,' Beatrice said as she put a bookmark in the middle of Pride and Prejudice and closed the book.

'Oh yes you do,' Lucinda said with a smile. 'I've heard you.'

'Babe you look…' Jake thought carefully as he watched Beatrice fiddling with her hair in the car mirror. 'You look perfect.'

'Liar. Lou will get off that plane looking glamorous and I'll look like a…'

'A beautiful woman who has just had a baby, has two lunatic five-year-olds and a husband who loves her.'

Beatrice smiled at Jake as he finished strapping their son into the car seat. They'd first met outside the Forbidden Planet comic book shop on Charing Cross Road. To say they met was not entirely correct. She'd been walking past carrying a Frappuccino when Jake had walked out of Forbidden Planet with his nose deep in a comic book as he bumped into her.

He'd stood there in horror as the brown coffee stain spread across her pristine cream silk blouse. Beatrice had been too stunned to speak whilst Jake repeatedly apologised. He'd promised to pay for the dry cleaning and Beatrice had given him the address of where she worked. A week later he turned up at her office with a Selfridge's gift voucher and a Frappuccino. They'd been together ever since.

'I still don't understand why you're picking her up. Doesn't she have people? I mean, how are you going to fit her, two kids, a baby and all of their stuff in our car?'

'We'll manage. Anyway, I doubt she has bought much luggage with her. She shipped most of her stuff over.'

'This is Lou we're talking about. It's not as if she'll be flying economy with a 23 kilo weight restriction.'

Lucinda checked again that her seatbelt was firmly fastened as the plane began its descent into London, Heathrow. For as long as she could remember she hated flying. Her brain just couldn't comprehend the physics of how this great metal beast of a plane managed to stay in the air. "Lift, force and drag. It's called fluid dynamics or the Bernoulli's principle. The plane's wing is shaped and tilted so that the air moving over it travels faster than the air moving underneath." Richard loved flying and had tried to explain more than once how it all worked. It was odd how she'd suddenly remembered that. It was 10.30am, but her watch was still on New York time, 5.30am. She looked across at Reece who was sitting upright but still out cold, tucked up in his blanket, with his bright red headphones still on his head. The boy had an amazing ability to sleep anywhere, whereas Katelyn was wide-awake with her forehead pressed firmly against the window as she watched London beneath her. Lucinda tried to focus on the film but finally gave in and turned her own head. The mid morning sun was spreading across London like butter on a freshly toasted crumpet and the River Thames snaked through the centre of the city. It'd been so long since she'd seen the city and she could clearly see London split in two. The South East where it had all began for her, the o2 arena, Docklands, which had expanded since she'd last seen it, and the West where she was heading. Her stomach flipped. She blamed it on the plane making its descent but she knew it was really anxiety as the plane flew over the South Bank with the London Eye standing resolute like an archer's target. She copied her daughter and pressed her face closer to the window as she spotted the iconic Wembley Stadium. When she'd left London the two ivory towers were still standing amongst the red and grey rooftops. Now an impressive arch stood in its place. Still iconic but not quite the same.

Beatrice stood with Sam in her arms watching the arrivals of Terminal 5. It was noisy and chaotic with families and friends screaming, laughing and crying as they reunited with each other. She could see the drivers standing, expressionless with their white placards waiting for their passengers. It brought back memories of a time when they'd returned home after a successful promotional tour of Japan. Beatrice had never seen so many people in one place and it took her a few moments to realise that the crowd of teenagers and photographers were screaming their names. 'Lucinda, over here. Jessica, Jessica…Auntie Bea. Auntie Bea.'

Beatrice was snapped out of her daydream by the voice. She saw Katelyn run through the waiting crowds closely followed by a trolley filled with four large suitcases being pushed by Reece, and his mother behind him pushing a second trolley with another four suitcases. Beatrice groaned and kicked herself for believing that Lucinda would be travelling lightly. She found a gap in the crowd and watched as Katelyn excitedly made her way over and didn't stop her as she threw her arms around her much to the bemusement of Sam who found himself squashed between them. Beatrice felt the overwhelming love radiate from Katelyn as she hugged her aunt.

'So you missed me then,' Beatrice said laughing.

'Of course I did. I always do. Ooh let me look at the baby. Can I hold him?' Katelyn said excitedly.

Beatrice removed Sam from his sling and handed him to his older cousin who immediately began to cover him in kisses, which caused him to gurgle happily.

'Oh my God Reece. Look at you.' Reece stood awkwardly by the luggage with his red headphones still on his head. 'For God's sake you're not too big to give me a hug,' Beatrice said as she hugged her nephew. She burst out laughing as he hugged her even tighter. When she let go of Reece she finally took a look at her sister. Lucinda had been determined to arrive in London in style and without giving any credence to the fact that she was now on a very strict budget. She hadn't even blinked when she booked the flights and took out her debit card to pay the princely sum of $20,000 for their business class seats, but she'd made sure that the pyjamas and luxury toiletries that British Airways provided were tucked away in their hand luggage. Beatrice took a close look at her sister standing statuesque in her Alexander McQueen heels, black skinny jeans and a turquoise blazer. There was no sign that Lucinda had just spent nearly 8 hours on an overnight flight. Her dark chocolate skin, with barely a line on it was freshly made-up and her hair was pulled back into a sleek ponytail. Beatrice's left hand immediately went to own hair and she began a feeble attempt to smooth down the split ends. There was no sign at all that this was a woman running away from financial disaster. 'So, are you just going to stand there gawping,' Lucinda said with a smile. Beatrice walked over and hugged her sister.

'You look amazing, sis. How was your flight?'

'It wasn't bad. I have no idea how people endure that flight in economy. You're not here on your own are you?' said Lucinda. 'You've got a driver, right?'

'Er, no. It's just me. I didn't think you'd be coming with all of this stuff. I thought that you shipped nearly everything over.'

'Bea, do you have any idea how much it costs to literally ship an entire brownstone townhouse from New York to London?' Beatrice didn't answer because she didn't know.

'Lou. I can't take all of this. I mean have the Range Rover, but it can't take all this.'

'Don't panic. I'm only joking. I've arranged for our luggage to be picked up and taken to the house.'

'Thank God for that. It's good to see you, Lou.'

'You too. It's been too long,' Lucinda said as she took the baby from Katelyn. 'He's very cute. Come on lets go.' Beatrice had no choice but to follow as Lucinda walked ahead leaving her with the luggage.

They'd been on the motorway for fifteen minutes before the excited chatter in the back seat died down completely. Beatrice glimpsed into the rear-view mirror and could see that her niece, nephew and son had all fallen asleep. She thought that Lucinda was asleep also but as she turned her head she could see that she was just staring solemnly out of the window.

'Well at least you didn't come back to pouring rain,' said Beatrice as she took out a pair of sunglasses from the glove compartment and put them on. 'I still can't believe that you're back at all.'

Lucinda didn't reply and smiled because she couldn't quite believe it either. The last six weeks had been so frantic that she hadn't had the chance to fully absorb the enormity of what was actually happening to her and her family. She was uprooting herself and her children from everything they knew all because she'd taken her eyes off the ball. Laziness, complacency and arrogance had got her into this position. 'It's a shame that dad couldn't come with you. You know how much he loves a trip to the airport,' said Lucinda.

'Well it's a good thing that he didn't. He'd have had to sit on the roof,' Beatrice replied.

They made small talk for the rest of the journey. Beatrice spoke about the twins and how much she despised her local mothers and babies group. Noticeably she didn't mention Jessica and Lucinda didn't ask. As Beatrice drove along the A40 and turned onto the Westway it wasn't lost on Lucinda just how much London had changed, but also how much it had stayed the same. As they turned into the familiarity of Notting Hill and drove past the large white Victorian houses the anxiety Lucinda had felt when the plane had begun its final descent overtook her again. As much as London had changed, Lucinda knew that it had an uncanny ability to show you for who you really were.

NINE

'DAD,' LUCINDA said as she fell into her father's arms.

'My girl,' Richard held onto her tightly. This was his star. He knew that you weren't supposed to have favourites but she was his first.

'Come on. Come in. We don't want to be making a spectacle of ourselves on the doorstep.'

They stepped into the house and Lucinda closed the door behind him. They looked at each other and the same thought passed through their minds. *You've lost weight*. Though neither said it, Lucinda and Richard could recognise the signs in each other. That there was something inside, eating away in both of them. Richard followed Lucinda through the hallway, which still smelt of paint and varnish. It was all very white. Even the oak floors, which had been stripped back, had been whitewashed. He felt as though he was walking through a hospital corridor.

'So, dad what would you like to drink? Tea, coffee, juice or…' Lucinda stopped abruptly as she turned and looked again at her father, watching intensely the new lines on his face. 'Or perhaps you'd like something to eat?'

'No. I had a big breakfast,' Richard lied as he followed her into the kitchen. The kitchen had been recently decorated and fitted out with new white gloss cabinets, granite worktops and the largest cooker that Richard had ever seen. It wouldn't have surprised him if the cooker had cost more than his own car.

'It's not really you is it?' Richard said as he walked around, opening and closing the cupboard doors and running his hand across the worktops. Lucinda smiled as she watched her dad.

'I'm not a fan of all this white gloss and steel. It's a bit too cold for my liking. Definitely not my taste. But it's only for a time until I can get back into my own house.'

'When will that be?'

'Not sure yet. I was planning to go to the estate agents this afternoon but there's so much to sort out first.'

'Well, take it easy. You only got back yesterday. You've got plenty of time. I can't believe that it's been so long since I've seen you, Lulu. I only ever see your head on Skype.'

'What can I say? Thank god for Skype. How's mum? I called her cell phone but…'

'Oh, she's moderating exams today so she probably won't get round to calling you back until lunchtime. Anyway, where are my grandchildren?'

'Sleeping. They're still adjusting to the time difference. You know dad, you didn't have to come over. I was planning on coming later once the kids had emerged from their cave.'

'Don't be silly. I wanted to see you. It's been too long and you don't have a car.'

'God, don't remind me. I need to sort that out too.

Anyway, we would have got a taxi.'

'A taxi? You shouldn't have to waste your money on taxis.'

'Dad, money isn't a problem. Now. Are you sure that you don't want something to drink? Thank God for Bea and online shopping that I've actually got something to offer you.' She knew she was rambling but she'd never been able to lie to her father so if he asked her she'd just blame it on jetlag.

'Fine, do you have any green tea?'

'Green tea? You?'

'Yes green tea? Don't look so surprised.'

'You're the man who puts three sugars in his tea and calls a Mars bar breakfast.'

'It's your mother's idea. She's got me on a detox health kick.'

'Health kick? You won't last a week. Is this why you've lost so much weight? Detox?'

'Yes, something like that,' Richard said quietly. She decided against pushing it any further and busied herself with making the tea whilst her dad wandered into the garden. He had so much running through his mind. The appointment with the oncologist the day before had left him with more questions than answers.

'Have you spoken to your sisters?' Richard asked as he took the hot cup of tea from Lucinda. It was quiet in the garden. The only sounds came from an occasional car driving past and Vanessa Feltz's voice drifting out of the radio from her neighbour's kitchen window. It was nice. Peaceful. A time for confessions.

'Not all of them. Bea picked us up from the airport. Emma left me a message this morning.'

'And Jess?' Richard asked as he took a sip of his tea, knowing full well that there was a better chance of José Morhinio walking through the front door than there was of Lucinda and Jessica having a civil conversation.

'No dad. I haven't heard from her.'

'Life is too short to waste it on petty fights, but nevertheless, Lulu I'm happy to see you.'

Lucinda smiled. He almost sang her nickname, Lulu. When Jessica had stopped calling her Lulu, it'd hurt. 'Anyway, I really am pleased that you've come home. I won't ask why you've come back. I'll leave those questions to your mother.'

'Dad, you know what I'm like.'

'You're impulsive.'

'Exactly and a change is as good as a holiday.'

'A holiday means that you go back at some point. You bought a one way ticket.'

'Actually, it was a return. They're cheaper.'

'Do the twins know that it's a return ticket?'

'You're having a laugh aren't you? Katelyn would be on the first plane back. All that I've heard from her for the past month is that I'm ruining her life.'

Richard laughed. 'She obviously takes after you then. When you were fourteen you were constantly telling your mother and I that we were ruining your life.'

'Sorry about that. Thankfully, Reece isn't too bad. His life solely consists of either sitting in his room with his headphones on or playing Black Ops online on his x-box so it doesn't make a difference if his friends are in London or back home in New York.'

'And Paul? How is he? I heard about his …problems.'

'Paul is experiencing some financial difficulty but you know him. He'll bounce back.'

'But he's still able to support the kids? I mean financially, not just take them out to McDonalds.'

'Dad, he's doing his bit. Don't worry. We wouldn't be here if there were problems.'

'Baby girl, I'll always worry about you.'

'What about you? Should I be worrying about you?' Lucinda asked, because he didn't look like a man who was enjoying retirement. She'd always known her dad to be a strong and able man but she wasn't blind. She'd watched how he moved, and how he spoke, and she knew. 'It's come back, hasn't it?'

Richard nodded, not at all surprised that Lucinda had been able to see through the smokescreen.

'Oh God. Where?'

'Pancreas this time. Stage two. It's all confirmed,' Richard said as he leaned back in the rattan chair and took a deep breath. Every time he said it, he tried to absorb the enormity of what he was saying, but it felt good that he'd told her. Good that he didn't have to hold it in anymore. The one good thing about his Lulu was that she wasn't one for amateur dramatics. She could deal with this.

'What does stage two mean?'

'It means that it hasn't spread to my lymph nodes yet but it's large.'

'So, what are your options?' Lucinda asked as she took hold of her dad's hand.

'My consultant wants me to start chemotherapy. If I don't, they're saying that I probably won't make it until Christmas. If I have the chemo and maybe surgery then there's an 18% chance that I'll last another 12 months.'

'18%. Are you sure?' Lucinda said, as she pulled back, shocked at the numbers.

'I know. I'd get better odds with the lottery.' Lucinda gave her dad a sharp look.

'Sorry love.'

'How long have you known?'

'About six weeks.'

'And do the others know?' As Richard nodded, the call from the unknown UK number that Lucinda had received suddenly made sense.

'And you've had a second opinion. Actually don't even answer that, mum would have made sure that you got a second opinion. So what do you want to do?'

This is what Richard wanted to hear and he knew there was a reason why he wanted to speak to Lucinda alone. She was impulsive but she was also practical and, at times, could put her feelings to one side and ask the question "What do you want?"

Richard looked into his daughter's eyes, which were an exact copy of his. 'What I want is for you and your sisters to sort out this nonsense.'

'Dad, stop it. This isn't about me or Jess, Emma or Bea. We're grownups, we'll sort it.' She'd only been back 24 hours and her south London lilt had returned. 'I'm asking about you.' Lucinda took a breath and asked the question that she knew her mother and her sisters would never ask her father.

'Do you want to do this? Do you want the treatment?'

'I don't think that I do, Lulu. It was horrible the last time. I hated feeling so dependent on your mum. The stress. The pain. The headaches. It was too much. It was horrible for Emma too, having to live with that.'

'But you got through it.'

'I did. But it was just in one place then. Nice and contained and manageable in my prostate. But now it's in my pancreas, one of the worse places that you can get it. I can't take the pain as it is. I don't let your mum know how bad it is.'

Lucinda watched the anxiety and the pressure of what he was going through etched in her dad's face. She wasn't going to cry. It wasn't what her dad would want to see. Instead she'd do what she did best. Throw money at the problem.

'What about a private consultant. Harley Street. I could pay.'

'No. You're not paying for anything.'

'But you don't have any private health insurance, so let me…'

'Lulu, this isn't America. I don't need private healthcare. There's nothing wrong with the NHS. They didn't kill me last time.'

'It wasn't in your pancreas last time,' Lucinda replied. 'Have you told mum any of this? How you're feeling.'

'Not yet.'

'Are you going to?'

Richard took a sip of his tea and looked at his daughter. 'What do you think?'

TEN

12 September 1997

'Are you sleeping with him?' Jessica asked as she stood watching Lucinda pack. She had no intention of helping her. There was no way that she was going to help her after what she'd just done to them.

'Why would you assume that I'm sleeping with him?'

'Because you don't get something for nothing, Lou. As if he's going to whisk you off to the States and promise you the world without getting something in return.'

'And you think what he wants is between my legs? Don't judge me by your standards,' said Lucinda as she slammed her suitcase shut. She looked around her bedroom for anything else that she needed to pack. It was odd she had bought the house almost a year ago but it hadn't been lived in. Euterpe had been touring and recording continuously for the past two years. There had been no time for her to lay down roots, let alone pick curtains and carpets. She was simply moving clothes and shoes from one end of the room into her luggage. She'd never even had time to place anything on hangers. Lucinda couldn't look at Jessica. She'd convinced herself *that Jessica would understand, that they'd never shared the same dreams but inside she knew that wasn't true.*

'You must be delusional to think that I'd support you. How could I support you with this?' Jessica shouted. She had been tolerant up to now hoping that Lucinda would turn around and say it was just a joke. That she wasn't really leaving the group.

'Do you know how hard it is to break into the States, Lou? Do you know how many bands and singers have tried and failed but we did it. Us. You, Beatrice and me. Euterpe. The three of us. Together.'

Beatrice didn't say anything as she entered the bedroom. She could hear the shouting from downstairs. In fact it had been non-stop shouting since Lucinda had made her grand announcement just two weeks after they'd won a Brit Award for Best British Group. Now they were no longer a group.

'Why don't we all just sit down and talk about this calmly?' Beatrice said as she closed the bedroom door and sat on the king-size bed.

'Bea. There's nothing to talk about. I've made up my mind.'

'Lulu, of course there's something to talk about. You can't make a decision like this without discussing it with us.'

'I don't know why you're wasting your breath,' Jessica said as she joined Beatrice on the bed. 'But there are people we're responsible for. What about Sal and everything that he's done? What about the record company?'

'What about them? We're out of contract. They're not losing any money and there's no reason why they can't sign just the two of you. Euterpe doesn't need three of us.'

'But Euterpe is the three of us. It always has been. If you do *this Lou then that's it. There's no more Euterpe. It's over,' Jessica said coldly.* Lucinda stared back at her sister, suddenly consumed with anger. She stopped what she was doing and turned and faced her two sisters. Beatrice felt herself lean back in an effort to distance herself from Lucinda's fury. She had never seen her eyes so dark and so angry before.

'Why do you even care?' shouted Lucinda. 'You never really wanted this and Beatrice definitely didn't want it. I had to practically break her arm just to get her to sing back up. This was my dream, no one else's and you all made it because of me. No one else. Me.'

'You're a selfish bitch,' Jessica said, her voice calm but cold. 'I can't believe that we're even sisters.'

ELEVEN

JESSICA WAS glad, that like politics, the celebrity world had entered its very own silly season. If they weren't falling out of nightclubs with people they shouldn't be with, then they were assaulting the paparazzi or harassing Jessica's staff about the lack of exposure they were getting despite attending every envelope opening ceremony. It was Jessica's ex husband, Christopher, who had convinced her to start the agency. He knew that his wife wasn't made for a life of domesticity. Coincidentally, that same week Jessica had received a call from her ex backing singer, Jackson. Unfortunately for him he'd been caught in flagrante with the lead singer of Utopia; who were the boy band of the moment. After years of being the tabloid's favourite bad girl, Jessica knew how to handle the media.

'Have you been listening to a word I said?' Christopher said as he popped the last California sushi roll into his mouth.

Jessica looked up at Christopher with a blank face.

'I might as well have been speaking to the wall,'

Christopher said.

'I'm sorry. I just want to sort out this stuff for Jo Lucas's people. I met them for lunch yesterday and they're already breathing down my neck.'

'I doubt that you ate anything,' Christopher said under his breath as he wiped his hands with a napkin and threw it into the bin. There weren't many couples that would still be able to work together after a divorce but Christopher and Jessica had managed it.

'Sorry, what did you say?' asked Jessica as she reached for her phone, which had been vibrating on her desk. She looked at the name on the screen and pressed decline.

'I was saying that we're going to have to make some changes. We're running out of space as it is. The staff are being run ragged…Jess, will you pay attention.'

'Oh for fuck's sake,' Jessica said as she read the email that had just arrived. 'I can't believe that he's gone and done it again.'

'Who are you talking about?'

'Sebastian Roycliff. He's just been arrested for possession of drugs. He's such a fucking idiot. He's supposed to be opening at the Donmar tonight.'

Christopher sighed. 'Well, he won't be opening anywhere if we don't find someone to represent him, but Jess, where is your head at?'

'Just give me a minute,' Jessica said as she walked out of the office and went to speak to Angelique, a statuesque blonde who nodded efficiently at what Jessica had to say before grabbing her bag and leaving the office.

'It's so bloody hot in here,' Jessica said as she turned off the malfunctioning air conditioning unit and opened the window. 'I hate the summer. It's as if the heat turns everyone mad. Right, I'm here. What were you saying?'

'If you'd been listening to me I was saying that Wendy is going to be on annual leave for the next two weeks from Wednesday, and then Anthony, Michelle and Natalie have got leave scheduled.'

'I wouldn't have authorised for them to have leave all at the same time.'

'Well, you have, and our diary is absolutely manic – and that's not even taking into account the inevitable last minute crisis that always lands at our door.'

'How was I supposed to know that bloody Sebastian was going to go on a mini drug run? Where is Wendy anyway?' Christopher picked up his iPad and opened his calendar. He was a good looking man and Jessica wondered why he was still single.

'Wendy is currently swanning around Westfield for the launch of that X-Box football game and then she has a meeting with the directors of that eco-design company who I swear are only about 12-years-old.'

'I thought that you were doing the X-box thing,' Jessica said, as she took out a bottle of water from the mini cooler behind her desk.

'No Jess,' Christopher said, clearly exasperated. 'We had a meeting last Monday and talked about all of this stuff. Your mind is clearly elsewhere. What's happening? Is everything alright at home?'

'Of course everything is alright at home,' Jessica said rather too quickly and forcefully.

'Well something is going on. This isn't like you. Talk to me,' Christopher said softly.

'It's dad. He's…well he's not well again and the signs aren't good, Chris.'

'Oh fuck, Jess, I'm so sorry. If there's anything that I can do.'

Jessica waved her hand at Christopher and indicated for him to sit back down as he tried to get up and reach her. The irony wasn't lost on her that she was telling her ex husband about her father's condition whilst her current husband still remained clueless.

'And Lucinda is back in town.'

'Ah,' Christopher said as he leaned back in his chair.

'I'm surprised that Lena hasn't told you considering she worships the ground that woman walks on.'

'Lena hasn't told me anything, other than that she wants me to pay for her to go on a film course in New York in July.'

Jessica rolled her eyes. 'I've already told her that's out of the question. She's too young.'

'So did Lulu come back because of your dad?' Jessica stiffened with the ease and familiarity of Christopher saying her name.

'When has she ever done anything for other people? It's just good timing on her part. Who knows what she's up to but I'll tell you one thing, she definitely didn't come back for dad.'

'How long is she here for?'

'According to Bea she's back for good.'

'Wow. Lulu is back in town. It'd be good to see her. It will be good for you to see her too. Just make sure there aren't any sharp objects around.'

'You're not funny Christopher.'

He laughed as he got up from the chair. 'Lulu is back in town,' Christopher repeated as he walked out of the office. If Jessica didn't know better she could have sworn that there was a spring in his step.

'Maybe grandma has gone out,' Katelyn said without lifting her eyes from her mobile phone.

'No, she's in,' Lucinda said as she lifted up the brass knocker but stopped as the front door jolted open.

'Grandma,' Katelyn screamed as she ducked under her own mother's arm and straight into Felicia's arms.

'Bon Jé,' Felicia said. Lucinda couldn't help but smile as she saw how much her mother's face lit up when she saw her grandchildren.

'We thought you'd gone out,' said Katelyn.

'No, I was in the kitchen and the radio was on and bloody hell, Reece, you've shot up.' Reece gave his grandmother a hug, squeezing her so tight that she felt herself lift off the ground.

'I'm not that tall. I'm only 6ft 1.' They all stood in the hallway as Felicia watched the two grandchildren who she hadn't seen for over five years.

'God, I could cry but I won't.' Lucinda closed the front door and faced her mother.

'Hi mum.'

'You left it too long,' Felicia said as she hugged her daughter. Lucinda hugged her back but couldn't help feeling that her mother didn't have the same warmth in her voice that she had for her grandchildren.

'So, you're home,' said Felicia as she sat at the kitchen table with Lucinda. Her mother had clearly been busy that morning as the kitchen counter was filled with plates of Lucinda's favourite foods: aubergine and saltfish, fishcakes and fried bakes.

'Your aunt Sarah came back from Grenada last week and brought back cocoa. I've even got some mangoes and avocados left if you want to take some home. God knows how the woman got it all through customs,' Felicia said as she poured Lucinda a cup of steaming hot cocoa tea from the blue teapot. Lucinda took a sip and sighed satisfactorily as the smooth, rich, sweet Grenadian chocolate hit the back of her tongue.

'That tastes so good. I can't remember the last time I had this.'

'Maybe if you came home a bit more often you wouldn't miss it so much,' Felicia said as she poured two more cups of cocoa tea then went out to the garden and handed them both to Katelyn and Reece who were playing with the dog. The dog had never had so much attention. Lucinda didn't say anything as she ripped apart a fishcake and dipped it into the homemade pepper sauce.

'How's work?' Lucinda asked when her mum returned to the table.

'Busy,' Felicia replied as she stirred her tea. 'But at least it's exam time so it's not too long to go. I suppose that it's good timing really.'

'Because of dad.'

'Of course because of your dad. I mean, it's just me and him here now.'

'Well, I'm here. You don't have to do it all on your own.'

'You're here,' Felicia repeated slowly as if she was about to embark on a complex lecture about the economic structure of ancient Greece. 'But how long are you here for before your feet start itching again?'

'Mum, don't do this. I'm here. The children are here. It's a new start for all of us.'

'I'm not doing anything, my dear.'

'Of course you're not, mum,' Lucinda said with a wry smile. 'Look. I'm not going to get itchy feet. I'm not going to uproot the kids just because I don't like the water pressure in my shower and I'm not going to leave whilst dad is…' Lucinda stopped talking as Reece and Katelyn came back into the kitchen with their empty cups.

'When is grandad coming back?' Reece said as he picked up a handful of fishcakes and began to demolish them.

'He's only at your auntie Beatrice's house so he should be back soon. So, are you happy to be here?' Felicia said as she stroked Katelyn's hair in the exact same way that she used to do with Lucinda.

'Give me a week and I'll let you know,' Katelyn said as she began to pull apart a fried-bake.

'You sound just like your mother when she was your age.' Lucinda rolled her eyes but she supposed she should have been grateful because she knew that her mother was being quite restrained.

'So, what's your plan?' Felicia asked Lucinda.

'Mom is going to make a new album,' Reece answered for his mum, which surprised Lucinda, as she didn't think he could hear anything through those headphones, which seemed permanently attached to his head.

'You're doing what?' Felicia said.

'And Auntie Jessica is going to help her.' Lucinda gave her son a look, which he recognised as the sign to shut up.

'You've spoken to your sister?'

'Not yet.' Felicia watched Lucinda. She knew there was a lot more going on here even though Richard had tried to dismiss any talk of there being more to Lucinda's return.

'So, you're going to record again? Perform?'

'Well, one step at a time, mum. But yes that's the plan.'

'Why?'

'What do you mean why? It's what I do. It's what I'm good at.'

'But you haven't done it for so long. Things have changed.'

'Mum things haven't changed that much, people still appreciate good music. I still have fans out there.'

'Where?' Katelyn said.

'Don't be facety,' Lucinda said sharply. 'I have friends and it'll work.'

'Well for your sake I hope it does because *crapo smokes yuh pipe* if it doesn't,' Felicia said as she picked up a fishcake, dipped it in the pepper sauce and ate it.

If Lucinda didn't know better, she could have sworn that her mother had already gone to Ladbrokes and placed a bet on her comeback being an epic failure.

TWELVE

LUCINDA WAS still reeling from her mum's comment when she got home.

"*Crapo smoke your pipe if it doesn't.*" She'd always hated it when her mother said that. As though it would kill her to wish her luck instead of telling her that she was about to enter Dante's inferno. It infuriated her.

The first two attempts to call Jessica had failed and Lucinda wondered when Jessica had changed her phone number, completely cutting her sister out of her life. She had to call Beatrice in the end, to get Jessica's number. As she dialled the number she crossed her fingers and said a quick prayer that Jessica would pick up.

'Jessica. It's me. It's Lou.'

Lucinda heard Jessica take a sharp inhale of breath and could almost hear the words running through Jessica's brain. *Why didn't I press decline.* Instead Jessica said, 'I don't usually pick up unknown numbers but I thought you were someone else.'

'Sorry, I'm afraid that you've got me. How are you?'

'I'm fine. How are the kids?'

'They're good. They're looking forward to seeing you,' Lucinda answered as she sat down on the stairs and waited for Jessica to stop behaving as though she was talking to a debt collector.

'As I said, I'm busy. So what do you want?' Jessica said coldly.

'I've spoken to dad. He's told me,' Lucinda said ignoring the sternness in Jessica's voice. She knew her sister didn't want to talk to her but to hear that forcefully in her voice, hurt.

'Has he told the twins?'

'No, he wants to tell them all together. I don't know, safety in numbers I suppose.'

'So now you know I really don't see what there is for us to talk about.'

'Look, Jess,' Lucinda said finally having enough of Jessica's obtuseness. 'We're going to have to see each other at some point. So I was thinking that if you were free tonight, we could meet. Just the two of us.'

'Fine,' Jessica replied but only in an effort to get Lucinda off the phone.

'Good. Hopefully we can finally sort things out once and for all.'

'Let's get one thing clear, Lucinda. The only thing that we have to talk about is dad. Other than that, there's absolutely nothing that we have to sort out.'

Jessica leaned her head against the shower wall and let the water beat down on her shoulders. She'd been standing there for at least fifteen minutes with the hot water scalding her skin, trying to forget about the conversation with Lucinda. It'd annoyed her that Lucinda had sounded so confident and sure of herself, as if the past five years hadn't happened. It pissed her off.

She finally stepped out of the shower, took the shower cap of her head and wrapped the thick cream towel around her. She wondered why she was even making the effort as she wiped the condensation off the bathroom mirror and watched her reflection. She was only 42 yet she felt much older.

'What are you doing home?' Jessica said as she instinctively pulled her towel around her tighter at the sound of Andrew's voice, surprised to see him standing in the doorway. His blue Hermes tie was slightly askew and he had the tell tale signs in his eyes that he was recovering from a liquid lunch.

'It's a bit early for you isn't it?' he continued. 'I mean, it's only 7pm, don't tell me you actually came home to cook dinner for your husband?'

'You can talk. I can't remember the last time that you came home before midnight. I should call the newspapers and let them know,' Jessica replied as she squeezed past him and walked over to the chest of drawers in the bedroom.

'Don't get too excited. I only came to change my shirt,' Andrew said as he walked up behind Jessica, put his arms around her and began to remove her towel. 'But that doesn't mean I haven't got time for a quickie.'

'Well, I haven't,' she said as she pulled back the towel,

grabbed her underwear from the drawer, went back into the bathroom and locked the door.

'What is with you? I'm not asking for an eighteen hour tantric session,' Andrew shouted.

Jessica put on her underwear and silently cursed that she hadn't picked up the rest of her clothes, which were laid out on the bed. After she'd finished moisturising, she did her make-up and then plugged in the straighteners. 'Not bad,' she said as she looked at herself when she was done. She turned sideways and viewed her profile in the mirror. She couldn't remember the last time that she'd even stepped on the elliptical machine or used the rowing machine in the basement. It wasn't as though she'd got fat; she was running around like a blue arsed fly for 18 hours a day but she was definitely slacking. Her once firm stomach had softened and she could see the delicate folds of love handles beginning to form.

Neither Jessica nor Andrew said anything to each other as she came back into the bedroom and continued getting dressed.

'You look nice,' Andrew finally said as Jessica put on her Jimmy Choo flats and picked up her bag from the bed. She didn't reply as her phone beeped to let her know that her cab was arriving in 10 minutes. She still hadn't told him that Lucinda was back or that she was meeting her that evening. It wasn't as if they had all sat down at the dining table and had anything resembling a family dinner where they would discuss what was happening in their lives. She looked into his eyes and wondered what his reaction would be, whether he'd be surprised or pleased. If he had any brains at all, he'd remain indifferent.

'I'm meeting Lucinda.' She watched his eyes intently for a reaction.

'Oh she's back is she,' Andrew said as he got up and opened the bedroom door. 'Tell her that I said hello.' There was no mistaking the slight flicker of a smile before he walked out the door. She stood in the room for a few minutes waiting for the sound of the front door being opened and closed before she went downstairs. The house was deadly quiet as Lena, who was in the middle of her GCSE exams, was locked in her bedroom studying. She resisted the urge to pick up the dog, who was asleep in his bed, just so she could receive a few minutes of genuine affection from him.

Jessica walked down the stairs into the living room and looked through the shutters to see the familiar black and white sign of the Addison Lee cab waiting on her road, with its hazard lights rhythmically flashing away. Jessica walked into the kitchen, opened the wine cooler and pulled out a bottle of vodka. 'Just a quick one,' she said as she filled a tumbler with vodka.

Lucinda had been waiting for forty-five minutes and was now on her second glass of Pinot Noir. The restaurant was busy for a Wednesday night and Lucinda had quite enjoyed watching couples, friends and business acquaintances sitting at the other tables. She wondered what their conversations were about. She'd always been intrigued by people and she revelled in the fact that when she sang she could effectively be in control of the emotions people felt, although she felt repelled when someone had told her more than once that they'd conceived their child whilst listening to a Euterpe song.

As she sat and waited she was more than aware of a few heads turning to look at her and then those heads frantically met together as the same question passed between their lips. 'Is it her? I'm sure it's her.'

Jessica looked at her watch again. She was late and she knew that Lucinda was the sort of woman who prided herself on always being on time or annoyingly early. That was one thing that they'd always say about Euterpe. Thanks to Lucinda they had never left anyone waiting. As the cab turned into Smithfield's market Jessica asked herself again why she had agreed to have dinner with Lucinda. Dinner was a commitment. Dinner meant sitting at a table for a minimum of two hours. She should have suggested a pub. She should have suggested an underground car park. Anything but dinner.

Lucinda felt her before she saw her. Sal, their old manager, had always said that the LeSoeur sisters walked with a presence. She'd never quite understood what it meant when people said that but when she turned her neck and saw how the conversations stalled and the waiters stopped when Jessica walked through the room she now knew exactly what he meant. Lucinda stood up as Jessica approached unsure of what the etiquette was now that they'd technically been estranged. Should she hug her, kiss her on the cheek? She couldn't just shake her hand and then sit down. That would be ridiculous. The decision was made for her when Jessica walked up to the table and immediately sat down.

'You look well,' Jessica said, and annoyingly she actually meant it. Lucinda looked beautiful as she stood there and had caused more than a few heads to turn as she walked into the restaurant earlier wearing a floral print Chloe dress and gold sandals.

'My hair is a mess. The humidity is playing havoc with it,' Lucinda said as she pushed back the black curls from her forehead and sat down with the sad realisation that there wasn't going to be the onslaught of screams and hugs that normally went on between sisters who hardly saw each other.

'I like your hair. I always thought that you had the right face for short hair,' Lucinda said as she indicated for the waiter to come over. 'You're ok with red aren't you?'

'Yes, that's fine thanks. How are the twins?'

'They're good. I think that they're pleased that we're here. It's good for them to be here with their family. I mean look at Lena and Katelyn. They've hardly got off the phone with each other.'

Jessica couldn't deny that. Lena didn't have any siblings and she often thought that she was being selfish by not having any other children. To rob her of the sisterly relationship that she had with Katelyn would be cruel. Both sisters breathed a sigh of relief as the waiter came over and took their orders.

'So, why are you back?' Jessica asked as soon as the waiter left.

'Talk about getting straight to the point.'

'Well there's not much point in trying to make small talk. So, why are you back?'

Lucinda said nothing as she lifted her wine glass to her lips. As she did so, it occurred to Jessica that Lucinda was giving her the same look that her clients did when they were being challenged and they didn't like it.

'I outgrew New York.'

'You outgrew it?'

'Yes, I outgrew it and anyway, London is a better environment for the twins.'

'So, you're doing this for them. It's not all about you.'

'Not everything is about me.'

'Could have fooled me,' Jessica said bitterly. They'd both decided not to have starters and had moved straight to their main course. They'd both chosen a medium rare fillet steak however whilst Lucinda went for a smoked garlic hollandaise sauce, Jessica chose a classic peppercorn sauce.

'And now that daddy is sick,' Lucinda said ignoring Jessica's tone, 'It's more important that we're close by.'

'That would be a first. You barely called when he was ill the first time around and now you sit here telling me that you want to be with the family. Do me a favour Lucinda…'

'I did what I could. I mean for Christ sakes, he wasn't dying and I was going through a divorce. I couldn't just pick up and leave.'

'You're just making excuses.' Lucinda took a bite of her steak and as she ate she tried to focus on the bigger picture. She wanted something from her sister and she wasn't going to get it if she fought back, but she was the oldest and she wasn't used to just sitting back.

'Jess as much as I prefer arguing with you as opposed to

sitting here in complete silence I didn't invite you out to dinner to spend the entire evening being a target board for all of your digs.'

'If that's how you felt you could have sent me an email.'

'Dad wants us to behave like sisters so it's the very least we could do for him. You haven't spoken to me for five years, Jess. The only reason that you're sitting here now is because dad is ill. At least being out in public, sitting at a table, forces you to be civilised.'

'Don't pretend for one single minute that you're here because of dad. You're not doing this for dad, Lou. I know you. You always have an agenda for everything you do,' Jessica said angrily. Her raised voice caught the attention of the diners around them. Lucinda sat back and waited for the moment to pass. If she jumped too much then Jessica would know that there was more truth to that statement then she realised.

'I have no agenda Jessica,' Lucinda said slowly as she cut into her steak.

'I don't believe you and I don't trust you.'

'Are you going to be like this for the whole dinner? Because quite frankly, sweetheart, you're behaving like a spoilt brat,' Lucinda said finally having enough of her sister.

Jessica opened her mouth to answer but stopped. 'Are you paying for this?' Jessica asked as she reached for the side dish of sweet potato chips.

'I suppose so. Why, is that a problem?'

'No. Not for me. It's just that I read that Paul had gone bankrupt.'

'Paul's business isn't my business.'

'I'm just making conversation.'

'Well change the subject.'

They sat eating with nothing more said between them. Jessica felt grateful for the food. In fact if it wasn't for the fact that her head had been spinning from the effects of vodka on an empty stomach, when she'd entered the restaurant she'd never have sat down to eat. They used to be close as sisters. Yes, they'd fought like cat and dog when they were younger but Jessica had always known that Lucinda would defend her to the ends of the earth. Being so physically close to her now but with none of the warmth and love that once was, Jessica would have to be made of stone to admit that it didn't hurt.

'I know that dad wants us to be one happy family but I doubt that's going to happen.'

'You're not even going to try?'

'Why should I be the one who has to try after what you done? You're delusional, Lucinda.'

'I'm delusional? None of what happened was my fault and you know that,' Lucinda said sternly. 'For the love of God, Jess, why can't you just let it go and move on?'

'Unfortunately, I can't let go of my own flesh and blood stabbing me in the back.'

'When are you going to stop walking around with bloody blinkers on? I didn't stab you in the back. I've never stabbed you in the back. Why are you here if you really feel that way?'

'Because I reckon that enduring an hour with you is much better than putting up with mum and dad having a go at me because I won't make amends with my sister.'

From the way that Jessica was attacking her steak, Lucinda

knew that as soon as dessert was over, if they got that far, her sister would grab her bag and head out of the restaurant before she had a chance to enter the first digit of her pin number in the chip and pin machine.

'Jessica. I know that I'm asking a lot but I want this dinner to be the start of new beginnings for us,' Lucinda said as she took the slim leather cardholder from her clutch bag.

'I'm prepared to be civil for dad but that's it,' Jessica said as she downed the rest of her wine; grateful that the bottle was now empty.

'I also need a favour.'

'You want a favour from me? I knew you wanted something.'

'Don't sound so pleased with yourself.'

'Lucinda, I'd never in a million years do you a favour.'

'Jessica, I'm talking business not honouring family obligations.'

'I'm surprised you even know what the word *honour* means.'

'You're being facetious.'

'And you're a bitch.'

Lucinda could do nothing as she watched her sister collect her bag and stand up.

'I haven't seen you or heard from you for five years and now, all of a sudden, you're back and mum and dad are acting as though you're the fucking messiah. Whatever it is that you want, I'll never help you. Not even when you haven't even got the fucking decency to apologise for acting like a slut.'

THIRTEEN

IF LUCINDA didn't know better, she could have sworn that Jessica had been drinking well before she stepped into the restaurant. You didn't spend nearly 10 years practically living, sleeping and travelling in planes, trains and coaches with someone without knowing the signs. The taxi driver didn't seem interested in talking, although he kept taking sneaky glances in his rear-view mirror, and that suited Lucinda fine as they drove through the city. For the first time she felt as though she was leaving a part of herself behind. No matter how angry you were with your sister. No matter how much pain they may have caused each other, the sisterly bond still should have remained. But it was broken. So Lucinda did what she did best and pushed the sadness and anger she was feeling into a box and then she began doing the calculations…the same calculations that she'd been doing non-stop since she'd realised the extent of her financial mess. She had to stop herself from laughing out loud as the word budget formed on the edge of her tongue. Even though it was the buzzword in these times of financial austerity, it'd never ever formed part of her vocabulary.

She'd signed a six-month lease on the house and hoped she'd be back in her own home by then. If she *budgeted* properly then she could probably make it to the beginning of the New Year without anyone knowing that she was living on borrowed time. For the first time she understood what it felt like when people looked at their bank account and their heart sank when they realised they had another 10 days to payday.

'You're her aren't you?' the taxi driver said as he stopped at the traffic lights on Lancaster Road. He turned around and lifted his Ray bans to the top of his head. He couldn't have been more than thirty-five and looked as though he should have been sitting in a boardroom as opposed to driving a black cab through the streets of London. Even his accent suggested someone who had benefited from private school and a university education. 'You're her aren't you? Lucinda from Euterpe.'

Lucinda sat back in her seat. She could be walking up and down Fifth Avenue naked and hardly anyone would ask if she'd once been a member of the biggest girl band in Europe; but now that she was home.

'Yes. Yes I am. I'm surprised that you recognised me.'

'Recognise you? I knew as soon as you poked your head through my cab window. I just thought it'd be a bit rude to ambush you.'

'That's fine. I really don't mind.'

'I had you plastered all over my bedroom door,' the driver said as the light turned green, but he was prevented from driving off as a procession of horses from the local riding school trotted into Hyde Park. 'But Beatrice was my favourite.'

Lucinda laughed. They all had a favourite and she was more than used to fans telling her that they preferred one sister over the other.

'How long have you been driving a cab?' Lucinda asked as she lowered the volume on the TV in the back of the cab.

'Only five years.'

'Five years? That's not long. What did you do before?'

'I was an associate at Lehman brothers. Was there for about 3 years before the crash. Went into work at eight and I was watching myself on Sky news at eleven. Weirdest day of my life.'

'And you decided to become a cabbie?'

'Not straight away,' he replied as he continued onto Notting Hill Gate, driving past people standing outside crowded pubs or sitting at cafe tables enjoying the best of London on a summers evening. 'I tried looking for another job but I was just one of a thousand other associates traipsing through the city banging on doors. After a year of getting nowhere, my savings were running out and then a mate suggested this. So here I am. I don't mind it really. I've met all sorts of people but funny enough you're my first pop star.'

Lucinda sat back and pondered what the cabbie had just told her. Everyone had a story. Everyone's life was subject to change.

Lucinda turned the key and pushed open the front door. The smell of the house was not yet hers and it unnerved her but then she heard the excited and combined voices of her baby sister and the twins coming from the reception room. All of their voices running over each other. Even Reece was joining in and he usually ran from a room that had more than one woman in it.

Her relationship with Emma was an odd one. The truth was that they had not grown up together but that didn't stop her from being immensely proud and protective of her baby sister and doing everything she could to keep Emma out of the battles she had with Jessica, but that was difficult to do when you were almost 3000 miles away.

'Lulu is that you?' Emma shouted out.

'Who else would it be?' Lucinda felt as if the wind had been punched out of her as the full force of Emma came at her.

'Let me look at you,' Lucinda said as she pushed her sister gently back.

'Bloody hell, you sound like gran. *"Bon Jé, let me look pon you,"* Emma said in a convincing impression of their maternal grandmother. Emma was 31 but looked five years younger. Her shoulder length hair was jet black with the occasional streaks of auburn. The dye had struggled to cover the streaks of grey hair that all of the LeSoeur sisters had been cursed with from an early age. She wore a navy maxi dress with a single gold bracelet. Lucinda instantly recognised it as the one their parents had bought them all on their 18th birthday. From the look of her, Emma had been spending a lot of time in the gym or she'd become close friends with Gwyneth Paltrow.

'You look amazing,' Lucinda said. 'Gorgeous and amazing. What have you been doing?'

'Spinning classes, running around like I've got a rocket up

my arse and having no time to eat. Oh and spanx. I'm being held together by big support knickers and have probably cut off the circulation in my legs. Also, I've got a new weave. I was going for a Gabrielle Union sort of look. What do you think?' Emma said as she flicked her hair.

'I love it. You look great.'

'You don't look too bad yourself for forty something.'

'What can I say? Support knickers and a good concealer. What time did you get here?'

'About eight. I was in Birmingham for a book launch and then I had to go to Manchester and then got back from Edinburgh this morning. It's been hectic. Anyway, I was in the area so I thought, *Em you've got no excuse. Go and see your sister.*'

'Nothing new then. Well at least two of my sisters are pleased to see me.'

'To be honest, I'm surprised that Jess agreed to have dinner with you at all.'

'Well the world is full of surprises little sister.' Emma winced. She hated being called *little sister*. There was a lot more to her than that title. They walked into the front room where two empty pizza boxes sat on the coffee table and the twins were stretched out on the sofas.

'Hi mom,' the twins said in unison although neither of their heads lifted from their iPads.

'Make sure that you two clean this up,' Lucinda said as she hooked arms with Emma and led her out to the garden, which had easily become her favourite place in the house. She stopped at the fridge. 'What do you want to drink? Wine, sparkling water, juice, smoothie or do you want tea?'

'Tea?' Emma said, screwing up her face. 'No thank you. Do you have beer?'

Lucinda pulled out a bottle of Kronenberg and handed it to her sister. She decided that she'd have one too.

'So how was dinner?' Emma asked as she followed her sister into the garden.

'How do you think it went? We ate, we drank, we argued. So all in all a success I think.'

'What is it with you two?' The question was a genuine one from Emma because considering her ability to automatically side with Jessica she was still none the wiser about what had actually taken place between the two of them.

'I don't know. I haven't actually done anything to her.' And for the first time that night, Lucinda actually spoke the truth.

'Your garden furniture is better than the sofa in my flat,' Emma said not so subtly changing the subject. 'In fact I don't even have a sofa or cushions or curtains for that matter,' Emma said as she slipped off her sandals and sat down on the sparse cream cushions of the garden chairs. She wriggled her toes on the cool grass. 'I have a balcony which is the size of your downstairs toilet. Absolutely ridiculous.'

'But it's yours and that's the main thing,' Lucinda replied as she took a sip of beer and actually felt relieved as the ice cold liquid slipped down her throat. It was just what she needed on this humid night.

'I'm sorry that it's taken me so long to visit,' said Emma.

'That's fine. You've been busy. I didn't expect you to drop

everything just for me.'

'Even so, you've been back for over a week now and I should have seen you and the twins sooner. So, I'm sorry.'

Lucinda was slightly taken aback. She hadn't been expecting this at all. After all if anyone should have been apologising it should have been her.

'So, how are things with you after…'

Emma held her hand up to stop her sister from asking the question that she knew was always on everyone's lips. Lucinda stopped. The last thing that Emma was looking for was sympathy.

'I'm fine and I'm moving on. I've got a new flat and a job which I actually enjoy.'

'Even though you're running around like a blue arsed fly?'

'I haven't even had time to pull my knickers out of my arse. Anyway, I didn't come here to talk about me. I came to see my big sister and find out why she's come home. So go on then. Tell me. Why have you come home? Is it because of dad?'

'Dad? No, I didn't even know about dad until I got back, which I still think was slightly out of order. He could have told me earlier.'

'Lou, it's not something that you tell someone over the phone.'

'Even so, it's not nice knowing that you're the last to know. I can't believe that this is happening to him again. It doesn't seem fair.'

'You weren't here the first time, Lou. You have no idea what it was like. Having to live with him whilst he was going through that, seeing him so ill, but you're here now. So…'

Emma looked at her sister with a steely determination, 'why are you back? Is it anything to do with Paul?'

'Oh my God. Why does everyone think that it has something to do with Paul?'

'Because he's bankrupt and a couple of months later you've hotfooted it home.'

'Emma, I did not hotfoot it home. It was always my plan to come home eventually.' It scared her how easily the lies rolled off her tongue.

'Really?' Emma said, making no attempt to disguise the disbelief in her voice. 'After all this time. Just like that?'

'It wasn't just like that,' Lucinda lied again.

'So what are you going to do? Mum mentioned that you were going to make music again.' Lucinda wasn't at all surprised that her mum had immediately called her little sister and told her of Lucinda's plans.

'That's the plan. I can't sit on my arse doing nothing.'

'Hmmm, why change the habit of the past fifteen years,' Emma said with a smirk.

'You really should have respect for your elders, Em.'

'I'll have respect when you start telling the truth, Lou. Just because I'm the *little sister*, as you've so kindly reminded me, doesn't mean that I'm living in a bubble and that I need to know my place.'

'I never said that.'

'You didn't have to.' Like the breeze that had suddenly swept across the garden so had the temperature quickly heightened between Lucinda and Emma.

'You're not in trouble are you?' Emma asked as she

swallowed the last of her beer and put the empty bottle on the table. Lucinda focused her attention on the blue bottle and watched the little beads of condensation trickle down. 'I mean, everyone in America is always getting in trouble for not paying their taxes. You're not running away from the IRS are you?' Lucinda felt her body sink down with relief and the beginnings of laughter rise from her stomach.

'No, no I'm not in trouble with the IRS,' Lucinda said as she began to laugh.

'Are you sure?'

'Ems, honestly, I'm sure,' Lucinda said as she wondered how much longer she'd have to hold on to her lies.

FOURTEEN

JESSICA STILL hadn't made it home, even though she was the first one to walk out of the restaurant and only lived twenty minutes away. She'd thought about heading back to the office but tonight was the first time in months that she'd left before 10pm and that wasn't right considering she had a teenage daughter at home. Instead she distracted herself with a quick trip into Little Waitrose on Highbury Corner buying things she didn't really need before beginning the walk home. It was almost eleven o'clock when she arrived at her house. It'd been the first thing that she'd bought after the divorce. Neither she nor Christopher wanted to live in a house that held the memories of the beginning or ending of their relationship so they amicably sold the house in St John's Wood and split the profit. Jessica had wanted to be closer to her family but not too close that her mother could drop in whenever she felt like it; so she chose Islington. She loved her house but instead of rising up to greet her the house sunk back and told her to prepare herself.

As she walked through the front door the first thing she

saw was a picture of her second wedding day as they stood on the steps of Marylebone Town Hall. It'd never occurred to her that she would remarry. She was laughing in those pictures as the white confetti floated down in front of them and Andrew leaned over and kissed her on the cheek. That was a moment of happiness frozen in time. Now she walked past it as though it didn't exist. She put the shopping bags on the kitchen counter and leaned against the island unsure what she should be doing. On the outside she was the epitome of calm but inside she was a jumbled up mess. She wasn't able to compartmentalise and put her emotions in neat little boxes, the way that Emma and Lucinda did. Without turning on any lights she reached into the wine rack and pulled out a bottle of red.

She packed away the shopping and then went upstairs, showered and changed into a vest and shorts before returning downstairs where she drunk her wine in the quiet and coolness of the living room. Jessica only realised that she had dosed off when she heard the sound of footsteps on the staircase.

'Andrew,' Jessica called as she rubbed her eyes and walked out into the hallway. She stopped in her tracks when she saw Andrew standing in the middle of the staircase with a mulberry holdall in his right hand.

'I didn't think that you were home,' Andrew said.

'Why would you…?' She stopped when she noticed two suitcases and his suit bag on the bottom of the staircase, waiting to be claimed by their owner.

'What's going on? Why are all these bags downstairs?' She had no idea why she was even asking the question. It didn't take a genius to work out that he wasn't just going on a business trip.

He walked down the rest of the stairs and placed his bag on top of a suitcase before taking a breath. He was 10 years older than Jessica and from their early days of dating had been almost regimental in his approach to his appearance. She had never been able to read him. In the beginning that made him dark, mysterious and attractive and it made her immune to the other features of his personality, such as the arrogance and the vanity. He didn't look like a man who was trying not to hurt his wife's feelings, but he had an excellent poker face.

'I'm leaving you.'

'You're doing what?'

'I'm leaving you.' He said it as though he was merely telling her that their online food shop was being delivered at three o'clock instead of two. Jessica felt her legs begin to shake. She had trained herself not to be shocked by anything but this was about her. Not some soap star that had been caught freebasing cocaine off her personal trainer's chest.

Jessica stood there dumbfounded. She knew that their relationship had changed. She had lost count of the times Andrew had returned home late from work or simply not all. There had been more weekends away where he said he was playing golf than she cared to remember. The facts that he was always shopping and had just splashed out on a Porsche were no surprise to her. Andrew was larger than life. Whether it was shopping, drinking or gambling these were all parts of his personality, but how did he have the audacity to leave her?

'You can't leave me. We've just done a photo-shoot for

Living magazine for Christ's sake. You can't leave me Andrew,' Jessica said not knowing where the strength or the desperation in her voice had come from. Andrew just laughed; a bitter but pitiful laugh that immediately made her regret saying those words.

'You're so absorbed in yourself. This isn't even about you.'

'Self-absorbed. Me? I'm not fucking self absorbed,' Jessica said as she uncontrollably shook with rage and tears formed in her eyes. This shouldn't be happening. If anyone was to end this marriage it should have been her.

'Who is she?' She'd wanted to sound strong but the words came out choked and weak.

'What makes you think that it's another woman?'

'Because I know you. You wouldn't be leaving me if you didn't think you were off to bigger and better things. Who is she?' Jessica shouted.

'It could be that you just bore me Jess.' The coldness of the statement struck her more than when he'd told her that he was leaving her a few minutes earlier.

'I bore you? No, no. That can't be the reason. It has to be another woman.'

'Think what you like. I'm not going to stand here and argue with you,' Andrew said as he pulled his car keys out of his pocket and walked to the front door.

'Where are you going?' she said as she followed him to the front door.

'That's really no concern of yours. The next time you hear from me will be from my solicitor,' Andrew said as he walked out, slamming the front door behind him.

She stared at the front door as though it would be able to give her answers. Jessica ran to the living room towards the large bay windows. As she peered through the shutters she could see Andrew loading up the boot of his Porsche. She resisted the urge to run outside and hurl abuse at him but she had no idea what she'd be fighting for. As the car drove away, Jessica slumped down to the ground and for the first time in years she had no idea what to do next. She could call Beatrice, Emma or Wendy but what would she say? How would she explain it? Another marriage over. It always came in threes. First her dad, then Lucinda and now Andrew. She felt that her life was running through her fingers. She should be able to manage a crisis like this but this was her life and the rules that she applied to clients didn't apply to her.

FIFTEEN

IT COULD have just been living in London in the summer that was giving her an illusion of sun drenched false hope. They'd been back in London for three weeks and Lucinda had to admit that the rhythm of London life suited her; that ability Londoners had to just do their own thing and not be forced into any boxes. That kind of life suited Lucinda perfectly…until she opened up the next screen on her laptop. Her budget. The figures weren't adding up. You've been such a fool the voice inside her head told her again. She ignored it and clicked onto the iTunes music store.

'I must be out of my fucking mind,' Lucinda said out loud as she scrolled through the iTunes top ten. Firstly, she didn't have a clue who half of the female artists were, and secondly, when she listened to a sample of their music, the only thing she could conclude was that the music they were making was simply noise. To make matters worse, she wasn't even sure what genre of music she fell into. What was she? Pop, R'n'B, Soul? She definitely wasn't a new artist but she didn't want to be relegated to the confines of adult contemporary classics. For starters, she wasn't even sure what that was.

Lucinda didn't like labels despite her penchant to purchase them. As far as she was concerned, the Brit and Ivor Novello awards, gathering dust in the garage, proved that Euterpe was a group who won awards for making good music.

She'd never thought that she'd have to reinvent herself, especially after the success of her first solo album. She had even been nominated for a Grammy but lost out to Erykah Badu in the best female R'n'B performance category. Lucinda had never wanted to be marketed as an R'n'B singer but the record company and her husband pushed her and she wasn't surprised that her second album was critically and financially mullered. She'd been visibly uncomfortably in dresses that were too tight and weaves that were too long. There were parties with hip-hop stars and music executives that she didn't want to go to and she was fighting against girls, who were just girls, but who had the steely determination of seasoned pros who were willing to be exploited. Lucinda recalled the night that she'd bumped into Ruby Nestor. When they first met Ruby had been a naïve 18-year-old, doe eyed and fully clothed. Two years later she had the familiar look of someone who was self-medicating themselves as she stood at another party wearing a halter-top that barely contained anatomically out of proportioned breasts and a skirt that showed there was absolutely nothing underneath.

Lucinda was dragged out of her thoughts by her phone ringing. Since she'd come back, her phone had hardly rang and the texts usually told her that she was entitled to £3,498 because she'd recently had an accident or that there was a PPI payment waiting for her. If only.

'You sold the house,' Paul said.

'Well hello to you too, Paul.'

'How could you sell the house?'

'Forget about the house. Where have you been for the past three months?'

'It wasn't three months. I can't believe that you sold our house.'

'It was my house to sell and quite frankly I have no idea why you feel that you have the right to question me about my financial affairs when you couldn't even handle yours.'

There was silence, as Paul knew there was no appropriate response, so Lucinda decided to fill in the gaps. 'How did you get my number?'

'Reece had the decency to let his father know that his mother had kidnapped him.'

'I did not kidnap the children, Paul. You were the one who disappeared off the face of the earth.'

'I had my reasons.'

'You ignored your children.'

'I've emailed them and told them that I'll make it up to them.'

'Bollocks you will.'

'Look, Lou. I've clearly hit a nerve…'

'Hit a nerve? Are you out of…'

'Let me start again. How are you? How are the children?' Lucinda took a deep breath. It was only the fact that she wasn't paying for the call that made her stay on the line.

'They're fine. I'm fine. What happened to you, Paul?' Lucinda said gently.

'Bad business decisions.'

'That bad you had to file for bankruptcy?'

'Chapter 11 means nothing. It's tactics, baby.' Lucinda rolled her eyes. She'd heard that more than once during their marriage.

'You should have told me that we…sorry that you were in trouble.'

'I know, I know,' Paul said with a sense of exhaustion. 'I'm sorry that you had to find out the way you did. I'm sorry that you felt you had no choice but to sell the house. I'm sorry for everything.'

'Shit happens,' Lucinda said, as she felt overwhelmed with empathy for her ex husband. 'Anyway, if I know you, you'll bounce back. So where are you?'

'Atlanta. There's a new artist I'm looking at.'

'The last artist you looked at was conveniently on her knees between your legs,' Lucinda said, unable to help herself.

'Hey, there's no need for that,' Paul said, clearly amused. 'This is legit. So when are you and the kids coming home?'

'What are you talking about? We're not coming home. We're here for good.'

'But I thought that you were just in London for the summer.'

'You really are delusional. I didn't sell the house just to fund a summer trip.'

They spoke for a few more minutes with Paul promising to send her some money once he was back on his feet and to think about coming back to New York before Lucinda ended the call. The conversation had made her feel sorry for her ex-husband and even more sorry for herself. Lucinda got up and walked over to the large silver fridge and saw that it was filled with food. She became slightly offended by the luxurious items staring back at her. Bottles of champagne, a small tin of caviar, smoked salmon; everything from the cheese, to the carrots and milk was organic. The old New York Lucinda would have thought nothing of opening a bottle of champagne at eleven in the morning. Instead she reached for the bottle of orange juice. The champagne would have to wait until there really was something to celebrate.

Lucinda only had the sounds of radio 2 for company, as the twins were already out after she forced two fully loaded oyster cards into their hands and told them to find their way around London. She wasn't confident that they'd end up on the right end of the Metropolitan line so she called Lena who'd just finished her exams and arranged for her to meet her cousins. Lucinda walked through the house, barefoot and still in pyjamas. Every room was a reminder that she didn't have much time left. She constantly worried that any moment now the landlord would tell the estate agents that he was selling the house and that she'd have to leave. Where would she go? She couldn't live out of hotels and she wasn't prepared to be separated from her children. The very thought caused anxiety to grip her stomach as she walked into her bathroom and turned on the shower.

The sky was a clear bright blue with only the vapours left behind by planes on their way to Heathrow. There was a cool breeze in the air and it rustled the leaves of the trees that had long lost their cherry blossom. It only took Lucinda ten minutes before she found herself outside her house. She pushed the wrought black iron gate, which wasn't on the latch and instantly swung open. She walked up the stairs, trying to ignore the overflowing, green wheelie bin. She wrinkled her nose in disapproval at the front door, which clearly needed repainting. She lifted the chrome knocker not quite believing that she was knocking on the front door of her own house. She waited, but there was no answer so she knocked again, harder, before bending down and pushing open the letterbox. Even from the hallway she could see that the house was in complete disarray. There were baskets of clothes that had just been dumped in the hallway and shoes scattered across the floor. Lucinda slammed the letterbox shut and tried to lean across to look through the large bay windows.

'What the hell do you think you're doing?'

Lucinda jumped at the sound of the Irish-accented voice behind her. She turned around and found herself face to face with a tall white man who didn't look like he'd slept much recently. 'I asked you what the hell are you doing?'

Lucinda looked down at the carrier bags in his hands and the keys that he held in his left hand. 'This is my house,' Lucinda answered straightening herself up.

'I'm sorry.'

'I said that this is my house.'

'Are you off your head? This is my sister's house. Do I need to call the police?'

'Why on earth would you need to call the police?'

'Oh let me think. There's a crazy woman knocking at my sister's front door, looking through letter boxes, forcing open windows…'

'I wasn't trying to force open the window…'

'And telling me that this is her house. You don't think that would be good enough reason for calling the police?'

Lucinda stared back at him, swelling with anger. His green eyes never left her face as he pulled his phone out of his jeans pocket.

'You know what, I'm going. I don't have to stand here and listen to this.'

'I suggest you do that,' he said as Lucinda walked back down the stairs and closed the gate behind her, making sure that she placed it firmly back on the latch.

'For the record. This is my house. I own it. Your sister is renting from me and when you've stopped ranting and raving like an idiot you can tell her that I'm speaking to the estate agents today and I want her out,' Lucinda said as she stormed off down the road.

He was left speechless as he watched the stranger walk away whilst thinking this was the last thing that his sister needed.

SIXTEEN

IT TOOK Lucinda two hours and an uncomfortable, hot and sticky tube journey from Notting Hill to Waterloo before she calmed down. She understood now what it meant when people said that it felt like the whole world was conspiring against you. As she pushed open the glass doors of the office building and told the receptionist who she was, Lucinda prayed that things were about to change.

'I cannot believe that Lucinda LeSoeur is sitting in my office after all these years,' said Sal as he sat on the grey pastel sofa in the corner of his office.

'Why are you wearing shorts?' Lucinda asked as she looked down at his tanned but hairy legs. 'It's not very professional.'

'What are you talking about? They're Ralph Lauren. Anyway, you're wearing shorts.'

'That's because I have the legs for it,' Lucinda said as she crossed her long legs, which she knew always caught Sal's attention. She was wearing a pair of yellow DKNY shorts and a white linen vest. One thing that Lucinda could do was pull a look together. Although this was one was pulled together whilst she was in the middle of an angry huff.

'That is double standards. So, what can I do for you, Lulu, because if I remember correctly, the last time we saw each other you said that the next time you saw me you'd stuff a Grammy award up my arse.'

Lucinda couldn't help but laugh out loud as the memory of that moment flashed before her eyes. 'I'm sorry. I was a bit angry the last time I saw you.'

'That's an understatement.'

'Anyway, there's nothing to worry about. I never did win one and if it makes you feel better. I apologise.'

'Look,' Sal said as he suddenly stood up and slapped his hands together as if he was gathering a group of five year olds to line up properly. 'Why don't we get out of the office and take advantage of the nice weather before it disappears and I've got to pack my shorts away.'

Sal's office was next door to the Old Vic theatre in Waterloo and in ten minutes they were walking along the South Bank.

'They had a fake beach here last summer,' Sal said as they walked past the growing queue of tourists waiting to board the London Eye. 'They had stripy deck chairs and even a Punch and Judy show.'

'You're joking?' Lucinda said as she stopped at a row of pop up food stalls. 'I can't believe how much the South Bank has changed. I remember when the only food truck around here was the ice-cream man selling hot dogs from his van.'

'But it's nice to see that some things haven't changed,' said Sal as he pointed across the river at St Pauls Cathedral.

Lucinda looked across and watched the sunrays bouncing off the top of the majestic cathedral and then catching the ripples of the River Thames. The river sparkled in the sunlight and looked cool and inviting. It was these moments that made Lucinda realise just how special London was. With the exception of the extra three stone that Sal had piled on, which had settled mainly on his stomach, he hadn't changed. He still had the same cheeky grin and large, bright blue eyes. His thick, curly brown hair was in desperate need of a cut but he looked well. He'd been the manager for the group since he'd discovered their demo tape amongst the reject pile of the record company where he'd been temping that summer. His boss had not been interested – he'd said that no one was interested in girl bands. Sal had taken it upon himself to call the number on the inside of the tape cassette and then turned up, uninvited on their doorstep and had begged Lucinda to let him manage her group. Jessica said no, he didn't look like he could manage a tuck shop. Beatrice wasn't really interested as she was convinced that the entire venture would go nowhere. But Lucinda had liked him because he was enthusiastic and more importantly he was offering his services for free. No one had been harder working as Sal was in those early days and no one was more devastated then he when Lucinda had decided to call it a day.

'I spoke to Bea about a month ago. Sent a pressie for her baby. Nice little Burberry number,' Sal said as they sat at an outside table of a bar that was close to Blackfriars Bridge but nicely tucked away from the tourists. Lucinda wasn't surprised that Sal was still in contact with her sisters. He and Beatrice had grown close and she knew that nearly all of his clients were on Jessica's books. There was an unbroken trust between them all.

'It's funny though. She didn't say that you were coming over,' he said.

'It was a last minute decision. I decided it was time for a fresh start,' Lucinda said in a well-rehearsed speech.

'And that's why you've called me, right? You want a fresh start,' Sal stated rather than asked as he ordered a club sandwich for them both and a bottle of sparkling water. Lucinda looked at him surprised as she remembered all of the occasions when Sal was more than the life and soul of a party.

'Sparkling water? Really Sal?'

'Three years sober, Lulu.'

'I had no idea.'

'Well, I had to buck up my ideas after I woke up in the front seat of my car, engine running and the contents of my wheelie bin on the bonnet. To this day, I have no memory of even getting into that car. I could have killed someone. I could have killed myself. Petrie threatened to take the kids and move back to Portugal and live with her parents. So I fixed up.'

'Fuck.'

'Yeah I know. Who would have thought? Salvatore Alinari. Sober. But don't think that you don't have to drink on my account. I watched Petrie knock back half a bottle of sauvignon whilst I sipped at my virgin bloody Mary last night. Me, I've already lost two stone and I'm thinking about a triathlon next year. Don't roll your eyes,' Sal said before Lucinda had even had a chance to think about it.

Lucinda changed her order from a white wine to a diet coke and decided that there had been enough small talk.

'Sal, I need your help.'

'Well, I didn't think you were coming to see me just to say hello and tell me that I got fat. So what is it?'

'I want to make a comeback.'

'Why?'

'What do you mean why?'

'It's a good enough question. Lou, seventeen years ago your lawyers sent me a lovely fax telling me that it was over. Within that time you threatened to assault me with a musical award and sent me a couple of Christmas cards. I think that the least you could do is tell me why. Do you need the money?'

'No, of course not. There are loads of reasons but mainly I need to have a career. I need to give my kids something to look up to. I want to try again.'

'But I thought that you weren't interested in the music business. I read that interview you gave a few years back.'

'That was years ago. I don't even know why I gave that interview. I need to make music. I need to work. I need a manager.'

'You want me to manage you?' Sal said not making any effort to hide his surprise.

'Who else would I go to? You've known me for nearly twenty-five years.'

'Don't say it too loudly.'

'You manage three artists who are in the top ten right now. You're respected, you know me and I trust you not to screw me over.'

'Lou, the music business isn't the same as it was.'

'I know that, Sal. In fact I know that better than anybody. Fuck it, I'll even do a reality show if I have to, if it means that I'll get my name back out there.'

Sal looked at Lucinda quizzically. Instinctively he knew that her words weren't fed by some burning desire to reignite her passion for music.

'It's a different world out there, Lulu. It's harsh. I'm trying to find space for talented artists who are competing with robots produced from the talent show factory and singers who think that they're being artistic because they go on stage and perform in their knickers whilst they're groped by a dwarf in a gimp outfit.'

'It's not that bad.'

'Clearly you don't watch MTV love,' Sal said as he stuffed a chip into his mouth.

SEVENTEEN

THE PAIN started in the middle of his back towards the left and then hit a nerve, which caused a sharp shooting pain to travel down his left leg. This caused Richard to jump out of his sleep and reach for the nearest thing to him, which was his wife's right arm. He couldn't breathe and he was scared now that he could feel the warm breath of death on his neck. Yes he believed in God and he wanted to believe that there was an afterlife but he couldn't recall the last time that he'd entered a church of his own accord, without it being for a wedding, christening or more often than not recently, a funeral. As the pain gripped him again the thought ran through his mind that this could be it. As if a light has just been switched off and a room had been plunged into darkness.

'What the...' Felicia shouted out with the shock of being abruptly woken up out of her deep sleep by her husband's right arm involuntarily slapping her in the face. 'Oh my God Richard. Richard what's wrong?' He couldn't answer as his face contorted into a grimace of pain and sweat began to emerge from every pore of his body. Felicia pulled back the sheets and saw that his t-shirt was drenched in sweat. She scrambled out of bed, grabbed the phone on the bedside table and dialled 999.

Felicia sat in the ambulance and watched her husband wither with pain with an oxygen mask on his face. The painkiller that they had given him whilst they were in the house was having no effect, so they'd given him a shot of morphine. After a few minutes Richard began to calm down, giving Felicia the opportunity to hold onto his hand. The last time she had been in an ambulance she couldn't have told you if up was down or down was up as she was gripped by wave after wave of contractions as her waters had broken in Columbia Road flower market with a young Beatrice at her side. The journey to Guys Hospital seemed to take an eternity but in reality it was less than fifteen minutes. As soon as they arrived, she'd been ushered to a waiting area with uncomfortable red, metal chairs whilst they rushed Richard to the urgent care unit. It was only when the double doors opened half an hour later and Jessica walked through that Felicia even remembered that she'd called her.

'Oh Jess, you didn't have to come down here,' Felicia said in a quiet voice. 'I shouldn't have called you.'

'Don't be silly, mum. I wasn't going to leave you here on your own.'

'I would have been fine. Anyway, I'm not the one who needs to be fussed over,' Felicia said as she pulled her own cardigan tighter around her and became aware that she was sitting in a hospital waiting area in her pyjamas and the trainers that she usually wore to do the gardening.

'So what happened? How is he?'

'I don't know. I didn't even know that he was in any pain when we went to bed last night. But you know your father. His leg would have to be hanging off before he'd consider even taking a bloody pain killer...but one minute I'm asleep and the next thing I know your dad has slapped me in the face and he's screaming in pain.'

'What do you mean he slapped you?' Jessica had never known there to be any sort of violence between her parents. Of course there had been arguments. Her mother's voice usually overpowered her husband's, and on a few occasions Richard had stormed out and spent the night on his sister's sofa, but there had never been violence.

'Jessica, don't be ridiculous. How could you even think such a thing? It wasn't like that. Your dad just thrashed out with the pain. And he was in so much pain, Jess.' For the first time, Jessica saw the years etched in her mother's face. Her eyes were swollen from a lack of sleep and the tears that she'd shed whilst she was waiting for news of her husband. 'I shouldn't have called you. I should have known that you would have come here and you have enough on your plate. I know how busy you've been.'

'Mum, please, don't worry about it.'

'Did Andrew drive you?'

Felicia didn't notice her daughter flinch at the sound of her estranged husband's name.

'No. There's no point in both of us being here.' The truth was that she had called, texted and emailed him. Whether it was out of pride or misplaced obligation she'd persevered for almost two weeks but he hadn't replied. Not once. She'd even lied to Lena, telling her that he'd gone away on a last minute golfing holiday for two weeks. If Lena had been paying any attention then she would have realised that Andrew should have returned home yesterday. Jessica had become the sort of woman that she despised. She'd never been the sort of woman who chased. But now she wanted to know what her husband was doing and whom he was doing it with. She had no control over the answers and it'd become quite obvious that he wasn't prepared to give her any.

'Mrs. LeSoeur?' Both women's heads turned in the same direction at the sound of their name. 'How is he?' Felicia asked as she reached for her daughter's hand as Dr. Simpson walked towards them.

'He's comfortable. We've given him morphine to address the pain he was experiencing and we've started him on a course of antibiotics.'

'But he couldn't breathe.'

'His lungs are fine. There are no issues there. As far as we can tell the cancer hasn't spread to his lungs or any of his other organs. He has the beginnings of a viral infection but we suspect the breathlessness was caused by anxiety.'

'Anxiety?' said Jessica. 'You're saying that my dad had a panic attack? He doesn't do panic. Not my dad.'

'How could that be anxiety? He couldn't breathe,' Felicia said, talking over her daughter. The doctor took a step back.

'It's not unusual for patients to experience panic. I suspect that a diagnosis like this would be difficult for him to get his head around.'

Felicia stared at the doctor not convinced by what he was saying. Anyway, he looked far too young to be talking to her about her husband.

'We're going to keep him overnight,' the doctor said, looking at his watch. 'Sorry, for the rest of the day and if there are no other issues he can go home tomorrow.'

'No other issues? He has cancer, not an ingrown toenail,' said Felicia sarcastically. 'Can I see him?'

'Of course you can. He's asleep at the moment and we're obviously monitoring him so don't be alarmed by what you see.' Felicia didn't thank the doctor as she walked around him and through the double doors.

'You're more than welcome to go in also,' Dr. Simpson said to Jessica.

'I will, thank you but I wanted to ask you something first. You said that the cancer hasn't spread to his other organs. That's good news, isn't it?'

'In the sense that the cancer has slowed down its growth, yes. But it's still aggressive and without treatment it'll undoubtedly cause your father to deteriorate. Obviously, if he was to embark on a course of chemotherapy and radiotherapy…'

'What do you mean *if* he was to embark? Hasn't he already started?'

Doctor Simpson knew he'd gone a step too far but the long working hours had pushed protocol to the recesses of his brain. He'd been up for 36 hours straight and he could feel the burning sensation of tiredness. 'I've been working with Dr.

Marcus, who is…'

'I know who he is,' Jessica replied abruptly.

'And your dad hasn't started…well to be exact, he hasn't made a decision about whether he wants to start treatment. I can't say anymore than that. In fact, I shouldn't even have told you that,' the doctor said embarrassingly, scratching his head.

The brief silence was broken by the beeps of Dr. Simpson's mobile phone. He mumbled his apologies again, jogged down the corridor, and disappeared around the corner. Jessica didn't know what to do with the news she'd just heard. It was all too much for her and she wanted to scream, but as she looked down at her leggings with the dried paint on them any screaming would most likely result in her being carted off to the psychiatric ward. There was so much going on and she was starting to feel that familiar sense of unfairness rising through her body. It was too much responsibility for her and she didn't know why it had all landed at her feet. No one wanted to spend money on long distance calls to the States so her mother had taken to calling Jessica when there was something on her chest or when she simply wanted to rant about her father's inability to return home after a night out with her uncle in a sober state. Even Beatrice and Emma had started coming to her when they wanted to talk, complain or wanted advice. It angered her that Lucinda's departure had meant that all of the responsibility had been dumped on her.

'Do you know, when I first met your dad I thought he was the most ignorant and annoying man on the planet. He hassled me for weeks until I agreed to go out with him and he was always doing something: playing football, basketball, badminton. I thought that when we had you girls he'd slow down. Girls are safe, I thought. They don't want to hang upside down on monkey bars or hurtle down hills on their bikes, but that didn't happen at all. He was still running around after you four. Now look at him,' Felicia said as she stood over her husband's bed and rested her hand on his forehead. His forehead was the only place not covered by tubes or wires. His breathing had regulated, and his blood pressure and heartbeat were now stable. But the machines still beeped in a rhythm that was not yet comforting.

'Why hasn't dad started his treatment?' Jessica asked as she stood by the door.

Felicia kept her eyes focused on her husband, too embarrassed to look at Jessica.

'I don't know what's wrong with him,' she said softly. 'I want him to fight not just lie there and do nothing. He's never just done nothing.'

'When he gets home we'll talk to him. Maybe we can get Lucinda to pay privately. She might as well do something useful.'

'We're not burdening your sister with paying for treatment.'

'How's paying for dad's treatment burdening her? She's loaded. Let her take responsibility for once. You've always…'

'Jessica, stop! Not now and not here,' Felicia hissed at her daughter. 'Maybe you should go home. I'll stay. I'm not leaving him alone to wake up in a strange hospital bed.'

Jessica walked out of the hospital building and took a deep breath forcing her to embrace that moment of calmness before London became fully awake. The city hadn't yet warmed up and there was still a chill in the air despite the sun rising hazily above her and the birds cheerily singing their song. She walked in the direction of the multi-storey car park not noticing that Dr. Simpson had hurriedly hidden the cigarette behind his back when she'd walked past.

I'm always alone, she said to herself as she opened her car and sat down. As she put the key into the ignition the radio came on. All of the presets were talk radio. She'd stopped listening to music stations a long time ago. Her anger had made her so resentful and bitter about the artists who dared to grace her radio with their sometimes not so dulcet tones. They had literally been on the edge of greatness. That was what the music journalists were saying before Lucinda decided to leave. The abandonment had ruined everything. Jessica had texted Beatrice before she left for the hospital and there were now four missed calls from her. She hated herself even more for being disappointed that the missed calls weren't from Andrew. She had pretended that their marriage was perfect and had done nothing to stop it from completely falling apart. In the privacy of her car, she could admit that. Even with a wedding ring on his finger he'd still behaved like a single man. He went on holiday without her. He hardly consulted her on anything from the purchase of his Porsche to the installation of the plantation shutters, and as for sex Jessica couldn't remember when she had last initiated it but that had never stopped him from taking it.

EIGHTEEN

'SO YOU want to die? Is that what you really want?'

'Well, if you keep carrying on like this, I may not make it to the end of the week.'

'Stop it. Just stop it. For once will you take things seriously instead of making stupid jokes?' shouted Felicia.

Richard didn't answer as he stood in the middle of their bedroom and peeled off the blue t-shirt that he'd been wearing when the pain had taken him. The stale smell of sweat ran into his nostrils as he pulled the t-shirt over his face and threw it in the direction of the clothesbasket in the corner of the room. He missed.

'So, is that what you want? To die?' Felicia said again.

'Of course, I don't want to die,' Richard resignedly said as he sat down on the old armchair next to the bedside table. It felt as though the cancer had picked up an oyster card and was on a fast train round his body.

'You're going to start the treatment,' Felicia said defiantly.

'Shouldn't that be my decision to make?'

'No. You can't be trusted with something this important.'

'Don't talk to me like I'm one of your students, Fliss,' said Richard. But there was no fight in his voice.

'I'm going to make something for you to eat. Maybe you should rest or think about what you're doing with your life. At least what remains of it.' She walked out of the room leaving Richard alone in their bedroom. He didn't even remember his wife repeatedly asking him what was wrong or telling him that she was going to call for an ambulance. He didn't recall the paramedics coming into his bedroom or when they inserted an IV into his left arm or placed the oxygen mask over his face. At some point he must have blacked out. That was the only explanation for it. It wasn't as though he had just dozed off. It had been so easy to let the blackness sweep over him. As he sat in the chair he wondered if death would come over him so quickly and just as sweetly.

Felicia wasn't sure if the tears falling down her face were angry tears or the sadness that she felt at the thought of losing him. She hated fighting with her husband. But this wasn't a fight about him not putting the rubbish out again. She couldn't stay quiet. She had already lost one daughter because she didn't fight hard enough. She wasn't prepared to lose her husband too.

If anyone ever asked Lucinda what London landmark made her feel as though she was really home, she would say Westminster Bridge. Actually it happened as soon as she saw the Houses of Parliament. When she drove across the bridge she observed that nothing had really changed. It was still packed with tourists making their way aimlessly along the left side of the bridge whilst the locals who knew better, walked with their eyesight focused straight ahead as they talked into phones or hailed taxis. She wasn't in love with the car she was driving. When she lived in New York she had her choice of cars. The Land Rover evoque, which was the family car, or her beloved Audi R8. She had to stop herself from crying when she handed the keys back to both but reality had bitten hard when she arrived home. Buying oyster cards for the twins was one thing; queuing up at a bus stop or having to endure the crowded Central line was something completely different. To most people, twenty thousand pounds was a windfall but Lucinda had reverted back to type when she'd handed over her debit card and watched the salesman punch in the five digits into his chip and pin machine. As she drove the second-hand BMW cabriolet off the forecourt in Holland Park and headed in the direction of Park Lane with the roof down, she inexplicably felt powerful. It was stupid that buying a car would make her feel that way but it did. She felt as though she was regaining control. Despite Sal's initial reservations about her so called comeback, his need to think about it overnight had resulted in a 12-page email headlined "Lucinda's Payback" in homage to his favourite artist of all time, James Brown. Lucinda would have been lying if she'd said that she hadn't been excited by what she read, which meant only one thing. She was one step closer to getting back into that recording booth.

Lucinda wasn't sure what to expect when she drove into the

driveway of her childhood home. It was a large Victorian house on the top of Royal Hill in Greenwich. She had flashbacks of her poor dad having to spend the first week of his summer's annual leave painting the wooden frames of the windows and putting a fresh coat of gloss on the front door. If she looked closely she could still see the initials that she and her best friend Ramona had painstakingly written with Tippex on the wall underneath her bedroom window when they were 12-years-old and bored one afternoon. When she thought about it, Ramona and Harrie were her only friends, which was either quite tragic or simply a reflection of how particular she was. She spoke to Ramona at least once a month but hadn't seen her for three years and now that she'd moved to Melbourne Lucinda wasn't sure when she'd see her next. Every part of this house included a part of her. She'd grown up in this house. Every room held a memory. Her proudest moment was when she and her sisters had given their parents a cheque to pay off the outstanding mortgage on the house. She'd been generous to a fault even though Jessica had said it was no more than her showing off, however she did genuinely like to give. She wanted her family to be cared for and to have the best and in the back of her mind she secretly hoped that Jessica would remember the good things that she'd done instead of focusing on that one decision and that awful night in her New York living room.

'Oh,' Felicia said as she opened the door.

'That wasn't the welcome I was expecting,' Lucinda replied.

'What are you doing here? You didn't tell me that you were coming?' Felicia said, still holding on to the front door.

Lucinda looked at her mum who looked as if she was seriously considering not letting her into the house.

'Mum, are you seriously not going to let me in?'

'What on earth did you think you were doing by talking your father into not having treatment? For God's sake, you've only been back five minutes and you're already causing trouble,' said Felicia as she left the door wide open, her daughter still standing on the doorstep.

'Where's dad?' Lucinda said as she stepped into the house.

'Upstairs,' Felicia replied as she stormed into the kitchen. Lucinda took the stairs two at a time. Her parent's room was the first room at the top of the stairs, their logic being that they'd be able to hear if one of their daughters tried to sneak out of the house in the middle of the night. Jessica had only been caught once, whilst Lucinda had never tried. The bedroom door was slightly ajar and the radio was on low. Her father's eyes were closed but she knew he wasn't sleeping. For starters the whole room would have been shaking with the force of his snoring if he was.

'Dad.' Lucinda walked in and sat gently on the bed.

'Hey baby girl. There was no need to come.'

'Don't be silly. How are you feeling?'

'Not bad. Considering. They've given me some painkillers. Not the good stuff.'

'No morphine?' Lucinda said with a smile.

'I wasn't even asking for that much. I may have to find myself a dealer.'

'You're terrible.' She leaned down and kissed her father's forehead the way he used to when they were younger. 'I'll be downstairs with mum.'

The look on Richard's face changed. 'Ah, about your mum. She's not in the best of…'

'Yeah, I gathered that by the way she left me on the front doorstep.'

She could smell it before she even opened the kitchen door; that familiar smell of thyme and sweet peppers that you could never find in any Caribbean greengrocers and which could only have come direct from Grenada, plus onions and coriander, all being simmered in the old trusted Le Creseut casserole pot.

'What type of fish are you using?' Lucinda asked as she walked into the kitchen.

'Monkfish,' her mother replied as she stood next to the cooker dropping white portions of fish into the pot.

'You normally use salmon or snapper.'

'Things change, Lucinda.' She barely looked up as she opened the cupboard to her left and pulled out a small pot of saffron. She took a few dried leaves out and dropped them into the pot.

'Mum, I didn't tell him not to have any treatment.'

'Oh please, Lucinda.'

'Mum, I promise you. I didn't. Dad and I talked. He told me what his options were and that was it.'

Felicia turned and looked at her daughter. 'But you spoke to him about it. You discussed it.'

'Well of course we did. What did you think was going to happen? He was hardly going to say *"Oh by the way, the cancer is back. Have you got any custard creams to go with this tea?"*

'You two are exactly the same.'

'I didn't tell him what to do, mum. I told him that it was up to him. I can't make the decision for him and neither can you.'

'So what you're telling me is that you're more than happy to be visiting your father in Hither Green Cemetery in six months.'

'I'm not even going to answer that,' Lucinda said as she sat down at the kitchen table and took off her denim jacket. This was the first time that she'd ever felt uncomfortable in her parent's home and it occurred to her, not for the first time, that she should just go. There was nothing said for a while, the only sound coming from the gentle simmering of the pot on the cooker and Eddie Nestor on the radio.

'You look *maga*,' Felicia finally said as she realised that there was nothing more that she could do with her hands so she sat down at the table opposite Lucinda.

'What?'

'I said that you look *maga*. You're too skinny. Why aren't you eating?'

'I have been eating and I'm not that skinny. I'm a size twelve.'

'More like an eight. You've never been an eight. Not really, but now you look like an eight. It doesn't suit you.'

'Thank you very much. Anything else you that you want to tell your skinny daughter?'

'Why haven't you been eating?' Lucinda looked at her mother amazed. The woman was unreadable. One minute she was accusing of her allowing her father to kill himself, the next she was acting as though she needed to be booked into a clinic for an eating disorder.

'I've had a lot going on, mum.'

'Is that why you've come running home?'

'I have not come running anywhere.'

'Hmmm.'

'Don't hmmm me. It's just life, mum. Sometimes life can be, well…it's just life. But that doesn't matter now. Everything is sorting itself out.'

'Do you want some?'

'Some what?'

'Broth, child. Do you want some?'

'I suppose so.'

Felicia sighed heavily, got up and took a bowl from the cupboard. She placed the steaming broth into the bowl as Lucinda watched and wondered what would be her mother's next line of attack.

'I've missed this,' Lucinda said as she broke off a piece of homemade bread and soaked every piece of it with the broth before placing it into her mouth.

'You should try making it yourself.'

'I do.'

'You do?' Felicia said making no effort to hide the surprise in her voice.

'Yes mum I do. I can cook you know. Katelyn likes it with salmon head. Takes after you like that. She even eats the eyes. Disgusting.'

'Nothing wrong with that,' she replied with a smile. 'You

need to talk to your dad.'

Lucinda put down her spoon. 'Mum, I'm not going to tell him what to do.'

'Lou.' Her mum seemed to have forgotten that she'd been so angry that she couldn't even look at her. 'He listens to you. Just talk to him again.'

'Why can't Jess or Bea, even Emma talk to him?'

'Because you and him are the same. You think the same and you don't want your children to be without their grandfather.'

'That's low mum.'

'Being six foot under is lower.'

Lucinda couldn't help it but she had to laugh. Her mum wasn't known to have a dry sense of humour or any sense of irony. 'It wasn't that funny.'

'Dad would have liked it.'

Felicia got up and began to prepare a bowl for Richard. 'I'm glad that you're home. I never liked the idea of you living on your own in New York.'

'I wasn't on my own. I had the twins.'

'You know what I mean. There's nothing like being close to your family no matter if you don't all get on like a house on fire.'

'We get on.'

'I'm not a fool. Jessica barely tolerates you. That's no way for sisters behave.'

'What has the doctor said about dad?' Lucinda asked in an effort to ignore what her mother was saying.

'He can manage the pain with the medication and the

cancer hasn't spread any further…'

'But that's good isn't it?'

'It means that it has slowed down for the moment but if he doesn't start chemo soon…well, you know the rest.'

Felicia stopped as the dog, which had been sleeping under the kitchen table let out a yelp, and ran towards Richard who was walking into the hallway. 'What are you doing? I was going to bring your food up to you?' Felicia said.

'Nah. I can't stay in that bed all day listening to LBC. Pure crazy people calling up that station, Lou. Anyway I'm not dead yet so there's no need for me to be laying flat on my back.' Richard eased himself onto the chair.

'So what happened to you?' Lucinda asked as she sat down opposite her father. Seeing him sitting up, she could see the loose skin around his throat and the entrenched lines on his normally smooth face. Richard took a spoonful of the broth and smiled as he felt it run smoothly down his throat. It was the first thing he'd eaten in weeks that he'd actually enjoyed. Felicia felt a small rise of hope as she watched her husband eat.

'Apparently I had a panic attack.'

'You, panic?'

'I know. But the doctors said the breathlessness was due to anxiety. They suggested counselling.'

Lucinda raised a cynical eyebrow at the image of her dad lying on a therapist couch. 'Dad, your idea of therapy is sitting in the Fox and Crown with Uncle Stephen.'

'That's what I told the doctor.'

'I think that mum will have something to say about that.'

'Your mum always has something to say,' Richard

whispered.

'I heard that Richard,' Felicia said as she opened the kitchen doors to let the dog out and to cool herself down. She was not enjoying this heat wave one little bit, which was a bad combination with the hot flushes she was still suffering from. Some days she just wanted to throw herself into the river and let the water wash over her. She thought that she would have finished it at this stage in her life. In fact when she thought back about the plans she and Richard had made for their life she realised that it could all come to an abrupt end, and no matter how efficient she could be, she wasn't ready for the end.

'Your mum told you that Jessica was at the hospital?'

'No. Beatrice told me. I'd have come if mum had called.'

'Have you seen her lately?'

'Who, Bea?'

'No, Jessica'

'Dad, you know that I haven't, not since we went to dinner. I haven't heard a peep from her.'

'She texted earlier and said that she'll be coming round later.' Lucinda knew her dad was purposely ignoring her. Apparently, he'd been more than just listening to the radio when he'd been upstairs resting.

'Well I'll be gone before she gets here,' Lucinda said sternly.

'Lulu, don't you think that it's time that you put the past to rest?'

'Hold on a second, it's not me holding onto things. I haven't done anything wrong.'

'But you're the oldest.'

'Dad, being the eldest has nothing to do with it and just

because I'm the eldest doesn't mean…'

'Doesn't mean what? That you shouldn't take responsibility?' Lucinda flinched at the tone in her father's voice. He was never the one to raise his voice in temper but you always knew when he'd had enough and apparently he had.

'I wasn't going to say that. I was going to say that I shouldn't be the one who has to take the blame for everything. Have you ever noticed how it's always the person in the wrong that's the first one to turn around and say that the innocent party should let bygones be bygones? Well, Jessica hasn't even got to that stage yet.'

'You're the eldest. You have to take responsibility for your actions.'

'There are no actions for me to take responsibility for.'

'You left.'

'And I apologised for that. Jessica is the one who's being stubborn. Do you think that I haven't tried to reach out to her?'

'You know what she's like. You have to be…'

'Oh please. Jessica isn't a china doll. She can handle herself.'

Lucinda and Felicia who'd been standing by the back door both jumped as Richard slammed his hand on the table.

'Enough,' he said.

Lucinda closed her mouth as she saw the fear in his eyes. Not anger like she expected but the fear of a man who may be leaving a fractured family behind.

'Life is short, Lucinda. I could either drop dead tomorrow

or I could outlive the bloody Queen.'

'Dad, I…'

'No. You listen. I'm your father and I want you to fix it, do you hear me?'

'Richard, maybe you should go back to bed,' Felicia said as she approached her husband.

'No, you want me to be more decisive. Well this is the decision that I'm making. I want my eldest daughter to fix this. I don't know why you've chosen to come back now Lulu and I don't expect you to sit here and tell me but you listen to me. You will fix this mess. Do you understand me? Fix it.'

NINETEEN

'YOU'RE REALLY efficient at taking your commission each month but when it comes down to actually doing your job you're less enthusiastic,' Lucinda said to the sales agent at Hemingway Glass Estate Agents. It seemed to be her day for dealing with teenagers. 'So, what is this for you? Work experience?' she asked sarcastically.

'Erm, no. I'm the assistant branch manager. I've been here for three years,' he said as he adjusted his glasses, which were slightly bent.

'Well done you. Assistant branch manager. Your mum must be so proud. Look, six weeks ago I gave your office clear instructions and six weeks later nothing has happened.'

'Ms. LeSoeur.'

'Don't Ms. LeSoeur me. I instructed you to terminate the lease but you've done nothing.'

'I can only…'

'Only what? Apologise. An apology is not good enough. I want them out now.'

'I'm sorry but that's not possible. We've served notice to

quit this morning. We even sent it by courier'

'What do you want a medal?'

'But the tenants are still allowed three months notice,' he said determinedly.

'I can't afford…look; it's simply not good enough. Three months from today,' Lucinda said as she stabbed at the fake wood desk with her finger. 'Three months is too long.'

'I'm sorry, but unless they agree to leave earlier then I'm afraid that you'll have to wait three months.'

Lucinda stormed out of the estate agents. She couldn't carry on like this. Financially she was starting to run out of purse strings to hold. She needed to get things moving but with children making music out of their bedrooms and a child telling her that she couldn't move back into her own house she could feel herself sinking into a hole.

'You will not cry Lucinda Angela LeSoeur,' Lucinda told herself as she got into her car and drove home.

'Are you happy?' Lucinda nearly jumped out of her car seat as the male voice shouted at her and the sound of his hand slamming onto the bonnet reverberated through the car.

'What the hell?'

'I said are you happy? You really are a heartless…'

'Stop it right there,' Lucinda said as she opened the car door and stepped out. It was him again. The same man who'd threatened to call the police when she went round to her own house the other day.

'Who do you think you are? Shouting at me in the street, attacking my car. Do you want me to call the police? Tell them that a crazy man is attacking women in broad daylight?'

The man took a step back as if he finally realised what he'd done.

'She's been through enough. She doesn't need this.' He thrust a crumpled sheet of A4 paper towards Lucinda. She took it recognising the estate agents logo. It was addressed to a Madeline Knight and was headed 'Notice to Quit.'

'It arrived this morning. Do you have any idea what it's done to her?'

'I'm not being funny but I have no idea who this woman is. And I have no idea who you are…'

'Owen,' he replied as he shifted his weight from one to the next as if there was something wrong with his back.

'What?'

'My name is Owen. I'm that woman's brother.'

'Oh. Well, Owen.'

'Do I know you?' Owen asked as he squinted his eyes. He was taller than Lucinda at 6ft 3 and looked as though he was still undecided about shaving off his beard or keeping it.

'No, we've never met. Well only the once when you threatened to call the police.'

'You haven't been into my restaurant?'

'Your what?'

'My restaurant, Geraint's kitchen on Portobello Road.'

'No, I haven't been there. Look, I'm sorry that I have to do this but I don't have much of a choice,' Lucinda said as she handed the letter back and walked towards the house.

'She doesn't need to be kicked out of her home. I mean, what's the hurry? You've got a roof over your head. She's doesn't need this. She's been through a lot.'

'We've all been through a lot,' Lucinda replied as she turned her back on Owen and walked into the house that wasn't quite hers.

* * * *

It was all very well and good that Ocado were happy to deliver your shopping for you but Beatrice wondered why that hospitality didn't extend to packing it too. She hovered between the hallway with the discarded shopping, and the twins watching TV in the living room and felt that she wanted to cry when Sam began to release the full force of his lungs. She started to wish that it'd been her instead of Jake who'd disappeared up the M6 to Birmingham on a two-day convention.

It wasn't that she couldn't cope. She was more than capable of coping; she was just knackered and bored. Of course she loved her children but being a stay-at-home mum had never been on her agenda. She'd stayed at home for twelve months with the twins whilst Jake only had to endure a total of three weeks with his new family before he was able to escape back to his regular life of the office and a quick pint after work. He seemed to think that a text a day was enough to show his support.

'Oh for crying out loud. Really? Now?' Beatrice said as the doorbell rang. She saw a silhouette through the stained glass and prayed it was someone she could slam the door at. She stepped over the bag of satsumas and opened the door.

'You wouldn't believe the morning that I've had,' Lucinda said as she stepped through the door. 'Honestly Bea, I've had enough.'

'What are you doing here?' Beatrice said, more than surprised to see her sister on her doorstep. 'Why didn't you call?'

'I did. I called you three times.'

'You did?'

'Maybe if you knew where your phone was. Bea, this place is a mess,' said Lucinda as she kicked a jar of baby food and watched it roll towards the wheels of Sam's pram.

'It's not that bad,' Beatrice replied unconvincingly.

'Hmmm, that's what hostages say when they've been with their kidnappers for too long. Where's Sam?'

'He's watching Teen Titans with the twins,' Beatrice mumbled.

'Aw bless him. He'll be watching Batman before you know it. Mum always said that the television was the best babysitter,' Lucinda said as she picked up the rest of the shopping bags and walked towards the kitchen. She stopped as she surveyed the chaos of the house. There were baskets of clothes that had made it out of the utility room but no further than the bottom of the stairs. The kitchen wasn't in a better state. The twins had abandoned their cereal bowls on the table with the cups of orange juice that they hadn't finished.

'Come on you two. You're going to help me clean up,' Lucinda said as she poked her head into the living room where Theo and Issy were sitting transfixed. After intense negotiations involving a trip to the park, Beatrice was surprised to see the twins stand up with no complaints and follow their aunt into the kitchen.

'God, I'm terrible. I should be reading them Keats or playing Canon in D,' Beatrice said.

'Please. Mum sat us in front of Crown Court TV and Crossroads. Your kids have got it good. Look, why don't you go upstairs. Have a shower. Make up your bed and I'll do what I can here.'

'Sam will need feeding in a bit,' Beatrice said, feeling unsure of what to do with Lucinda's generosity.

'That's fine. I'll give him some of that organic pumpkin and carrot stuff that I kicked on the way in, or some of this furry stuff. What was it, chilli?' said Lucinda as she lifted the lid of a plastic container. 'I think that's a kidney bean. I'm not too sure'

'God knows what it is,' Beatrice replied as she ran out of the kitchen and up the stairs.

An hour later, Beatrice emerged from her bedroom. She couldn't remember the last time that she had more than ten minutes to herself without a child calling her name or a baby pulling at her hair.

'Bloody hell,' Beatrice said as she walked into the kitchen. In the short space of time everything had been cleaned and put away, the dishwasher was on, and there was the faint smell of lemon fragranced Flash.

'Right I don't know what your parents have been teaching you,' Beatrice heard Lucinda say. 'But it's time to move onto some Hendrix.' Lucinda started to sing as the sounds of Jimi

Hendrix and his electric guitar filtered out from the living room speakers.

Beatrice stifled a laugh as Lucinda sang and danced with Sam in her arms whilst Issy and Theo threw various shapes around in the middle of the room.

'Come on Bea. You love this one,' Lucinda said. Beatrice couldn't help herself as she started to sing along at the top of her voice.

'Bloody hell. That was knackering,' Beatrice said as she sat down on the sofa once the song was over.

'Singing is good for the soul, Bea,' Lucinda said as she handed Sam to his mother.

'I can't believe that you did all this?' Beatrice said as she gently touched the clothes that had been folded up neatly into piles. The cushions had been placed back neatly onto the sofas. DVDs and books were back on bookshelves. Everything looked in order.

'Someone had to.'

'Jake's away.'

'Like you're going to tell me that it's any different when he's here,' Lucinda said as she turned off the iPod.

Beatrice didn't answer as she walked over to the TV and swiped a finger across the black edge, sweeping along a thick film of dust. 'God it is bad isn't it?'

'Get a cleaner.'

'Cleaners cost money.'

'And your point is what?'

'We don't have the extra money to spend on cleaners.'

'What do you mean you don't have the money? You're the

sensible one.'

'Don't overreact; we had to invest a lot of money to set up Jake's company. There was a lot of work to do on the house. There's savings and money put away for the kids so we're not broke. We're just being careful. Anyway, that's boring stuff. Let me put Sam down, I think you've exhausted him enough. I'll sort out lunch for us and I can finally have a conversation that doesn't involve Loom Bands, LEGOLAND, and Peppa bloody Pig.'

Beatrice couldn't cook and all attempts by her mother to teach her had stopped when Beatrice at the age of fifteen had caused a boiled egg to explode in the pan. She could warm things up really well but cooking, well that was beyond her. Luckily, she'd found Jake who could at least make a spaghetti Bolognese from scratch.

'What are you doing?' Beatrice asked as she came back into the kitchen.

'Making lunch,' Lucinda said as she cut up spring onions, chives and red peppers and put them into a bowl. 'Warm potato salad, haddock in pesto butter and baby spinach for us and cheesy pasta for the gruesome twosome over there,' who were in actual fact not being that gruesome as they stood at the kitchen table attempting to butter slices of baguettes that Lucinda had cut for them.

'I have haddock?'

'Oh Bea. In the freezer. You really need to defrost that freezer,' Lucinda said with a smile.

'That was so good,' Beatrice said as she pushed her plate away. 'I can't remember the last time I ate a meal without a baby sitting on my lap or with the twins behaving as if their dinner was an art project. Thank you Lou. So, tell me about your morning? What happened?'

'Oh God. Well, Sal put me in touch with a few producers'

'And?'

Lucinda huffed and picked up the empty plates. 'His name was Haven?' she said. 'Can you believe that? He looked about twelve and was producing, and I use the word loosely. He was producing from a studio in the basement of his parent's house in Clapham.'

'Clapham is nice.'

'Clapham is very nice but that's not the point. I've worked with top producers out of multi-million dollar studios and now I'm resorting to driving around London to make music out of someone's basement. We didn't even do that when we cut our first demo.'

'How much did that studio cost us?'

'Excuse me. That studio didn't cost you anything but it cost me two grand.'

'Did he really look about twelve?'

'Bea, his mum answered the front door and I nearly asked her if it was ok if Haven could come out and play.'

Beatrice laughed out loud. 'It couldn't have been that bad.'

'It was a complete waste of my time, Bea, and I don't have time to waste. I then went to the estate agents and then…you know what, never mind. I don't even want to talk about that. It was just so much easier before Bea. Now it's so hard,'

Lucinda confessed.

'But we were much younger then. We weren't even in our twenties when you were dragging us around dodgy London studios. I think you're brave to start again.'

'It feels more like stupidity than bravery. It doesn't even feel fun.'

'You're probably putting too much pressure on yourself. You've only just come back.'

'I know,' Lucinda replied unconvincingly. 'But I want to love it again. I read in the paper that they're holding X-Factor auditions at the o2 next week.'

'Absolutely not,' Beatrice said, outraged at the thought of Lucinda subjecting herself to potential ridicule. 'You're a million times better than that.'

'Well it's either that or find a job.'

'Doing what?' As far as Beatrice could remember, Lucinda had only three A-levels and that was it.

'Exactly,' Lucinda said. 'Doing what. At least you and Jess had the good sense to have a plan B. I couldn't imagine you sitting at home doing nothing.'

'Neither could I,' Beatrice said as she watched the twins playing outside. 'Neither could I.'

TWENTY

'WHAT DO you mean Andrew has gone?'

'Shhh, keep your voice down,' Jessica said she looked past Emma's shoulder and onto the office floor. She hadn't intended to be having this conversation but Emma had given her little choice after Lena had called her saying she was worried about her mum.

'So where has he gone?' Emma asked as she sipped on her mango and passion fruit smoothie and stared wide eyed at her sister. Jessica shrugged her shoulders.

'What do you mean?' Emma imitated her sister shrugging her shoulders. 'What does that mean Jess?'

'I don't know where he is? He just left.'

'What, last night?'

'No. Three weeks ago?'

'Three weeks?' Emma shouted.

'Emma! Keep your voice down.' Jessica said as a few staff members turned their heads.

'No wonder you look like shit.'

'What?'

'I'm sorry but you do. You've lost weight and your skin looks awful.'

'Thanks, Em. That's exactly what I needed to hear. Why don't you go ahead and give me another kicking whilst I'm down?'

'So why did he go?' Emma said, ignoring her sister's sarcasm. 'Is he having an affair? Are you having an affair?'

'Me! As you always say, I don't have time to pull my knickers out of my arse, let alone have an affair. I don't know why he went but he has.'

'Are you ok?' Emma said softly.

'I'm doing ok. Just don't say anything to mum or dad. They don't need this right now.'

'Does Beatrice know?'

Jessica shook her head. 'No. She's got enough on her plate and whatever you do, do not and I repeat do not tell Lucinda. The last thing I need is her gloating.'

'Why on earth would Lou be gloating and why do you think that I'd run off and tell her?'

'Because little sister, you have a big mouth. Just promise me that you'll keep this to yourself until I'm ready.'

Emma walked out of her sister's office and digested what she'd just heard. Despite the success of her parents and Beatrice's marriage it did little to convince her that marriage was a good thing. People didn't take it seriously. Jessica had had two marriages, and neither had made it past the seven-year mark. The clients she represented were getting married as soon as they dropped their knickers, and were filing for divorce as soon as they were back from their honeymoon. As she looked back at her sister's office she couldn't help but feel sorry for her. It wasn't nice to be abandoned. Emma knew that better than anybody. She woke her computer up and started to scroll through her emails, then she felt her heart stop and her stomach begin a series of somersaults. She hadn't heard from him for so long and now there it was. After all this time. An email from him.

* * * *

'I was thinking that maybe I should come back to work,' Beatrice said.

'Is this a joke?'

'No Anoushka, this is not a joke.'

'But you're on maternity leave?'

'I know that.'

'You haven't even done one keeping in touch day since you dropped.'

'You said that I didn't have to bother with that nonsense.'

'And you expressly said Beatrice, and I quote, "I want to take the year off Anoushka. I want to spend as much time as possible with my baby."'

'I know that's what I said.'

'"I want to be a proper mum. I didn't have enough time with the twins. I don't want my children growing up saying that I wasn't there." End of quote.'

'Thank you Anoushka.'

'Are you sleep deprived?' Anoushka said as she pushed her Prada sunglasses to the top of her head, revealing her own hazel, cat-like eyes, to take a look into Beatrice's.

'Of course I'm sleep deprived,' Beatrice said as she stabbed at her chicken Caesar salad with her fork. 'I've been sleep deprived since 2009.'

Beatrice had thought it was divine intervention when Anoushka had texted her the night before and asked her if she fancied meeting for lunch. She'd left the children with Jake, who was supposed to be working from home and had run out of the house as quickly as she could before Jake could change his mind.

'Are you skint? Because quite frankly I thought that I gave you quite a generous maternity package. I mean, I could have been a right bitch and given you 90% of your salary for six weeks and then £136.78 per week. Talk about being punished for being a woman, £136.78 couldn't even keep me in shoes.'

'Or Botox, but no, I'm not skint and yes you did give me a generous maternity package. Don't get me wrong we're not rolling in it, but I'm not on the verge of sending the kids out to rob from the rich either.'

'Don't knock the Botox darling. You could do with some yourself,' Anoushka replied as she tried to raise an eyebrow. 'Look darling, I'm more than happy for you to come back to work but I don't want you running off to a tribunal alleging that I forced you to come back.'

'Oh for God's sake. You're so bloody dramatic.'

'Please, I know what you new mothers are like. You act like motherhood is the hardest job in the world, but it isn't. You try running a business as successful as mine.'

'Anoushka, you had nannies.'

'So, I still had to organise them.'

Beatrice had long since stopped being surprised by the words that came out of Anoushka's mouth. They were sitting on the terrace of the fifth floor at Harvey Nichols. Anoushka had nodded acknowledgements to at least three former clients for whom she had handled multi-million pound divorces. McMillan LLP was one of the country's leading law firms that dealt exclusively with high profile individuals and Beatrice was one of her prized assets. Beatrice's demure demeanour was a cover for the Amazonian wonder woman who represented her clients in mediation rooms and courtrooms.

'Every time you've gone off and had a baby it's really pissed me off.'

'You make it sound as though I've been breeding like rabbits.'

'I just don't know why women want to do everything.'

'You did it.'

'Well, I'm me and not everyone is as great as me. Anyway, no one else is as good as you and if you want to come back early, that's fine with me. I got a call from Simon Wilby's agent this morning,' Anoushka said in a low voice. The fact that she smoked like a chimney and had developed a deep, huskiness to her voice, made that slightly impossible.

'Simon Wilby, the footballer? I actually think that Jake would leave me for him,' Beatrice said as she allowed the waiter to top up her champagne glass.

'Can hardly blame him. 100 caps for England. Leading scorer for Chelsea. Fifa footballer of the year, 2009, 2010, BBC Sports Personality of the year 2012.'

'I thought you didn't do football.'

'I do money, darling. And he's modelled for Tom Ford, what's not to love; especially when they're instructing the firm to handle their divorce and they make a specific request for you.'

'You're joking? He asked for me.'

'Why are you surprised? Look at who you represented before you disappeared into a world of pampers. Alexandra Powers, the tart from that cookery rubbish on BBC Two.'

'Sarah Cohen,' Beatrice added.

'Exactly, her. George Hunter. I'm not saying that Simon Wilby had the brains to ask for you personally; this is all down to his agent. So to be honest,' Anoushka said as she pulled out an e-cigarette from her YSL clutch bag. 'If you hadn't had told me that you wanted to come back, I was planning on calling you and offering you a bribe to come back early.'

'The bribery act has been in force for a couple of years. I can't take bribes.'

'Oh please. Anyone can be bought. By the way, I've been meaning to ask you, who's representing your sister?'

'What are you talking about? Representing my sister?' Beatrice said as she put her champagne glass down.

'Your sister, Jessica. In her divorce.'

'What divorce?'

'Don't tell me that you didn't know,' Anoushka replied as she managed to dramatically raise her eyebrows.

Two hours later, Beatrice had left Anoushka outside Harvey Nichols and jumped into a black taxi. It was almost four o'clock and the taxi quickly made its way through Knightsbridge, Park Lane and towards Charlotte Street. It wasn't the fact that Jessica was having problems at home that angered her; it was the fact that she had to find out the news from someone who wasn't family.

'Why the hell didn't you tell me?' Beatrice said as Jessica grabbed her by the arm and frogmarched her into a conference room.

'What on earth are you talking about?' Jessica said as she closed the door and switched the air conditioning on. The temp who was working on reception had no chance of stopping Beatrice as she burst through the main doors after she'd buzzed her in. Thankfully the office was nearly empty, as everyone seemed to be out seeing clients, or more realistically skiving, due to the weather.

'I'm talking about you. Your husband. The divorce.' Beatrice slumped herself down in the corner couch as the sudden rush of energy that she'd felt when she'd left Knightsbridge and jumped in a taxi suddenly escaped her. 'Why is it so hot in here?'

'The air con is playing up. How do you know about that?' Jessica took out a bottle of water from the chill cabinet and handed it to her sister. 'Have you been drinking?'

'You're a fine one to ask if I've been drinking. I had lunch with Anoushka.'

'That explains it.'

'Don't change the subject, Jessica'

'Did Emma tell you?'

'Emma? No. Does she know? Why am I always the last to

know?'

'You're not the last to know. So who told you?'

'Anoushka told me. How many times have I told you? This legal world of ours is very small. Nothing stays quiet for long.'

'I thought he might have changed his mind,' Jessica said solemnly. 'I thought that he would have come home by now.'

'What the hell happened?' Beatrice asked as she kicked off her shoes. 'You never said that you were having problems.'

'We're not having problems. It's just a thing that we're going through.' Beatrice stared at her sister open mouthed.

'Jess, when I make Jake sleep in the spare room because he comes home at two in the morning steaming drunk even though he told me that he was just going to the pub for a quick pint to watch the first half, that's a thing. When your husband instructs one of the top divorce lawyers in the country that's not a thing.'

'What ever happened to client confidentiality?' Beatrice looked at her sister as though she'd turned into Hydra and grown an extra head.

'You work in PR. You know there's no such thing as confidentiality. You need to stop burying your head in the sand. He's instructed Curtis Miller Solicitors. Anoushka just happened to be speaking to one of the senior partners when he let it slip that Andrew had instructed them.'

'He's just having a moment. He'll be back.'

'So he's moved out?'

'He packed his bags about three weeks ago.'

'Three weeks and I'm only finding out now. Sis what's going with you? This isn't like you.'

Jessica leaned back on the couch and took a deep breath. She'd spent many a sleepless night pondering that same question. The arrival of her eldest sister had stirred something deep inside of her. Combined with the news of her father and Andrew's out of the blue departure she felt as though she was in the middle of a hurricane. She thought she'd be able to throw herself into her work but they were so busy at the moment that she felt her own business was about to swallow her up.

'Everything is such a mess, Bea. Our life was not meant to be like this.' Beatrice suddenly felt herself sobering up when she saw her sister's eyes redden and fill with tears. 'I mean there's dad and Lucinda is back fucking swanning around…'

'Jess stop. Come on. We can't be…You can't be falling apart. You don't do that.'

'It's just so shit at the moment,' Jessica sniffed as she reached over for a tissue from the box that was on the oak coffee table. 'It's all so fucking crap.' At that moment, Jessica's mobile phone began to ring. She recognised the number instantly as one of the showbiz desk from *The Daily Post* and wondered which one of her clients was about to grace the sidebar of shame.

'Jessica LeSoeur speaking.'

'Hi, Jess it's Elizabeth Chandler.'

'And what can I do for you?' Jessica said as she slumped back in her seat. In ten years she'd never known Elizabeth, the showbiz editor, to call up just to say hello.

'Well, I'd like a quote actually.'

'A quote. I can't believe that you're actually asking for one.

That's not like you. You're usually so apt at making them up, Liz.'

'Very funny, Jess. We're running a story on your impending divorce and current business problems. So I thought considering how long we've known each other that a quote from you would be appropriate.'

'Liz, once again you've got the wrong information.'

'Oh Jess, are we really going to play this game? We've known each other for far too long. We have a reliable and verified source that your husband, and this will be your second husband Andrew, is divorcing you and that there's a dispute over the business. *"Jessica LeSoeur, ex member of 90's girl group Euterpe in the middle of £25 million divorce battle."* It's a bit long for a headline but I think it'll be effective. So, any comment?'

TWENTY ONE

'£25 MILLION. Is your sister really worth £25 million?'

Jake liked to pretend that he was above salacious gossip and couldn't care less about the rich and famous but Beatrice had caught her husband on more than one occasion stealing her copy of *Allure* magazine and flicking through *Heat* magazine when they were in the supermarket.

'If Jess is worth £25 million I wonder how much Lucinda is worth?' he continued as Beatrice handed him a bottle of beer. It'd been hot and humid all day and Beatrice had jumped straight into the shower when she'd returned home. She felt exhausted. The combination of a champagne fuelled afternoon and the bombshell of Jessica making front-page news for the first time in nearly 20 years had been overwhelming. She'd forgotten what it was like to be caught up in the middle of a media shitstorm.

As soon as Jessica had put the phone down on Elizabeth Chandler it was as if all hell had broken loose. Emma had come running at full pelt into the conference room almost immediately after Jessica had put her phone down, having received her own phone calls from The Daily Post, *Evening Standard and Grazia* magazine. One by one the rest of the staff members followed.

The story had already made the online edition of The Daily Post and would be in the paper edition the following morning. It'd already been discussed on Sky News Press Preview.

'So how much do you reckon Lou is worth then? Forty or fifty million?' Jake asked as he continued to swipe through The Daily Post article on his iPad.

'I have no idea how much Lou is worth. It's not my business to ask,' Beatrice said as she sat at the kitchen table with a large glass of water. 'But there's no way Jess's business is worth £25 million. From what Jess tells me it's probably worth about twelve to fifteen million.'

'Twelve to fifteen million. You say that as though you're talking about a hundred quid. I mean what's our net worth, Bea?'

'God I don't know.'

'I'll tell you what it is. About £12.50, a bag of Doritos and the 6 pack of Kronenburg in the fridge.'

'Things aren't that bad.'

'Oh yeah. We've got the kids. How much do you think we'll get for that bunch of rug rats upstairs?'

'Who'd want them? They'd ask for a refund.'

'So where has this figure of £25million come from?'

'The business, her houses, savings, the office building, royalties…'

'Hold on, royalties? They can't be that much. You get the

odd cheque every couple of years but it's hardly enough to keep me in converse trainers for the rest of my life.'

'You're such a comedian Mr.Ashcroft. Have you ever considered stand-up? Jess and Lou's royalty cheques are a lot more substantial than mine.'

'Why is that? Look babe, I've never pried into what happened financially and I never thought that you'd made enough to sit on your arse forever, even though it's a very nice arse indeed,' Jake said as he leaned over and squeezed Beatrice's bum.

'You're such a perv.'

'And you're an amazing singer, baby cakes.'

'Yeah, but I didn't write the songs. I just provided the oohs and ahhs in the right places. I wasn't sitting up night after night writing lyrics and composing musical arrangements. That was Jessica and Lucinda, and to be honest I wasn't really interested, so it's not as if I've been robbed or anything.'

There was nothing said for a while as outside rumbled with the sounds of thunder and a few seconds later, the kitchen lit up as lightening struck. Both Beatrice and Jake held their breath and watched the video baby monitor but with the exception of baby Sam kicking up his legs, it barely bothered him. The heavens above suddenly opened and rain began to fall signalling a temporary break in the heat wave. Beatrice watched the rain fall outside the kitchen window suddenly taken back to when she was 15 years old and she stumbled upon her two sisters in the so called *good sitting room*. Lucinda was on the piano and Jessica on the floor with a notepad scribbling down lyrics. Even though she'd loved listening to them, she'd never had the same passion as them.

'Do you miss it?' Jake asked, recognising that far-away look in his wife's eyes.

'I probably missed performing more than anything and it was glamorous, to a point. But the truth is that I travelled the world and I never really saw it. I don't have any stupid pictures of me standing on top of the Statue of Liberty, or sitting under the Eiffel Tower. We spent years travelling in the back of coaches and sleeping in hotels. I was scrutinised over my weight, my clothes, and my hair. Don't get me wrong, there were some amazing times but you spend your life living in a bubble and permanently on show, like a moving goldfish bowl. I don't think that we would have survived if we'd carried on.'

'So you'd never want a reunion?'

'God no. I honestly think that Lucinda doing a runner was the best thing that ever happened to us. Can you imagine if we'd carried on? I doubt that I'd have had the life that I have with you now, and to be honest, I wouldn't change that for the world, even if we're only worth a bag of Doritos and a six-pack of beer.'

Jake leaned over and kissed his wife. 'I don't know. I could get used to being a celebrity husband like David Beckham. Staying at home whilst you sing for our supper and follow you around with the kids, smiling politely at the cameras.'

'Shut up. You would have hated it. Sleazy men ogling me whilst I withered about on stage.'

'Bea this was the nineties, I've seen the videos and you never withered.'

'Yeah but if I was still in the game I'd have to compete with

Miley Cyrus and Rhianna. Can you imagine me sitting naked on a bloody wrecking ball?'

'Yes, I can see you sitting you naked...'

'You're obsessed. At least there were still some rules when we were around. It was look but don't touch. But now, it's Facebook, Twitter and Instagram, which I just don't get. If we were still in the game they'd know what colour my knickers were before I'd even put them on.'

Jake laughed and got up to close the kitchen doors. 'I was thinking of taking the twins to my mum and then go into the office tomorrow.'

'Do you mean your shed in the garden or the real office?' Beatrice always found it funny when her husband said that he was going to the office because as far as she could work out he spent his working day drawing and writing comic book scripts and his office attire consisted of jeans, trainers and an assortment of t-shirts. She'd only seen him in a tie on three occasions, their wedding, his nan's funeral and the twins' christening.

'Don't mock the shed. I'm going to the real office so taking them to my mum's and giving you a break seems like a good idea to me. You could go shopping or something.'

Beatrice tried to hide her surprise at the suggestion. Jake's relationship with his mum was delicate, made even more so by her leaving his father and his younger brother, Daniel when they were 14 and 9-years-old. 'I'm trying babe. She can't make it up with me but she wants to try with the kids, so...'

'Speaking of work,' Beatrice said as she followed Jake into the living room and onto the sofa strategically placed in front of the 50 inch television.

'What about it?' Jake replied as he flicked the channel until he came to Sky Sports News.

'I spoke to Anoushka about coming back?'

'What now? Sam is not even six-months-old yet.'

'I know and it kills me to have to leave him but I'm only on full pay for 6 months and then it's reduced by 20%.

'We have savings and it's not as if we have a mortgage to pay.'

'And I want them to remain as savings, Jake.'

'You can always jump on a wrecking ball.'

'Enough with the wrecking ball. I'm serious. I'm going mad at home. I want to pick up a bag that isn't filled with baby wipes. I want to wear beautiful clothes. I want to speak to grown up's Jake.'

'I thought you loved being at home with the kids.'

'I do but…I've never been one to just sit at home and there's more to me than just being a mum. Anyway, we still have bills to pay. You can't afford to keep us'

'I may not be able to drag a wild boar through the house every night for dinner but I try.'

'Sorry, I didn't mean to hurt your feelings but you know what I mean.'

'You didn't hurt my feelings. I would have made a rubbish hunter. But what about Sam? I'm not happy about putting him in a nursery when he's still so young.'

'Well, Sam has to go to nursery at some point and I was thinking that maybe your mum could help out a bit. Don't look at me like that. You didn't think twice about dropping him off two minutes ago.'

'I know. Fine. I can hardly stop you.'

'Thank you, sweetheart,' Beatrice said as she kissed him on his cheek. 'It'll only be part-time at first.'

'Are you going to represent Jessica?'

'I wasn't even thinking about representing her.'

'Bea, come on. This is me you're talking to.'

'Fine. I can't let that bastard take her for everything she's worked for. I just can't Jake.'

'Even so, don't let her walk all over you Bea. It wouldn't be the first time that Jessica has made you do something that you didn't want to do.'

'Jake, I do know how to stand up for myself.'

As if on cue, Beatrice's phone began to beep signalling the arrival of a text.

'I know you do,' Jake said as he picked up her phone. He shook his head as he read the name on the screen. 'I just want you to remember that you're not in Euterpe now and the world doesn't revolve around your sisters. This is real life Bea and you're allowed to say no.'

TWENTY-TWO

'LOU, CAN you hear me properly?'

'I can hear you perfectly but it'd help if you actually turned your video on. Bloody hell, even my gran can use Skype and she's 84,' Lucinda said as she stared at her iPad and waited for her best friend to appear on screen. For someone who was fiercely bright she was amazed at Harrie's inability to master technology.

'I hate Skype. I don't know why you can't pick up a phone.'

'A phone isn't free.'

'Can you see me now because I can see me and I'm not looking so hot in Technicolor. God, I can see my roots. Hey there you are. Hi honey.'

'Hello sweetie.' Lucinda settled back onto the bed and lifted up her glass of wine to salute Harrie.

'So how are you? How's London?'

'London is unbearably hot. Can you hear that noise? That's a fan, Harrie. No one has air-con.'

'Good God no. How do you cope?'

'With ice cold Sauvignon Blanc.' Harrie laughed and gave two thumbs up.

'So give me the news. How are the twins?'

'They're really good. Once they realised that their summer holidays had started early they loved it even though I did get them a tutor just to shut my mother up…and the news is that I've signed up with my old manager.'

'Well that's progress.'

'And I've been writing again.'

'Oh my God. Really? Actual song lyrics.'

'Yes. Harrie. Actual song lyrics and music too. This house actually came with a piano. It's been really good for me, even, cathartic. I just need to get into a studio. For some reason the record companies aren't interested in a forty something woman from an old girl group from yesteryears.'

'Please girl. They know nothing. There's a market for everybody.'

'And Paul called me.'

'What the hell for?'

'Wanted to know why I sold the house, and when I was coming home.'

'But no sign of a cheque. Well, I wouldn't feel too sorry for him. For someone who's supposed to be on skid row he's been running around town acting like he's won the goddam lottery. It makes me sick to my stomach. I haven't had a chance to tell him though. Every time he sees me he runs off quicker than Usain Bolt. The wanker.'

Lucinda laughed out loud. Harrie had declared "wanker" to be her favourite word the first time that she heard Lucinda use it.

'Anyway,' Harrie continued. 'I wouldn't get too excited about him running around as if he's got access to the federal reserve. Remember what I always say about New York City.'

'Smoke and mirrors honey. Smoke and mirrors,' Lucinda said.

'How are you doing for money?'

'I'm doing ok. There are less people to impress here. But I won't lie, Harrie. It's hard. The money from the house will only last so long. I have to find something quick. Things will be a little better when I get into my house but that won't be for another two months.'

'Like what? I mean from what you're saying no one is prepared to invest in you and put money into an album.'

'Thank you for your bluntness.'

'I'm sorry hun, but at a time like this you need someone to be blunt.'

'I even asked Sal about Celebrity Big Brother.'

'You've got to be kidding me.'

'Nope. Desperate times call for desperate measures. But apparently I've already missed the boat on that one.'

'You'd do that? A reality show, warts and all.'

'Harrie, I'd do anything.'

They talked about other things, New York social gossip, Lucinda's family, and Harrie's surprise pregnancy, and then they told each other 'I love you' and ended their Skype call before Harrie saw the tears that were falling from Lucinda's eyes. She missed her best friend who was the closest thing she had to a sister. She'd lost count of the amount of times that she sat in this house wondering if she'd done the right thing taking the children away from everything they knew. As she walked into the hallway, she saw the glow coming from under her son's bedroom door and heard a series of explosions, followed by the sound of his voice barking orders into a headset as he played Black Ops on his Xbox. Next door, her daughter's bedroom door was slightly ajar and she stopped as she heard her daughter's own voice sounding like hers as she sang along to Nina Simone. She was always amused by her daughter who from an early age had dismissed the bubble gum pop in favour of her mother's music collection resulting in more than one scratched record in her vinyl collection, which was currently being stored in the garage. She briefly wondered how much the collection was worth. She knocked tentatively on her daughter's door.

'Hey baby girl. Can I come in?'

'Sure mom.' Katelyn lowered the volume of her iPod dock and shifted along the bed as her mum sat next to her. She was still only 14 and when she wasn't throwing a teenage tantrum about something insignificant, she was a sweet, soft natured, intelligent girl.

'What are you doing?'

'I was talking to Janis on Facetime. She said that you were on Skype with Auntie Harrie.' Janis was Harrie's oldest daughter. She was only a few months younger than Katelyn and they were as close as Lucinda and Harrie were. 'Did you know that Auntie Harrie is having a baby?'

'I did.'

Katelyn wrinkled her nose at the thought. 'You wouldn't

do that, would you? Have another baby?'

'With who? Believe me, having another baby is the last thing on my mind. Anyway, I didn't come in here to talk about babies. I just wanted to see how you are. And to ask you if you're happy?' Katelyn looked at her mum quizzically for a moment and then squinted her eyes in the same way her mother did when she knew that there was something more behind the question

'Are you happy?' Katelyn asked.

'Excuse me? I asked you first.'

'I'm not the one who sold her house and grabbed her two children and ran off halfway around the world because we're not as rich as we used to be.' Lucinda opened her mouth to respond but couldn't think of an appropriate lie. 'Mom. Reece and I aren't stupid. Actually, Reece is stupid but I'm not.'

'Don't talk that way about your brother.'

'Ok fine. But I am happy. I was pissed…'

'Hey, language.'

'Sorry, annoyed about leaving New York, leaving my friends and stuff like that but I like being here. I like being near to Grandma and Grandpa and finally getting to know my aunts and cousins. London is cool. Reece's friends exist in a virtual world so to him nothing's changed.'

'I'm doing my best to make everything right,' Lucinda said as she lay on the bed.

'I know, mom. We wouldn't have moved if you weren't. And it's not like dad was about to win any Father of the Year awards.'

'You shouldn't talk that way about your father. He's still your father.'

Katelyn sighed. 'I know. He keeps telling me that in his emails but he's not here and you are. You're really quite loud.'

'What do you mean?'

'You. Singing. When you sing it fills the house.'

'Thank you but it's not going as well as I thought it would.'

'You know what you should do…'

'Don't you dare suggest The Voice or X-Factor.'

'God mom, no. I was watching this programme on ITV called the Big Reunion. Here let me show you.' Katelyn reached for her MacBook and opened up the Internet. 'They got all of these old groups from the nineties for a big concert.'

'Old?'

'Yes, old. I haven't even heard of any of them. In fact I wasn't even born when…

'I get your point, thank you very much. Not that it matters. I doubt that your aunts would be interested in a reunion.'

'But that doesn't stop you, does it. People love retro and vintage stuff. I was reading about in my magazine. Retro is in.'

'Katelyn. I'm neither retro or vintage.'

Katelyn rolled her eyes. 'Mom, you're overreacting. I'm just saying that you can put on a show. Something small and intimate. Not Wembley stadium or that place in Greenwich which Auntie Emma took us too.'

'You mean the o2.'

'Yeah not there, but somewhere smaller, with you and your piano just like Nina Simone. Except maybe not so angry. What do you think?'

'I think my darling daughter that you may be on to something.'

TWENTY-THREE

IT WAS going to be one bitch of a hangover. Jessica could still taste the wine at the back of her tongue as she slowly rolled over onto her back. She hadn't even made it into her own bed and had passed out on the sofa. The empty wine glass was lying on its side, stained red with the remnants of the wine reminding her of the failed promise she'd made to herself. With the benefit of hindsight she was glad that Lena wasn't here to see her in this state. It was her phone that had woken her up at the ungodly hour of 8.30am. She pulled it out from where it'd been wedged in the back of the sofa with the remote control and what looked like half a bag of now melted chocolate buttons. There were various emails from newspapers and magazines wanting to buy her story, and two texts from Barclays with an update on her bank balance; for the first time ever she wished that the numbers were a great fat zero, as that way Andrew would leave her alone. The second text was from Lucinda. She was about to delete it when the phone vibrated in her hand. Jessica must have still been drunk because she didn't press decline.

'I suppose that you're calling to gloat.'

'No, Jess. I haven't called to gloat. I just wanted to see how you're doing?' Lucinda said as she sat down on the bottom step and took off her trainers. 'I've seen the papers and I just thought…'

'You thought what?'

'I know that it can't be easy.'

'This is anything but easy,' Jessica said as she opened the shutters of the front window and immediately closed them again when she noticed a couple of photographers holding cups of tea whilst they waited outside. 'I'm sure that you'd love the whole world knowing your business but I don't.'

'You're more than welcome to come to me if you want to get away from things for while,' Lucinda said.

'Unlike you, Lou, I can't just pick up and run whenever things don't go my way. I have responsibilities,' Jessica snapped back. She walked into her kitchen and started opening cupboards looking for anything that would put an end to the pounding headache that had started to form in the middle of her forehead. She vaguely remembered eating half a bowl of porridge yesterday and a bag of popcorn but she didn't think anything of nutritional value had entered her stomach. Lucinda didn't rise to the bait as she stretched out her legs. 'Jess, I just wanted to see how you were doing and to let you know that I'm here for you, ok?'

'It's funny isn't it?'

'What's funny?'

'Well, everything was fine until you came along. Dad wasn't ill…'

'For crying out loud Jessica, you're just being…'

'And my marriage was fine.' Lucinda took a deep breath and started to silently count to ten.

'There were no problems with my marriage. We were happy.'

'Happy? People don't walk out of their marriages when they're happy.'

'But as soon as you stepped foot in London, everything starts going to shit. I'm such a fucking idiot. I don't know why I didn't see it earlier…'

'Jess, your marriage problems have…'

'They have everything to do with you. What did you do? Email him before you left. Tell him that you wanted to finish off what you started.'

'Seriously Jess, you better stop right there.'

'Stop what? How long have you been fucking my husband, sister?' Jessica spat out the last word as she reached for the bottle of wine instead of the bottle of water at the back of the fridge.

'Have you been drinking or are you on drugs? I'm not…'

'I bet it started as soon as you came back. Is that why you kept sending your kids to mum and dad's, so you could fuck Andrew in your bed?'

'You've gone too fucking far. I haven't spoken to or seen that man that you call your husband. You really are a delusional cow. I told you from day one that he was a dog but you didn't want to see it. You believed all the bullshit that came out of his mouth over your own flesh and blood. You have no idea what he tried to…'

'I don't want to hear anymore of your lies, Lucinda. I know this has something to do with you. I know that...' Jessica didn't get a chance to say anymore as the call came to an abrupt end. She stared at the phone in her left hand and the wine bottle in her right hand. She threw the phone to the other end of the kitchen and watched as it hit the tiles as she slid down to the floor.

Lucinda ran to the bathroom and washed her face. She was so angry and she couldn't stop the tears that sprung from her eyes. After all these years, Jessica was still holding on to the lies that Andrew had told her, even though he'd walked out on her and had laid bare their lives for the world to see. She got dressed and headed downstairs to the front room. Earlier she'd gone for a run to clear her head and give herself room to think, but now it felt just as congested as it had when she woke up that morning. She sat at the piano and played a few scales to warm up. Then she began to play the song that had been forming in her head for the past few weeks.

'You said that I was a star,
But I was no more than dust and light,
I was supposed to shine brightly but the eclipse came and took my light
I fell down to earth with nothing to break my fall
I tried to stand up but my power was gone.'

She could feel the emotion of the song rising from the pit of her stomach. It was the only thing that felt right and natural to her. It put a soothing blanket over Jessica's words.

'Mom, there's someone at the door for you,' Reece said as he suddenly appeared at Lucinda's side with a half eaten croissant in his hand. She hadn't even realised that he'd come into the room or that someone had been knocking at the door for several minutes.

'Who is it?'

Reece shrugged his shoulders. 'I don't know. Some woman.' Lucinda wondered if it was a reporter who had tracked her down looking for *a close member of the family* to give them information on her sister's marriage breakdown.

'You sounded good mom,' Reece said as he threw himself onto the sofa and turned the TV on.

Lucinda opened the front door prepared to give the reporter or whatever they were a mouthful but she stopped when the slender red-headed woman turned around. She was definitely not a reporter. She was wearing the world recognised uniform of a new mother, black leggings, vest and an oversized cardigan. She wasn't wearing any makeup and when she put her hair behind her ears, Lucinda could see a faint scar running from her temple to her chin. The woman immediately pulled her hair back over her ear and smoothed it down. She had the same intense green eyes like her brother.

'Was that you?'

'Excuse me?' Lucinda asked as she wondered what this woman hoped to achieve by turning up on her doorstep at ten o'clock on a Saturday morning.

'Was that you singing?'

'Yes, it was.'

'It sounded amazing. Painful but amazing.'

'Can I help you or do you just randomly go around knocking on people's front doors offering a musical critique?'

'I'm sorry. I'm sorry. Yes, my name is Madeline and you're trying to kick me out of my house.'

* * * *

'How old is your baby?' Lucinda asked as she placed a cup of tea in front of Madeline who was now sitting in her kitchen, looking around, clearly not impressed with the decor.

'Abigail is six months and teething. I don't think I've slept for two days,' Madeline answered with a smile. 'And Joshua is 5.'

'Same ages as my niece and nephew,' Lucinda replied as she sat down in front of Madeline knowing she was about to hear a story that she wouldn't like.

'I left my husband two years ago. He gave me this,' Madeline said as she pulled back her hair to reveal her scar. 'And this.' She lifted her right cardigan sleeve and revealed a faint four inch scar. 'There are three metal pins holding my wrist together.'

'I'm sorry,' Lucinda said, not quite sure what she should be saying. To apologise didn't seem enough.

'It's ok. Joshua was 3 when I left. Owen my brother, whom you've met, he found the house for me. His flat was too small for a nervous wreck of a sister and a lunatic three-year-old.'

'You don't have to tell me all of this. I appreciate that none of this is easy.'

THE SISTERS

'I just want you to understand why this house has been important to me,' Madeline said firmly as though she'd been practicing. 'We had been there for almost a year, Josh and I, when my husband calls me out of the blue. Tells me that he wants to see Joshua. Wanted me to forgive him. Said that he'd had counselling. Anyway, like I fool, I went to see him. Owen told me not to and well…I ended up with a broken wrist and he gave me Abigail as a leaving present.'

'I don't know what you expect me to…'

'That house is the only place where I've felt safe with my children. My brother is only around the corner. I can't leave. Not yet.'

'I'm sorry. I really am and believe me if I was in a position to…I just can't. I need my house back.'

Madeline nodded. 'I'm sorry about Owen by the way. He's a bit overprotective.'

'Please don't worry about it. I'd have done exactly the same thing if I were him. Family is important.' Suddenly as if a thousand light bulbs had gone off in Madeline's head, she looked straight into Lucinda's eyes and she broke out into a smile.

'I know who you are. No wonder Owen kept saying you looked familiar. He had to listen to me playing your album on repeat when I was 16. My best friend and I even sang your song at our college talent show. You were in Euterpe, right? Oh my God. This is so cool,' Madeline said excitedly as she took a sip of her tea. 'Wow.'

'And I'm kicking you out of your house,' Lucinda said embarrassingly.

'I'm not being funny but what's wrong with this one?'

'It's a long story and not one that I'm prepared to go into with a complete stranger.'

'Fair enough.' The two women said nothing for a few minutes and just drank their tea.

'I can't believe that I'm sitting in Lucinda from Euterpe's kitchen,' Madeline said with a giggle. 'Can you believe that this is the first time I've been out of the house all week? It was like when I first moved in. I was scared shitless of leaving the house in case he found me, and the annoying thing is that I had a really beautiful house in Crystal Palace. We'd bought that house when it was a wreck, and we spent two years doing it up, making it perfect. It was what I did before I became a mum. I'm an interior designer. I loved knocking things down and building them back up again. Unfortunately I went and picked a man who decided that he liked knocking me down too. He was nice in the beginning but it starts with a push or a pinch and then…sorry. You don't want to hear about all of this.'

'It's ok. If you want to.'

'It's odd. I feel like I know you.'

'I'm kind of used to people saying that.'

'Anyway, what I wanted to say to you was this. We're in the process of selling the house. The Crystal Palace one. Apparently, I'm a millionaire. He was being a right arse about the house until the one across the road sold for something stupid and the next thing I know my lawyer is telling me that my decree nisi is in the post and that he's offering me half the proceeds from the house.'

'Oh lucky for you. So what are you going to do now?' Lucinda tried her best not to sound envious.

'I'd love to buy your house…'

'That's not going to happen…'

'Don't worry about it, I can't afford it. I half considered going back to Ireland and living with my parents but that would just give me a nervous breakdown. Owen is helping me look for somewhere else but I just need some more time.'

'Well how long do you need?'

'I'm asking for another three months on top of the six weeks that I've got left.'

'Madeline, I really can't do that.'

'Lucinda, please. We've accepted an offer for the Crystal Palace house and if everything goes ok, I'll have my share in about 6 weeks. I promise you that if I don't find anywhere by then I'll go. Even if it means that I have to tell Owen that he's going to have share a bunk bed with me for a couple of months, or God forbid I book a flight back to Ireland.'

Lucinda looked around at the kitchen that didn't belong to her and at the woman who had decided to spill out her life story to a complete stranger. She didn't owe this woman or her children anything. Keeping a roof over Reece and Katelyn's head was her only priority. Not Madeline.

'Ok,' Lucinda said before she had a chance to do more calculations in her head.

'What? Really?'

'Yes, really. I need good karma. So you can stay but only for an extra three months, and after that. I'm taking my house back. Is that clear?'

'Yes. Yes, absolutely. Thank you,' Madeline said as she reached out and hugged Lucinda and then quickly let go as she noticed the time on the clock on the oven door.

'Bloody hell, I better go. The kids have probably driven Owen mad by now.' Lucinda got up and followed Madeline to the front door.

'The estate agents are going to put this in writing. Not that I trust them to even put a poster on a wall.'

'That's fine. Honestly, I keep my word. Thank you'

'You're welcome.'

'I bet that your sisters are really happy to have you as their sister,' Madeline said before she turned and walked down the stairs.

'Not really,' Lucinda said softly as she closed the door.

TWENTY-FOUR

'HOW ABOUT an interview?'

'Who with?'

'*The Daily Post, OK magazine. The Mercury. The South London Press.* The newsletter for my son's karate club. Anyone who's prepared to talk to you.'

'Sal, they're only interested because they think I'm going to give a tell-all about Jessica. That isn't going to happen,' Lucinda said.

'But it'll get your name out there again. You know how these things work, Lou. We need to raise your profile and it might be worth a couple of quid.'

'I said no. I'm not going to talk about my family's business for a couple of quid. What sort of person do you think I am?'

'Fine. Fine be like that,' said Sal as they walked together through Portobello Market which was packed with shopped and idle walkers.

'It shouldn't be this hard, Sal,' Lucinda said as she stopped at a record stall and started to flick through a box of records. She smiled, as she pulled out a Jim Reeves album, pristine in a plastic sleeve. 'Every Sunday morning, without fail, my dad would put this on. It used to drive us mad but he loves it. "The man knows how to tell a story," Dad would always say. I could sing *Welcome to My World* in my sleep. Have you got a tenner?' she asked as the stall owner placed the record in a bag. 'Don't look at me like that.' She held up the bags of food she was holding in her canvas tote bags and tried to wave them in front of Sal's face. 'I've spent all my cash and he doesn't take cards.'

'Nah love. Hard cold cash for me,' the stall owner said as he handed the plastic bag to Lucinda.

'I hope you've got something to play it on?' Sal said as he pulled a crisp ten pound note from his pocket. 'I can't remember the last time I saw a turntable.'

'So, what's the plan?' Lou asked as they walked through the market and turned right onto Kensington Park Road where Sal had parked his car.

'I thought the newspaper interview was a good plan but…'

'No Sal, not unless they want to pay me more than just a couple of quid to talk about me and me only. I don't need the headache.'

'But you need the cash right? Look Lou, this game is hard. Times of austerity and all that crap, and no disrespect but you're a bit too old to think that you can upload a video of you singing on YouTube in the hope of a record company throwing money at you.'

'I wouldn't even know how to start uploading a bloody video and it's not about the money…well it is, but it's more than that.'

'Well, whatever it is you need to stop being so bloody stubborn. Swallow your pride a bit. The Lucinda I knew from back in the day would have done anything, within reason, but you'd worry about your pride and what people thought later.'

She said nothing as she noticed someone familiar crossing the road towards her. 'I'm not being stubborn. I just need to do this the right way. I don't need to be adding anymore drama to my life.'

'Speaking of drama. How's Jess doing? I texted her the other day but I haven't heard from her.'

'You're better off asking Beatrice.'

'You and her still not good?'

'Far from good.' She stopped as the person she'd seen crossing the road appeared at her side. 'Hello Owen. You're not going to start shouting at me in the street again are you?'

Owen began to visibly redden. He rubbed at his beard and smiled embarrassingly. 'No. I'm not. I'm sorry about that.'

'Everything all right, Lou?' Sal asked with one hand hovering on the door handle of his Jaguar.

'Yeah, everything's fine. There's nothing for you to worry about.' Lucinda said as she kissed Sal on both cheeks.

'Ok then. Well, let me know if anything isn't fine,' Sal said as he opened the driver's door and got into the car. 'By the way, I'm going to email you the details of another producer. I've managed to talk him round to meeting you.'

'Talk him round? I don't want to work with someone who you've had to talk around.'

'Stop being stubborn. Give him a go. You're both just as pretentious as each other. You might actually get on,' Sal said as he revved the engine and drove off.

'Interesting guy,' Owen said

'That's a polite way of putting it. So, can I help you with anything or are you just in the habit of following people?'

'I wanted to say thank you for what you did for Maddie. I mean, I acted like a bit of a git…'

'As I said, that's a nice way of putting it.'

'I know. I'm sorry. It's just that she's my little sister and she's…'

'She's been through a lot. I know, she told me.'

'She did?' Owen asked, surprised. 'She's not one to open up to strangers. She's a bit of a closed book, my sister. Anyway, I had no right to behave the way that I did. I'm sorry. It's your house and you can do with it what you want.'

'Apology accepted. Your sister is a nice woman. I hope that everything works out for her.'

'Me too. She's had it hard but you made her day. Even if you'd told her to pack her bags and go right now, you'd have still made her day. I remember having to take her and her mates to Tower Records in Piccadilly to pick up tickets to one of your concerts.'

'Did you now?'

'Yeah and my dad made me take her to the concert as well. Thought they were too young to go on their own.'

'So you weren't a fan then?' Lucinda said.

'Not really. It was a good show though and I'm not just saying that. Anyway, I'm sure you've got things to do.'

'Just cooking.'

'You cook? I thought you'd have people to do that for you.'

'I don't know why everyone thinks that I have *people*. I'm more than capable of cooking myself, thank you very much.'

'Sorry, no offence. I'm sure you're a very good cook but I'm better.'

'You're really full of it aren't you?'

'Just a bit. Look, I was a prat to you before. Bang out of order as Madeline keeps reminding me. So as a thank you and an apology I'd like to invite you to have dinner with me at my restaurant tomorrow night.'

'Dinner. With you?'

'I promise you it won't be that painful. I mean I'd understand if you said no.'

Lucinda thought about it for a minute. Since she'd been home she'd done nothing except run around London trying to put her life in order. There had been no fun, so she surprised herself by saying, 'No. I mean, yes. Dinner would be great.'

'Oh, ok then' Owen replied, equally surprised. 'Tomorrow at eight. My restaurant is called…'

'I know, Geraint's kitchen.'

'That's right. It's just at the end of Portobello Road, the Enbridge Road end. Is that ok for you?' Owen said with a smile.

'That's fine.'

'Great. Well, I'll see you tomorrow.' There was an awkward pause as they tried to work out the appropriate way to say goodbye. Instead they both nodded at each before Lucinda turned and walked through the park. She started to smile to herself, as she knew he hadn't moved and was still there watching her.

TWENTY-FIVE

'Fans were left devastated after it was announced that the lead singer of Euterpe, Lucinda LeSoeur has left the group just three months after entering the American Album charts at number one with their second album "Second Strike." Lucinda LeSoeur issued a statement saying that she had left for professional reasons only but that her sisters supported her in her decision and that they remained as close as ever. The remaining band members, Jessica and Beatrice LeSoeur were unavailable for comment.'

Jessica moved the curser to the beginning and watched the newsreader deliver the bad news again. She didn't know what had possessed her to start googling old videos of Euterpe. She was hoping that they'd have been forgotten, but she'd been surprised as she clicked on numerous fanzines' sites and Twitter accounts dedicated to her old life. They had been the top feature on the nine o'clock news that Sunday night. Jessica and Beatrice had watched the news in a Paris hotel room with Sal, not quite believing that Lucinda had so abruptly pulled the brakes on their career. Jessica still had trouble remembering what she'd done after she'd stormed out of the hotel room. It had infuriated her to hear the newsreader say, "the sisters remained as close as ever." What a joke! The only thing that she could remember was that she'd booked a flight to Ibiza and had gone on a three-day bender with a DJ friend of hers. Ironically, when she'd returned home, their last single, which had dropped down to number 46, in the charts, had climbed back up and was number one for six weeks. It'd been years since she'd stood on the periphery of fame and scandal, but Lucinda had made sure that she'd placed her back on the cliff edge again. Somewhere in the back of her brain she knew she was blaming the wrong person for what was going on in her life but it was easier to use her as punching bag. She'd happily project her anger at Andrew but she still had no idea where he'd disappeared to.

'Why aren't you at work?' Lena walked into her mother's bedroom and looked around. The shutters were closed despite the fact that at nine in the morning it was already 25 degrees and the sun's rays were hitting every window on the south-side of the house. It was a good question. Jessica was never late for work and had never taken a day off, not even when she was ill with bronchitis and could barely walk 10ft without stopping for breath and wheezing like an old man.

'When did you get in?' Jessica said ignoring the question. Lena pulled open the shutters and opened the windows, letting the sun's rays hit almost every surface in the room. She looked over with a look of disgust when she noticed the light spattering of dust on the dressing table.

'About half an hour ago. Auntie Lou dropped me...'

'She did what? Why was she dropping you off? You were

supposed to be staying with your dad.'

'Mum. Your fight with auntie Lou is not my fight. It's nothing to do with me or Katelyn or Reece. Just because you two are fighting doesn't mean that I can't go over there.'

'You were supposed to be with your dad. That was the agreement. You wait until I speak to him,' Jessica said unconvincingly.

'Why aren't you at work?' Lena asked again.

Jessica didn't answer as she got out of bed and started to straighten the duvet. Lena looked down at her mother's feet, walked over and picked up an empty wine bottle that had been poking out from under the bed.

'At least Auntie Lou isn't drinking herself into oblivion every night. I'm not surprised that Andrew left you,' Lena said angrily.

'How dare you talk to me like that! What exactly has that woman been filling your head with?' Jessica shouted at her daughter.

'She didn't fill my head with anything. I'm the one who lives with you. Just because I'm 16 doesn't mean I'm stupid.'

'I never said you were stupid.'

'Well, you're treating me like I am and you make Auntie Lou out to be a really horrible person, but she's not. She cares about you.'

'Lena, stop talking and get out of my room right now.' Jessica grabbed the wine bottle out of Lena's hand. They stared at each other. The same defiant look in their eyes.

'You're so busy blaming everyone else for what went wrong that I bet it hasn't occurred to you that the only reason I went to stay with dad is that I didn't want to be around you.'

Lena stormed out and slammed the door behind her. Her daughter was the last person she ever thought would talk to her like that. How dare she question her, criticise her and take Lucinda's side over her? Jessica threw the wine bottle and watched as it smashed against the pale blue walls. A small trickle of red wine began to snake its way down the wall before it settled into a small teardrop pool on the skirting board. She just wanted silence. To be able to hide away from it all like last time, but Andrew was making it impossible. £25 million! She knew she had to get herself together. She'd spent literally the rest of the weekend on the sofa watching bad movies and drinking. The only thing that she'd eaten was half a Chinese takeaway. Things had to change, but right now she could only take one step at a time. She had go to work but first she had to sort out a new phone because from memory it was still in pieces on the kitchen floor.

'It feels different when it's happening on your own doorstep. Look at them. Blood thirsty parasites,' Meghan said as she leaned over the wall and looked down at the paparazzi outside the agency's front door. Emma looked across at her friend who'd dragged her out to accompany her on her cigarette break. They were both on what was laughingly called a roof garden. There wasn't a pot plant or any decking on site but there was a bench and a table and chairs, which some of the staff members had nicked from the skip when the cafe next door had been doing their renovations.

'You'd think that they'd have had enough by now.' Emma said.

'Now Ems. You know better than that. They're like new born babies, they always want feeding. Oh shit,' Meghan said as she realised that Emma had suddenly gone quiet. 'Ems. I didn't think.'

'Don't be silly. I'm ok. You can't keep walking on eggshells around me forever.'

'I know but…I should have thought. Are you sure you're ok?' Emma nodded even though she could feel her eyes were starting to burn with tears.

'It was the first thing that I thought about when I woke up. I can't believe that it has already been a year.'

'You should have taken the day off.'

'God no. I couldn't think of anything worse than to spend the day moping around my flat. Us LeSoeurs don't do moping.'

'Speaking of LeSoeurs, I think your sister has just arrived.' They both leaned over to see the paparazzi swarm like bees as Jessica stepped out of a cab. She rushed through the crowd as they repeatedly called her name. They were used to Jessica standing boldly in front of them and reading out statements for her clients. It'd been a long time since they'd had to make do with a photograph of Jessica trying to hide her face.

You wouldn't have thought that anything was wrong as she walked boldly through the office. Whilst she'd willed herself to shower and dress for work she'd made a decision. It wasn't about what she was going to do with her life; that was too much to think about, it was about Phoenix PR. She was proud of what she'd built but she knew she couldn't cope with everything that was going on and if she wasn't on the ball there was a danger that she could lose it all.

'You want me to do what?' Emma asked as she sat in front of Jessica. An hour after Jessica had walked into the office the paparazzi had disappeared when they'd received news that Heather Stone, who was just 17-years-old and was being touted as Britain's next big thing, was due to arrive at West End Police Station after being arrested for assaulting her own mother. Jessica should have been at the police station with her but had sent Meghan along in her place. The last thing Jessica felt like doing was acting as an appropriate adult to a moody teenager. She was hardly the best choice when she could hardly communicate with her own child. She'd pushed paper around her desk and made a call or two giving the appearance that she was a woman in control before dragging Emma out for a late lunch.

'You heard what I said,' Jessica replied as she swirled the ice around her tall glass of vodka and tonic.

'I heard you but I think you've made a mistake.'

'I haven't made a mistake. Anyway, it's wasn't solely my decision.'

'Well, in that case you've all made a mistake. I'm not ready for all of that responsibility.'

'You're more than ready.'

'You actually want me to become a director of the company?'

'Well not just you. Wendy has agreed to become a director also...'

'Has this got anything to do with your divorce?'

'Of course not. It's a business decision. Nothing more than that.'

'And you want me to be in charge of the reality TV and wags division.'

'You really have to stop calling it that.'

'But why now? I mean you've got Christopher and Wendy...'

'And we can't do it all. Do you have any idea how much the business has grown over the last five years? When I first started I had just two clients and then something happened. It was as if the bubble had burst and anyone who'd even just had five minutes let alone fifteen minutes of fame started knocking on my door. Emma, you're level headed, smart and you know exactly how this business works. You've always known how it works.'

'They'll say that it's nepotism. That I only got the job because you feel sorry for me.'

'I'm giving you a promotion. It's as simple as that. Look, if I had any doubts about you, you wouldn't have got past the reception area. Wendy would have chucked your CV in the bin and I don't feel sorry for you. Well, I do but...you know what I mean.'

Emma nodded as she thought about what her sister had just said. It was always playing in the back of her mind that her job was no more than a sympathy vote but she knew that wasn't true. She'd been at Phoenix for over two years and had applied for the job with hundreds of other people. Any sympathy that had come afterwards had been brief.

'So, I'll be in charge of the wags…sorry Celebrity and Personal PR division?'

'Yes.'

'Complete control?'

Jessica downed her glass of vodka and tonic and started to pick at the Tuna Nicoise Salad that had remained untouched for the last half hour.

'Don't get carried away. I'm still in charge, and yes you'll have complete control. The same way that Wendy has control of the film, books and publishing division, and the same way that Christopher has control of the sport division. I'll carry on with the corporate and media PR division and I've decided that we'll have to recruit someone to head the music division.'

'Why all the changes? Don't tell me again that it has nothing to do with the divorce?'

'I told you Ems, it's just business. Nothing more than that.'

TWENTY-SIX

'HE SHOULD have let us pick him up from the hospital,' Emma said as she took the remainder of the shopping bags from the boot of her mother's car. 'He's so stubborn.'

'I don't know what's wrong with him. He seems determined to do all of this on his own,' Felicia said as they walked into the house. The sounds of cricket commentary escaped from the living room accompanied by Richard's soft snoring. 'He's been sleeping a lot. A lot more than last time.'

Emma stood at the living room door watching her father stretched out on the sofa with a newspaper on his chest, gently sleeping. 'Same ol' same ol,' she said under her breath before she followed her mum into the kitchen.

'I made a cake this morning,' Felicia said as she started putting things away. Emma dumped the bags on the kitchen counter and opened the ancient quality street tin that her mum used for a cake tin.

'Mum, this is a fruit cake. I hate fruit cake.'

'Not that one. That one's for Beatrice. Open the other tin. I made you a carrot cake.' Emma opened the tin and inhaled the scent of cinnamon, nutmeg and vanilla as her mum handed her a knife and a plate. She watched Emma as she cut into the cake. She could clearly remember that day last year when she'd found her last daughter trying to make her way down the stairs but having to stop just under the photograph of her paternal grandfather as the pain tightened every muscle in its vice like grip.

'Do you mind if I stay tonight?' Emma asked as she carefully sliced the cake and placed a large piece on her plate.

'What sort of question is that? Of course you can stay.'

'I just didn't fancy being on my own tonight. You know the funny thing is that I didn't even want to get married and have babies. I know that I'm not supposed to say things like that but it's the truth. Children weren't even on my radar, mum. I'm a free spirit. I wasn't ready to be tied down.'

'It's nothing to feel bad about. Children were the last things on my mind when I fell pregnant with Lucinda. I'd just graduated from LSE and I was enjoying my summer. The problem was, I enjoyed it a little too much because one month after starting my masters I found out I was pregnant…'

Felicia stopped talking as she diverted her attention to the kettle. Now wasn't the time to tell her daughter that she'd been in denial about the pregnancy for nearly four months and it was only as she sat in the abortion clinic with a nurse explaining to her in detail what exactly they'd do to remove the unborn child from her womb that Felicia had walked out. She'd always fully advocated a woman's choice to choose but at that point there was only one choice she could make. Richard had always told Lucinda that she was a lovechild but Felicia had never told her daughter that she'd never really wanted her.

'Mum.' Emma looked up from her plate to see her mother standing in front of the kitchen window, staring into the distance. 'Mum, are you ok?'

'Of course. I'm fine. So you were saying…'

'I was just saying that it was different with you. You were excited about having a baby. I didn't even know. There are days where I don't think about it. It wasn't as if I was picking nursery colours and test-driving prams but when I realised what was happening…well, I wanted him more than anything.' Emma subconsciously moved her right hand to her stomach.

Felicia didn't say anything because this was the first time in a year that Emma had begun to talk about it. She'd been so determined to get on with her life and had ignored any attempts to talk about it. Emma had even avoided Beatrice for a few months whilst she'd been pregnant with Sam.

'Anyway, that was then and this is now and right now I'm worried about Jess.'

'I'm sure that there's nothing to worry about,' Felicia said as she glanced at her watch. She didn't like him to sleep for too long. It scared her.

'She's drinking again. A lot.' Suddenly it was as if the world had stopped and everything had gone quiet. Even the fridge seemed to have dulled its monotonous hum.

'Jess has always liked a drink. She's like your father. … I'm sure that it's not as bad as you think.'

'Mum, it's one thing having a glass of wine after work to wind down, but it's another thing to knock back two double vodkas before I've had a chance to open a can of coke.'

'Emma...'

'She's been late for work and you know what she's like, Mum. Jess has never been late for work since that place opened, not even when she first started out and she was running it from her front room. Lena hasn't even been staying at home.'

'What are you talking about?'

'She's been staying with her dad. The only reason that she's back at home is because Christopher is in Italy with his new girlfriend.'

'How do you know that?'

'Lena phoned and asked if she could stay with me for a couple of days.'

'That doesn't mean anything? She's sixteen, she's on holidays.'

'Mum. Stop it. There's something going on and it's not just this thing with Andrew. Ever since Lucinda came back, Jessica has been acting weird.'

'Well, you know what those two are like. Look, your sister is just going through a bad time, that's all. I don't think there's any need to panic.'

'Mum, I remember what she was like the last time she was going through a bad time.'

'That was entirely different.' They stopped talking as they heard the sound of the downstairs toilet being flushed. 'Don't you mention a word of this to your father. You hear me.'

'Mum, we can't ignore it.'

'Emma, there's nothing going on with Jessica. You're

making a big thing out of nothing.'

Emma shook her head, every instinct in her body telling her that her mother was wrong.

'What's done in the dark will always come to light. Isn't that what you always say, mum?'

* * * *

'Are you going on a date?' Katelyn asked as she stood in front of her mother's open wardrobe and started going through her clothes.

'It is not a date,' Lucinda replied as she picked up the white sleeveless chiffon blouse from the wardrobe door and held it up against herself whilst staring at her image in the mirror.

'Well, if it's not a date why have you changed three times?'

'I haven't changed three times. The first dress had a stain on it.'

'I don't mind you going on dates. In fact I think you should go on dates. I mean if I have to wait until I'm 16 the least you can do is go out and enjoy yourself.'

Lucinda stopped midway from removing her shorts and stared at her daughter as she took a pair of hologramic Jimmy Choos from their box and placed her feet in them. 'Hey, they fit,' Katelyn said as she begun to strut up and down her mother's bedroom.

'You're mad.'

'Like mother like daughter. So what's he like? Your date?'

'For the umpteenth time it's not a date. Its just dinner. To …well…to apologise and he's, I don't know. He's just a man.'

'Who has asked you to dinner. I think the blouse with this skirt.' Katelyn handed over a pale blue pleated midi skirt. 'Ooh, and definitely these shoes.'

'I've told you this isn't a date.'

'That doesn't mean you can't look nice. Isn't that what you always say? Always look your best.'

Half an hour later, Lucinda was finally ready as she put the finishing touches to her outfit with a spritz of her favourite Chanel perfume. She actually felt resentful for leaving Katelyn as she'd really enjoyed spending the time with her daughter whilst she'd got ready for her *'not a date'* date. That was one of the blessings of moving from New York. She'd spent so much time trying to keep up with the New York Jones that she'd forgotten to keep up with her own children. She silently said a prayer and thanked God for allowing her the time to get to know them.

'So, whilst you're on your date,' Reece said as he sat on the bottom step near the front door watching his mother step into her ballet flats.

'It's not a date," Katelyn said as she sat down on the step behind him. 'It's an apology dinner.'

'Yeah right. Mom is going on a date.'

'I give up with you two,' Lucinda said as she picked up her keys from the hallway table.

'Anyway, whilst you're on your date,' Reece continued. 'Eating in a nice restaurant, what are we supposed to do? I mean you don't expect us to fend for ourselves do you?'

'So what you can't put pot on fire?' Lucinda replied in a

Grenadian accent reminiscent of what her mother would tell their father when he'd bang around the kitchen saying there was nothing to eat. 'I've already made your dinner. The chicken curry is on the cooker and the roti is on the side covered with a tea towel.'

'Ah, you made roti,' Reece replied as his eyes widened. 'Did you make that pumpkin and shrimp thing?'

'Everything is there Reece. Now only give the roti skins 30 seconds in the microwave otherwise it'll just turn into concrete.'

'Cool, enjoy your date,' Reece said as he ran into the kitchen.

'You know, mom if the singing thing doesn't work out you can always become a chef,' Katelyn said.

'My cooking isn't that good.' Lucinda put her hand on the door handle to open it but immediately jumped back as someone determinedly knocked on the front door very hard.

'Hi, Auntie Lou,' Lena said as Lucinda opened the door, surprised to see her niece standing on the doorstep.

'Lena, I didn't know you were coming over. Do you have to knock the door so hard? You sound like the police.'

'Sorry Auntie Lou. I texted Katelyn earlier and said that I was coming round. It's ok isn't it?'

'Of course it's ok.' Lucinda opened the door wider for her niece to step through but didn't say a word when she noticed the large holdall that Lena was holding in her hands. 'Have you eaten?' Lucinda asked as Lena kissed her cheek and she noticed the puffiness around her eyes.

'I had something at lunch-time.' If Lena was anything like

her mother then something was nothing more than some chocolate and a bottle of juice.

'Well, your cousins are about to stuff their faces in the kitchen so why don't you join them?'

Lena nodded and began to walk towards the kitchen. 'Oh and Lena, make sure your mum knows where you are.'

'I will.'

Lucinda walked out of the house and closed the door, knowing full well that there were better odds on her being selected to lead England in the World Cup then of Lena calling her mother. So she did the responsible thing and texted Jessica with the certainty that Jessica wouldn't text her back.

TWENTY-SEVEN

JESSICA HAD left the office in a temper. In fact, she'd spent the rest of the afternoon in a state of silent fury. She hated not being in control and felt like a puppet whose strings were being pulled in four different directions. The one place that should have been her sanctuary felt as though it was closing in on her. The paparazzi hadn't come back. She knew better than anybody that notoriety only lasted for so long and they were hardly going to stay just to get a picture of someone who used to be famous. Wendy had called and told her to come to the book launch party of another celebrity who hadn't picked up a book since Johnny and Jennifer's Yellow Hat when they were 6-years-old but Jessica had refused and said she was going to take the evening off, go to the gym and watch some rubbish on TV. Her intention quickly dissipated with the arrival of Lucinda's text whilst she sat in the back of the cab as it turned onto Pentonville Road. First her husband, even though she didn't have any actual proof, and now her own daughter was deserting her for her older sister. She leaned towards the open car window in a fairly useless effort to fan the flames of the temper that had been swirling and building inside of her since the moment she'd opened her eyes that morning. By the time the cab had pulled up onto her road she'd managed to talk herself into going for a run to clear the cobwebs in her head, but that intention was quickly swept away when she saw the thick white envelope on the doormat.

'Jess you need to calm down,' Beatrice said as she balanced baby Sam on her left shoulder and held her phone to her right ear. The last time she'd heard Jessica this angry was when Lucinda had walked into the dressing room and announced, *"I'm leaving."*

'Don't tell me to calm down. How can I calm down when everything I've worked for is being taken out from underneath me?'

'Jessica,' Beatrice said firmly. 'Stop pacing and sit down.'

Jessica did what she was told and sat down in the middle of her living room floor with the contents of the white envelope held tightly in her left hand.

'Who the hell does he think he is, Bea? How the fuck can he think that he's entitled to my business?'

'What exactly did the solicitors send you?'

'He didn't build this. I did. The bastard.' Beatrice placed the baby on the sofa next to his brother and sister who for once were sitting quietly in their pyjamas flicking through their dad's comic books whilst Jake sat in his armchair flicking through the TV channels.

'Are you still there?' Bea asked as she closed the living room door and sat down in the quiet of her kitchen.

'Yes, I'm still here.'

'Right, so tell me what they have sent you.'

'Divorce petition, application for ancillary relief, acknowledgement of service and some other bits of crap. I still can't believe he's doing this.'

'Right, I want you to scan and email everything to me, ok? Do it as soon as you get off the phone.'

'He wants my house, Bea. He didn't contribute a penny to this house, and the pensions, share accounts…'

'Jess, stop it. There's no point making yourself even more upset. He's not worth it.'

'How the fuck can I stop?' Jessica said as she started to scan the page that listed her possessions like a shopping list. She'd read it in a blind fury 15 minutes earlier, but now as she sat on the cool wooden floor and the calmness ebbed through her she noticed the last entry, which clearly wasn't an afterthought but had been placed there to reiterate the fact that Andrew intended on getting absolutely everything.

'This is just priceless,' Jessica said as she stood up and walked towards the kitchen. 'Fucking priceless.'

'What are you talking about?'

'He wants my fucking royalties.' She hesitated as she opened the fridge door and stared at the bottles of white wine on the middle shelf.

'What? Euterpe's royalties?'

'Can you believe it? The nerve of that poor fucking excuse for a man.'

'No wonder The Daily Post called it a £25 million divorce battle. The bastard,' Beatrice said as she took off her lawyer hat and replaced it with her sisterly heart. 'Look, send me everything and we'll talk about it tomorrow morning. I've got to sort Sam out and get the twins into the bed. It'll be alright. I'll look after you.' The lump that had formed in Jessica's throat stopped her from responding. She knew alcohol wasn't the answer but right now she wasn't looking for answers.

'I love you sis,' Beatrice said as she ended the call. Jessica stared again at the itinerary. She couldn't believe that Andrew was going after her business; the business, which had saved her. Jessica's working life revolved around the world of the celebrity but she was more than content to leave the limelight firmly at her office door, whereas Andrew had craved and insisted upon it. She'd stopped being Jessica the party girl from Euterpe years ago, but he wanted to be married to the girl he'd only known from music videos and newspaper gossip columns. As she took out the corkscrew from the drawer she chided herself for being so complacent in her marriage. *'More fool me,'* she said out loud as she pushed the hard metal into the cork and began to twist. Andrew behaved like a big-spender but he'd been barely solvent when they first met. The big warning sign had been glaringly obvious when three weeks after proposing Andrew asked her to help him out with a £35,000 tax bill. She had duly complied and from the moment she'd authorised the online payment he'd held fast onto the age-old adage of "what's mine is yours." He'd started their marriage with debt collectors breathing down his neck but now he was hoping to leave it as a lottery winner. She should have been the one who'd chosen to end their marriage but pride and stupidity had stopped her from doing that and now the choice had been taken away from her. Again, first Lucinda and then Christopher, and now that fuckwit of a husband. She leaned against the fridge door and took a mouthful of ice cold wine enjoying the feeling as it tickled the back of her tongue and worked its way down towards her stomach. It was pitiful really. A 42-year-old woman drinking alone in her kitchen whilst her only daughter sat in her estranged sister's house. As for her husband, she had to stop thinking about where he was or what he was doing. How he felt was clearly typed out on the papers that were now strewn across her kitchen counter. Royalties. She hadn't thought about the Euterpe royalty account for years. There was no reason to. Jessica LeSoeur was doing perfectly well on her own. She didn't need Euterpe but that didn't stop her from looking again at the itemised list.

'Fuck me,' Jessica said out loud as she traced her finger along the column. £4,786,985.28. If she really wanted Andrew off her back she could just give him that and get the full clean break she'd had when she divorced Christopher but there was no way she was going to do that. It hadn't occurred to her for one minute that the royalties were that much but as she traced her finger back to the account details it became clear that no matter what her feelings about her past she couldn't hand over nearly five million pounds because this was a joint account and Lucinda's name stood proudly above Jessica's.

TWENTY-EIGHT

LUCINDA HESITATED, which was unusual for her, as she wasn't a woman known for hesitation. She'd changed into her heels at the side of the pub opposite and walked tentatively towards the restaurant. It was a warm summer evening. Music and laughter seemed to drift out of every open window and car that drove past. She had spent a good fifteen minutes googling Geraint's Kitchen restaurant and much to her disappointment had found nothing but good reviews. Even *The Times* had described it as "simplicity at its rustic best, which rises above the pretentiousness of its neighbours." She'd wanted to be at least 10 minutes late but reminded herself that this wasn't a date so she didn't have to worry about following the rules. The doors to the restaurant were wide open as well as the windows that ran along the side. The restaurant was packed and a few heads turned as she walked past the window. She stopped briefly as she spotted Owen step out of the doors, check his watch and look in the opposite direction. Lucinda checked hers again, a silver Cartier watch that had been a gift from her paternal grandfather on her 18th birthday. All of the grandchildren had got one when they had turned 18 and there were 11 of them. Her cousin Daryl had been convinced that their grandfather had stolen them and was just offloading them to the grandchildren one by one.

'You're here,' Owen said as he turned to his right and saw Lucinda walking towards him.

'I'm not late am I?'

'No, no of course not.' He leaned towards her and kissed her on the cheek and then took a step back as he wondered if he'd done the right thing. Lucinda smiled and quickly chastised herself for enjoying the scent of his aftershave a little too much.

'Your restaurant looks really nice and it's busy.'

'I bet that you googled me or went on Tripadviser.'

'I forgot about Tripadviser? What does it say; did someone give you two stars because their toilet seat wasn't warm enough when they sat down?'

'Even worse, there was no one around to wipe their arse. Come on let's go in,' Owen replied with a laugh as he put his hand gently on Lucinda's back. There was no mistaking the look of pride on Owen's face as he walked into his own restaurant and said hello to his staff.

'Hold on a second. This isn't an odd way of you carrying out staff appraisals is it?' Lucinda asked as she followed Owen up a set of stairs where along the wall were black and white photographs of Hollywood legends. 'Oh look, my mum's boyfriend,' Lucinda said as she stopped at a photograph of Steve McQueen and admired it for a few seconds. 'I think he's the only man that my mum would have considered leaving my dad for.'

'Well she'd have to have fought off my mum first,' Owen said with a grin.

'Is that you?' At the top of the stairs was a large photograph of four men sitting at a table looking exactly like a modern day version of the rat pack. Owen sat in the middle of the group, all four laughing, with bow ties hanging loosely around their necks. He had his arm around a man who was obviously his brother, a black man who looked like he'd heard the best joke in the world and a Chinese man leaning back and holding a bottle of Jameson whiskey.

'Yep that's me. Madeline took it the night we opened the restaurant. That's my older brother Geraint. He lives in San Francisco.'

'Oh, you named it after him?'

'Well I kind of had to. He gave me the money with a proviso that as long as I didn't name a plate of scallops after him, he wanted his name somewhere in this restaurant so I thought I'd stick it on the door. He couldn't really complain about that.'

'So, you're close?' Lucinda asked.

'Yeah, we all are. I suppose no different to you and your sisters. So, whilst we're here this is my best mate, Daniel.' Owen pointed to the black man on his left. 'We've been best friends since the day we were born. My mum and his mum went to school together. They didn't even let a little thing like my mum and dad moving to Ireland break them up, and that in the corner is Jiang my mate since uni who described this picture as the worst Benetton advert ever.' Lucinda laughed again. 'They're all nuts but I wouldn't be without them. I'm telling you, you're lucky that Daniel is away on holiday and that Jiang's wife had a baby the other day otherwise they'd be falling over themselves to be here.' At the top of the stairs the door opened to the roof, which was an extension of the restaurant downstairs. There were only six tables and with the exception of one in the corner they were all filled.

'Wow, this is gorgeous. I wasn't expecting this,' Lucinda said as they were approached by a waiter who clearly didn't have a clue who she was as it was unlikely that he was even born when Euterpe had first appeared on Top of the Pops. They were led to their table and Lucinda took her seat completely aware that the couple on the table they'd just passed had clearly recognised her.

'Does it ever bother you?' Owen said as he handed her the menu. 'Complete strangers watching your every move.'

Lucinda shook her head. 'To be honest it rarely happens these days.'

'Really,' Owen said clearly surprised. 'But you and your sisters were all over the place. You even did a Pepsi commercial.'

'I thought you said Euterpe wasn't your thing?'

'Well, you wasn't but neither were the bloody Spice Girls and you could hardly ignore them could you?'

'That's true, we were everywhere and it did get ridiculous just before we broke up. Photographers everywhere, anyone who spent more than a minute with us or so *called close friends* selling their stories to the newspapers. I couldn't even go to Tesco's without being followed by five or six people who were far too interested in the contents of my shopping basket. My parents had to put up with all sorts turning up at the front door. My mum teaches Classics at UCL and for three years in a row her classes were oversubscribed. It's as if they thought that we'd appear as guest lecturers one day or mum would show them family photographs.' Lucinda shook her head at the memories and opened her menu.

'Isn't it a bit weird eating in your own restaurant? Aren't you tempted to run downstairs and check that everything is ok?'

'Not really. Even though this is the first time I've done it. I'm trying not to be so much of a control freak but I also wanted to show you that I wasn't a complete loon who runs up and down screaming at women in the street. I'm sorry about that.'

'You don't have to apologise again. I completely understand why. It couldn't have been easy for your sister.'

Owen took a deep breath as though he was trying to get rid of the memories of the past.

'You really have no idea what goes on behind closed doors and when it's your own family it's even worse. There are four of us all together. I've got another brother, Ethan. He's only eighteen, and he's visiting Geraint in San Francisco right now, supposedly as part of his gap year, which is crap because Geraint is going to spoil him rotten for the next few months before he packs him off. But Maddie is the only girl and we've always looked after her but when that…shitbag of a husband of her started to…well, she just cut off. Always making excuses as to why we couldn't come round to the house. Funny thing is she wasn't protecting him, she was protecting us. She told us that if we knew then it was more likely that she'd be visiting us in prison and having to look after a paraplegic at home. Still that didn't stop Geraint from jumping on the first plane to London and showing that arsehole how it felt to be a punching bag.'

Lucinda sat back and watched Owen closely. She wasn't expecting him to be so open but he was and that made a refreshing change from what she was used to. She didn't feel as though she had to put on an act with him.

'Sorry, this was supposed to be an apology dinner not a listen to how screwed up my family is.'

'You're family isn't screwed up. At least you talk to your brothers and sisters.'

Halfway through her main course of lobster ravioli Lucinda decided to open up to a man who had been no more than a stranger shouting at her in the street a few months ago. For all she knew Owen would be selling his story to the newspapers for his 12 pieces of silver before she'd stabbed a fork into her dessert.

'You're not close?' Owen said as he refilled Lucinda's wine glass.

'Not how we used to be. Beatrice and I are close and I'm just Em's big sister. But Jessica and I…well, she's going through a bit of tough time but we're not close at all. She pretty much hates me.'

'Because you left.'

'Amongst other things. Everything isn't always how it appears to be.'

'So why are you back? Must have been a good life in New York.'

Lucinda thought about telling the well rehearsed lie but she found that she didn't have the energy for it. She was sitting having a dinner with a man who didn't want anything from her. He didn't seem in the least bit interested in who she used to be and was quite content with the woman she was. So she did something that she hadn't done since she'd returned back to London. She spoke the truth.

'I'm broke.'

Owen put down his fork and sat up a little bit straighter. 'You're what?'

'Not broke, broke. I mean I could pay for my dinner but I'm just not as…put it this way, I wasn't as smart as I should have been. I got complacent and thought that someone else would keep me, which is really annoying when I sit here and think about it.'

'We all make mistakes. Why do you think that I had to go cap in hand and ask my brother for the money? My divorce practically cleaned me out.'

'You're divorced.'

'Five years now. Big mistake that was. I did the most stupid thing and married someone out of guilt. She was pregnant and I thought I should be a man, be responsible. Turns out that the baby wasn't even mine.'

'Wow…that's just…I don't even know what to say.'

'I know. If I hadn't overheard her talking to him on the phone I'd never have known. They worked together. He was her boss. Such a bloody cliché. Everyone thought that I was the bastard though, for leaving her, but the truth always has a way of coming out.'

'Well, I stopped being responsible. At some point I even stopped being myself. The old me would never have got herself into such a stupid mess. Always make sure that you have your *"vex money"* that's what my gran always says.'

'Vex money?'

Lucinda began to laugh.

'It basically means that if someone is taking you out and then it doesn't go well and your vexed with them, then you always make sure you have some spare cash so you can get home. There you have it. Vex money.'

'Oh, I see. "Full of vexation come I, with complaint" I like it.'

'*A Midsummer's night dream.* You're full of surprises,' Lucinda said amused.

'Can't help it. I did an English degree. I even thought about acting for all of five minutes until I was lured away by a crème brûlée. So do you have your vex money?'

'No need, I can walk home and anyway, you haven't vexed me yet,' Lucinda said as she felt Owen's leg brush against hers.

TWENTY-NINE

'YOU LOOK like shit Jess,' Wendy said as she pulled up a chair towards Jessica's open window and lit a cigarette in complete disregard to the health and safety regulations. 'Maybe you should take a little break or at least get some collagen. There's that place on Windmill Street who can do it for you in 30 minutes.'

'Unlike you, I don't want to look permanently surprised,' Jessica replied as she turned on her computer and poured herself a glass of water, dropping in an Alka-Seltzer.

'It's a lot better than looking as though you've spent the night with Islington Green's finest.'

Jessica pulled out the small mirror that she kept in her top drawer and took a look at the reflection she'd been avoiding for the past few weeks. Her skin looked awful and it felt rough. Despite the whitening drops she'd used her eyes were still bloodshot and puffy. She'd been sleeping but it had been a drunk sleep and meant that she'd awoken at 5am with the taste of wine still in her mouth.

'Are you depressed?' Wendy said as she pulled on her

cigarette.

'No, I'm not bloody depressed.'

'Then in that case you're going to have to pull yourself together. This isn't like you. I've never seen you like this, all despondent, angry and perpetually hungover.'

'I'm not hungover. I'm just not feeling great and I didn't sleep well.'

'You're forgetting that I'm one of your closest friends and I know you. You don't fool me, Jessica LeSoeur.'

'Wendy, I doubt that you'd be skipping along the rooftops if your bastard of a husband was trying to strip you of everything.'

'Firstly, I'm gay, secondly Karen wouldn't dare and thirdly I told you to get a pre-nup.'

'Don't Wendy. I keep asking myself why I didn't get a pre-nup. I was so stupid.' Jessica turned towards the glass door and looked out towards the rest of the office. There were only a few people milling about as the majority of them had already made their way to the conference room for the staff meeting, but it was everything she had. Phoenix PR Agency was hers. She had built it from the ashes of Euterpe and she'd made a success of it despite her initial hesitations.

'Are you two coming or do you want me to chair this meeting all by myself?' Christopher said as he poked his head through the open door.

'Just give us a minute,' Wendy said as she picked up the red makeup bag from Jessica's desk and began to take out foundation, concealer and mascara. 'Actually make it fifteen.'

'You're such a bitch,' Jessica replied with a hint of a smile.

'Of course I am, sweetie. Now go and wash your face and let's see if I can sort you out. I didn't spend all those years at the Selfridges makeup counter for nothing.'

Emma deleted the text messages one by one whilst she waited. She'd tried to delete them without having to read them but the last one refused to co-operate:

It would be lovely to meet up again. For old time's sake. What about tonight?

She hated that he said "for old time's sake" as though the last time they'd met had been a joyful occasion. The last time she'd seen him had been through a haze of burning tears and a violent wind that at times felt as though it was going to pick her up and throw her across the embankment along with the last shred of dignity that she tried to hold onto. Emma scrolled through the list of contacts, found his name and deleted him. She should have done it last year after he'd ignored every one of her phone calls and texts whilst she sat in her bedroom suffering from cramps which served no more than a painful reminder of the child that was no longer there. Emma put her phone away and tried to pay attention to the conversation that was taking place around her. She didn't do nerves. It seemed to be a family trait but she knew this meeting was about her and not about the rumours that'd been circulating ever since Jessica's marriage woes had made the headlines.

'Jam donut or almond croissant?' Meghan said as she placed her breakfast selection in front of Emma and took a seat next to her.

'Couldn't you find anything healthier?'

'How about an apple turnover? That will count as one of your five a day. So go on then, tell me, what's going on?' Emma tore a piece of the croissant and placed it in her mouth to stop herself from answering. She knew that she was being given this promotion purely on merit, however she wasn't sure how the other members of staff would see that considering more than half of them had joined the agency years before her and were more than capable of managing the department. Emma suddenly felt self-conscious about the dress and shoes that she was wearing. She'd chosen her outfit carefully that morning and thought of her outfit more like a suit of armour than a DKNY dress. All heads turned and conversations stopped as soon as Jessica, Wendy and Christopher walked into the room. Only Emma noticed that her sister was wearing a little bit more makeup than usual, but she still looked tired and as though she was carrying the weight of the world on her shoulders.

'Morning everyone,' Christopher said as he sat at the table on Jessica's right whilst Wendy busied herself with making a cup of coffee for herself and an even stronger one for Jessica. 'I know this isn't our usual monthly meeting but I thought it'd be better for everyone to hear the news directly from us instead of the usual round-robin email.'

Jessica scanned the room. Usually she relished having the staff's full attention but today, despite Christopher being the one doing the talking, she knew all eyes were on her. She gently touched his arm and gave him a look that he recognised far too well. 'I'll hand things over to the boss.'

'Thank you,' Jessica said. She cleared her throat and began, her voice firm.

'So, for the first time in years I've managed to make it into the papers, which I will openly admit hasn't been much fun but I'd like to thank all of you for the hard work you've put in over the last few weeks. I know that on top of everything else we've had to deal with, it hasn't been easy.' Whilst Jessica spoke, Emma had a flashback that it was similar to the speech that Jessica had given to the crying fans outside their publicist's office once the news had broken of Lucinda's departure.

'She's making us all redundant, isn't she?' Meghan whispered to Emma just before she stuffed the rest of the jam donut into her mouth.

'Shut up,' Emma whispered.

'Now, I don't plan on keeping you all here any longer than necessary so I'll get straight to the point. We've been lucky to have had a very successful first quarter. That shouldn't be too much as a surprise as you've all been incredibly busy. That has meant that we've had to make some changes. We have plans to expand the agency further, which will obviously take time, but to get things moving we've decided to make some changes to management.'

Everyone's shoulders visibly dropped with relief as they all realised that no one was being issued with their P45 and a cheque.

'Emma has agreed to accept the position of Head of the Celebrity and Personal PR division effective immediately.'

Jessica said it so quickly that Emma didn't even get a chance to prepare herself for the stunned silence that followed or for the glare that came from Angelique and Milo sitting directly opposite her as they quickly realised that Emma was now their direct boss. Emma sat up a little bit straighter and smiled as she saw Angelique turn her head and whisper something into Milo's ear.

'I'll be sending an email outlining the changes in more detail but rest assured that there will be no change to what you do, just changes in who you report to. Angelique, Milo, Gary and Megan could you please stay here as I'm sure Emma will want to have a few words with you. Everyone else, thank you.'

Emma watched the room empty out until she was left behind with her staff. Emma almost laughed out loud. She had completely neglected to consider the notion that she would be in charge of staff. Emma glanced at her friend Meghan who was grinning like a Cheshire cat and gave her an encouraging nod.

'I wasn't aware that they were recruiting for a new head of a department,' Angelique said before Emma had a chance to even open her mouth. 'I thought that they'd have recruited externally or at least hold an open competition. I'm sure that there are some rules about this.'

'Oh shut up, Angela,' Meghan said, knowing that calling her by her actual given name would annoy her even more. 'Congratulations Emma. I think that it's an excellent choice.'

'Me too,' Gary said. 'So boss, tell us what's new?'

'So it was a date,' said Harrie.

'No, it wasn't a date. Bloody hell, you're worse than the kids.'

'Hold on a second, unless things have changed since I last had a date, I'm sure that when a man buys you dinner, walks you home and then kisses you on the doorstep, that counts as a date.'

'It wasn't that sort of kiss.'

'Was there tongue?'

'For God's sake, Harrie,' Lucinda said as she switched the phone to her other ear and started to take sweet potatoes out of the fridge.

'You didn't answer my question. Was there…'

'Yes there was, ok?'

'Oh my God. I'm so proud of you, I could cry,' Harrie said before she started laughing down the phone. 'Was it good? I mean it has been so long since you kissed someone that you think being licked by a dog is good.'

'You really are disgusting. Yes it was good…'

'Are you going to see him again? Did he text you?'

'Yes he texted me.'

'Lulu, this is awesome. I knew that going back to London would be great for you.'

'Harrie, it was one date not the bloody royal wedding. Anyway, things haven't changed that much. I still haven't found anyone who wants to record me.'

'You wouldn't think that it'd be so difficult – anyone with a MacBook in their bedroom is a producer. I thought Sal was helping you.'

'He is helping me and he's doing his best but everyone he has sent me to see just haven't got me. I feel as though I'm getting too old for this.'

'You're not too old. You're just being too fussy.'

'I'm not fussy…I'm just,' Lucinda replied distractedly as she turned over the pages of her notebook and started to go through the list of ingredients.

'What are you doing? Because you're hardly paying any attention.'

'Sorry, I'm just going through a recipe.'

'Oh I wish I was there. What are you making.'

'Sweet potato pudding. My mum used to make it all the time when we were younger.'

'Lou, if none of this works out you can always cook for a living. I mean, you're a good cook. You're the only woman in New York City who would actually cook at her own dinner parties.'

'Cooking at home is entirely different to cooking for the world and his wife.'

'A portfolio lifestyle, baby. Perhaps all of this is teaching you that you need to diversify.'

'It was a lot easier when Paul just gave me money.'

'Yeah and that's how you got into this mess in the first place.'

They talked for a few more minutes as Harrie updated Lucinda on who was sleeping with who, how she was thinking of booking a holiday and how much she missed her closest friend.

'I miss you too. You're the only one who doesn't judge me,'

Lucinda said just before Lena walked into the kitchen, still in her pyjamas.

'Please, honey. None of us are saints. Right, I have to go. I'm taking that husband of my mine to the airport. I'll speak to you soon. Love you.'

'Love you too,' Lucinda replied. Before she put her phone on the counter she noticed a text, reminding her that her phone bill of £46.92 was due to be taken out of her account in 7 days.

'Afternoon.' Lucinda said as she glanced at the kitchen clock. Lena pulled up a stool and sat down in front of her aunt.

'We were up late. Katelyn is still asleep.'

'Nothing new there. So, how long do you plan on staying?'

'Why, do you want me to go?' Lena said defensively as she leaned over the breakfast bar and switched the kettle on.

'No, I'm happy for you to stay. More than happy, sweetheart but I'm not sure if your mum will feel the same way.'

'She couldn't care less.'

'I'm sure that's not true.'

'She probably didn't notice that I've even gone. All she cares about is herself. I mean look at how she treats you, auntie Lou.'

'Look whatever is going on between me and your mother has nothing do with your relationship. I know that it's not easy being a teenager…'

Lena rolled her eyes. 'And this is a hard time for you, I mean you're waiting for your exam results, the divorce, your grand...' Lucinda stopped as she remembered that Lena, in fact none of the grandchildren, had been told about their grandfather's illness. Even though it was nearly three months since he'd been diagnosed and he was attending weekly chemotherapy sessions, they were still in the dark having been told stupid stories that their grandfather was ill with the flu or that he had a stomach bug. Lucinda still didn't see the point. At least tell them now and prepare for the worse as opposed to being told that their grandfather had dropped dead one day.

'Your grandparents are there for you. You're luckier than most. You've got an amazing support network, which includes your mum,' she said.

'I'm not bothered about the divorce. I don't know why mum even married him; he wasn't horrible or anything like that. He was quite funny sometimes but mum wasn't happy with him. It's probably why she's drinking so much.'

'I'm sure she's not drinking that...?'

'Auntie Lou, I've read the stories online. I know what mum was like when she was famous, before she had me. She'd make out like you were the crazy one but really it was her.' Lucinda didn't answer because she knew Lena was speaking the truth. She had witnessed for herself when Jessica went off the rails and how she loved the fame and all of its trappings. Jessica disappearing on a week's bender wasn't unusual and she was more than happy to dapple in the various illicit selections in the club toilets or a darkened room of an after party.

'How much is she drinking?' Lena shrugged her shoulders because she honestly didn't know but she knew from the recycling bin that her mum was drinking at least a bottle of wine a night. 'She has been drinking in her bedroom and she hardly eats.'

'Ok, sweetie. It's probably time that I spoke to her.'

'Good luck with that,' Lena said with a look on her face that made her look much older than her 16 years.

THIRTY

RICHARD LEANED his face against the cold porcelain toilet seat exhausted. 'Perhaps I should just sleep here,' he thought to himself as he slowly turned around and sat down on the bathroom floor. The blinds were half open and the sunlight was streaming through to the spotless bathroom. He'd always thought it strange that the brightest room in the house was their guest bathroom; he used to think that it was a waste, but now that he was spending so much time there, he appreciated it. He continued to sit for a while, enjoying the warm sunshine on his face. It reminded him of the last time he and Felicia had visited Grenada. He had laid on a piece of land, which was the same land he used to play cricket as a young boy, and watched the clouds float overhead whilst Felicia had paced around saying she wasn't sure about moving to Grenada for good and maybe just a holiday home for now. They had made so many plans over the last few years, especially with Felicia due to retire in a year's time, but now it seemed that the only planning he'd be doing would be for his funeral. He stood up making sure to avoid his reflection in the mirror and the scales in the corner. He didn't feel as though he'd made any significant improvements. Yesterday had been his fourth chemotherapy session and as always he felt fine for the rest of the day but the following morning his familiar friends of nausea, temperature, a banging headache and constipation returned. If he wasn't sitting on the toilet trying to go then he had his head in it bringing up the little food that he'd managed to get down a few hours before.

'How are you feeling?' Felicia asked, knowing full well that he wouldn't tell her the truth.

'I feel like shit.'

'Oh,' Felicia said surprised at his forthrightness. 'Would you like a cup of tea?'

Richard shook his head.

'I was thinking of making some oxtail soup that would help you with…'

'Lord no. You know I hate oxtail.' He sat down in his armchair and picked up the Evening Standard from the floor.

'Did you know that Lena is staying with Lucinda?' Richard said as he started to flick through the paper.

'What?' Felicia said without lifting her head from the book in her lap.

'I don't know why I bother. You never listen to me. Our granddaughter, Lena, is staying with Lulu.'

'Why?'

'Lulu didn't say.'

'When did you speak to her?'

'Whilst you were out spending a small fortune in

Waterstones.' Richard pointed at the plastic bag on the floor on the sofa, the contents spilling out onto the floor.

'They had a deal on.'

'They always have a deal on. Speaking of deals, Virgin have a deal on for flights to Grenada.'

'Richard you know you can't go on holiday…'

'I don't want the next time I go to Grenada to be in a wooden box, thank you very much.'

'Stop being so dramatic. Anyway, what did Lucinda want?'

'She wanted to talk to me about the grandchildren. She thinks I should tell them.'

'And I think she's right. Reece, Katelyn and Lena should know what's going on. They're not babies, so you should tell them. They'd hate you for it if you didn't.'

'I know. I'll tell them,' Richard said as he turned the pages of the newspaper in his hand. 'I hate these bloody newspapers and their damn stories. Why don't they just leave her alone?'

Felicia had already skimmed through the third story that week about Jessica, this time intimate details about her non-sex life with Andrew and her turbulent relationships with the actor, Devon Miles and the club owner Otis Leigh from her Euterpe days.

'You should know better than to read it. Just throw it in the bin.'

Richard kissed his teeth and turned to the back pages. 'And England can't even win a damn cricket match.' He screwed up the paper and threw it on the floor.

'I should go and see her,' he said. 'She hasn't been around for a few weeks.'

'Don't be silly; I'm sure she's fine. You know the child has a lot on, she doesn't need us...'

'What's the point of being a father if I don't do my job and make sure she's doing ok?' He looked at his wrist and turned his watch so he could see the face. When Lucinda, Jessica and Beatrice had bought it for him it'd slightly pinched the skin on his wrist when he'd closed the clasp, but now it moved freely around his dry skin. 'What time do you think she'll get home?'

'You're not going all the way up there Richard.'

'It's only Islington, not Kathmandu.'

'I don't care if it's just across the street. You're in no state. You've just had chemo and your immune system is weak. It's not worth it.'

'Checking if our daughter is ok isn't worth it?'

'You know exactly what I meant,' Felicia said sternly. She looked up at the framed photographs on the wall, the three eldest daughters sitting together for their primary school picture, and Jessica not at all pleased about being squashed in the middle. Those were the memories that she wanted her husband to hold onto, not make new ones of a daughter who was angry and struggling to cope.

'I'll go and see her.'

Richard sullenly folded his arms and turned on the TV. He had to bite his tongue to stop himself from saying it wasn't fair. 'I just want to see if she's ok.'

'I know you do. I'll make chicken soup instead and bring her some of that.'

'Just don't put...'

'I know, I know,' Felicia said as she got up, walked over to her husband and kissed the top of his head. 'I won't put any dasheen in it ok, you silly man.' Richard smiled and grabbed hold of his wife's hand and squeezed it tightly.

Felicia knew she was taking a chance by turning up at Jessica's house unannounced but she didn't want to give her the opportunity to tell her that she wasn't home. She took a step back and looked up. The shutters and all of the windows were open and she could faintly make out the sound of the television. She knocked on the door and waited. It occurred to her that she couldn't remember the last time she'd been to Jessica's home. She, Lena and Andrew, when he felt like it, always came to them. In fact they all did, preferring the luxury of being waited on by parents who always thought that they didn't see them enough. Lucinda was different though. As much as Felicia hated to admit it, Lucinda would have been the one who threw open her doors to welcome her family. She lifted up the brass knocker and knocked again. The paint beneath the knocker was starting to peel away. If Richard had seen it, he'd have got back in his car and driven to Wickes. He was proud of his daughters and wouldn't have liked to see anything that would have laid them open to criticism. Felicia placed the canvas bag with a plastic container filled with slightly warm soup on the step and pushed open the letter box when the door suddenly swung open causing her to stand up quickly.

'Mum, what are you doing here?' Jessica said more than surprised to see her mother on her doorstep.

'Well, if Mohammed won't come to the mountain…' She

stopped as she took a close look at her daughter and felt her breath stop in her throat. She was dressed in her pyjama bottoms and a faded Back to the Future t-shirt that she was sure had belonged to Jessica's first husband.

'What's going on with you?' Felicia asked. Jessica walked away from the open door and picked up the large wine glass, which she'd left on the hallway table. Felicia slammed the door behind her and walked straight to the kitchen. She stopped when she saw the sight of dirty cups and plates in the sink, and the overflowing recycling bin with empty wine bottles on the floor next to it. There was an empty bread bag on the worktop and blackened bananas in the fruit bowl. Felicia didn't even want to leave her homemade soup in the kitchen but she cleared a space on the kitchen table and left it there.

'I thought you had a cleaner?' Felicia walked into the living room and moved a few dresses that were still in their plastic dry-cleaning bags on the sofa and hung them on the back of the door.

'She's on holiday.'

'That shouldn't stop you from cleaning up. I didn't bring you up to live in a pig sty, Jessica LeSoeur. Where's your daughter?'

'Mum, did you come here for a reason or just to harass me because I really don't need it?' Jessica said deliberately not answering. She sat down and turned up the volume on the TV. Felicia walked over and once she'd worked out how, turned the television off. She glanced over at the wooden coffee table and saw the bottle of wine that was still two thirds full.

'You know your father wanted to come round and see you. He's as sick as a dog but his only concern is you. I'm so glad he didn't see this.'

'Has something happened?'

'No, nothing has happened to him but the lord knows what it would have done to him to see you like this. What are you doing to yourself?'

'I'm not doing anything to myself.'

'Jessica, I saw all of those bottles in the kitchen and look at you, it's only eight o'clock and I'm sure that's not your first bottle. What are you doing to yourself?'

'Mum, in case you haven't noticed, my husband has left me.'

'So'

'What do you mean so? Mum, my husband has left me and is trying to take me for everything I own.'

'*Blouse and skirt* Jessica, that doesn't mean you have to fall apart. I didn't bring you up like that.'

'Please mum, this isn't about you. This is my life, not yours.'

'So you're going to drink it away are you? Look at yourself in the mirror. This isn't the woman you're meant to be. Instead of picking up a bottle, why don't you come to your family?'

'Family.' Jessica spat the word out as if the wine she'd just taken a sip of was arsenic. 'Family is the reason why I'm in this mess.'

'What are you talking about?' Felicia said as she took a step back from her daughter whose eyes were now wild with anger.

'Why don't you ask your precious daughter, Lucinda. This is all her fault.'

'What has your sister got to do with anything? She's only been back in the country for five minutes and you won't even talk to her and I know she tried. For God's sake, why can't you put Lucinda leaving behind you? It's in the past. It happened. Leave it alone.'

'That's a bit rich coming from someone who teaches classics. Leave it all in the past. What a joke.'

'You know what, you need to put the drink down and have something to eat. I bought soup for you.'

'I don't want any bloody soup. Soup isn't going to stop Lucinda from ruining my life again.'

'Jessica, let it go. Why can't you talk to your sister? Why don't you try?'

'Try? Mum, Lucinda only tried because she wanted to cover up what she's doing.'

'What are you talking about? You're not making any sense.'

'Well, let me make it clearer for you. As soon as Lucinda came back Andrew packed his bags and left me. Now why do you think that was?' Jessica stood up unsteadily on her feet whilst Felicia said nothing as she reluctantly tried to absorb what Jessica was saying about her sister. 'You and dad have always put her on a pedestal. You think that sharing the same blood allows you to ignore her faults.'

'Stop it. Your father and I have always treated you the same.'

'No, you haven't. Dad acts like the sun shines out of Lou's arse and you just tolerate us.'

'You know what, child, I'm going to go home before you say something you're going to regret.'

'It's not the first time you know. You all think this is about Lucinda breaking up Euterpe.'

'I'm going home.' Felicia turned and walked out of the living room.

'She slept with him, mum,' Jessica shouted at her mum's back. 'Five years ago, your precious daughter slept with my husband and she's doing the same thing now.' Felicia spun around and without thinking slapped Jessica on the left side of her face. Jessica staggered back in shock as the stinging spread through her face as though she'd fallen onto a pile of nettles. Despite Richard leaving the disciplining of the girls to his wife, as he knew he was too soft, Felicia had never hit any of their daughters. There had been the occasional smack on their legs when they had been naughty toddlers and when Beatrice had aged five stuck a knife in the toaster causing her to fly off her stool as the toaster sparked in front of her but she'd never hit her daughters until now.

'Your sister,' Felicia said her voice cold with anger 'wouldn't do anything like that. She's a lot of things but I know her and she wouldn't…'

'Why don't you ask her and watch her lie in your face,' Jessica said as she pushed her mum out of her house.

THIRTY-ONE

FELICIA FELT sick as she drove home that evening. She'd never seen Jessica that way. This angry, bitter woman was unknown to her. As she approached the Old Street roundabout she wondered when exactly she'd become no more than a casual observer in her daughter's life. Felicia was under no illusion that she wasn't a natural mother. She'd never wanted children. Whereas other girls had been pushing dolls in toy prams and spending hours combing their doll's hair or pretending to be mum when they played in their Wendy houses in the nursery, she'd always had her nose in a book and her father's words ringing in her ears. 'Education is everything, Felicia. You won't have anything if you don't have a good education behind you. Children can wait and if they're not meant for you then don't worry but make sure you have an education behind you.' When the girls came one by one she'd tried to install those same values in them but even she could see that there was something else driving Lucinda and Jessica, more than encouraged by their father who believed there was nothing wrong with trying anything once. Richard had been like that at university. He was supposed to be reading physics at university but had only stuck with it for one term before he switched to a mechanical engineering degree with the delusional idea of designing planes for a living. Felicia had tried to convince him to aim for a more stable and realistic career but he was like Lucinda and when he put his mind to something he did it, which was why he'd spent over thirty years working in the aerospace industry. Felicia recalled how furious she'd been when she found out that Lucinda and Jessica had convinced Beatrice to join them. Thank God, Emma had been so much younger than them and Felicia had been able to hold onto her and steer her in the right direction. She'd hoped that when Emma had taken a place at Warwick University to study History that she would have maintained an academic course in her career and had been disappointed when she'd left a career in publishing for PR. At least Felicia could still boast to her friends about her daughter the lawyer.

'What sort of woman are you?' Felicia said over the noise of the car radio. The sound of a car horn beeped repeatedly as she sat at the traffic lights that had now turned green. It was almost nine o'clock but she wasn't ready to go home and have to lie to her husband's face. She'd texted him whilst she sat in her car outside Jessica's house and tried to calm down. He was more than content sitting at home watching repeats of Grand Designs. She loved her daughters. All four of them were strong, beautiful women and even though she may not have always agreed with their lifestyle choices they hadn't, when she really thought about it, done anything to disappoint her. So instead of taking the first exit off the Old Street roundabout and heading home she drove completely around ignoring the sounds of a car horn as she cut in front of a Ford Focus and headed towards Notting Hill.

'Is that it? Isn't there anymore than that?' Lucinda asked as Katelyn adjusted the laptop screen so her mother could see.

'Nope, that's it.'

'It's a rubbish site. The only thing that's on it is a photograph of his arm on a mix desk. Are you sure that he's even a real producer?' said Lena who'd walked back into the dining room with another slice of sweet potato pudding, which she'd liberally covered with whipped cream.

'And what sort of producer advertises on gumtree?' Katelyn continued as she clicked on a link that went back to his website.

'A poor one.' Lena sniggered as she took a spoonful of pudding. 'Auntie Lou this is the best thing that I've ever eaten.'

'Thank you, sweetie,' Lucinda replied as she clicked on the "about" section of the website, which was only four lines long.

'You should sell it.'

'Sell what?'

'The pudding. Or go on the Great British Bake Off.'

'She's obsessed with that programme,' Katelyn replied as she refreshed the page in the hope that something new would appear on the website.

'Everyone watches it, Katie. It's the best programme and auntie Lou is a great cook. My mum doesn't cook like this. Then again I can't remember the last time that she actually cooked.'

'Mum, I don't think that you should go and see this Carter man. He doesn't even have a surname. Just Carter the producer.'

'Who advertises on gumtree' Lena added. Lucinda wasn't afraid to admit that she'd been equally as dubious as her daughter and niece when Sal had called her a couple of hours ago and told her that he'd arranged a meeting with an up and coming producer called Carter.

'I don't want anyone who is up and coming. They won't have a clue what to do with me,' is what Lucinda had complained whilst Sal had sat in front of her eating his second slice of sweet potato pudding.

'You can't afford anyone else,' Sal had replied bluntly. *'And anyway, he owes me a favour.'*

It was bad enough that Lucinda felt like a charity case but even worse that she was going to see someone who most likely had no interest in working with her. Things could be worse, she told herself. At least she had a roof over head and she wasn't in such financial dire straits that she couldn't afford to feed and clothe her children. She just had to remind herself that unlike the old days she didn't have access to an enormous reservoir of cash, but even then the reservoir of cash was just an illusion that Paul had successfully kept up for many years. No matter how much you tried to keep up with the Jones', the Jones' would eventually move away. The door knocked loudly almost causing the three of them to jump out of their skins. Lucinda wasn't expecting any visitors, now that Madeline and Owen had stopped their impromptu visits.

Lucinda walked up to the front window and slightly pulled apart the organza curtains. The sky had already transformed into a silky navy colour with only a few streaks of blue and wispy grey clouds breaking up the palette. The streetlights had turned on and they gently illuminated her mother's face. She had the look of a woman who was being driven by unknown forces and looked surprised to find herself her standing on Lucinda's doorstep.

'Mum, what are you doing here?' Lucinda said to her mother, who seemed reluctant to step over the threshold considering what had taken place just a few hours before.

'I've just come from your sister's house.'

'Which one?'

'Jessica. She told me…she told me some things,' Felicia said as she suddenly found herself shaking.

'Mum, maybe you should come in.'

'I really don't want to believe the things she has told me.'

'And you shouldn't. Look, come into the house.'

Felicia stepped into the house but stopped when she heard her grand-daughter's laughing.

'Lena's here,' said Lucinda.

'I know,' Felicia replied without looking at her daughter as she walked into the living room.

'I'll be in the kitchen,' Lucinda replied, wondering if her mother believed what Jessica had told her considering she hadn't even kissed or hugged her. She busied herself with putting things away and wiping down the worktops. Reece was out with Jake who was more than happy to take him to the launch party of a comic book artist he knew who'd just released his new book. Lucinda suspected that both Reece and Jake needed to escape the ridiculous levels of oestrogen that were part of their daily lives. Her phone beeped on the table, signalling that her battery was dying and that there were texts awaiting her perusal. The first was from the elusive Carter letting her know that Sal had already arranged a session for her at his studio in New Cross and that she must be there no later than 3 o'clock on Friday. She took a deep breath and told herself that it was a good thing, and then she opened the second text from Owen. She liked his text messages, which contained absolutely no text abbreviations or emoticons whatsoever. He was just saying hello and that he'd call her later once he'd finished work. Owen had called her almost every night since their *not really a date*, date.

'It's hard to believe that they're almost women now,' Felicia said as she walked into the kitchen and closed the door firmly behind her. 'Reminds me of you and your…' She stopped when she realised what she about to confront her daughter about. That old taboo that you'd usually find in a soap opera but not in your own lives. Lucinda opened the doors leading out to the garden to avoid the feeling of claustrophobia and the change in atmosphere when her mother walked into the room.

'Mum, I did not…' She didn't want to even say the word. To speak it would give the lunacy of Jessica's words credibility. 'Nothing has ever happened between Andrew and I.'

'Why would she say that you've been…been having an affair. He's your sister's husband for crying out loud. Don't you have any morals?'

'Mum, I'm telling you, nothing happened.'

'Then why is she in such a state? The child could barely stand up when I saw her.'

'Look, if Jessica wants to drink herself into oblivion then that's up to her. I'm not taking responsibility for that, not when I haven't done anything wrong. Mum, you raised me better than that and even if I was to take someone else's man, I wouldn't touch my own sister's. I'm not some kind of dog. I know that you've never thought highly of me, that I practically ruined Jessica's and Beatrice's lives, but I never in a million years thought that you'd think so lowly of me.'

'I don't think…'

'Of course you do. Why else are you here? If you didn't believe that there was a slightest grain of truth in what Jessica has told you then you wouldn't be here now asking me if it was true.'

Felicia looked down at the ground, suddenly feeling the heat of shame rise through her, unable to look at Lucinda. Jessica was a mess. She'd seen that for herself but she'd learnt a long time ago that there was some truth amongst the chaos of a person's drunken rants. She dragged a chair away from the table, not even wincing as the wood scraped against the tiles. She sat down suddenly emotionally and physically exhausted by everything that was going on around her. Most mornings when she heard Richard being sick in the bathroom she just wanted to pull the sheets back over her head. Her sister always told her that there wasn't a textbook on anyone's lives. Felicia had always dismissed it as nothing more than New Age ramblings of a sister who believed in the power of crystals and cupping. But it was true. At this moment, as she sat at the table, she would have killed for a chapter entitled "what to do when your husband has cancer, your daughter may be an alcoholic, and you feel that you've failed them all."

She looked up gratefully as Lucinda placed a steaming cup of tea in front of her.

'Have you eaten?' Lucinda asked. Felicia thought for a minute. 'Well, I made soup for your father and brought some for your sister, but I didn't even eat myself. What stupidness.'

'That's the problem with being strong. Sometimes you forget about yourself.'

'Hmm, that's true. I never wanted to be the strong one. I'd much rather be like your Auntie Anna and have other people be strong for her.'

'Sometimes we don't get a choice in the roles we're given.'

'I told her that you'd never do such a thing. It's beneath you.'

'Thank you. Mum, I won't lie to you. The last time Jess came to see me in New York with Andrew, something did happen…'

'I don't think that I want to hear…'

'No, not like that. Not even close to that. For crying out loud, I didn't even like Andrew as a brother-in-law let alone enough to drop my knickers for him. Jess thought that something had happened when I promise you that nothing ever did. I tried to talk to Jess afterwards but she'd rather believe that idiot than her own sister.'

'And you haven't seen him since you've been back?'

'I haven't seen him or heard from him. Mum, the chances

of that man calling me are slim to none. I don't know why they're getting divorced but it has absolutely nothing do with me. I wouldn't do that to my worst enemy, let alone my own sister.'

Felicia said nothing as she absorbed what Lucinda was telling her. The historian in her wanted to probe deeper to find out what had happened in her daughter's past to shape their present into something unrecognisable but she pushed that aside and tried to reach the side of her that she'd always fought against. That of the mother.

'Your father is right, you know. You need to fix what's broken.'

'Even though I'm not the one who broke it?'

Felicia nodded. 'You're a fighter, Lou. You've never been one to sit back and see what happens.'

'You'll be surprised,' Lucinda said with a huff.

'I think I'm past being surprised and I don't want to hide anything from your father, but…'

'I know, what happens in the darkness and all that stuff.'

'Just try and fix things before the light shines too bright.'

THIRTY-TWO

Five years ago

'I had to literally twist your sister's arm to get her to come here. I said to her, 'Jess come on we haven't seen your sister since the wedding. A week in New York isn't going to kill us. The business isn't going to collapse just because you decide to go on holiday.' Andrew pushed his dessert plate aside, which had been scraped clean of its chocolate and raspberry torte, and reached for the decanter of cognac to fill his glass. Jessica took a look at her sister and shook her head as Lucinda stifled a laugh.

'It wasn't like that Lulu. We spent two weeks in the Maldives.'

'That was a year ago, babe.'

'I told him that we could take a long weekend somewhere but he insisted on coming here with me,' Jessica said as she reached for her own glass, which her husband had just refilled with wine. She hadn't wanted to drink that much tonight but she'd had enough of listening to Andrew tell her that she was too much of a lightweight and didn't know how to enjoy herself.

'Well, I'm happy to have you both here. It's so quiet with the kids away with their dad. That's the only thing I hate about the divorce…when the kids have to go. But anyway,' Lucinda said as she stood up to clear the plates from the table.

'You shouldn't be doing that? Where's your maid lady?' Andrew asked as he reached into his jacket and pulled out a cigar without once taking his eyes off Lucinda.

'She's my housekeeper, not a maid, and she has gone home. It's not her job to wait on us hand and foot and if you're going to smoke that then I suggest you go outside,' she said with a smile. Andrew removed the silver tiffany lighter from his pocket, lit the cigar, got up and walked in the direction of the terrace that led off from the dining area. Jessica got up with her wine glass and followed her sister to the kitchen.

'I'm sorry about him. He can be so obnoxious sometimes.'

'Don't apologise for him. I can handle myself. Anyway, it's only for a few more days,' said Lucinda as she loaded the dishwasher and slammed the door shut.

'I know but I wanted this to be our time together, you know. I mean…' Jessica felt her tongue thicken as she tried to get her words out. It'd been a long time since she had drunk this much and it had quickly gone to her head.

'I was so tired of being angry with you and with dad being ill, it just…'

'Put things into perspective,' Lucinda said.

'I need to be less emotional. I need to be more like you Lulu and learn to compartmentalise.'

'It's not as easy as you think. Anyway, I was thinking of coming over to see dad but he kept telling me that there was no point, he's doing fine and he will come and see us. Stubborn man.'

'Daddy is doing fine. They caught it early, so he's doing

alright.'

Lucinda poured herself a glass of water. Since divorcing Paul she'd been determined to cut down on her drinking, not that she was getting obliterated every night but it'd been easier than dealing with her life falling down around her.

'And your right. It did put things into perspective. I mean Euterpe was years ago. We were kids; we were bound to split up at some point. I think that I was just pissed that you got in there first.'

'I thought I was doing a good thing…Look we've got our spa day tomorrow and we can talk about it more when you have a sober head on you.' Jessica took a look at the glass with its velvety red liquid and put the glass down. 'I've probably had a bit too much. Will you tell that husband of mine that I've gone to bed?'

'Of course,' Lucinda said as she walked over to her sister, linked arms with her and walked her towards the staircase. At the bottom of the stairs, the sisters hugged each other.

'Love you, Lulu.'

'Love you too, Jess.'

Lucinda went back into the dining room and cleared it of the wine bottle and glasses; she noticed that the terrace door was shut and that both Andrew and the decanter of cognac had disappeared.

'I never thought that I'd be married to a member of Euterpe.' Andrew was standing in the living room staring at a photograph of Beatrice, Jessica and Lucinda taken at the Radio One studios at the moment they'd found out they were number 1. Beatrice's face was one of shock, whilst Lucinda and Jessica hugged in that *moment of pure ecstasy. Lucinda was surprised that she'd actually cried that afternoon.*

'Well, stranger things have happened,' Lucinda replied as she sat down on the sofa, removed her shoes and turned the TV onto BBC World News. She was knackered after spending most of the day on her feet. She should have listened to Vivienne who repeatedly told her that that was the point of the help, but Lucinda wanted to do something that would make Jessica think of home and good times and not make her feel that Lucinda had something to prove. Andrew carried on looking at the pictures on the nicknamed wall of fame He touched the platinum record award for their first album and let out a low whistle before picking up the Brit award and then the Ivor Novello awards that were displaced prominently on the shelves. A strange feeling took Lucinda as she watched Andrew touch her things without permission.

'Your sister won't put any of this stuff up. She has it all hidden away in the back room as though she's ashamed of it.'

'Everyone's different. Our dad would have them displayed in his driveway if he could get away with it, whereas mum is quite happy for them to stay in the good room.'

He walked over and sat down close to Lucinda.

'You two aren't that different though. You've both got your fiery sides.' Lucinda shifted along the sofa as Andrew pushed his right leg towards her. 'But I always thought that you were the sexier one.' He put his hand on Lucinda's bare leg.

'What do you think you're doing?' Lucinda said as she pushed his hand of her leg and stood up, regretting that she'd taken off her shoes as Andrew towered over her.

'Come on. I've seen how you were looking at me and couldn't wait to get rid of your sister. Packed her off to bed like a good little girl. You're a smart one.'

'You're out of your mind. I'm off to bed.' She turned to walk away but he grabbed her arm and pulled her tightly towards him so that she could feel his erection pressing against her hip.

'Come on. When's the last time you've had some? You're a divorcee now. You must be desperate for it.'

'Get the fuck off me. No.'

Andrew spun Lucinda round and pushed her to the sofa. Before she could scramble back up, he was on top of her. She could feel his hot cognac fuelled breath combined with the heavy musk of his cigar against her neck as he tried to kiss her. There was nothing that she'd done to give him even the slightest hint that she was interested. She felt his belt buckle on her thigh and tried to push him away as he eased himself up to move his hands away from her breasts and under her skirt. She kicked out as she felt his hand inside her knickers.

'What the hell is going on? Lucinda!' Jessica screamed as she stood in the doorway. As quickly as he'd managed to get on top of her Andrew had rolled himself off and was standing in front of his wife.

'It's not what you think babe. Your sister…'

'What the hell do you think you're doing?' Jessica said as she pushed past her husband. Lucinda sat up and adjusted her clothing as she tried to stop herself from being sick, right there on the floor.

'Jess, your husband…oh my god,' Lucinda said as her legs suddenly gave way and she sat back down.

'You just couldn't help yourself, could you?' Jessica shouted, alcohol obscuring all of her sensibilities.

'Was that your plan, to get me drunk so that you could fuck my husband? You selfish bitch.'

'That's not what happened. Your husband tried to…'

'I don't want to hear it,' Jessica said as she lunged at her sister in a blind fury. Andrew grabbed her by the waist and pulled her back.

'Come on, Jess. Don't listen to her,' Andrew said.

'Take your fucking hands off me. You disgust me,' Jessica screamed in Andrew's face.

'You need to leave,' Lucinda said.*' You need to get out of my house. Jess, this isn't what you think.'*

'Don't Jess me. I know exactly what I saw you do, you conniving dirty bitch.'

Lucinda stood up, propelled by anger and the injustice of what had just happened.

'Your husband just tried to rape me you delusional, drunk cow.'

'You came onto me,' Andrew shouted back as Jessica slapped Lucinda around the face.

'I never want to see you again. As far as I'm concerned you're not my sister. No wonder Paul left you. I feel sorry for your kids. You're a pitiful excuse for a mother.'

THIRTY-THREE

BEATRICE DIDN'T like change and she definitely wasn't impressed that during her maternity leave Tanya had moved into her office. Beatrice felt like a visitor as she logged into her computer and she wondered if perhaps she had bitten off more than she could chew. She had chosen her outfit carefully and had even splashed out on a pair of Saint Laurent shoes but she didn't feel as though her armour was strong enough as she left the house earlier that morning. Beatrice didn't want to admit that she had lost her confidence as she looked down at the box of files next to her desk but it was too late to turn back now.

'They told me that you weren't coming back for another six months,' Tanya said as she walked into the office and scanned Beatrice like a human x-ray machine.

Beatrice ignored her as she looked around the office that had been hers for 12 years, not quite believing that this woman had the cheek to take down the pictures on the wall and the personal items from her desk. It was as if she hadn't left the last time she'd been on maternity leave. She couldn't believe that

Anoushka had allowed this to happen. It wasn't that she wasn't used to sharing an office, as she'd shared an office with her closest friend, Preena for seven years until she decided that law was no longer for her and was now charging the women of the city a ludicrous amount of money to provide them with life coaching.

'I've found that women who come back from maternity leave aren't really committed. So I'm sure it won't be too long before you return home,' Tanya said as she sat down on the chair, adjusted its height, pursed her thin lips together and turned her back. Beatrice resisted the urge to pick up the brown archive box and smash it into Tanya's head.

'Morning Beatrice. We were told that these cases have been allocated to you,' said James, as he walked into the office carrying a box of files. Sarah, the trainee solicitor who was standing behind James, nodded meekly and put the box down next to Beatrice's desk.

'I supposed I was asking too much to think that I could start gently,' Beatrice said ignoring the huff that came from Tanya.

'Why would you want to when you're going to be representing Simon Wilby?' James said as he walked back out of the office and picked up a third box. He placed it on Beatrice's desk and started to pull out the files. 'I mean, you're actually going to meet him.'

'Sometimes the most famous people are the most boring. He might have the personality of a fly,' Beatrice said.

'That's blasphemy,' James said with a serious look on his face. 'I won't accept it. He's a legend.'

'Who are you working with at the moment?' Beatrice asked, knowing how tedious it could be working as a paralegal. The moments of glamour and excitement were rare, even if you did work for one of the top family law firms in the country who had represented royalty.

'We're unallocated. Driftwood.'

'Both of you?'

Sarah nodded and in a barely audible whisper said, 'Cruella didn't want us. Said that we were worse than frog spawn.' James smiled and discreetly pointed at Tanya who had shoved her headphones into her ears as soon as the pair had walked in. Beatrice covered her mouth with her hand and tried not to laugh.

'If I ok it with Anoushka, how about you both work with me? It's the least you can do after dumping me with all of this stuff. James, you can have the honour of Simon Wilby. Sarah, I've got a client meeting this afternoon in the city, so you can come along with me to that. How does that sound?'

Both of them nodded their heads like obedient puppies before bolting out of her office. Beatrice looked over at the pile of files that had been unpacked and shook her head glad that Tanya still had her back to her. She silently prayed that she hadn't been right when she'd said that most women returned home.

The black cab pulled up next to Mansion Hill tube station and both Beatrice and Sarah got out. Sarah had asked her sensible questions about the case and hadn't said a word when the taxi driver turned around as they sat at the traffic lights in New Change and told Beatrice that she looked familiar; like one of those girls who used to be in a group whose name he couldn't remember.

'Isn't it a bit strange representing someone you know? My tutor in law school warned us against it.'

'So did mine and I'd usually run a mile but this is different,' Beatrice replied as they walked along Queen Victoria Street. The recent thunderstorm had cooled down the summer air and a soft breeze swirled around them. It was only 11 o'clock so the traffic moved steadily along the roads, and there weren't a million and one people rushing out of Cannon Street Station, in the middle of rush hour, trying to make it to work on time. They reached the revolving glass door of the office building that was no different to the other buildings they had passed with the same faux marble exterior walls and a simple brass plaque on the wall. Sarah and Beatrice headed to the lifts and up to the fifth floor to Bacall Fields, the firm of accountants that she and her sisters had used when they received their first advance from the record company. They'd been recommended several accountant firms by the record company but Lucinda had put her foot down; she didn't like the idea of Concave records being involved in every single part of their professional lives. When Beatrice had first entered the offices of Bacall Fields they'd been above a funeral parlour on the Old Kent Road. Thomas Bacall had opened the door himself whilst his partner, Calvin Fields had been in the back room haggling with their landlord over payment of the rent. Beatrice remembered telling Lucinda that she had another thing coming if she thought that she'd trust a couple of accountants who looked like they found their degrees in the bottom of a cereal box with their money. Lucinda had pushed her through the doors and she hadn't looked back since.

Bacall Fields had certainly come a long way since their days on the Old Kent Road, which they were still quite proud of, shown by the battered road sign that they'd *acquired*, that now hung on the reception area wall.

'Hello Beatrice. It's been so long. You look fantastic. I'd never have guessed that you'd had a baby. How are you?' Phoebe said as Beatrice and Sarah walked onto the fifth floor.

'I'm well, Phoebe. It's good to see you. Why are you sitting in reception?' Beatrice asked. Phoebe tutted and flicked back her long brown hair. 'Bloody temp. She was here last week no problem and then Monday morning she's a no show. Two days later I get an email from her. She had an offer to go to Marbella. Too good to turn down apparently. Your sister is already here. I've placed her in the conference room. Tom is just finishing off with another client but he'll be with you shortly. Do you want anything? Tea, coffee, water?' Phoebe said without taking a breath as she got up and walked authoritatively through the corridor.

'Tea, thank you. Sarah?'

'The same, thank you,' Sarah said softly.

'You need to learn to speak up love. You're swimming with sharks now,' Phoebe said as she opened the door to the conference room.

Jessica had been waiting in the conference room for twenty

minutes. She felt nervous and sick that her life was out of control. She spun the gold bangles around her left wrist, and pushed them down but she could still see the red wings of the small butterfly tattoo on her wrist. She ran her fingers along the tattoo. It had been her bright idea. Emma had been on the verge of a nervous breakdown as she paced around Jessica's garden convinced that her life was over as she waited for her A-Level results, due the following day. Jessica's solution had been to ply her baby sister with wine to try and take her mind off things. Lucinda and Beatrice had also been there, although Lucinda had stuck to sparkling raspberry and cranberry juice as she was still breast-feeding her four-month-old twins who were on their first international trip and were being looked after by her parents. The birth of the twins – and Jessica's daughter a year earlier – had eased the tension between them. However, it wasn't as good as it used to be. Lucinda's departure for a new life was still fairly raw but it had got better. Jessica still wasn't sure how she'd managed to convince her sisters to get into a cab to Nunhead, which reminded Beatrice of being dragged around to all sorts of dodgy underground clubs in South East London to perform. They'd all left the small shop with the peeling posters on the wall and the metal bars on the window, with butterfly tattoos on their wrist. Euterpe's second number one had been a ballad called 'Butterfly Soul,' which Edgar the tattooist, despite looking like the recruiter for Hell's Angels, had surprised the girls by putting their album on the CD player and humming along.

Thomas pushed aside the pages of Jessica's financial portfolio that he'd printed out earlier that morning and looked directly at Jessica.

'I'm not being funny but how could you not realise that you had this much money in the bank? I mean, how could you miss four million quid?'

'I didn't miss it,' Jessica sighed. 'I just kind of forgot about it. It wasn't as if I had to live off the royalty cheques. The business was doing well.'

'Forgot about it? I wouldn't have forgotten about four million,' Thomas said as he took his glasses off and cleaned them with his sky blue tie. Sarah silently agreed with him. 'Well, it's not quite the £25 million that's being quoted in the papers but it's close. Your house has increased in value but then again everyone's house is increasing in value. Do you know that your house is probably making more money a day than you do?'

'Great,' Jessica said sullenly. 'Can't I just sign the house over to Lena? I mean it'll go to her eventually.' Beatrice shook her head whilst Sarah diligently made notes. She hated this part of divorce law, dragging over the coals of her client's finances.

'Not a good idea.'

'But I don't want him getting my house.'

'I know you don't, but giving your house away to try and reduce your assets isn't smart and I wish I could say that everything they've put in their ancillary relief application was wrong but it's not. Jess, financially you're the equivalent of the ravens at the Tower of London. You're not going anywhere.'

'I was hoping the numbers were wrong.'

'Excuse me, I never get things wrong. Anyway, look on the bright side. You can reduce the amount of the account a bit. Just tell Lucinda to take her share of the money. I'm sure she wouldn't turn down a couple of mill.'

'I doubt that she'll be interested,' Jessica said, causing Beatrice to look at her sister and wonder why on earth she would be so defiant. 'Can't I just put the money into one of those tax avoidance thingy's?'

'Talk to your sister about that. She's the lawyer. She'll tell you why hiding your assets is a bad idea. Personally, I haven't got a problem with hiding money from the taxman,' Thomas said bluntly. 'How could you let this happen Jess? What was the first thing that I taught you and your sisters? Protect your assets. Haven't I always told you that?'

'How was I supposed to know that my husband would turn out to be the devil?'

'Well, the devil was an angel once but that's no excuse Jess. You should have protected yourself.'

Jessica got up and stormed out of the office.

'I better go after her,' Beatrice said. 'I'm so sorry.'

Thomas looked at Beatrice and shrugged his shoulders. 'It's not your fault Bea. Some people just can't handle the truth.'

THIRTY-FOUR

'YOU CAN'T hide the money from her Jess,' Beatrice said as she sat across from Jessica in a restaurant in St. Pauls. She'd sent Sarah back to the office whilst she seized the opportunity to find out what was going on with the sister who used to have so much fire and whose gregariousness she once envied. Instead she pitied the woman who sat in front of her drinking double vodka and tonic and pushing the risotto around her plate.

'I know you're going through a rough time.'

'My husband is trying to financially ruin me and he's sleeping with my sister. That's more than just a rough time.'

Beatrice started coughing and spluttering as the bread she'd just swallowed decided to take a different direction. She grabbed the glass of water in front of her and took a couple of gulps.

'I don't know why you're so surprised,' Jessica replied without looking up from her plate. She put a small spoonful of risotto into her mouth and slowly chewed. She'd been trying to eat more but it was difficult when your stomach was filled with so much anxiety.

'Lou would never do that. You've got it wrong.'

'Well it wouldn't be the first time, would it? She tried it on with him before, the last time I visited her in New York. She's a devious little...'

'Stop it, Jess. I know Lou. That's not like her...'

'If you saw what I saw then you wouldn't say that.'

'And what exactly did you see, Jessica? The last time you were in New York Lou had just got divorced from Paul. She was a mess, you know she was. She'd caught Paul with that skanky...' Beatrice stopped as she felt her temperature begin to boil. 'You know what Lou is like. With her yoga and her Buddhism like Tina bloody Turner. She believes in karma, she'd never have done that to you. Never.'

'You're wrong,' Jessica said shaking her head. 'You've all been sucked in by her. I saw her...Five years ago I walked in on her and Andrew, she practically had her knickers on the floor.' Beatrice picked up the white linen napkin that she'd placed on her lap and threw it on top of her half eaten meal. She'd suddenly lost her appetite.

'You need to pull yourself together and ask yourself what exactly you saw because I'm telling you there's no way that our sister would do that to any of us. We worked hard to get through all of that Euterpe stuff and there is no way that she'd stick the knife in by sleeping with Andrew. For God's sake, she didn't even like him. You were the only one who thought that the sun shone out of his arse.'

'Are you calling me a liar?' Beatrice looked at the glass in her sister's hand, the slice of lemon moving daintily amongst the ice cubes as the vodka swirled around the bottom.

'I'm not calling you a liar, Jess but you'd stopped drinking before you had Lena, stopped being Jessie the party animal and then as soon as you met Andrew it started up again. So if you were as drunk then as you are now then all I'm saying is that you made a mistake. I'm going back to work. They were right when they said you shouldn't represent your family.'

Jessica watched her sister walk out of the restaurant and past the window as she headed in the direction of Ludgate Hill. She felt sick and angry. Angry about the position that her estranged husband had put her in, angry that her mum and now Beatrice were telling her she was wrong. She'd kept this secret to herself for five long years and every time she allowed the footage to replay in her head, something was always different. On some nights she pressed play and she saw her sister on her knees between Andrew's legs with his hands pushing down on her head. Other days she saw Lucinda naked sitting on top of Andrew as he called out her name. Some days it was even cruder as Lucinda was bent over the sofa with Andrew thrusting away behind her as he pulled onto her hair and Lucinda looked at Jessica with a smile on her face. Jessica shook her head as she tried to get rid of the latest image in her head as though she was removing pictures on an etch a sketch. It was the image of Lucinda trying to push Andrew off her, as she screamed no.

'Did you know that I've run a marathon?' Richard said as he rhythmically tapped the arms of the chair.

'Oh yeah. I've done it twice. What was your time?' said Dr.

Marcus as he squinted at the scans on his computer screen.

'This isn't a competition you know. Six hours 12 minutes. Anyway, I was a cancer survivor and I was running with my brother-in-law. I was hardly going to be breaking any records.'

'It's a great achievement. I walked like John Wayne for a week.'

'It's all Lance Armstrong's fault. If he can do seven Tour de Frances then I can do one little marathon, I told myself. If I'd only known. Hey, if I had what he had I probably could have run the marathon in half the time.' Richard looked around the room that he'd sat in many times before and wondered what news he was going to hear today. He'd surprised himself by being in a good mood. There was no nausea or thumping headache greeting him that morning and he'd felt like his old self. He'd even stepped on the bathroom scales and had put on two pounds. He wanted to hear good news. He needed good news. 'So, doctor. What is it?'

'Well, the good news is that the tumours haven't spread but I'm still concerned about your lymph nodes, even though they appear to be clear.'

'So the chemo is working then? That's good isn't it?'

'Yes, good but not good enough. The growth has stopped but the tumours haven't reduced in size, which is what I'd want to see before we even contemplate surgery.'

'So what…more chemo? I've had four cycles already.'

'I know you have and I know it's hard.'

'You've got no idea how hard it's been. If my head hasn't been down a toilet then I've been sitting on one. I'm sick of drinking soup but it's the only thing that I can keep down for more than an hour. Monday was the first time in months that I ate something and kept it down and you know what it was? A deep pan pizza with peppers, sausage and extra cheese. I thought that even if I couldn't eat it, I just wanted to smell it. I managed two and a half slices.'

'That's good. It's when you're not eating that I've got to be worried. Look Richard, I know that you're not going to like it but I'm going to suggest five more cycles of chemo…'

Richard groaned as he thought about what he'd have to go through again. 'And radiotherapy. If the tumours have reduced in size as I'm hopeful they will, then we'll discuss surgery, ok?'

Richard said nothing as he thought back to what he'd been researching online as he slowly ate his pizza the night before.

'What about alternative therapy? I was looking up some stuff online.' This time it was Dr. Marcus' turn to groan. He had nothing against alternative treatments and he supposed that if he was the one sitting in that chair he'd want to consider all of his options, but still, he was a doctor of medicine. He believed in the science not in chanting, crystals and mythical herbs that were probably no more than dried coriander leaves.

'There are treatments, medication from America.'

'That has mostly likely not been approved by the FDA, but go on.'

'You're probably right. I'm not sure how shark cartilage would be a cure for cancer. I might as well swallow a pack of Tic Tics but even so…'

'Even so, you want to consider your options. I understand that.'

'So, you don't mind if I give them a go?'

'I do mind actually, but I've known you long enough to know that you're stubborn and will probably do it anyway. So, take this. I don't want you going to any old snake charmer.' Dr Marcus took a card from his desk drawer and handed it to Richard. 'That's Dr. Stone. He's a friend of mine and has a practice on Harley Street. I'll let him know to expect you.'

As Richard drove home with the card of Dr. Stone in his wallet he suddenly felt the urge to turn the car around, drive to Brighton and do a Reginald Perrin. He knew that it was a stupid idea, as Felicia would find him in five minutes. He'd tried to avoid this for as long as he could. The same way that he harboured the fantasy that Dr. Marcus would call him up one day and tell him that it was all a mistake, but he knew that day wasn't going to come. He could hear their voices before he'd even put his key into the front door. The laughter and excited chatter of his three grandchildren floated through the open window of the front room. He didn't want to be responsible for stopping that laughter.

'Hey Pops,' Reece said as he walked out of the living room as Richard closed the front door behind him. He gave his grandad a tight hug and a kiss on the cheek, which made Richard laugh. He couldn't believe how tall he was. He'd run up and down the hallway when Paul had called him to tell him that the first twin to be born was a boy. He and Rachel were twins so he wasn't at all surprised when Lucinda had first called him to tell that she was pregnant with twins but it'd been so long since there had been boys in the family.

'Where's your grandmother?' Richard asked as he kicked off the black air force ones that Reece had persuaded him to buy when he'd decided to take his grandfather to Westfield one afternoon.

'In her office talking to Uncle Noah on Skype. They've been talking forever.' Reece rolled his eyes, as he knew better than most what it was like to be caught up in a conversation with his great uncle who had a habit of turning up on their doorstep unannounced, even though he lived in Toronto. Richard put his arm around his grandson and led him back to the living room.

'Come on, I need to you talk to you all.' Reece took a look into his grandfather's eyes and knew that the delights of the biscuit tin in the kitchen could wait.

Lena's large eyes widened and filled with tears whilst Katelyn squinted her eyes and began to chew on her bottom lip as she processed what her grandfather had just told them.

'Are you dying?' Reece asked. He was like his father and didn't believe in beating around the bush. He needed facts. He could deal with facts.

'No…no I'm not. But the odds aren't good,' Richard answered truthfully. The three grandchildren had squeezed themselves onto the two-seat sofa as if to insulate themselves from the news.

'And they're sure?' Katelyn asked.

'Yes, they're sure.'

'I told mom that you'd lost weight and she told me not to be rude.'

'Does my mum know?' said Lena who'd finally found her voice as she blew into a tissue that Richard handed her.

'Yes, she knows. They all know.'

'Oh great, so we're the last to know?'

'Well, I haven't told the dog yet,' Richard said with a grin. He wanted to take the sadness away from their faces. His grandchildren were so precious to him. Lena had been the first one and he remembered the mixture of emotions that he'd felt the first time he'd seen her in the hospital. There was intense love and then the realisation that he was being confronted with his own mortality, when he wondered if he'd ever see her graduate or be at her wedding when he saw her in Jessica's arms. It had made him wonder how much time he had left but he'd dismissed it, but now as he watched the faces of his three grandchildren he found himself asking the question again.

'We're only just getting to know you,' Katelyn said softly. He could feel his heart breaking at Katelyn's words.

'Hey. I'm not gone yet. Who knows how long I may be around for?'

Lena got up from the sofa, went over to him and sat on his lap just like she used to do when she was younger when she'd curl up and cocoon herself in his arms.

'I don't want you to die, grandad,' she whispered into his ear.

Richard swallowed hard and held onto his first grandchild. Memories flashed back of Lena climbing into his lap when she was three-years-old in her pink pyjamas and straggly toy rabbit, which had lost an ear and whose leg was barely hanging on and insisted that he read *Winnie the Pooh* for the hundredth time.

'Come on you three. I don't want you all sitting there depressed and miserable. I'm still here and the good news is that the chemo is working. The cancer hasn't grown.'

'What about alternative therapy?' Katelyn said as she looked up from her mini iPad. She'd been busy googling once she'd decided that she must do something to help her grandfather.

Richard began to laugh. She was so much like him and so much like her mother. She knew how to be practical and get things moving.

'What are you talking about?' said Lena.

'I'm looking at options for grandpa. There's all sort of things that he could try. Homeopathic remedies, acupuncture…'

'Yeah right, like putting needles in grandad's stomach will be the miracle cure…'

'Oh my God. That's gross,' Reece said as he read over his sister's shoulder. 'Hey grandpa how about this. Shark cartilage. An actual shark.'

The three grandchildren looked at their grandfather wondering why he'd burst out laughing to the extent that tears were starting to escape from his eyes.

'It wasn't that funny,' Reece said as he stared at his grandfather.

THIRTY-FIVE

LUCINDA SIGHED again as she took another look at her surroundings. If it wasn't for the ticket machine and the traffic warden sitting under a tree on a partially collapsing brick wall as he occasionally looked at his watch there was no way she'd believe this was a legitimate car park. She didn't want to get out of her car. During the entire drive from Notting Hill to New Cross she'd tried to ignore the fluttering in her stomach and the bile in her throat. She definitely wasn't pregnant so the only thing she'd put it down to was nerves and she'd never suffered from nerves before, not even when she'd stepped out on stage at Wembley Stadium in front of ninety thousand people. She had literally felt electricity flow through her whilst Beatrice always had to have her head down a toilet before she went on stage, and it wasn't unknown for Jessica to knock back a Jack Daniels and coke before she picked up the microphone.

She pulled down the sun visor and looked into the mirror. Hair, makeup, everything was perfect and she'd taken care with her outfit but it wasn't about the outside it was all about the inside. The last time she'd stepped into a recording studio was almost 14 years ago in Atlanta. She and Paul had arrived in a back of a limousine at the ridiculously sized mansion of the pint sized Booker Heritage, the twins had been left with the nanny whilst Booker and Paul had tried to mould her into something that she wasn't. She didn't want to compete with Aaliyah or Brandy or Monica and she had no intention of reinventing herself like Mariah Carey. She knew her sound and she was her own competition. Her voice was her power but Paul and Booker didn't think that was enough. It was no surprise that her second album flopped and found its way to the bargain bins of record shops.

Notting Hill had been filled with sunshine when she'd left her house that morning but a dark cloud had followed her and the skies in South East London darkened. She was determined that the dark cloud wasn't going to be an omen but then she remembered that it had poured down with rain more than 25 years ago when she, Jessica and Beatrice had got off the train at Deptford train station and walked to a narrow Victorian building behind the halal butchers, which laughably had a brass plaque on the door that said that they were at the music academy. Adam, the owner, had unconvincingly told them that Bros, Squeeze and Mica Paris had recorded in his studios. Just five minutes up the road was the Deptford Albany where Euterpe had performed at numerous talent nights before there was even a hint of a record deal. The arrival of a text message pulled Lucinda out of her daydreams. It was from Owen telling her good luck. He was the one surprise she hadn't been expecting when she'd made the decision to return home. It made things so much easier knowing she could talk to someone who didn't question her truth. Maybe she should have been more honest in the beginning instead of trying to put a gloss on everything.

'Right, Lou, let's do this. What's the worst thing that could possibly happen?' she said out loud. There was no answer to give because as she'd already concluded, the worst had already happened to her. She took her umbrella from her taupe Birkin bag and pushed the plastic bag of books out of sight, under the passenger seat. She was being forced into the position where she wasn't only re-establishing a career but now had to make a living.

"If one direction doesn't work for you then change the course of your life" was a mantra that her grandmother had tried to drill into her head the first time Euterpe had gone on a UK tour.

'Always have an escape plan, Lulu,' Grandma Celia had said as she kissed her on the forehead then wished her good luck. Lucinda finally got out of the car, paid an extortionate amount of money into the ticket machine, warned the traffic warden not to give her ticket and crossed New Cross Road that as far as she was concerned was in desperate need of gentrification. She found herself staring at a door with grey peeling paintwork and no door handle. It was nothing more than an exposed keyhole next door to a cafe that she swore used to be a Wimpy. The heavy drops of rain that had started to fall formed the question in her head about whether she should turn around and go home. Reluctantly she pressed the unlabelled buzzer and waited. No answer. She pushed again and waited, pressing herself against the door to shield herself from the rain. Suddenly there was a loud click and she fell into a dark hallway. She kicked aside a pile of pizza menus and minicab cards and stared ahead at the bare light bulb that starkly illuminated the steep staircase with its threadbare, stained carpet.

'Come up,' said a disembodied voice from somewhere upstairs.

'Sal has sent me to a bloody crack house,' Lucinda said as she wondered if her bag contained any anti-bacterial gel as she placed her hand on the banister barely held together by two rusty brackets. When Lucinda reached the top of the stairs she was surprised with what she saw and felt like one of Doctor Who's assistants when they first stepped into the tardis. There was no door and she walked onto a brightly lit room with stripped back but scratched floors, the hallmarks of microphone stands and drum kits being dragged back and forth across the room. The rainstorm had been brief and streaks of sunlight shone through the large bay windows that were slightly open causing a cool breeze to circulate the room and the sounds of south London traffic to provide the soundtrack. There was a piano that reminded her of the one that occupied the good room in her parent's house, keyboards, a drum set and on the left hand side of the room was a rack stacked with a bass guitar, rhythm guitar and a classic guitar. In the centre of the room there were three microphone stands. And to the right of the room she could see through to the recording booth.

'Sal said he wasn't sure if you'd turn up. Said you could be a bit difficult. I don't get on with difficult.'

'Difficult,' Lucinda said as she turned around to face a tall, slender man who she suspected didn't step out into daylight. He had thick, curly black hair and he kept his hands across his face as if he was still making up his mind about whether this meeting was a good idea or not. 'I'm not difficult. I just have standards. Lucinda LeSoeur,' She held out her hand, which he shook firmly.

'I'm Carter.' Lucinda raised an eyebrow as she waited. He huffed and finally said, 'Carter Rea.'

'It's nice to meet you Carter Rea,' Lucinda said with a smile.

'Well, you're here on time. I hate it when people take the piss. Would you like a drink?'

'Just water thank you.'

'That I can do.' He disappeared into a small kitchenette and returned a few minutes later with a large glass of water and a cup of tea. He handed the water to Lucinda and sat down on the battered leather sofa in the corner of a room.

'How old are you?' she asked.

'What?'

'Look, the last couple of producers looked like it was their first day wearing their big boy pants.'

'So,' Carter said, ignoring the question as he stretched out his legs and wriggled his feet. He wasn't wearing any shoes or any socks. 'Your last album was crap.'

'Oh.'

'I don't know what you were thinking because that sound

wasn't you. Your first solo album was a lot better. Not great, but better. I liked the last four tracks. *Play it slow. The Angel. Like Clockwork* and your cover of *Sinnerman* was …well it could never touch Nina's version…'

'No-one could ever touch Nina,' Lucinda said as she watched Carter carefully.

'But I liked it. The Euterpe stuff. I wasn't really into that manufactured, sweaty R'n'B stuff.'

'Hold on a second. Number one, we were never manufactured and number two, Euterpe was never sweaty R'n'B. Who were you into?' Lucinda took a look at his blue t-shirt with the logo for a karate club that had closed down eight years ago and his loose fitting jeans with the frayed hems. 'Don't tell me, Red Hot Chilli Peppers, Onyx, Radiohead a bit of Bowie and Wu Tang Clan.'

Carter grinned at her over his cup of tea. 'Something like that.'

'I bet you've got a Boys II Men album in your collection though. I wouldn't be surprised if you had a special Take That, Eternal and All Saints mixtape hiding in the back.'

'Alright, alright you can stop there. So Sal said you're planning a comeback. I usually work with new artists or established artists, not someone who hasn't had a hit for nearly twenty years.'

'Are you always this rude?'

'No, just honest. Maybe if someone had been honest with you then you wouldn't have made that last pile of shit.'

'I hope you don't talk to your mother or your girlfriend like that,' Lucinda said.

'Of course not. My mum would just tell me to shut up and I'm single.'

'I'm not surprised.'

'So what do you want me to do for you, Lucinda LeSoeur formally of Euterpe, Lucinda of my solo career didn't go to well. How do you want me to help you?'

'I want to perform, I need to perform. I've been working on some songs but I need some help. It can't sound like anything I did before…'

'You don't have to worry about that with me…'

'I didn't think that I'd have to. Look, I've done this before, I know how this game works and I've done my fair share of acting like I've lost a brain cell, being dressed so that I'd fit in, arguing with record executives who simply have no clue. I need to be me. I've got no intention of doing what I did before but then again I don't want to compete with everyone who has appeared on X-Factor.'

'And you don't want to sound like every generic sound on the radio,' Carter said as he sipped his cup of tea.

'Exactly. Look, despite what you think, when my sisters and I started out we had our own unique sound. We weren't pretending to be a British version of En-Vogue and we definitely didn't feel the need to compete with anyone who came after us.'

'You definitely had your own unique sound. I lied earlier on, I saw you and your sisters perform at a roadshow in Great Yarmouth. My dad always said that I had the most random taste in music. Your song Electrify could sum up the summer of 93. I know it sounds like a cliché but me, my brother

Adrian, and his best mate Ben travelled down to Devon the summer after I finished my GCSEs in our grandad's battered Volkswagen camper and that was our theme tune for eight bloody hours.'

'GCSEs…God. How old are you – 37? Don't look at me like that. I have a brain for figures. Surprisingly. Well, you held up well.'

'The secret is plenty of water and running. So what are you looking for? What sort of sound?'

'I don't want to sound like I've been auto-tuned!'

'I don't do auto-tuned. Look around you. Do I look like I do auto-tuned?'

Lucinda smiled and glanced around the room before focusing her attention on the wooden floorboards with the numerous scratch marks, the peeling varnish, and the boards that had been replaced and fitted smoothly amongst the familiarity of the old.

'I want my sound to be stripped back. I want it to sound raw but mature like whiskey that's been soaking in an oak barrel for fifty years. I want people to have that same feeling that I get when I listen to Nina but when we're done I don't want ITunes to put me in a box. That is what I want.'

There was no mistaking the excitement that flashed across Carter's deep brown eyes as he put down his cup of tea on the battered wooden crate that functioned as a coffee table.

'You know what, I've got the best idea. I know exactly what you need. Come on, let's get you in the booth.'

THIRTY-SIX

'I THINK you should take some time off,' Christopher said as he closed the living room door. Jessica looked at her ex-husband, as she stood barefoot in her work clothes. The house had been quiet again when she'd returned home that evening. Even though Lena had finally returned home after spending almost two weeks with Lucinda. It was as if the gods were playing a cruel joke when Lena had told her that staying with her aunt felt like a real home. Jessica had refused to look at her and simply told her that she'd prefer it if she stayed with her dad.

'You're going through a hell of a time at the moment, Jess. I wouldn't wish this on anybody but you're not coping at all. It's going to kill you if you carry on like this.'

'Who are you to tell me that I'm not coping? I'm managing things perfectly well.'

'Come on, Jessica. This is me you're talking to. I was married to you, remember. I know when you're not coping.'

'I am coping,' Jessica said defiantly as she sat down on the sofa.

'Knocking back a bottle of red every night and letting your daughter do what she wants isn't coping.'

'Don't you dare accuse me of being a bad mother!'

'I'm not saying that you're a bad mother. I'd never say that,' Christopher said as he sat down on the sofa next to her suddenly feeling overwhelmed by the situation. His new girlfriend, Patricia had told him that he shouldn't be getting involved and that he should just leave Jessica to work out her problems on her own but he couldn't do that. He'd lost count of the amount of times that Patricia had told him he wasn't responsible for his ex-wife. But he wasn't that type of man. Yes, they were divorced, but she was the mother of his child and also his friend.

'You're not a bad mother,' he said softly. 'No one in their right mind would ever accuse you of that. But you're not being the best you can be whilst you're in this state. Look at yourself, Jess. The last time that you were like this was…'

'That was different. Entirely different, Christopher.'

'I know it was different last time…'

'I didn't have the business for starters and I definitely didn't have a husband who was trying to strip me of everything I owned. I think I more than deserve to have a drink now and again.'

'But it's not just now and again, is it? You know you can't just have a drink now and again, which is why you stopped drinking in the first place.'

'It's not that much. You're just overreacting.'

'It is when our daughter is finding the empty bottles and picking up broken wine glasses and having to cover you up with a blanket because you've passed out on the sofa again. You're drinking during the day and from the look of things I wouldn't be surprised if you were drinking in the morning also.'

Jessica looked away at Christopher as shame and embarrassment burned through her. She couldn't even remember any of that happening. The last time that she'd spoken to her daughter was after she'd peeled the luminous pink sticky note from the fridge covered in Lena's handwriting saying she was staying at her grandparents for a couple of days and taking the dog with her. And then she'd received the text message that she was with Lucinda.

'I'm not an alcoholic, you know,' Jessica said, with no conviction at all.

Christopher didn't say anything as he watched Lena's baby photograph on the wall. He had the same one sitting on his hallway table. He wanted it to be the only one as he tried to ignore Patricia's not so subtle hints about wanting a baby.

'I'm not Christopher,' she said more forcefully. More for her own benefit than for his.

'I heard you.'

'The timing is just so wrong with everything. I know they say that bad things come in threes but this is ridiculous.'

'Lucinda coming home isn't a bad thing and before you open your mouth and say anything, I'm not taking sides but one thing I know about your sister is that she'd do anything for any of you.'

'Please, she just thinks about herself.'

'Jess, no one is a bloody saint. You can't sit there and tell me that you're not being selfish. Not everything is about you. You're on the verge of losing clients. Good ones.'

'What are you talking about?' Jessica said as she stood up a little bit straighter.

'Don't get me wrong, people are fickle and there's no such thing as bad publicity but not everyone likes the idea of the person who's supposed to manage their publicity taking up more column inches then they are. Mary Temperly has been bending Wendy's ear about moving across to The Visum Agency.'

'She wouldn't do that. She's been with me since the beginning,' Jessica said as she stood up and began to pace around the room.

'She wouldn't go…'

'She's not the only one. Evan Caine called Emma this morning and told her that he'd heard the agency was going under and that he may have to look elsewhere unless Emma wanted to work for him exclusively.'

'This isn't right. It's not fair. It's all Andrew's fucking fault. I've got to do something.'

Christopher got up, took hold of Jessica's shoulders and looked directly into her eyes. Despite the tough exterior that she put up, he knew she was vulnerable. He'd always wondered why people whose interior resembled a crème egg put themselves in positions where they were at risk of being attacked and criticised. He wasn't surprised that Jessica had hidden behind the shields of her agency. When he'd met her she was still brittle after the sudden split of Euterpe. They'd met at a birthday party for Kelvin Spring White who'd just signed for West Ham almost three months after Lucinda had left for New York. Jessica had arrived at the party with a friend and had proceeded to do what she did best, party and loudly proclaim that everything was fine.

'You can't control everything, Jess. Sometimes you have to stand back and let things take care of themselves.'

'But I'll lose everything and I'll be a laughing stock.'

'No one is laughing at you. You've got to let people help you and you've got to know when to let go.'

* * * *

Emma breathed a sigh of relief as she closed the office door behind her. To say that the last few weeks had been crazy was an understatement. It made her wonder more than once how her sisters had ever coped with the consequences of fame. Social media wasn't even a concept when they made their first appearance on Top of the Pops. There was no such thing as instant fame, no one re-tweeting everything you said or did or selling a napkin that you were supposed to have used on eBay. The most that Emma had ever had to put up with was catching a fan obsessed with Beatrice rifling through their dustbin when she was 11-years-old. She'd breathed a second sigh of relief when she saw the email from Jessica as she walked towards Tottenham Court Road station. Emma had known that she might as well have been talking in the wind and that Jessica wouldn't listen to her younger sister telling her to take a break so the task had befallen on Christopher. She was taking 10 days off work and from the text that followed from

Christopher; Jessica would be spending the entire time at the Bellevue clinic in Brighton, one of the most exclusive rehabilitation clinics in the country. It was the only clinic that had a waiting list despite the exorbitant fees they charged. Celebrities who revealed that they'd gone to *rest* at the Bellevue was the equivalent of confirming that you'd just received the latest bag from Hermes and that Aston Martin had just named a car after you. It was almost eight o'clock when Emma took a deep breath and stepped onto the sweltering Central line train still packed with a combination of lost tourists and people wearily making their way home. As she got off at Notting Hill Gate it occurred to her how much her life had changed in such a short space of time. Six months ago she was living in her parent's house in her childhood bedroom, Jessica was *happily* married, Beatrice was about to drop and talking about being stay at home mum and Lucinda was the sister she never saw but always received a birthday present from. Now here she was, knocking on her front door.

'How much,' Lucinda said as she sat at the kitchen counter with her laptop opened in front of her. 'I only want to hire it for one night, not buy the place.'

'It may sound a lot but it's the going rate love.'

'And I have to use the house band?'

'Yep'

'And you only have capacity for 300 and you want eight grand?'

'Yep, can you fill it with 300 people?'

'Please, I sold out Wembley Arena,' Lucinda said as she put

the phone down. She closed down the document with the lists of clubs that she'd spent most of the afternoon calling. There was no way she could afford the West End prices that they were asking of it. She opened her online bank statement and looked at it again. Well, she could afford it but she also needed to feed and clothe her children and in reality her funds were evaporating fast. When she'd left New York she'd had what most people would call a small fortune in her pocket. She'd arrived in London with £300,000 and change but now she was looking at a balance of £214,876.92. As she looked at the balance Lucinda had no idea how she'd managed to spend nearly a hundred grand in a few months. The Chanel ballet pumps that were on her feet should have given her a clue but she'd hardly done anything except pay the rent and made sure that the kitchen cupboards and fridge were full. She hadn't been on one shopping trip and had been living as frugally as she could. As she scrolled down the page every arrow was red and showed a debit. There was nothing coming in and that scared her. It was all very well and good having nearly a quarter of a million pounds in the bank but when you had no income and no safety net it might as well have been twenty pounds in the bank. Eventually the money was going to run out.

'That's so loud. I could hear it going off as soon as I came through the door. How could you sit here with all that noise?' Emma said as she walked into the kitchen trying in vain to ignore the repetitive beeps of the oven timer signalling her arrival

'Oh shit,' Lucinda said as she jumped off her chair and ran towards the oven to turn off the timer and pick up the oven gloves. She pulled out the terracotta tagine from the oven and lifted the lid. Immediately the kitchen was filled with the warm smell of lamb, cinnamon, tomatoes and apricots.

'That smells delicious. Even though you didn't have to cook for me,' Emma said as she walked over and kissed Lucinda on the cheek.

'I could hardly have you come over and then shove a cardboard box with a pizza in your face.'

'I only ever eat home cooked food if I'm at mum's. I'd rather starve than eat anything Beatrice cooked. Where are the kids?'

'They're at the cinema with Lena. She gets her exam results tomorrow and has turned into a wreck.'

'So, she's still staying here?'

'Not officially. Technically she has gone home but more often than not she's here,' Lucinda said as she switched on the kettle and busied herself with preparing the cous cous. 'Well, what am I going to do? I could hardly kick out my own niece and tell her to go home.'

'And Jessica was ok with that because to be honest, she's not exactly singing your praises?'

'That's a bloody understatement. Considering that she's telling everyone who will listen that I've been sleeping with her husband,' Lucinda said no longer feeling the need to keep this part of her life secret. She was fed up with it all.

'Is this a joke? Because if it is then I'm telling you now that it's not a good one.' Emma said.

'No it's not a joke.'

'You didn't did you?'

'Of course not Ems. What do you take me for?'

'So why is she saying that you did? Something must have happened. I mean it's not the kind of thing that you make up. Especially about your own sister. I mean how much would you have to hate someone to…'

'Emma, I'm going to tell you the same thing that I told mum. Nothing happened between that fool of a man and me. Nothing. Jessica made a mistake. It's as simple as that. Ok?'

'Well, I have to ask,' Emma said as she picked up a fork and pierced a piece of lamb. 'So you didn't sleep with him?'

'Emma! No I did not.'

'Fine. There's enough going on with this family without us turning into an episode of Eastenders.'

'Are you sure that you haven't got anything else to say?' Lucinda said surprised by Emma's reaction. She'd thought it would have been more screaming accusations and at that moment she didn't have the strength to defend herself anymore.

'Nope not a word,' Emma said as she took another piece of lamb.

'Thank you,' Lucinda said as she slapped Emma's hand away and placed the top back on the tagine. 'Leave it alone.'

'I can't help it. It's so good. I can't believe you can cook like this.'

'What can I say? I have lots of time on my hands. Actually, that's something I want to talk to you about. I know it's not your…' The sound of the door bell interrupted Lucinda.

'Can I borrow your laptop quickly? I just want to check something. Is that ok?'

'Yeah it's fine. Anything to stop you picking at the tagine. The password is Asteria97,' Lucinda shouted out as she left the kitchen and went to the front door.

'Bloody Greek mythology,' Emma muttered under her breath. She blamed their mother for Jessica and Lucinda's obsessions with Greek mythology as she typed in the password. She was surprised that their mother hadn't named them all after Greek goddesses. The home screen disappeared and immediately Emma was faced with Lucinda's bank statement.

'Oh crap.' She knew she should have closed the screen down and respected her sister's privacy but Emma was and had always been inquisitive. She raised her head as she heard the sound of two voices in the hallway and then the sound of steps. She clicked on the document folder, knowing that perhaps she was going too far but she wanted to know what her sister was hiding. She opened a letter from Lucinda's old accountant in New York and read it.

'Oh Lou,' Emma said again. 'How can you have no money?' She quickly closed the folders and logged on remotely to her work computer as she heard footsteps walking down the wooden floor of the hallway. Emma could feel the shame of knowing she'd invaded her sister's privacy but also the satisfaction that came with knowing you'd just been proven right.

'Ems, I'd like you to meet a friend of mine,' Lucinda said. 'This is Owen. Owen this is my little sister, Emma.'

'Little? Just *sister* will do,' Emma replied as she stood up and shook Owen's hand.

'Even if Lou hadn't said anything I would have known you

were sisters. You've got the same eyes. It's nice to meet you. I've heard a lot about you.'

'You have? Well, Lou has been keeping secrets because she hasn't mentioned you at all,' Emma said.

'Well, she can tell you all about me in the two minutes that it'll take for me to use the toilet,' Owen said as he gently touched Lucinda's waist and walked out.

'How long has he been coming round? He didn't even ask for directions to the loo.'

'So, he's been here before. That doesn't mean anything.'

'I saw the look that he gave you. Don't tell me it doesn't mean anything. Where did you find him?'

'It's a long story,' Lucinda replied as she started to take plates out of the cupboard and place them into the oven to warm them up.

'Well sis, I'll tell you one thing. There's no way that anyone could believe that you were doing anything with Andrew, not after seeing Owen. I'm surprised that you didn't kick me out as soon as he walked in. I'd have dragged him upstairs by now. Then again, I wouldn't have bothered. Right here on the kitchen table would do.'

'Emma stop it,' Lucinda said as she burst out laughing just as Owen walked through the door.

'So, Owen, why don't you tell me all about yourself?' Emma said as she tapped the kitchen table loudly.

'What do you want to know?' Owen said as he pulled out the bar stool and sat down next to her.

'Well firstly, do I need to buy a hat anytime soon?' Emma said with a grin.

THIRTY-SEVEN

'HOW COME Lulu is the only one that you taught to cook?' Emma asked as she sat on her old bed and folded clothes which she couldn't remember even buying and definitely didn't have anywhere to put in her new home so she was disposing of them by placing them into the charity bag.

'I didn't teach her how to cook. The only one I taught was you,' Felicia replied as she checked through the items on her list.

'Mum, I wouldn't call that teaching. You just told me to stand there and watch.'

'And that's exactly how my mother taught me. No, your dad's mother was the one who really taught Lucinda when she used to go and stay for the weekend.'

'Well, if Lulu's comeback doesn't work out then she should cook for a living because what she cooked last night was out of this world.'

'She brought your father round some sweet potato pudding the other day. I haven't made that for years and he ate every last bit. I didn't think that she was paying any attention when she was sitting in the kitchen with that blasted Walkman in her ears scribbling in her notebook.'

'So you're sure that you want to do this today, mum? Because I can think of a hundred other things that I'd rather do on a Saturday morning instead of wandering around bloody Ikea. I always come out of that place with an injury. I don't know why I just couldn't order stuff online.'

'Because if you did that my darling daughter I promise you that this time next year you'll still be eating your dinner with the plastic cutlery that you took from Pret a Manger.'

'Hmm, most likely. So where's dad?'

'Gone to the Oval with your uncle Stephen.'

'He shouldn't be out gallivanting with uncle Stephen, not when he's doing chemo. Why didn't you stop him?'

'Me, stop your father? I've got more chance of stopping a runaway train. Anyway, it's good that he's out. Keep himself motivated. The worst thing he can do is to sit there and wallow. That's more likely to kill him quicker than any cancer.'

* * * *

'What's wrong with you Emma LeSoeur?' Felicia asked as she lowered the volume of the car radio. Her daughter who could usually talk at a 100 miles an hour was unusually subdued.

'Aren't you fed up with all of the secrets in this family?' Emma replied as she stared out of the car window as they drove through Crystal Palace.

'What are you talking about? We don't have any secrets.'

'Of course we do, mum. Jessica has hers…'

'No she doesn't.'

'Mum, Jessica is an alcoholic. She's tried to hide it for years and now look at her. In bloody rehab.'

'What on earth are you talking about, rehab? Lena said she was going to a spa for a week.'

'A spa? No mum. She's not. As I said, keeping secrets…and as for Lou.'

'Oh please Emma, I don't want to hear any more about Lou.'

'I'm not going to slag her off, I'm just saying that I could never work out why she decided to come back. She hasn't lived here for nearly twenty years.'

'Seventeen years actually.'

'Whatever, but haven't you ever wondered what she was running from?'

'What makes you think that she's running from anything and even if she did why would it matter? The main thing is that she's here and your niece and nephew are here and that can only be a good thing for your dad. Having all of you around.'

'I know that's a good thing but I'm just sick of all of the secrets. I mean didn't you ever ask yourself why Lou was renting?'

'You know why. She's waiting for the tenants to move out.'

'So, she could have bought another house. You and dad drilled it into us that the best investments are property but she sold her house in New York and came here.'

'What do you mean she sold it?' Felicia said as she tried to focus on the Ikea chimneys looming in the distance, approaching her as quickly as the truths that were coming from her daughter's mouth.

'She sold her house in New York and then she came here and rented. She didn't buy another one, which I would have done, but she's had to rent. Now why do you think that is? People only run away from two things, mum; bad relationships and debts.'

Felicia distractedly drove twice around the roundabout before another driver beeped her.

'Your sister isn't a woman who runs.'

'Mum, open your eyes. Paul is bankrupt and Lou hasn't done anything since the turn of the millennium except be a real housewife.'

'You know, despite what he did, I always liked him. He was always generous and confident.'

'He was a bullshitter.'

'Emma, watch your mouth.'

'Oh mum, you know that he was. For a woman who had three daughters who were literally global superstars and now has daughters who work with every A list to Z list celebrity you can shake a stick at, how can you be so rubbish at keeping up with gossip? And for someone who's a lecturer I do question your ability to keep up with current events.'

'Emma, I teach classics. I talk about dead people, events that changed the world, not what Lady Gaga wore on her latest album cover or the fact that someone saw Idris Elba walking down the road.'

'He's quite a nice guy actually,' Emma said as she got out

of the car and closed the door. 'I hate this place,' she said as she looked up at the familiar blue and yellow sign. 'I saw her bank statement, mum.'

'Whose bank statements?'

'Lucinda's,' Emma said suitably shamefaced.

'Emma, what is wrong with you?'

'It was by accident.'

'Accident my foot. If I was your sister I'd have pelted you so far out of the door that you wouldn't even have seen daylight.'

'She's skint mum. Not so skint that she can't feed the kids and she can obviously rent a house in Notting Hill but she's skint. I told you people only run away from bad relationships and debts and Lucinda's running away from both.'

THIRTY-EIGHT

'HAVEN'T ANY of you lot heard of a recession?' Lucinda asked as she pushed aside a pile of dirty napkins on the bar that was still sticky with beer.

'And you haven't heard that the time of austerity is behind us.' Pete replied as he stuffed a piece of toast into his mouth. 'Lou don't get me wrong, I'm happy that you want to play in my club but Dougie Mills jazz club isn't a charity mate.'

'I know that. But it's just a silly amount of money that you're asking for, Pete. I mean it's not as if you won't make any money from the ticket sales.'

'When's the last time you sold out a concert on your own, Lou? I can't take the risk.'

'But you know me. I can sell out a show.'

'Yeah, with your sisters you could. Now if you were talking about us hosting a Euterpe comeback show then you would have something to negotiate with but you on your own, sweetheart I can't do it. Anyway, it's not just my club anymore. I've got partners now and they ain't as sympathetic as me.'

'I'm not asking for sympathy. I'm asking for a deal.'

'I can't give you a deal, Lou,' Pete said sympathetically. 'The problem is that the majority of people who come into the club won't have a clue who you are unless they happen to be driving home at three in the morning and Magic FM is playing.'

Lucinda felt sick as she walked out of the club on Wardour Street. She thought that after spending all of Friday and most of this morning calling venues trying to find anyone who would be prepared to give her a deal, that showing up in person might change their minds but it hadn't worked. When Euterpe had started out that had been Sal's job. Organising venues, making deals with club managers and hiring musicians. It was only now that she truly recognised how many bridges that she had burned, personally and professionally. She leaned her head against the wall, took a deep breath and tried to stop the tears that were threatening to spring from her eyes. She hated the feeling that she was begging but she didn't want to think about the worst case scenario. Even she could see that she had been an idiot for trying to keep up the lifestyle that she'd become accustomed to and also not to appear as a failure in front of her parents. All she needed was just one opportunity to get herself back into the public eye.

'You've got to spend money to make money, Lou,' Owen said as he broke eggs into a bowl and then pulled a handful of fresh chives from the pot on the windowsill.

'Only people with money say that,' Lucinda said as she

picked up a bag of coffee beans and started to make coffee. 'You couldn't just have a normal coffee machine could you?' she said, as she fiddled about with the buttons on the large silver machine

'Don't take out your frustrations on my coffee machine, thank you very much. Look, you have to think positively about all of this. Pass me the spring onions.'

'That's all I've been doing since I got here but positivity doesn't pay the bills, Owen. If I don't get this sorted then I'll just be surviving, living hand to mouth. I've never had to do that before. God, I should be at home, not here, doing…I don't know…'

'Look you. There's nothing wrong with you being here. Life goes on, just because you've hit a curve.'

'Curve? More like a fucking earthquake. You know what Owen, sometimes life is just eggs, it doesn't matter how much you try and jazz it up with spring onions and chives and paprika, they still remain eggs.'

'You haven't tasted my eggs, love,' Owen said as he kissed her. 'You have the money, Lou. Spend it.'

'I can't take the risk.'

'Hold on a second. The other night, I listened to your sister spend the whole evening telling me how determined you were and wouldn't let anyone tell you no, not even your mum. How you were the one who harassed the record companies to take you and your sisters on. You're a fighter and you're brave.'

'I'm not so sure about that.'

'You take chances. Bloody hell, you even took a chance with me. I never expected you to say yes.'

'You got lucky there. I don't know Owen, I just don't know what the right thing is to do now.'

'Yes you do. What does your heart tell you?' Lucinda closed her eyes and thought about it whilst Owen dropped rashers of bacon into a sizzling pan. She could see it now, the memory as clear as though she was stepping out on stage right now. The heat of the lights upon her face, the sounds of the crowd as they shouted out at her name. 'I want to perform at Ronnie Scotts,' she said as she opened her eyes.

'Really?'

'Yep, that was one of the last places that we performed at before I left and it was such a great night. You have no idea what it's like to be on stage and to hear people screaming out your name.'

'I screamed out your name,' he replied as he placed the plates on the table and then took the cups of coffee from Lucinda and kissed her.

'Not like that. Why is your mind always in the gutter?'

'It's what you like about me.'

'But you should know what I mean. It's like knowing that people are coming to your restaurant because of you. Do you know how much of a buzz it is knowing that people have come to see you? That they spent their money, listened to your albums, they know the words of every song and when you're on that stage, something takes over and you know your purpose. My gran always said that every child comes into this world with a secret. That's why their fists are closed when they're born and that secret that you're holding is your gift. You came here with a purpose and being on that stage is mine.

Don't get me wrong, I love my kids, they're my life but just sitting at home whilst they're at school, I wasn't fulfilling my purpose.'

'Then I don't get it. Why did you leave? If you were so happy why go solo and disappear to the States?'

'I never wanted to leave, not really. I never really wanted to be a solo act but I met Paul. I suppose that it was the right time and Paul talked a good game.'

'But Lou, you don't strike me as the sort of woman who would let anyone talk you into something that you didn't want to do.'

'It wasn't about me. Leaving Euterpe wasn't about trying to make some amazing solo career.'

'So why go?' Owen asked as he placed a plate in front of her.

Lucinda inhaled the coffee's aromatic scent and took a sip. 'I had to save Jess. It wasn't about me. I had to look after my sister. She was partying too much, drinking too much; Euterpe was going to kill her. So I had to leave. I had to save my sister.'

If someone had told Jessica that nearly twenty years later she'd be back in rehab she'd have told them that they were lying but here she was in Brighton, in a grade II building overlooking the sea, being forced to talk about her relationship with alcohol. Jessica hadn't slept since she arrived and it had only just dawned on her how much she'd been using alcohol to self-medicate and that she had a problem. She'd always believed that because she'd always got up and gone to work in the morning, that she did not have a problem. She had always functioned. She ran a successful business, a happy marriage and had a wonderful daughter. She had made it and moved beyond the woman who used to be in a girl group and knew how to party. Now she was exhausted, emotionally and physically, and the work hadn't even begun yet. Her life was falling apart and if it wasn't falling apart then an estranged husband, who felt he was entitled to everything that she represented, was picking it apart.

'So, how are you feeling?' Candice asked as she curled up on an armchair next to Jessica. Despite the fact it was 25 degrees Celsius, Candice was still wrapped up in a hoodie with the sleeves pulled down over her hands. Jessica had thought that the famous photographer had disappeared to Miami for the summer and was surprised to see her in the room next to her. Candice had told her on her first night that her bulimia had returned and she'd become more than reliant on her painkillers that she'd taken after an operation on her back, three years ago.

'Honestly, I feel as though I'm trying to grab bits of my life out of the drain and it doesn't even feel like any of this is happening to me,' Jessica said.

'That's how I felt when I came in here. Like I was a visitor in my own fucking life. I never thought that I'd be the type of person to be addicted to anything. I thought I was stronger than that. It's all a facade really. So have you thought anymore about staying longer?'

'I have but I can't do it. I've got five days left and then I'm going home to sort my life out. I mean my daughter got her exam results on Thursday and I wasn't even there.'

'How did she do?'

'Oh God, I'm so proud of her,' Jessica said as she suddenly found herself crying. 'She got all 10 GCSE's, 4 A*, 4 As and 2 Bs. I should have been there. Not here. I should have been with her.'

'Count yourself lucky that she even called you.'

'I know. I just can't stop feeling that I've disappointed her. I never wanted her to be disappointed in me.'

'I don't think she is, Jessica. For fucks sake, we're only human, not fucking wonder woman. Picking you up from the bathroom floor when you're covered in your own vomit won't make her proud but coming here, telling her that you've made mistakes and that it's ok to make mistakes but that you're getting help, that'll make her proud.'

THIRTY-NINE

'LUCINDA. I have something that you may be interested in. They won't pay you.'

'So why would I be interested?'

'Just listen to me,' said Sal. 'Allure magazine. You've heard of it?'

'Funny enough I've got a copy in my hand,' she replied as she turned the magazine over to look at its cover, noticing it had a beaming Naomie Harris on the front.

'See, this is a sign. Well, I was talking to their features editor, Lily, who's a really nice woman I met last night at a book launch. She's just came out of a messy divorce like you…'

'My divorce wasn't messy. You must be confusing me with my sister.'

'Whatever. Anyway, I was telling her all about you and she said she was working on a feature about high profile women from the nineties…a kind of where are they now and we got talking about you. She loved you lot by the way.'

'Unfortunately, you can't put love in a pot to boil Sal.'

'Stop being a moody cow. She wants to do a whole piece about you, possibly make you the cover story.'

'Really? A cover?' Lucinda said standing up as though as she'd been jolted with a cattle prod. 'She wants to do a cover story on me?'

'See, that grabbed your attention. So what do you think?'

'I think that I'd be a fool to say no. I can't remember the last time I was on a cover.'

'Pride magazine, November 1999. I've got a head for these things.'

'It wasn't that long ago was it?'

'Afraid it was. So, you'll do it?'

'Of course, I'll do it.'

'Excellent. I'll give her a call and tell her people to call your people.'

'Sal, you are my people,' Lucinda said as she burst out laughing.

'Oh yeah, I am. Speak to you soon, chick.'

It wasn't a lottery win but it was definitely what she needed. An opportunity to get back into the public eye. It was as if the universe was finally listening and giving her a break. She was tempted to strip off her clothes and run screaming, naked around the garden, except it wasn't her garden and she wasn't that close to her neighbours.

'Thank you, God,' Lucinda said as she kissed the magazine cover as though it was a magical talisman.

'What are you so happy about?' Richard asked as he walked into the living room and picked up his wallet from the coffee table.

'Nothing, just life. So, are you ready?'

'Ready for anything.'

'Have you told mum where we're going?'

Richard looked at everywhere in the room, in a misguided effort to avoid Lucinda's eyes. 'Dad, you haven't told her, have you?'

'She'd only tell me that it's a stupid idea and a waste of money.'

'And when she's finished cussing you, she'll call and cuss me out and tell me off for encouraging you.'

'Which is why I need you to do me a favour.'

'What's that?'

'Can you pay for the doctor today? You know what your mum is like. She'll go and check the bank account online and then ask why I'm giving a Harley street doctor £300.'

'I should refuse for making me an accomplice.'

'I promise that I'll never ask for anything ever again.'

'Fine, stop panicking,' Lucinda said as she burst out laughing at her dad's pleading eyes.

'Don't worry about it, I'll pay for it.'

The drive to the doctors went quickly as they talked about everything except the cancer, which was perfectly ok with Richard. Ever since his family and friends had found out that he was ill again, he felt as though they were treating him as if the grim reaper was taking him out that very afternoon every time he stepped out of the front door.

'So tell me what's happening with you. I feel like I've hardly seen you,' Richard said.

'I've just been busy, dad. I've been at the studio with Carter every other day.'

'And it's going well?'

'Dad, it's going so well. I haven't felt this excited about music for God knows how long. I've just been asking myself "what have I been doing to myself all of these years?" I've wasted so much time. Ooh, let me play you what we've been working on.' Lucinda connected her iPhone and waited for the music to fill the car. With the roof down, the warmth of the sun on their faces and Lucinda's strong but smooth voice filling the car, encapsulating how they both felt as they drove along Park Lane. Richard closed his eyes and began to nod his head in time to the music.

'That's really good, Lulu. So good, I like it. Lord, it reminds of me when I first heard you sing. You were only nine-years-old and you were singing along to my Al Green album.'

'I think I scratched up that album.'

'You did, playing Love and Happiness over and over again, and I heard you and I told your mum, "that girl can sing."' Lucinda smiled as they pulled up at the traffic lights at Hyde Park Corner. As soon as her song finished she selected Al Green.

Richard began to sing along loudly as Al Green launched into "Love and Happiness".

'Well I definitely didn't get my talent from mum. Go on dad, sing,' Lucinda said as they headed towards Harley Street.

Lucinda had been holding it in for the past twenty minutes

and had even asked the doctor a series of well researched questions on behalf of her dad but now she was struggling and was convinced she'd burst if she didn't leave the doctor's office quickly.

'If you wanted to begin the treatment then we could start straight away. I firmly believe that treating cancer is a multi-step process. I wouldn't advise you to stop with the chemo and radiotherapy but I'd recommend a course of Laetrile along with complementary therapy like acupuncture and Gerson therapy,' the doctor said as he spoke to Richard but kept his eyes firmly on Lucinda as she tried to keep her composure by keeping her eyes fixed on the floor.

'Well, thank you doctor,' Richard said as he nudged Lucinda with his knee. 'I'll give it some thought.'

'The sooner the better obviously, but think about it overnight and let me know.'

As soon as the black glossy door closed behind them Lucinda collapsed into laughter. 'Oh my God. I don't know how he could say all that with a straight face.'

Richard began to laugh also as he watched his daughter lean against the railings to try and compose herself.

'Come on dad. What were you expecting?'

'I don't know. Something a bit more futuristic.'

'Dad, that office was not the starship enterprise. But saying that you can always give it a try. What's the worst that can happen?'

'True, true. Oh well.'

'Why don't we go and get some lunch. We can drive up to St Christopher's place.'

'Don't be silly, it's only a short walk.'

'Dad, we don't have to. Ok if you're sure,' Lucinda said as she saw the determined look on his face. She linked arms with him and they began to walk. It never ceased to amaze her, the love that she felt for her dad. No matter how old they got, it never went away.

They found a restaurant but decided to sit outside in the square, which was already bustling with diners.

'I know you're disappointed,' Lucinda said as they handed their menus back to the waitress.

'I was just expecting something a bit more than shark cartilage capsules, sticking needles in my belly and illegal medication.'

'Dad, the second one wasn't illegal; it's just not authorised in the EU.'

'That's illegal to me.'

'It's authorised in the States.'

'Money making scheme if you ask me. How much was it again, $500 for a month's supply? What's that in pounds?'

'Just over £300.'

'See, nothing more than a snake charmer peddling his wares and you couldn't even keep a straight face. I need to be a bit more practical. Life just becomes a lot clearer when can see the thread of life unravelling before your eyes.'

'You can always have an eco funeral if you want to be practical. We can bury you in a cardboard box in the garden, next to mum's roses. It'd only cost you a hundred quid,' Lucinda said, laughing when she saw the laughter lines crease around her dad's eyes.

'She's going to think that the cancer has gone to my brain.' They said nothing for a while as their food arrived. Richard looked down at his steak sandwich and almost cried as the smell of caramelised onions wafted up his nose. He didn't think he could manage the whole sandwich but he wanted to at least try

'Do you regret not having boys, dad?' Lucinda said as she cut her sandwich in half.

'Why would you ask that?'

'I just wondered. Every man wants a son to carry on his name.'

'I suppose it'd have been nice to have a boy around, especially when you girls were teenagers and were somewhat hormonal. Jesus Christ it was stressful and then your mum was…' Richard thought about the right word.

'Pre-menstrual.' Lucinda grinned at her dad's embarrassment.

'Five of you. It was like living in a war zone. The screaming, doors slamming and then you'd start playing Morrissey and The Cure really, really loudly. Even to this day, when I hear Morrissey my blood runs cold.'

'Sorry about that.'

'And then the boys started knocking the door; ringing the house. Jessica would be sneaking out of the house. I don't know what was worse; you lot discovering boys or all the photographers at the door when you became famous. There 'aint nothing in the parenting manual for that. I should have written a book. "How to cope when your children become famous." To be honest I don't know how you girls even managed to sit down in a room together and write music.'

'I don't know either actually. I can't even remember the last time the four of us were in the same room together.'

'Well, you will fix that. I know you will. But I don't regret not having boys. I don't regret having you girls. I wouldn't change it for the world. You girls are my life,' Richard said as he reached across the table and squeezed Lucinda's hand.

FORTY

AS THE cab travelled into London Jessica felt that wide eyed anticipation that normally came when you'd been out of the country for several months and you were returning home. She expected to see changes. New buildings going up or old buildings being taken down. She wanted the London that she knew to be bathed in the light of a setting sun but the reality was that she'd only been away for ten days not ten months and there should have only been one change; the change within her. She'd fooled herself into thinking that abstinence would be an easy thing but it was as though she had forgotten everything she'd learnt from her first rehab stint. She'd found that alcohol was something that she craved. She used it as a crutch, as a way of telling herself that it was just another way of relaxing; a liquid yoga. Ten days sober was not enough. She knew that and she also knew that the battle to regain herself would not start until she had stepped out of the cab, opened her front door and walked back to her life.

Jessica had arrived home a day early and knew she'd be

alone. Lena was still living a hobo lifestyle and Jessica honestly couldn't remember if she was spending the night with her father, aunt or grandparents. That thought had pained her. Richard and Felicia had always made sure that their children had a stable life and hadn't been keen to send them here there and everywhere. The girls had to beg just to stay the weekend with their aunts or grandparents when they were young. It was only once they discovered the freedom of their travel cards that they begun to spend weekends away, but it hadn't been encouraged.

It was 8.05pm and the sky had not yet completely given itself away to darkness but Jessica could see that the hallway light was on. Jessica watched the light, feeling confused. There was no way that Lena would be home and far as she was aware there had been no emergency that would require either Emma, Beatrice or her parents to be at her home. Her heart stopped in her chest and her stomach sunk when she saw the car. The gleaming silver Porsche was sitting defiantly two doors away from her front door.

'Please God, no,' Jessica said as she walked towards the car praying that it belonged to someone else. But the residential parking permit on the windscreen with her door number written on the front and the personalised number plate, which she'd always hated but had never had the guts to tell him that it was pretentious and egotistical, was displayed proudly in black and yellow.

'What are you doing in my house?' Jessica said calmly, which surprised her considering that she could feel herself shaking with rage as she watched Andrew walking territorially around the living room.

'That's not a very nice welcome for your husband,' Andrew said with a smug grin on his face.

'You're not my husband.'

'Well until the court says otherwise, I am. So the least you could do is say hello.'

'You want me to say hello? The last time I saw you, you were walking out of this house and telling me you wanted a divorce so forgive me if social niceties go out the window. So answer me, what are you doing here?'

'I'm here to pick up the rest of my things.'

'There's nothing here for you.'

'This house is here and anyway, I thought we could talk about the divorce?'

'We have lawyers. There's nothing for us to talk about, so get out.'

'Come on Jessica, there's everything to talk about. You're at risk of losing your house and your business to me. Plus, I know where you've just been on your so-called holiday, so I think we should talk, don't you?'

'Are you out of your fucking mind? You have no right to anything.' Jessica shouted as she marched up to Andrew and pushed him firmly in the chest. 'You didn't make me. I made me. I did all of this. Not you.'

'You were nothing when I met you. Just another washed up wannabe singer from yesteryear. I gave you status,' Andrew said as he grabbed Jessica's arms and squeezed tightly.

'You're delusional. You pursued me. You wanted me. I'm

the one who gave you status not the other way round, Andrew. Now let go of me.'

'You've always had an overinflated image of yourself. I picked you up from the shelf of obscurity.' As soon as Andrew let go, Jessica slapped him round the face. Andrew rubbed at his face but still smiled a mocking, arrogant smile. 'I'll get everything, Jessica. Look at you. You're cold, irrational. Just my luck to pick the frigid sister but then again Lucinda wasn't up to it either. She was putting up quite a fight. She was lucky you came in when you did.'

Jessica stepped back stunned 'You didn't. How could you…' She didn't know what to say. It wasn't Andrew's betrayal that hit her the most; it was the fact that she was now face to face with the truth. She had been the one who had betrayed her sister.

'You really are pathetic, Jess. I should have left you ages ago. You know I actually came here to make a deal with you.'

'Get get out of my fucking house before I call the police.'

'Give me the agency and you can keep this house and your pathetic royalties.'

'I'd rather see you dead then give you a penny. I'll kill you myself rather than give you anything. Now get the fuck out of my house,' Jessica screamed, her whole body convulsing with rage.

* * * *

Jake put his arms around his wife and kissed her neck. 'We haven't had sex for ages.'

'And this is how you plan to seduce me, by whining about it?' Beatrice said as she turned around and kissed her husband as he adjusted the pillow behind his head.

'I'm too tired to give you the full Jake Ashcroft seduction routine. You're just going to have make do with begging.'

'But you're not too tired to actually have sex.'

'Do you know if Theo doesn't come back in here demanding that I read him another story and Sam manages to sleep for four hours straight we may actually have time for a quickie with no interruption?'

'You're obsessed.'

'I'm not. I'm just horny especially when my wife is looking so sexy.'

Beatrice looked down at her grey cotton pyjama bottoms and white vest with the black dye stain on it and shook her head. 'You're not right in the head if you think this is sexy.'

'Of course it is,' Jake said as he rolled over and laid on top of his wife. 'Don't answer it,' he said as Beatrice's phone began to ring and vibrate across the bedside table. He placed his hand inside his wife's pyjama bottoms and felt his way between her legs. Beatrice groaned as she felt his fingers pushing gently inside of her and she began to pull off his t-shirt. He could feel himself hardening and was desperate to be inside his wife when Beatrice's phone began to ring again from the bedside table. 'Jake, I should…'

'No Bea, just leave it. Come on. I just want to be inside of you,' he whispered into her ear.

The phone stopped ringing for a second time and then almost immediately begun to ring again.

'Oh for God's sake,' Jake said as he rolled off Beatrice, exasperated and grabbed the phone off the table. 'It's Jess,' he said, handing the phone to Beatrice and walked off into the en-suite bathroom. 'Bea, I don't think I can handle this anymore.'

'Jess, what's happened? Are you ok? Are you hurt?' She suddenly felt fear as she heard the anguish in her sister's voice.

'Andrew was here.'

'What the hell was he doing there? Did something happen? Did he hurt you?'

Jessica looked down at the faint swelling on her left wrist.

'No, no. We argued, I slapped him. I've just been wrong about so many things, Bea. I've made such a big mistake'

'What happened, Jess?'

'He just wanted to wind me up by walking in here like he owned the place and then he told me…Oh Bea, I've been such an idiot. I couldn't blame Lou if she never wanted to speak to me again. How could I do that?'

'Sis, you're not making any sense. Do you want me to come over? Or Jake can…'

'No. Don't be silly. You've got the kids. I'll be fine. Honestly. I've got a locksmith coming tonight…I'll be fine. I'll call you tomorrow, ok?'

'What's happened?' Jake said as he came back into the room and noticed that his wife's face was suddenly devoid of colour and her forehead was wrinkled as she tried to comprehend what had just happened. 'Bea, what's wrong with your sister? You look like you've seen a ghost.'

'You need to go over there. I've never heard Jess sound

frightened before,' Beatrice said as she began to shake.

'Leave it to me. You've done enough,' Jake said as he sat down next to Beatrice and held her tightly.

FORTY-ONE

'YOU'VE GOT the look of someone who has just heard their voice for the first time,' said Carter as he stepped out from the control booth.

'Did it sound ok? Because I wasn't quite sure,' Lucinda asked as she picked up her cup of hot lemon tea.

'Was it ok? You know that it was more than ok. All in one take too. I don't know what you've been so worried about.' Lucinda couldn't stop the smile that was spreading across her face. She could feel her cheeks start to ache but she couldn't help it. As the bright, intense light from the super moon seeped through the studio and illuminated the microphone stand, making it appear that it was glowing with angel wings, Lucinda felt as though she was given some form of heavenly approval.

'It's the first time in years that I've felt excited. I feel like I'm buzzing. Thank you.'

Carter looked at Lucinda with a quizzical look on his face. 'You don't have to thank me. I'm just doing what you paid me to do.'

'Come on. It's more than that and you know it. You've been amazing, Carter.' There was no question about it. Carter was talented and he instinctively knew how to bring out the best of her voice. When he'd played back the first recording of an acoustic set of the song that she'd written after she'd arrived home, she was surprised at how much her voice her changed. It was still recognisable as her voice but it had developed a haunting, melancholy huskiness to its tone. It had unnerved her at first but as Carter had said it was richer because of her life experiences.

'So, when you come back we'll record the next two tracks with the band,' Carter said.

'Sounds good to me. I can't wait.'

'It's good to see you excited.'

'I am. I really am. I just need to finalise the dates for the show and confirm the venue and then I'm good to go,' Lucinda said, however not convincingly enough to hide the uncertainty in her voice from Carter. Not after he'd spent the last few weeks listening to every nuance of her voice. He could tell when she was in pain, if she was singing from genuine love or overwhelmed with the enthusiasm of trying something new.

'What's wrong?' he asked as she sat down next to her on the sofa as Lucinda began to pack away her things. She took a deep sigh and looked upwards. 'I just don't want all of this to be for nothing. I mean I've loved working with you. I love to sing. It's all consuming and I just want people to hear me. I know that everyone thinks it's just about making as much money as you can, and I won't lie. Before I stepped on that plane that was the only thing that was going through my mind. Just do what you can to make as much money as you can but it's not about that. Not really.'

Carter nodded in understanding and leaned back into the sofa, the aged leather creaking beneath him.

'I wasn't supposed to be doing this,' he said. 'The music thing. My dad wanted me to have a career in something stable. He's an actuary, my mum's a dentist and they wanted me to have a secure career. Anything but music.'

'So what happened?' Lucinda asked intrigued by the impending confessional.

'Did what I was told. Went to Oxford university.'

'I'm surprised you didn't bump into Beatrice. That's where she went.'

'Really, small world. Anyway, went to uni, got a degree in History and Economics, got a job in an investment bank and hated every single minute of it.'

'You were a banker?'

'Yep, an overworked, depressed, investment banker. I lasted three years and one day I woke up and said "I'm not doing this anymore. I want to make music." So, I took voluntary redundancy and here I am.'

'Wow, I knew there was something about you.'

'Yeah, a rebel. Dad went mad, mum went madder. Thought that I was throwing my life and education away. But this makes me happy. Even if it doesn't make me rich at least I'm doing something that makes me get out of bed in the morning and I'm excited about my day.'

'Have they got over it yet? I think my mum regrets the day she ever agreed to put a piano in the house.'

'My dad still thinks that this is just a blip and that I'll get over it. It's been ten years; it's not going to happen. So Ms. LeSoeur don't worry about a thing.'

As Lucinda drove home she sang along, at the top of her voice, with every song that came out of her car speakers. For the first time in a long time she could actually say that she was happy, she even laughed when the opening lines of the Gwen Guthie club classic *'Ain't nothin goin on but the rent'* blared out of the speakers. Lucinda was still singing when she arrived home. It was almost 11pm and she wasn't surprised that the twins were still up but she was surprised to see Jessica sitting in her living room with a cup of tea in her hand as though it was the most natural thing in the world.

'Hi mom. How was the studio?' Katelyn said, sprawled out on the sofa watching High Fidelity and ignoring the absurdity of the fact that the aunt whom she'd barely seen since she arrived in London was sitting next to her.

'The studio was fine,' Lucinda said calmly.

'Hello Lou,' Jessica said as she stood up. It had taken her two days to find the courage to contact her sister but every time she'd picked up the phone she knew that a phone call simply wouldn't do and there was no guarantee that Lucinda would even have accepted it. So she'd taken the chance, knowing that her sister deserved more respect than that. She'd driven from Islington to Notting Hill in the hope that her sister wouldn't slam the door in her face. The icy tension between the sisters was enough to draw Katelyn's attention away from the television.

'I think I'm going to watch the rest of this in my room,' Katelyn said as she unwound herself from the sofa, walked up to her mum and kissed her on the cheek. 'Be nice,' Katelyn whispered to her mum. 'Night, Auntie Jess,' she said before running up the stairs two at a time.

'What are you doing here, Jessica?' Lucinda asked once she'd heard Katelyn's door shut.

'I needed to see you. To speak to you.'

'You could have called.'

'I could have done but…' She searched for the words. 'A phone call wouldn't have been enough.'

Lucinda didn't move away from the door as she watched her sister from a distance. She wasn't wearing any makeup and she could see the dark circles under her eyes and her face looked anguish and drawn.

'Mum said that you've been away, but you don't look like you've been on holiday. Not unless you took a ten day city break to Helmand Province.'

'Lou, I'm…'

'Have you eaten?' Lucinda asked, not feeling quite ready to hear whatever Jessica had come all this way to tell her, especially after the last time they'd spoken, which had left their relationship beyond repair.

'What?' Jessica replied, confused that Lucinda hadn't yet grabbed her and demanded that she leave.

'I said have you eaten?'

'No, I haven't. I had something at lunch but it wasn't much.'

'Right, come on then,' Lucinda said as she turned and walked into the kitchen leaving Jessica with no choice but to follow her.

FORTY-TWO

LUCINDA BUSIED herself with taking out the remainder of the butternut squash and spinach rotolo from the fridge. As always she'd cooked too much and feared that she and the twins would be eating it for a whole week. She turned on the radio to fill in the silence as Jessica stood patiently by the island not sure whether she should be sitting.

'Would you like some wine? I've got a shiraz already opened,' Lucinda said as she waited for the ping of the microwave.

'No thanks. I'm not drinking…I've stopped drinking.'

'Oh, ok. Well, I've got diet coke or cranberry juice.'

'I'll take the juice,' Jessica replied as Lucinda prepared the drinks and only sat down once she'd placed the plates on the table. Jessica felt her stomach rumble as the smell of rich, spicy tomato sauce combined with butternut squash, basil and oregano wafted up her nose. She sat down and took a mouthful of pasta not quite believing the sensation in her mouth. 'Oh my god. Lou, this is so good,' Jessica said after her first mouthful. 'I never knew that you could…'

'There are a lot of things that you don't know,' Lucinda replied coldly as she poured herself a glass of wine and sat down to eat.

'Why are you here?' Lucinda asked as she topped up her glass unable to take the pretence of the silence anymore. 'Because I'm surprised that you're here in my house eating in my kitchen. I thought you had no intention of speaking or seeing me again.'

Jessica pushed her plate away and diverted her eyes away from the large wine glass that Lucinda was bringing to her lips.

'I came to apologise. To tell you that I was wrong. I was wrong to take Andrew's word over yours.'

Lucinda raised an eyebrow. 'You were wrong? You were wrong to take his word. Is that it?'

'What do you mean is that it, of course that's it.'

'Jessica, you weren't just wrong. You betrayed me.'

Jessica looked down at the table. 'I know.'

'You took his word over mine. I'm your sister and I'd never have done anything to hurt you. Never, and you believed him over me. How could you do that?'

'Lou, I know and I'm sorry.'

'It's not enough. Saying sorry is not enough. So what happened? What made you see the light? Because it definitely wasn't anything I said.'

'He told me,' Jessica said unable to stop the hot tears that were streaming down her face.

'Oh great, so you only believe me because that shit of a man told you. Thank you, Jessica. Thank you very much. Do you know what damage you did? I had mum here looking at me as if I was a piece of shit under her shoe, Beatrice calling me asking if it was true. Even though she said she'd never believe it, do you have any idea how it feels to have your own family doubting your words and questioning your truth? I've done a lot of things that I'm not proud of but I'd never do what you did to me. Never,' Lucinda said as she got up angrily from the table and walked towards the garden doors, suddenly finding the room and conversation suffocating. She walked barefoot into the garden still holding her wine glass and took a deep breath and closed her eyes as the soft, warm breeze swept over her.

'You hurt me, Lou. You hurt me when you left me,' Jessica said softly as she stood next to her sister. 'It was always us. We did everything together and then you left me.'

'And that made you believe that I'd try and sleep with your husband. Come on, Jess. You can do better than that.'

'Lou, I'm trying, I'm really trying. I've been stupid, I've been blind and I've been a fool. I accept all of that. Even worse I put someone else before my own sister. I should never have done that.'

'Jess, I left you. I left Euterpe but I never stopped being there for you. I left Euterpe for you. Not for me.'

'I don't understand.'

'You were going to kill yourself. You were drinking too much, partying too much. Every time you disappeared to some after party I was worried sick that I'd wake up to find out that something had happened to you. I couldn't let you do that to yourself so I had to leave. Jess, I loved being in Euterpe. You and me we lived and breathed music and there was nothing I loved more than creating music with you and performing on stage with you and Bea, that was my life. I didn't really care about going solo but when I met Paul and he told me what I could do if I stepped out on my own I thought it'd be the best thing for you. I didn't plan on doing a Diana Ross and turning us into Lucinda LeSoeur and Euterpe. I never wanted that. I just wanted to save you.'

'I thought that it was all about you, and when I saw Andrew on top of you, it was easier to believe that you did that to me instead of blaming him.'

'Well, you wouldn't would you? You were so self-absorbed, so far up your own arse that it was easier to blame everyone else but you. It was easier to blame me.'

Jessica said nothing, knowing that everything Lucinda was saying was true. 'I'm sorry that he tried to hurt you.'

'You don't have to apologise for him. Don't you dare do that. I may want to kill you right now but I'm not having that,' Lucinda replied as she suddenly felt exhausted and sat down.

'I'm sorry that I didn't behave like a sister. You're my big sister Lulu and I'm sorry,' Jessica said as she sat down next to her.

Lucinda said nothing. She'd never wanted to fight with Jessica and she'd learnt a lot over the past few months to know that life was too short and too unexpected to focus on the negative or the frailties of others.

'Say something Lou,' Jessica said.

'I'm glad that you've stopped drinking.'

'I could lie and say that I'm glad too, but I'd kill for a sip of your wine.'

'Well tough. Stick to cranberry juice.'

'He never wanted me you know. He just wanted…actually I don't know what he wanted.'

'Yes you do. He saw a cash cow. Simple as that. If it wasn't you it'd have been someone else.'

'He wants everything, Lou. Everything that I've worked so hard for. When Christopher and I got divorced it was reasonable.'

'That's because Christopher is a decent human being and Andrew is a cunt.'

'God, I hate that word.'

'Find a better word to describe him and I won't use it.'

'You're right he is a cunt.' Jessica looked at her sister and for the first time since she'd walked into her house, laughed.

'He came to me the other night saying that he'd let me keep the house and our money if I gave him the agency.'

'Tell him to go and fuck himself. Hold on,' Lucinda said as she realised what Jessica had said. 'What do you mean our money? I don't have anything to do with this.'

'He wanted our money, Lou. Our royalties,' Jessica replied. 'Lou, what did you think was happening with the royalties?' Lucinda turned towards Jessica, suddenly feeling confused, stupid and drunk. She hadn't seen a royalty cheque for over 12 years. It'd never occurred to her that she was still receiving royalties. When she'd walked away from Euterpe in her head she'd walked into a world where her husband was providing for her so she hadn't given a second thought as to what was happening with the profits from her old life.

'We're still getting royalties? I hadn't even thought…?'

'Are you serious? Of course we do. It was business. Andrew did teach me something. They used our music for advertising cars, game shows, there were the greatest hits that we were contractually obliged to release five years ago. Euterpe is still making money, even if we'd stopped being Euterpe. I can't believe you…'

'I just didn't think…'

'Well, I just assumed that you just weren't interested in a couple of quid because as you told me every time Paul took a piss he earned money.'

'I think I was drunk when I said that.'

'Probably, but I thought that if you were putting Euterpe behind you then I didn't want anything to do with you or our past either. So I hardly paid the account any attention until it appeared on the divorce application.'

'Well how much is in the account?' Lucinda asked.

'£4million, 728 thousand and 32 pence.'

'You what?'

'With interest, it's probably a little bit more than that.'

Lucinda couldn't say anything, as she felt overwhelmed by what Jessica had just told her. She felt as if the dove was flying towards her with the olive branch.

'Lou, are you ok?'

'I'm fine,' she replied as she swallowed the rest of her wine and sat up a little bit straighter as she tried to get her head together. 'Nearly five million.'

'Yes and Andrew wants it.'

'Well he can fuck off.' Jessica smiled at her sister's words.

'What does he think we are, a bloody cash-machine?'

'To be fair, I couldn't believe it was that much. It makes me wonder why I stopped song writing. Even after you left. But Lou, the reason why I'm telling you this is because…'

'Half of it belongs to me.'

'Of course it does. I'd imagine it's just small change to you though.'

Lucinda threw her head back and laughed loudly causing the dog in next door's garden to bark back.

'Small change? If only you knew, Jess. If only you knew.'

FORTY-THREE

'WHAT ARE you looking at?' Richard asked as Felicia quickly closed the laptop.

'Nothing. Just emails. Work ones.'

'Since when do you hide work emails? Show me.'

'Honestly, darling, there's nothing to see,' Felicia replied as she got off the bed, firmly holding onto the laptop. Richard moved towards the door and blocked her. He knew that over the past several weeks Felicia had been keeping things from him but he'd thought it was nothing more than her being overprotective and not wanting to be stressed by whatever was going on in their daughters' lives. That hadn't stopped him. He was their father after all. Just because they were all now grown women didn't mean that he'd relinquished the title. 'What are you hiding from me?'

'I'm not hiding anything from you.'

'Of course you are. You never close your laptop when I come into the room, not even when you're ogling over pictures of that Luther man.'

'Bloody cheek. I don't ogle over pictures of him and his

name is Idris Elba not Luther.'

'Whatever, is this about Jess?'

'What about her?' Felicia asked as she put her laptop down on the bed and watched her husband.

'I do have Twitter you know. What else am I supposed to do when I'm hooked up to that chemo machine for hours.' Felicia took a deep sigh and sat back down on the bed.

'It's not true. It can't be,' she said as she opened the laptop and entered her password. The screen opened up to *The Daily Post* showbiz page. *"Jessica LeSoeur took drugs whilst her nine-year-old daughter slept in the same bed with her. Jessica assaulted her husband Andrew, when he confronted her drug dealer."* She shut the laptop again unable to continue reading the shopping list of slander against her daughter.

'Of course it's not true,' Richard said as he put his arms around his wife and held her. They'd been through so much together and it hurt him even more to see his usually strong wife look so resigned to a fate that they'd made for themselves. He glanced over to the clock on the bedside table. It was still only 8.45am. He'd forced himself to wake up early, take two and a half mouthfuls of a disgusting green juice concoction that Katelyn and Lena had blended for him last night and then walked the dog. The reality being that he'd sat on a park bench and watched the dog chase his own tail for half an hour before making the short walk home.

'It's far too early for the postman,' Felicia said as the sound of the doorbell travelled up the stairs to their bedroom. 'Alright, I'm coming,' she said as she unravelled herself from her husband's arms, took her kimono style dressing gown from the back of the door and went downstairs.

'Oh, what are you doing here?' Felicia said, more than surprised to see Jessica at the front door.

'Morning, mum. I just wanted to see you and dad before I went to work.'

'We're a bit out of your way aren't we?' Felicia replied, still holding onto the door frame.

'Mum, aren't you going to let me in?'

'Of course, of course. Come in. Do you want tea, coffee? I'm going to make one for your father.'

'Tea, thank you. I'm staying off the coffee,' Jessica said as she followed her mother into the kitchen.'

'Jess, what's wrong?' Richard asked as he came down the stairs and saw his daughter.

'Nothing's wrong, dad. I wanted to see you and mum. I was hoping I'd catch you before you found out from the papers.'

'It's not true is it Jessica? Don't tell me that you're doing drugs. Alcohol I can just about understand, but drugs…'

'Mum, just calm down,' Jessica said as she took hold of her hands. 'I promise you.'

'I know that things have been hard for you and that you haven't been coping…'

'Mum, stop. I haven't got a drug habit. For crying out loud, you know me. I can't even put Vicks up my nose, let alone snort cocaine every night. They're lies, all lies.'

Felicia stared back at her daughter, noticing that since the last time she saw her, her skin now appeared brighter and her eyes had regained their sparkle. She thought back to when she was pregnant with Jessica. How she'd lie in her bed at night and poke her stomach just to check the baby was still alive. This child would hardly move, compared to Lucinda who behaved for the entire nine months as though she was in training for a high jump competition and Beatrice who you could set a watch to as she turned around and kicked out every four hours just to let you know she was there, and also Emma who would kick so hard and push her tiny hands against Felicia's stomach as though she needed to get out right now. Jessica had been quiet and restrained.

'I have a problem mum, but it's not drugs.'

'Why didn't you just tell us that you were going to rehab? Do you think we care what the neighbours think?' Felicia said as she sat cradling the mug of tea that she had yet to take a sip from whilst Richard sat next to Jessica picking out black grapes from the box in front of him.

'As if you've ever cared about what the neighbours think,' Jessica replied. 'It all happened so quickly. Things had gotten too much for me and I was, well I wasn't listening. In fact, I've spent so long listening to other people that I've forgotten what my own voice sounds like.'

'So, how are you now?'

'I feel as though my body has been run over by a train and I'd much rather be sitting here with a vodka and tonic instead of tea.'

'Jessica!'

'Don't sound so shocked. You knew that I had a problem

I've always had a problem. I have to accept that I'm an alcoholic and I'm dealing with it. Oh dad, don't look like that. It's not the end of the world.'

'I know. I know but you're my baby.' Jessica squeezed her dad's hand.

'I'm sorry for everything. I'm sorry for being so selfish, for putting that man before my own family. I mean, I drove my own daughter away, what sort of mother does that make me?'

'Lena loves you. She understands and she's home with you now, that's the main thing, and once that man is finally out of your life you can move on,' Richard said. Jessica nodded as a lump came to her throat.

'I just don't understand why he'd say these things about you. I mean, what the hell is wrong with him. Christopher never behaved like this,' Felicia said as she finally took a sip of her tea.

'He's a bastard,' Richard said angrily. 'How dare he have the audacity to tell the papers that you're a habitual cocaine user and that you emotionally abused him throughout your marriage. You should have physically abused him. You should have cut off his…'

'Richard' 'Dad' both women said together, not quite believing what was coming out of his mouth.

'If I can't speak the truth when I've got one foot in the grave then when can I?'

'Thank you daddy,' Jessica said with a smile.

'What do your lawyers say?'

'Well, Bea thinks that we've got a good chance but who knows.'

'You have to think positive. Pray and be positive. You're a strong girl. All of my girls are strong. So be strong and fight, ok?'

'Alright dad. How are you doing? I haven't even asked.'

'I'm alright. I'm starting radiotherapy on Wednesday, so we'll see but as I said, positivity is the key.'

'That man,' Felicia said as she listened to his footsteps fade away as Richard went upstairs. 'Do you know that your aunt Rachel caught him and your uncle Stephen sharing a spliff in the garden shed?'

'You're joking. Dad and Uncle Stephen smoking weed?' Jessica said as she burst out laughing.

'It's not funny. Medicinal he said. Anyone would think that they were still in school. He makes me sick.' Jessica couldn't help but laugh as the image of her dad and Stephen formed in his head.

'I'm not saying that I approve but if it helps him.'

'Don't worry. I seriously doubt that dad and uncle Stephen are going to start freebasing in the kitchen or start a drugs cartel in the garden shed.'

'Stranger things have happened,' Felicia replied.

'Mum, I'm sorry. I can't believe that I…I wasn't myself when you came…'

'I understand. You don't have to apologise.'

'Of course I have to apologise to you. And, I've also apologised to Lucinda.'

'You have? When?'

'A couple of days ago.' Jessica thought it was sensible to leave out the part when Andrew came round to her home. 'I was wrong. So wrong, mum. I blamed her for so many things and I didn't think that she'd forgive me and I wouldn't have blamed her. I said some horrible things to her mum.'

'And how are things now?'

'We had a good talk. It's getting better.'

'That's good my angel. No matter what happens you'll always be sisters and that's a bond that can never be broken.'

'Where is she? She should be here by now,' Emma said as she paced around Christopher's office. 'I knew that I should have picked her up. Or we should have sent a cab round for her.'

'Will you stop panicking? She'll be here,' Christopher said as he turned his TV onto sky sports news and watched the scrolling yellow bar for football transfer news.

'You couldn't really blame her if she didn't come back. I'd do a runner too if I woke up to all that shit in the newspapers. What I don't understand is why he'd trash Jessica's name, ruin her business and then try and take that business from her. It's just stupid and Andrew isn't a stupid man.'

'He's not. He's just greedy. Ems, he doesn't want the business. I mean what the hell would he do with it? It's all just a ploy. He thinks that if he causes as much damage as he can to Jess' reputation that she'll just write him a cheque for whatever he wants. Simple as that.'

The pair of them said nothing to each other as they watched the office bustling into action. Despite the avalanche of negative press they were busier than ever. Since Jessica's leave, Wendy had taken on the mantle of dealing with all of the TV and radio requests for Jessica to tell her side of the story. Wendy was robust enough to tell them no, albeit not that politely. From the look on her face as she marched into Christopher's office she'd clearly had enough.

'This is why I do book publicity. It's so much easier knocking up some warm wine and cold sausage rolls for a book launch in a dodgy art gallery then putting up with this shit,' Wendy said as she dropped into the armchair. 'What a fucking nightmare. Was it like this when Euterpe broke up?'

'I think it was even worse. I had reporters hanging around my school trying to get an exclusive and the fans, oh my God, you'd have thought someone had died.' Emma shook her head at the memory. 'I don't know why anyone would want fame.'

'Well if they didn't want it, we'd be out of a job,' Wendy replied. 'I told her from day one to watch out for him but would she listen? No. But it could be worse. There's a lot of respect for your sister and no one believes any of that crap in the papers. Now if it were me they were talking about, no one would bat an eyelid. I don't think that I even ate during the nineties. I was on a diet of champagne and cocaine. Now look at me, spending weekends at a fucking yoga retreat and eating quinoa and tofu. I hate tofu.'

'As if you'd ever give up champagne.' Wendy, Emma and Richard both turned to see Jessica at the office door.

'You're here,' Emma said as she jumped up from Christopher's desk and hugged her sister.

'Of course I'm here. I'm sorry I'm late but I had to stop off at mum and dad's first but I'm here,' Jessica said as she hugged her sister back. 'I'm sorry,' she whispered into Emma's ear. 'I'll make it better.'

'Don't be,' Emma whispered back.

'Oh for God's sake, stop being so sentimental. Now that you're back you can answer your own bloody phone,' Wendy said as she pulled a cigarette out of her bag and lit up.

FORTY-FOUR

'I HAVE news,' Madeline said as she stood at the front door with a buggy that was being weighed down with shopping bags and a now seven-month-old baby who was trying to pull the head off her firefly cuddly toy. 'Joshua, get back here right now,' Madeline shouted after her son who'd wandered further down the road and now had his face pressed firmly against the window of a gleaming silver Mercedes.

'Don't let me tell you again. Get here now. Sorry, my dad came over last week and took him to a car show and ever since then he's developed a fascination with cars.'

'It's fine,' Lucinda said bemused by the sight. 'Why don't you come in? I'll make you a cup of tea. It looks like you need it.'

'So my news,' Madeline said as she placed the white china cup onto the coffee table and clapped her hands together, imitated by Abigail who was sitting happily on Lucinda's lap whilst Joshua had followed the sounds of Reece playing computer games on his X-box in the living room and had refused to follow his mother any further into the house.

'I wanted to tell you face to face,' Madeline continued, clearly excited by what she had to say. 'I've bought a house.'

'A house. So quickly…but I thought you needed more time.'

'I did but I don't know what's happened. The estate agent tried to explain it but to tell you the truth I stopped listening once he told me that my share of the old house was being deposited into my account in an hour, and that was…' Madeline looked at the clock above Lucinda's head. 'That was two hours ago. So right now you're looking at half a millionaire.'

Lucinda laughed at the sight of Madeline who was literally bouncing on the edge of the sofa. She was a changed woman from the one who'd knocked on Lucinda's door almost a month ago.

'So how does it feel?' Lucinda asked.

'It feels like I can finally breathe again. Do you know what I mean? Like I can finally see a future for myself again. I've been running around like a blue arsed fly all morning. I've had an offer accepted on a house in Streatham.'

'Streatham? But that's the other side of the London.'

'I know, I know. But I had to be sensible. I'd have loved to have stayed here in Notting Hill but if I did that I could only afford a poxy flat and most likely not been able to keep this one in pampers.'

'No, I understand. So, how soon do you go? Sorry. I didn't mean it to sound like that.'

Madeline laughed. 'It's fine. I know what you meant. Well,

thankfully there's no chain. The house is an absolute shithole, ooh, sorry Abi,' Madeline said as she leaned over and covered her daughter's ears. 'It's a shithole in a good way. I'm going to be doing it up. It's going to be amazing. I should be out of your hair in about 3-4 weeks. I have so many plans, Lucinda.'

Lucinda could hardly believe that she'd finally be going back to her home in a month's time. When she thought back to the state she'd been in when she first arrived home and the person she was; well it seemed unrecognisable to her. The pressure on her had been immense and she'd been in denial about what she was doing to herself. As she sat here now with a giggling baby on her lap and Madeline talking at a hundred miles an hour about her plans for the next chapter in her life she felt a tear fall down her face.

'Oh my God. What's wrong? Why are you upset?' Madeline said as she pulled a packet of tissues out of her bag and handed them to Lucinda. 'I haven't upset you, have I?'

'No, no,' Lucinda said as she gratefully took the tissue and dabbed her eyes. 'No, it's just been a tough few months and there were times where I felt like giving up. It's been so hard.'

'Well, if you want to talk about it, I'm here. I mean you've had to listen to me rambling on.'

'I got myself into a financial mess. That's why I had to come back. That's why I needed my house back.'

'Was it bad?'

'Pretty bad. I wasn't sensible and I used to be someone who was always sensible. I think after years of putting everyone else first that I just wanted to let go. Have someone look after me. Not have any responsibilities. Do you know what I mean?'

'Yep, definitely. I loved my job but my ex convinced me to give it up. Focus on doing up the house, he said to me. Focus on Joshua. It was just another way of controlling me but I convinced myself that it was ok. That it was no problem being a kept woman, but it was a problem. I ran away from that house with nothing except clothes for Joshua and my oyster card. It took two hours to get to Owen's flat. My first thought was to go to my parent's place but I didn't even have my passport. I had no money of my own and that never used to be me. I remember begging my dad to take me to the Woolwich Building Society to open an account when I was seven-years-old because they were giving away a pink piggy bank. I don't know, we all make mistakes I suppose.'

'We do make mistakes,' Lucinda said. 'Anyway, it's not all bad. Things are getting better, a lot better.'

'Of course they are. I mean you've got two beautiful children and you're making amazing music. Owen played me some. Sorry,' Madeline said when she noticed the confused look on Lucinda's face. 'It's really, really good and Owen likes it, which is saying something considering I'm positive that he deliberately broke my copy of your first album.'

Lucinda couldn't stop the smile that was spreading across her face. 'He's told me more than once that he wasn't our greatest fan.'

'Owen's musical repertoire stops and starts with football chants at White Hart Lane,' Madeline said dryly.

'Oh, he's not that bad.'

'You must really like him. He really likes you. I haven't seen him this happy in a long time and I've never known him to take a night off from that restaurant of his. Imagine if you became my sister-in-law!'

'Hold your horses, it's only been a few months. We might go off each before the clocks go back.'

'Nah,' Madeline said with a glint in her eye. 'I've got a good feeling about you two.'

When Madeline finally left, with a crying Joshua who wanted to spend the rest of the day with his new best friend, Reece, Lucinda allowed herself to fully absorb the changes that were happening in her life. She'd thought that Jessica telling her that she had nearly three million pounds waiting for her would have put her on cloud nine but she wasn't an idiot. At least not anymore and she wasn't placing her hopes on a large deposit into her account anytime soon, not when it had become a pawn in an acrimonious divorce battle. As far as Lucinda was considered, her financial position had not changed and the only financial lifeline was the one she had to make herself.

Beatrice should have been happy to see Jessica looking so much better but she couldn't dig into the happiness reserves. The anger had been building up within her for the past couple of weeks. That morning she'd snapped at Jake because he'd forgotten to turn the tumble dryer on the night before. Even the twins hadn't escaped a verbal onslaught from their mother as they played with their breakfast cereal, building God knows what on the kitchen table.

'I don't understand why you're not keeping my case,'

Jessica said as Beatrice sat folding a pile of clothes that she'd just taken out the dryer. Jake had seen the look on his wife's face when she'd returned home from work and had piled the twins into the car and taken them to Pizza Express. He'd asked his wife to join them but she'd flatly refused.

'Because it's not right, Jessica. Anyway, there's nothing wrong with Anoushka.'

'I know that there's nothing wrong with her but it has always been you. I don't want anyone else. This is a family thing.'

'Family. Please,' Beatrice snorted. 'It's only family when it suits you.'

'What are you talking about?' Jessica asked.

'I'm sick of being in the middle of your crap.'

'Bea, I don't understand.'

'You're just as bad as Lucinda with all of your secrets. Why didn't you tell me that you were going to rehab? Why did I have to find out from my bloody trainee? Even Emma knew and I didn't.'

'Bea, I didn't tell anyone that I was going to rehab. The only reason Emma knew was because Christopher told her. In fact he was the one who organised it. I didn't tell mum or dad, or Emma. I don't understand why you'd be angry about me going to rehab.'

'I'm not angry that you went to rehab. I'm glad that you got help. You were turning into a person that I didn't really want to know but it's all about you Jess. You being here is just about you.'

'You're not making any sense.'

'You're selfish,' Beatrice said firmly. 'And you always put me in the middle of your bullshit and I'm sick of it. You came here and you didn't apologise to me. You haven't asked me how I am. It's all about why aren't you doing this for me.'

'I didn't think you'd feel so strongly about handling the divorce.'

'Jessica this isn't about your fucking divorce. You and Lucinda are exactly the same. She decides to come home and I'm supposed to drop everything and run to her aide. You get yourself into a fucking mess and good old Beatrice is there again. Charmaine decides that there's more to life then supporting you two and low and behold what do you do, drag me into your bloody group.'

'Hold on, you're pissed about being in Euterpe? Is this about the money? The royalties.'

'No, it's not about the money. I couldn't care less about the money. I'm pissed off about the fact that you two have never once asked me what I wanted. You've always taken from me and then expected me to ask how high when you say jump.'

'That's not true. I've never taken advantage of you and neither has Lou.'

'Funny how you're defending her now.'

'I made a mistake with Lucinda. I've admitted that. I've apologised to her.'

'Yep, you've apologised to her but what about me?'

Jessica didn't say anything. This was not what she'd been expecting when she'd driven to Beatrice's home after work. The news that someone else was handling her divorce was upsetting and she'd thought it was nothing other than office politics, not that her sister was angry with her.

'I'm sorry, Beatrice.'

'You're only apologising because I'm shouting at you. If you didn't want something from me, then you wouldn't even be here now. I'm always the one running after you and I've had enough of it.'

'Maybe I should go.'

'There's no maybe. You should go,' Beatrice said as she turned her back.

FORTY-FIVE

'I'M SORRY Lou,' Sal said as he picked up his pint of beer and took a sip. Lucinda had worked out that she'd spent less than fifteen minutes in Sal's office since she'd arrived in London. Every time she'd got off the train at Waterloo station and made the short walk to his office, Sal had spun her around and taken her to the nearest restaurant, cafe or on this occasion the Windmill pub.

'I'm fed up with everyone apologising to me,' Lucinda said as she picked up her cappuccino.

'It should be against the law to drink hot beverages in a public house.'

'It's far too early to be drinking. It's not even midday.'

'It's 11.42am and it's roasting outside so that's good enough for me. Anyway, this is a non-alcoholic beer, hardly the same thing. I'm sorry though, Lou. I know how much you wanted to play at Ronnie Scott's but it's just not possible. They're fully booked until next year unless you want to do a matinee slot on a Wednesday afternoon. I'm sorry.'

'Fine.'

'Fine?' Sal replied as he stared at Lucinda. 'You're not going to kick off are you because I've been doing my best, trying to pull in favours left right and centre. Pissing off my other clients.'

'No, I'm not going to kick off. I'm grateful. I really am. Thank you for everything, Sal. I mean it, you've been amazing.'

'Oh,' Sal said, his face reddening from both embarrassment and pride. He couldn't remember the last time that any of his clients had told him thank you. They were docile and cooperative in the beginning but as time went by and fame grew, they began to make demands, throw tantrums that would embarrass most three-year-olds and stop showing any appreciation.

'Come on, Sal. I know that we have history. We go way back to the days of having to find a telephone box and twenty pence to make a phone call but you could have just told me no but you didn't do that. So, I'm thanking you.'

'You're welcome. I don't know what you're talking about though. You know that I'd have done anything for you. So, onto plan B.'

Lucinda groaned. She knew what plan B meant. 'Dougie Mills. I can leave it to you to sort out the details.'

'Of course you can. I've got your dates and the band's dates. Your website is nearly done, I'll send you the links right now so you can see it for yourself but it looks great. You've got another session with Carter this week haven't you?'

'Yeah, tomorrow afternoon.'

'Right, I'm sending Kelvin. He's a photographer who

fancies himself as the next Scorsese. You've also got the *Allure* interview coming up and I'm going to see if I can get you on the radio, see if I can call in a few favours with BBC London. It used to be so much easier back in the day.'

'Oh yeah, that was great fun traipsing around every dodgy tower block in London looking for pirate radio stations.'

'Remember that night at Loose FM on the top of those flats in the Stonebridge Estate? I've never run so fast in my life when that gang burst through the door.'

'The only thing I remember is one of them taking off his balaclava, winking at Beatrice and telling her she was fit and to come back next week and he'll take her out. What a joke.'

'Happy days,' Sal said nostalgically. 'So, I'll get on with Dougie Mills and take it from there.'

Lucinda left Sal shortly afterwards and made her way across Waterloo Bridge. It'd have been quicker to jump on a bus but as her dad always said, London isn't that big and everything is next door to each other. Whilst she was with Sal, there had been a missed call from Jessica. Lucinda had texted her back and told her that she was in a meeting. Despite Jessica's apology and their heart to heart she still wasn't ready to resume her older sisterly duties. How Jessica had behaved towards her had hurt her more than she'd cared to admit and she was finding that forgiveness wasn't that forthcoming. It was something she had to work through and the last thing she wanted was for the pain and resentment to eat away and dilute every bit of her life and consume her the way it had with Jessica

The receptionist looked up at the woman who looked remarkably similar to Beatrice. 'You're her sister?'

'Yes I am,' Lucinda said.

'But you haven't got an appointment.'

'Now, do I really need an appointment to take my sister out for lunch?'

'Well, no but I can't just let you through and anyway, she's got a "do not disturb" sign on.'

'Oh for the love of God. Can you just send her a message and let her know that I'm here please? Just email her and tell her that Lucinda is at reception.'

The receptionist shook her head and tapped away at the keyboard.

'Thank you,' Lucinda said as she sat down on the bright red chair in the waiting area and turned her attention to the wide screen TV that was currently showing BBC News.

'Lou, what are you doing here?' Beatrice said as she appeared at Lucinda's side. 'Has something happened with dad?'

'No, of course not,' Lucinda said as she stood up and kissed Beatrice on the cheek. 'I was in the area and I thought it'd be nice if I took you out for lunch.'

'Just like that?' Beatrice replied as she took off her glasses and brushed the strands of her fringe out of her eyes.

'Yes, just like that. We haven't really spent that much time together since I got back.'

'Has Jessica said something to you?'

'About what?'

'Never mind. Ok, give me a minute and I'll get my bag.'

'I'm sorry I haven't been a better sister to you since I got back. I had you running around all over London sorting stuff out for me and I've hardly spent any time with you. I've been so wrapped up in my own stuff that I forgot about you. I'm sorry about that, Bea,' Lucinda said as she poured a glass of sparkling water for herself and Beatrice.

'Is this why you're taking me out to lunch, because you feel guilty?'

'No, it's because I've realised that I owe you an explanation. Since I called you and told you I was coming home, I've never explained to you why.'

'It's not really any of my business.'

'Oh come on Bea. We're sisters, of course it's your business.'

'Are you sure that you haven't spoken to Jessica?'

'The last time I saw Jessica was when she came to my house a couple of weeks ago.'

'She said that she apologised to you.'

'She did.'

'And now you're apologising to me.'

'Yes, I am.'

'I kind of snapped at Jess. I probably went a bit too far,' Beatrice said as she indicated for the waiter that she was ready to order. She hadn't had any breakfast and had thought that the least Lucinda could do was to buy her an overpriced burger and chips.

'Is that why you have a face like thunder? Because to be

honest I've been waiting for you to snap at me too.' Lucinda said as she picked up the menu.

'You're lucky. If you'd come round yesterday to take me out to lunch I'd have told you where to stick it.'

'Wow.'

'Yeah, wow. I just felt like the middle sister being pushed around by you and Jess.'

'You're not really the middle sister, if anything Jessica is the middle sister. Then again there are four of us.'

'Don't interrupt me.'

'Sorry.'

'You're right. You called me out of the blue, told me that you're coming home and then assumed that I'd run around like your glorified assistant. I sorted out your house, schools for the twins, picked you up from the airport, even organised your bloody food shopping.'

'I know.'

'And not once did you stop and say thank you Bea. How are things with you, Bea? Is there anything that I can do to help you? I mean when you did come by it wasn't because you wanted to see me. I wasn't the first thought in your mind. You haven't even invited my family and me to your house for dinner. It was just like when we were younger. You and Jess would happily ignore me until you both realised that you might actually need me.'

'I didn't know that you felt like that. You should have said something.'

'Would you have heard me if I did?'

Lucinda thought about this for a few seconds. 'Probably

not. My head wasn't exactly in the right place when I came back. I'm sorry for making you feel like that. I'm your big sister. I'm supposed to look after you, not make you feel like you're nothing. You're the most amazing person I know. I couldn't be prouder of you.'

'Look, don't get me wrong, I should have said something to you both sooner instead of letting it all build up. God, I've been a bitch. Even Theo turned around to me last night and told me that I wasn't a very nice mummy. Can you imagine hearing that from a five-year-old?' Lucinda leaned over and brushed away the tear that fell from Beatrice's eye and ran down her cheek.

'You're a beautiful mummy. In fact a yummy mummy.' Beatrice laughed.

'I don't feel like one. It's bloody hard going back to work, dealing with dad and his cancer, you and Jess fighting, then Jess being in rehab, the twins, Jake and I feel fat. It's all too much.'

'God, maybe we should have been the ones who went to rehab.' The sisters said nothing for a while as the waiter arrived with their burgers. Automatically, Beatrice removed her pickles and placed them on Lucinda's plate whilst Lucinda repeated the gift by handing over her onions.

'They never listen. I hate onions.'

'You don't know what you're missing,' Beatrice replied as she placed a slice of onion into her mouth.

'That's disgusting. So how are you feeling now?'

'Better. When Jake came home last night, he handed me a box of leftover pizza and half a bottle of red wine and I sat in the living room on my own and watched old episodes of Sex in the City. I woke up late with a bit of a hangover. So you coming here today has helped a lot.'

'I'm glad,' Lucinda said as she mixed together her mayonnaise and ketchup and dunked in a chunky chip.

'So what's your explanation? You said you never told me why you came home. So, why did you come home?'

'I came home because I'm broke.'

'You're what? How can you be broke? Hold on.' Beatrice ducked her head under the table.

'Hey,' Lucinda said as she felt Beatrice lifting up her left foot.

'You're wearing Chanel ballet flats and your bag is Prada. How the hell can you be broke?'

'It's a long story,' Lucinda said as she bit into her burger whilst Beatrice looked at her astounded.

'Jake said that there was something going on with you. I told him that he was being overdramatic as per usual. Right, I better call work and tell them that I'll be running late. I hope you can afford to pay for that burger,' Beatrice said as she reached into her bag and pulled out her phone.

FORTY-SIX

'HELLO EMS.'

Emma stopped walking at the sound of his voice even though every muscle in her body was screaming at her to keep on moving.

'You haven't returned any of my calls or my texts messages,' Daniel said as he waved his phone in front of her. Emma moved to the side as a courier on a pushbike cycled past her and silently chastised herself for making the decision to cut through Soho Square. He pushed up his Ray Bans to the top of his head. As he smiled, a few wrinkles arrived at the corner of his eyes, which did nothing more than make him appear more distinguished. Despite standing 5ft 10 with the help of her heels, Emma still had to look up to Daniel. It was one of the things that had attracted her to him. He was 6 foot four and had the sort of body that was made for bespoke suits. He'd always turned heads when he walked into a room, which was not something that had gone unnoticed by him.

'So how have you been?'

'What do you want?' Emma asked as she folded her arms

defensively in front of her.

'Oh come on, Ems. It's been so long. I wanted to see how you were. I thought it'd be good to catch up. You know, for old time's sake.'

'You didn't return any of my calls or texts. You dropped me like a hot stone and now you're standing here telling me that you want to catch up for old time's sake.'

'Don't be like that, Emma. Come on, a lot has happened since then,' Daniel said as he took long strides to catch up with Emma who had turned and began to walk quickly towards Dean Street. 'Emma hold up,' Daniel said as he grabbed hold of her arm.

'Get off me. I can't believe you. Why can't you just leave me alone?'

'Why would I want to do that? We were close once.'

'So close that you lied to me and then completely blanked me when I told you about the pregnancy.'

'Come on. You know it wasn't like that. You make it sound like I dumped you as soon as you told me you were pregnant. Bloody hell, you didn't even know until you lost it.'

'That's not the point.'

'And you understood my situation and you had your family,' Daniel replied.

'What situation? I was supposed to be your situation.'

'You knew why I couldn't be there, Ems. Come on; don't make me out to be the bad guy. You knew my situation.'

Emma looked down at Daniel's hand seeing for the first time that his ring finger was now bare. The calls. the texts. It all made sense now why he was suddenly interested in making contact. 'So, what happened? Did you leave her or did she finally see the light and get rid of you?'

'What does it matter? It's over and you know full well that it was over for a long time. Look, Emma, instead of us discussing our business on the street why don't we go somewhere and grab a coffee? We can have a proper chat and talk about moving things forward with us.'

'You have got to be joking. I don't want to see you and I don't want to speak to you. You nearly broke me. Thank God I had my family. The next time you see me on the street you better walk away but if you ever touch me again, or ever try and contact me again I'm calling the police, do you understand? You're a despicable human being. I don't know what I ever saw in you.' Daniel didn't respond as he saw the steely determination of a woman who had finally recognised her own strength. 'Do you know something else though? I could have maybe found it in my heart to forgive you but not once did you act like a man. You didn't even have the guts to tell me to my face that it was over. In a way, I'm glad I lost the baby because at least there's no reason for you to ever be in my life.'

Jessica listened to the sounds of her heels on the tiles as she walked into the oncology ward at St Thomas' Hospital and headed towards treatment room number four. This was the place where her father had been visiting every three weeks for his chemotherapy and now radiotherapy treatments. She'd made a promise to herself to be more present in not only her life but also the lives of her family. Beatrice's verbal onslaught had done more to sober her up then her time in rehab. It had forced her to really take a look at herself, especially as she started from scratch to rebuild her relationship with her daughter and tried to slowly rebuild her relationship with Lucinda. As Jessica walked along the corridor she couldn't ignore the feeling that all eyes were on her, despite the fact that the headlines of her alleged drug use had now fallen away to Angelina Jolie and Brad Pitt's secret wedding, and Emma's client Amaya Summer revealing all about her holiday fling with a politician. This was her second visit and she knew her father was a creature of habit and would be in his usual bed next to the window, most likely thinking of ways to plot his escape. There were six other chairs in the room, all of them occupied with patients of varying ages, sex and race. Walking into the treatment room just reinforced how indiscriminate cancer was. It simply didn't care who it attached itself to. Whether you were three, twenty-eight or seventy years old. Black, white, Chinese or Indian, it held no prejudice.

A sixteen-year-old girl, whose head was wrapped with a brightly covered scarf concealing the fact that she had lost her hair, waved at Jessica as she walked into the room. The first time that Jessica had come, she'd arrived before Richard and had spent half an hour talking to this over excitable teenage girl who had been diagnosed with Leukaemia. She knew that it was the fact that this young girl was the same age as her daughter which had tugged at her heart, especially after she'd spoken to Freya's father, Liam, who was now a single father after Freya's own mother died of breast cancer at the pathetically young age of 38. Jessica couldn't imagine the pain of that loss.

'Hi Jess. You look better than you did the last time I saw you,' Freya said as she put down her iPad and took off her headphones.

'Thank you very much. I decided it was time to sort myself out. How are you doing today?'

'I'm alright I suppose. It's just so boring but I've got one more session and then they think I should be able to start college in a couple of weeks. I can't wait.'

'That's good news. Really good news. I'm not staying for long today but I've brought some things for you.' Jessica handed over the blue gift bag that she'd been carrying. Freya gasped as she pulled out several bottles of Ciate nail polish. 'O. M. G. Is this real?' Freya said as she pulled out an Alexander McQueen scarf with the familiar skulls motifs. The last time Jessica had visited, Freya hadn't been able to take her eyes off Jessica's own red and black scarf and had confessed her own ambitions to become a fashion designer.

'Of course it's real. I thought that the white and green would suit you better,' Jessica said as Freya put the scarf around her neck and continued to pull out magazines and then Freya's mouth dropped open when she pulled out the CD.

'It's The Junction's new album. This isn't out for another month and they've signed it.'

'Well I told them how special you were.' Jessica hadn't told Freya that The Junction were on her client list and the lead singer, Heath, had attended the same school as Lena and was actually one of her closest friends before he and his two cousins and best friend had decided to audition for Britain's got Talent only two years ago. Their popularity now rivalled that of One Direction and they'd been more than happy to comply with Jessica's request.

'They actually touched this and signed it. They wrote my name,' Freya said as she held the CD close to her chest and then looked it again. 'Thank you so much.'

Jessica kissed the top of Freya's head. 'You're most welcome sweetheart.'

'Her father will never forgive you,' Richard said as Freya waved the CD cover at him.

'Why?'

'I still haven't got over when you got that bloody Bobby Brown album. Every single day you played that album. Over and over again.'

'I wasn't that bad.'

'You were obsessed. So what will Freya be forcing her father to listen to?'

'The Junction's new album,' Jessica said as she sat on the chair next to her father's bed.

'When I saw you, my heart collapsed as if the roof came in,' Richard began to sing, loud enough to cause Freya to collapse into a fit of giggles, even causing Jessica to laugh.

'You have no idea how many times Freya has played that song. I'll probably die with that song in my head.'

'Dad, don't be so morbid.'

'I'm not. Anyway, it's nice to see you smile. You haven't done much of that lately. In fact I don't think any of us have been smiling much.'

'Well, it's been hard but it's going to get better, I promise you.'

'Does that include your relationship with your sister because I don't want to leave the planet not knowing if you two have fixed things?'

'Dad, stop with the death talk. We're getting there. One step at a time.'

Emma had held it together for as long as she could. She went back to the office and carried on with her work. She calmed down erratic celebrities who weren't impressed that their spotlight was fading. She talked firmly with journalists and negotiated exclusives. That was one thing about the LeSoeur women. They could put on a face and act as if they could fight the world with their hands tied behind their back and no weapons even though inside they felt that they were sinking in quick sand. The lunch she'd brought herself remained uneaten on her desk. Her stomach had dropped when she'd heard him call her name and her heart had begun to beat so fast that she honestly thought she was about to have a heart attack. Every time her phone had rung since she'd returned to the office she had to stop herself from jumping out of her seat but it hadn't been him. When the clock struck six-thirty and she found herself to be the only one left in the office she knew she had to leave. After all she couldn't very well spend the night in the office but she didn't want to go home even though Daniel had no idea where she lived.

As she walked slowly to Oxford Circus tube station and took the escalator down to the Central line she could feel herself grow cold and begin to shiver, despite the fact that it was at least 34 degrees on the underground and there was a gigantic blue fan circulating hot air into her face. Even though her head told her to grab a hold of herself she stepped onto the Westbound Central line and took the first tube heading to Notting Hill Gate.

FORTY-SEVEN

LUCINDA HELD onto Emma as she cried. It was the deep convulsing cries that children usually had a talent for. She still didn't understand what had happened. As soon as Lucinda opened the front door she'd found Emma with tears streaming down her face and visibly shaking. It took fifteen minutes for Emma to calm down and to finally find her voice.

'Shit, I've made a mess of your top,' Emma said as she pulled out a tissue from the box on her lap and blew her nose. Lucinda looked down at her vest, which was now streaked with mascara and foundation.

'Don't worry, it'll come out in the wash. Do you want anything to drink? I think that I've got some Jack Iron in the cupboard.'

'God no. Not the jack,' Emma said shaking her head at the thought of the over-proof rum that her dad always smuggled back from Grenada. 'But I'll have some wine.'

'Look, why don't you go upstairs to my room, have a shower, find something to wear and I'll sort out something for us to eat and then we'll talk.' Emma nodded, suddenly feeling weak and exhausted.

'I haven't eaten since breakfast,' Emma said as she picked up a slice of sesame prawn toast.. They were sitting in the garden sharing a Chinese takeaway and a bottle of red wine. Emma was glad she wasn't in the confines of her flat with the tiny balcony. At least here in this garden in Notting Hill with the still bright sky and the promises of an Indian summer she felt as though she could breathe.

'I think that all I've done is eat today. I met Beatrice for lunch earlier.'

'How is she? I've been meaning to go and see her. I've just been busy.'

'She's ok but I think she'd appreciate it if you went to see her. Maybe spoil her a bit. We just have to take the time for each other.'

'Is she ok?' Emma asked aware that there something wasn't being said.

'Yeah, she's fine. Just had a bad day that's all. So are you going to tell me? You don't have to if you don't want to.'

'No, I want to,' Emma said as she picked up her wine glass, took a sip and began to tell her story of how she fell for a married man who'd told her the world's oldest lie that his marriage was over, when in fact it had never really started, how he was neglected and how he wished he'd met Emma first.

'How could he do that to you? Even if he was married how could he not come to the hospital?' Lucinda said, as she sat there not quite believing what Emma was telling her.

'I asked myself the same question, Lou. It's the strangest

feeling to lie in a hospital bed being told that you're having a miscarriage when you had no idea you were pregnant in the first place. I spent ages blaming myself. For drinking, partying, working too hard.'

'But you didn't know. It's not your fault.'

'I know that now. But he treated me as though I was nothing and that hurt so much.'

'I should have come over.'

'To do what, Lou?'

'You're my little sister. I should have been there for you.'

'You called me. In fact you were quite annoying with your phone calls.'

'A phone call isn't the same. I should have been there with you. God, I've been an awful sister.'

'You've had your own problems. It couldn't have been easy for you. I saw your bank statement on your laptop the other day,' Emma said quickly. 'I'm sorry, it was just there.'

'Ah,' Lucinda said as she refilled her wine glass. 'You always were a nosy cow. So you know?'

Emma nodded. 'How bad is it? I mean it must have been bad for you to come back to London.'

'Let's just say that it wasn't great but I'm sorting it. But this isn't about me. It's about you. So how are you feeling now?'

'I really thought I was over him. I mean, if someone can treat you that badly then you should hate the ground that person walks on. You should want them to suffer through every level of hell and burn, not having them walking up to you in the middle of Soho Square. How can I still be in love with him?'

'Because it's your heart and your heart never does what your head tells it do. It just takes time. You can't beat yourself up about it.'

'I just feel like I'm betraying womankind and all that crap, plus the baby.'

'You're not. Never think that. Look, we've all done things that we're not proud of and I promise you that baby would know what a strong woman he had for a mother…and you know what gran would say, it just wasn't his time yet. It doesn't mean you didn't deserve the baby and it doesn't mean you won't be a wonderful mother someday and be with a man who loves, respects you and worships the ground that you walk on.'

'Preach it Sister Lucinda,' Emma said with a laugh. 'I hope that's how Owen treats you.'

'We're not talking about Owen.'

'Look at you. You're blushing. You must really like him.'

'I do actually.'

'Is the sex good? Because if the sex is rubbish then I suggest you call it a day now.'

'Emma! Yes, it's good. Bloody good,' Lucinda said with a laugh as she picked up a pork dumpling.

'I've missed you sis,' Emma said over the sounds of the children screaming hysterically as they jumped up and down on a trampoline two doors down.

'I've missed you too.'

'Since you've been back and with dad being ill I've thought a lot about what it was like growing up. I mean, who grows up with famous sisters? I'm not saying that we were Greenwich's answer to the Jackson Five but it was hard, Lou. You were my big sister but I never really grew up with you. I was only 9-years-old when you, Jess and Bea became famous. One minute I'm sitting at home watching Top of the Pops singing along to Snap's "The Power" at the top of my voice and the next week I'm sitting with dad watching you three sing "Electrify". I spent more time watching you on TV and reading about you in magazines than spending actual time with any of you. One minute it was all of us together and the next it was just me and mum and dad. It was like I went from being the baby of the family to an only child. You three were always on tour, or in a recording studio and then you left. I didn't really know you.' Emma took a deep breath surprised with what had come out of her mouth.

'I'm so sorry sis,' Lucinda said as she willed herself to stay strong. 'I can't even explain what that time was like. Before we got that first number one, before we were spending every waking hour in the recording studio, before I decided that Euterpe was going to be a success, I was absolutely besotted with you. I'd take you to school, read to you, and sing to you. You were like my little shadow. Do you know that when you were 3 you slept in my bed for a year? You refused to sleep in your own bed. Every time dad put you to bed you'd get up and come into mine. Even if I wasn't there mum said that she would still find you in my bed.'

'I don't remember that.'

'Well you were only little but you did. Mum was busy with work and dad was also working. Things weren't easy, we weren't rich. I remember that mum was teaching during the day and tutoring in the evening. It was difficult and that's why I worked so hard. I wanted to make things easy for everybody.'

'But Lou, it didn't seem that way. Not when Euterpe split up and you pissed off to New York. Don't get me wrong, I had a very nice side-line selling Euterpe memorabilia at school but I thought I'd get my big sister back.'

'Ems, there was so much going on. I thought I was doing the best thing for Beatrice and Jessica and I'm not ashamed to admit that I got caught up with the hype. Oh come on, you know what it's like. You work in PR. Look how easy it is to convince anyone who has ever stood in front of a camera that their shit smells of roses. I believed my own hype and I wanted more.'

'But what more could you want? You were rich. You were famous! You have talent and I'm telling you only about 20% of my clients have half your talent. Lou, I've been out with you. People are constantly looking at you and you haven't been on TV or sung a note for years.'

'Emma, no one under 25 knows who I am.'

'That's bollocks.'

'It's not bullocks. It's the truth. I've learnt to ignore the bullshit, especially after being married to Paul who was the biggest bullshit artist. He told me that I could be as big as Janet Jackson. No, forget that. His best one was that I could be the black Madonna.'

'The black Madonna?' Emma said as she put down her now empty wine glass. 'Lord have mercy.' She began to laugh uncontrollably.

'Come on, it's not that funny,' Lucinda said as she begun

to laugh along.

'Oh sis, if I haven't told you already, I'm really glad that you're back.'

FORTY-EIGHT

LUCINDA'S HEAD was pounding and the fact that Katelyn had decided to blast music from her room and Reece had been charging up and down the stairs as though he was possessed wasn't helping one little bit. When Emma had dragged herself from the bed at seven o'clock Lucinda had acknowledged her departure with an indecipherable 'bye' and covered her head with the pillow only to be woken two hours later by what felt like a hurricane shaking the foundations of her house. If she'd had her way she'd have spent the entire day in bed, hiding herself from the world whilst she watched bad TV, but as she heard the opening cords of Muse's *Starlight* blaring through the house she knew that wasn't going to happen.

'Katelyn Celeste Morgan, why are you playing music for the whole street?' Lucinda said as she pushed open Katelyn's bedroom door. She didn't have the energy to tell her that her bedroom looked exactly how her head felt. It was in complete disarray, with clothes everywhere and cardboard boxes on every available surface. 'Low it down,' Katelyn huffed as she turned down the volume on the dock station whilst Lucinda pushed aside a pile of clothes and sat down wearily on the bed.

'Don't take it out on me just because you've got a hangover. You should know better, mom.'

'I'm not hungover.'

'Yeah right. I saw the bottles that you and auntie Emma left in the garden. Despicable mom. Despicable,' Katelyn said with a laugh.

'Shut up you. Why are you packing?'

'You said we had to get everything ready.'

'Katy, anything could happen, we may not necessarily be moving out in the next few weeks.'

'What happened to "you need to be positive" and "don't waste energy worrying."'

'God knows, probably in the bottom of a wine glass,' Lucinda replied.

'Awww, my poor mommy, all hungover and miserable,' Katelyn said as she sat down next to Lucinda and gave her a hug. Lucinda smiled and kissed the top of her head, with the curls escaping from the loosening plaits. 'Are you nervous?'

'About what?'

'The interview. Today's the day isn't it?'

'Yep, today's the day. What's she going to think when I turn up looking like I had merlot for breakfast?'

'You don't look that bad,' Reece said as he arrived at the bedroom with a bagel stuffed in his mouth. 'Even though, you should have a shower you could knock out skunks with that smell, then again it could just be Katelyn.'

'Hey, shut up. Mom, tell him.'

'Please, you both need to stop. In fact considering you're

both up so bright and early you should go and buy your school uniforms today. You're starting next week.'

Both Reece and Katelyn groaned. 'I can't believe we have to wear a uniform. That's just archaic and wrong and a way of turning us into mindless drones,' Reece said as he sat down next to his mum.

'Drones. You think uniforms make you drones?'

'It's stifling our identities,' Katelyn added. 'Uncle Jake said it's just a way of indoctrinating us into a system.'

'I don't really think that you should be taking advice from a man whose uniform consists of Spiderman t-shirts that are older than you,' Lucinda said dryly. 'Right, as you've both pointed out that I'm not fit for purpose, I'm going to shower and get out of here and you two will go and buy your uniforms and anything else that you need for school next week. I've already printed out the list and stuck it to the fridge and if I haven't told you recently, I love you both very much.'

'Oh mom, you tell us all the time,' Reece said as he playfully pulled at her hair.

'And I'll keep telling you until I'm blue in the face. I couldn't have done any of this if you two hadn't been supporting me. I honestly couldn't have asked for a better set of children' Lucinda said as she kissed them both.

'I love you too mom,' Katelyn and Reece said together. They still spoke in unison as if their thoughts had merged into one.

There had been an attack of self-doubt and she'd taken out her phone twice, before she'd even stepped into the shower, to cancel the interview; but she knew that she would have been making a big mistake. She thought that she'd done quite a good job on herself even though she had to use her mascara to cover the grey hair that had decided to make a break from freedom from her scalp. Lucinda took a final look at her reflection in her mirror before she stepped out of the Borough High Street exit at London Bridge Station As she crossed the road towards Borough market, she asked herself again why she was feeling so nervous. She'd lost count of the amount of interviews she'd given over the years. Everyone from *Smash Hits* magazine to *The Guardian* had interviewed Euterpe, including early morning breakfast shows in Japan and once Jeremy Paxman on Newsnight. This shouldn't be a problem but she knew this interview was more than what she wanted for herself; it was her opportunity to finally close the door on her old life.

On reflection, Lily thought that arranging the interview for eleven o'clock had been a stupid idea. Her morning had been beyond manic as she battled her six-year-old son who seemed determined to extend his summer holiday by refusing to get dressed for school and her three-year-old daughter who was usually more than content to run around her nursery as if she owned the place, had suddenly developed separation anxiety and had howled the place down. The restaurant with views of the bustling market was serene with the soothing hum of satisfied diners but it was doing little to settle her nerves. She checked through the list of questions on her notepad feeling much more secure with a good old fashioned notebook and pen. Despite all of the googling that she'd done last night and the pleasure she'd experienced when she spent a good hour playing Euterpe's greatest hits loudly in the kitchen whilst the children ate their dinner, she was nervous. She took a look at her watch. Lily was early and because of her prior experience interviewing celebrities with an overinflated image of their own self-importance she'd resigned herself to the fact that she'd be waiting for a while as she pulled out her phone and turned on Candy Crush.

'That game is ridiculously addicted. I'm stuck on level 45 but somehow my son has managed to get to level 247. You're Lily right?' Lucinda asked.

'Oh my gosh, yes, yes. Sorry. It's not really very professional of me,' Lily said as she pushed her chair back.

'Don't worry about it. I'm sorry if I kept you waiting.'

'No you didn't keep me waiting at all. I was early and so are you.'

'My children and a hangover drove me out the house.' Lily felt her fears and nerves disappear with how warm and open Lucinda appeared to be.

'Hangovers are never fun but you know what the perfect cure is,' Lily replied as her stomach reminded her that the only thing that had entered her mouth that morning was half a cup of coffee and a custard cream.

'Well, if you don't mind and only if you join me,' Lucinda said as she sat down and picked up the menu. 'I could murder a full English.'

* * * *

Lily's ability to make the people she was interviewing feel as though they were with an old friend meant that breakfast had turned into a late lunch accompanied by Lucinda's insistence that they treated themselves to champagne cocktails. At no point did Lucinda even feel as though she was being interviewed as she sat there and spilled every detail of her life, unabridged.

'Now you promise me that you won't make me out to be an egotistical, new age, green juice drinking, my-life-is-so-perfect-bitch, like that article you wrote on Heather Wallis?'

Lily laughed as she thought back to last month's issue of Allure where she'd interviewed the model. 'I promise you; you're nothing like her. I was actually very nice about her. She was a lot worse.'

'Good,' Lucinda replied as they walked back towards London Bridge Station. 'Well, it was really nice meeting you, Lily. I really enjoyed myself.'

'Oh, honestly, it was my pleasure. I always wanted to meet you, in fact all of you. If my friends Alex and Chloe had had their way they'd have been here too.'

'I hope I didn't disappoint you.'

'No, you didn't and I promise you that the readers won't be disappointed either. I'll be in touch.' Lucinda watched Lily disappear into the crowds of commuters making their way into the station. She couldn't bear the thought of joining the chaos that always seemed to be around the station and decided to walk across London Bridge to Bank station. She stopped halfway across the bridge to look across at the river and the afternoon sun bouncing on the famous blue and white of

Tower Bridge. London was a part of her. It had never really left her. Even though she had made New York her home and it was the place where her children were born it had always felt temporary and she'd never felt as though she truly belonged. London was where her heart was and it was the city that defined her and showed her for the woman she truly was.

'Excuse me.' Lucinda turned around as she realised that someone was trying to get her attention. As soon as she took a look into the blue eyes of the man standing in front of her, she knew exactly what he wanted. She recognised that look, even though it had been years since she'd seen it. 'Hello, I'm really sorry but my friend here, Darren-'

'Hi, that's me,' said the tall, light skinned black man with incredibly sexy eyes. He raised his right hand and smiled.

'And I'm Brandon,' said the third male who was standing next to the blonde man whose name transpired to be Henry.

'Well, we're sorry to bother you,' continued Henry whose eyes were sparkling as though it was Christmas day. 'But we could swear that...' Brandon who quite clearly couldn't take anymore interrupted Henry. 'Are you her? I mean, are you from Euterpe? Are you Lucinda?'

'Bloody hell mate. Show some restraint,' said Henry.

Lucinda didn't know what to think. She couldn't remember the last time that she'd been accosted on the streets by fans. She was just grateful that it wasn't a Friday night and they weren't drunk. 'Yes I am,' she replied.

'Oh my god,' Henry said. 'We walked past you and Darren said it was you and I thought no way, it can't be.'

'Well, Darren was right.'

'Bloody hell. Who'd have thought? The first time we saw you was at our Fresher's Ball.' Lucinda threw her head back and laughed as she had a flashback of her, Jessica and Beatrice driving around all over England and performing at various universities before they had their first number one. 'Well there were a lot of fresher's ball. I'm surprised that you even recognised me.'

'Who could ever forget you and your sisters? I told myself that I was going to marry Jessica,' Darren said. 'I stood at the front of the stage hoping that she'd take a look in my direction.'

'I always liked Beatrice,' Brandon said. 'Sorry,' he added.

Lucinda laughed again. 'It's fine.'

'So are you performing again? Because quite frankly I don't know why you split up in the first place. You were excellent,' Henry said as he pulled his phone out of his pocket.

'Well things change. People change. You try different things,' Lucinda replied. 'But in case you're interested I'm going to be performing at the end of the month. I'm having a show at Dougie Mills in Soho. So, if you gentlemen want to come along then I could put your names on the guest list.'

Lucinda thought Brandon's eyes were going to pop out of his head. 'Seriously?' he asked.

'Yes, seriously. You don't seem like a bunch of stalkers.'

'That would be fantastic.'

'I've got a website. Why don't you email me and I'll make sure you're on the list?'

'That's amazing. Thank you. Would you mind awfully if we took a picture? I'll understand if you said no. You're probably sick of people asking.'

'Funny enough, it doesn't happen as often as you think.'

Lucinda spent another 15 minutes contentedly taking pictures with her mini troop of fans and then even allowed them to escort her to the station. When she finally stepped onto the tube, for the first time since she arrived, she didn't feel fearful about what was to come.

FORTY-NINE

'DOES YOUR sister know you have this?' Wendy asked as she inserted the memory stick into her laptop and opened the document, *'Lucinda's Kitchen*. It's not really imaginative is it? We'll definitely have to change that. We could always call it *the book I stole from my sister.'*

'Stop being facetious and just tell me what you think?' Emma said as she perched herself on Wendy's desk.

'What makes you think that she even wants to publish this?'

'Why else would you start writing a book if you didn't want the public to see it? Anyway, at least she's written it herself, which is a lot more than I can say for most of your clients. Half of them are only interested in talking about orcs, wizards and dragons, and the other half have never written their own name, let alone an entire book.'

'This coming from the woman whose latest client's claim to fame is a reality show about a dog beauty parlour.'

'What can I say? It's very popular. So what do you think?'

'I think that it's really good. I love how she has attributed a recipe to each chapter. She's a really talented writer and reading this is actually making me hungry,' Wendy said as she reached into her desk draw and pulled out a chocolate biscuit and a packet of cheese and onion crisps.

'I knew it was good.'

'But seriously, Ems, maybe this is just her own private musings. For all we know this may just be an exercise set by her therapists.'

'Lou doesn't do therapy. Music is her therapy. Look, we spent ages talking about what she wants to do. Don't get me wrong, she loves music, it's her life, but she wants to try other things. She's a brilliant cook, a fantastic writer and an amazing singer. She deserves this.'

Wendy looked at Emma quizzically. 'I gather that a lot has changed since she's been back. You and Jessica were hardly her biggest cheerleaders last year.'

'I know, but things change don't they and sometimes you think you know it all but you don't really. So, what are you going to do about this work of art here?'

'What do you think? Find a publisher, which shouldn't be that hard. I can think of a half a dozen publishers who would grab at this. If she's making a comeback, as you said, then this will be a great tie-in. Has she got anything else lined up?'

'She's being interviewed by Allure magazine today and I've been calling in some favours. In fact, I've got to check on one of them right now.'

'Go on, you crazy woman. It seems as though I've got some calls to make. Hey, before you go, you better give me her number. Someone needs to warn her that she's just acquired a book agent.'

'Sal, tell me that it's good news,' Emma asked as she walked down to reception to find him talking animatedly to their latest temporary receptionist.

'Did you know that April here is an actress and a singer?' he said as he leaned away from the desk.

'No, I never knew that,' Emma lied, knowing full well that every temp that had ever sat in that desk had thought it'd be his or her way into the world of fame. To her knowledge, since Jessica had opened the doors of the agency, it'd only happened once with their administration assistant, Duncan, who'd been scouted whilst he stood outside having a cigarette with Megan. The last time Emma had seen him was modelling in the pages of the Style section of *The Sunday Times* and a small role in the latest Christopher Nolan film.

'Sal, you didn't come all this way just to flirt with our staff,' Emma said as she kissed him on the cheek. It was funny to think that their lives were coming full circle. Sal used to be such a regular feature in the early days that it got to the point that their mother would set an extra place for him at the dinner table on a Sunday.

'Don't flatter yourself. I was only around the corner at the BBC, which is my news. Carter sent me a couple of tracks that he's been working on with Lucinda. Have you heard it?'

Emma shook her head. 'We didn't get round to it last night.'

'Oh, it's good. Really good. I knew Carter would be the right person for her.'

'Who's Carter?'

'Her producer. A really nice guy. If he stopped being so bloody precious he could be big really big. Hey, you never know it could still happen, especially once we release this. Anyway, Robert Elms is an old mate of mine.'

'Oh, I like him. I sent him a note and query once. Is he really your mate or did you stalk him at the studios?'

'He's a mate and he knows what he's talking about. He loves Lou's newest stuff, so to cut a long story short, he's offered to have her in as a listed Londoner and have her perform live.'

'Sal, that's brilliant. She's going to go nuts.'

'Oh, that's not all sunshine. One of the girls who used to work for me is a booking agent for Lorraine and Loose Women.'

'No way Sal.'

'Yes. As I told you the other day. I'm a bloody miracle worker and I've managed to get her on both. I don't know what it is but everything is falling into place. So now that I've told you my news would you like to give me the courtesy of telling me why you've demanded my presence?'

'Well, don't make yourself too comfortable because we're going on a trip.'

'You're just as bad as Lou. Can't sit still in one place.'

'Don't worry; we're not going far. I've had to pull a lot of strings and offer all sorts of bribes but I promise you that Lulu is going to love it.'

Once she'd arrived home, Lucinda decided to give herself

the night off. When she thought about it, from the minute she'd arrived home, she'd been on what seemed like a roller coaster, both emotionally and physically. As she laid in her bath with the warm scents of her Jo Malone pomegranate noir bath oil filling the steamy bathroom and the candles flicking silently on the windowsill, she recognised that what she had in her life was enough. She didn't have to revisit the dizzy heights of fame that Euterpe had reached and she didn't need the financial reserves that had once been at her disposal when she was living in New York. There was more to her than that. She wasn't a one trick pony, there were many facets to her that she'd either chosen to ignore or had convinced herself that they didn't really represent her. She wasn't a fool. She knew that she'd been in a better position than most people who recognised that they weren't financially independent and had hit rock bottom. Yes, she had had to hustle and make quick decisions. Yes, she had to budget and make changes to how she lived and viewed the world, but she hadn't been homeless. She hadn't arrived in London with her two children and been forced to bang on the council offices, demanding to be housed and then been forced to live in a B & B with damp on the walls and cockroaches for dinner companions. As she lay soaking in the bathtub she closed her eyes and said a silent prayer of thanks. Her children were happy and were due to start the next chapter in their lives, plus her own book of life was yet unfinished despite the surprise phone call from Wendy earlier that had made her want to hunt down her nosey little sister and kiss her. She did have to tell Wendy that she had no interest in becoming a celebrity chef but she was definitely up for what she had in mind.

'Yes, life is definitely getting better,' Lucinda said to herself as she stepped out of the bath and wrapped herself in a soft, warm towel. The house was quiet as the twins had managed to extend their shopping trip to an excursion to Islington and from their last text, were planning on a cinema trip with Lena. She couldn't remember the last time that she'd been truly on her own. Although Owen worked long and unsocial hours they'd been seeing a lot of each other. She was glad to, as Depeche Mode once said, *enjoy the silence.*

Her iPhone signalling the arrival of an email interrupted the silence. Her website and Twitter account had launched the day before and she'd been surprised by the number of emails she'd already received. It was hard to believe that she thought she'd been forgotten.

The first was from Carter sending her further versions of the songs that she'd recorded earlier that week. She wondered where he found the time to sleep; he seemed to be constantly working. The second was an email from Jake asking if she wouldn't mind looking after the children, as he wanted to take Beatrice on a surprise trip to Paris. However, it was the third email that surprised her. She wasn't expecting to hear from Lily considering that she'd left her only five hours ago, but there was a draft version of her interview. In the past she'd been used to giving an interview and seeing the finished article that bared no resemblance to what she'd said, but she remembered a story that Lily had told her about how an article she'd written had nearly destroyed her friendship with her best friend.

As Lucinda sat alone on her bed and read the article she realised again how far she'd come and what she'd been at risk of losing. Even more, she was amazed that she managed to come across so eloquent considering she was nursing a hangover and was stuffing her face with fried bread and an organic sausage at the time. As she finished the article and lay down on her bed she felt something stir within her that she hadn't felt for a long time. She felt at peace.

FIFTY

THE THOUGHT of seeing him again made her sick to her stomach. Her first reaction upon opening her front door to leave was to walk straight to the Tesco Express on the corner and buy herself a bottle of vodka but she knew that if she did that then all of the progress she'd made would have been for nothing. In retrospect, the short time away had been the best thing for her, even though when she'd come back she'd failed to recognise it. She'd hated the idea of attending Alcoholics Anonymous; the thought of having to sit in a room of strangers who she thought would be in judgement of her and ridicule her for following the clichéd road so familiarly travelled by those in the public eye. But it hadn't been like that at all. There were one or two raised eyebrows when it was obvious that she'd triggered more than one recessed memory but over the ninety minutes she'd just sat and listened. That had changed with week two when Jessica found her voice.

Everything that she'd been in fear of just melted away into the distance. She'd worked hard to resume her relationship with Lena, which required nothing more than her just sitting down with her daughter and talking openly with her. As Beatrice had told her a few weeks ago it was the fact that you kept something secret, not the secret itself that got you in the end. It was the energy that you spent trying to suppress it or denying that it ever happened that would eat away at you. Life was moving forward and she didn't really have any say in the matter. It was just the laws of motions in action and Andrew was another force that she had to contend with. There was no way that she was just going to sit there and let him use his whole force against her.

'Earth to Jess,' Beatrice said as she sat down next to Jessica in the waiting area.

'Sorry, Bea, I was miles away,' Jessica replied as she let Beatrice kiss her on the cheek. 'Oh wow, I like your hair. It really suits you.'

Beatrice grinned and smoothed down her hair, which had now been cut into a long bob. 'I wasn't sure about cutting it at first but I woke up one morning and just thought to hell with it. I need a change. Every time I looked in the mirror I just felt like an invisible working mother. I didn't feel like me. So, I did it. Told Kelly to cut it. She thought I was mad but I've had the same boring hairstyle for donkey's years and all I ever did with it was wrap it up in a ponytail. So there we have it.'

'Well, it looks really good. Bea, I wanted to say that you were right.'

'About what?'

'About taking advantage of you. You were right.'

'Jess. Look, forget that I said any of that. I was feeling

stressed, angry and overwhelmed and I took it out on you. I shouldn't have done that.'

'But it was all true Bea and you know it was.'

'Even so, I should have found a found better way to tell you instead of screaming at you whilst I had Jake's underpants in my hands.'

Both of the sisters burst out laughing. 'God, this has been a rough summer,' Jess said as she leaned back in the chair.

'I know, it's been absolutely nuts. Right, I've got to go to court in a bit. I just wanted to wish you luck. Not that you have anything to worry about.'

'Is he here?' Jessica asked quietly. Beatrice nodded.

'Arrived about twenty minutes go. I had to tell James that he was to call security if he saw me heading towards the conference room. He followed me down here to make sure that I was actually meeting you.'

'Every time I think about what he did to Lou and the things he's done to me. I can't believe that I chose him.'

'Don't even think about it Jess, he's not worth it and now you know what sort of man he is. Everything happens for a reason and Andrew showing his true colours has been the best thing for you.'

'It doesn't feel like it.'

'Look at where you are and the people who are in your life now. If he hadn't shown himself for what he was think about how different your life would have been.'

Jessica let Beatrice's words reverberate in her head as Sarah took her to meet Anoushka.

'Beatrice tells me that you were rather pissed off that I was representing you.' Jessica stood open mouthed as Anoushka appeared in front of her in a mist of Tom Ford perfume, balancing precariously on five inch heels. 'But let's not concern ourselves about that. Do you know that this is the first time that I've met any of the LeSoeur sisters? Are you all so tall?'

'I'm afraid so, except out of the four of us, I think that I'm the shortest. It's nice to finally meet you Anoushka. Beatrice tells me that you're very good.'

'Very good? Darling, I'm more than just very good. I'm absolutely outstanding. I mean, let's call a spade a spade. They call me a Rottweiler bitch behind my back, don't they Sarah?'

'I've never heard anyone call you that?' Sarah said, although they were both aware that this was a complete lie.

'My sister may have left that bit out.'

'Your sister is too nice but don't let that *butter wouldn't melt in her mouth* act fool you. She's a fierce one. Right, enough chit chat. Are you ready?'

The look on Jessica's face said it all and she followed Anoushka who quickly turned and strutted away down the corridor.

Jessica exhaled sharply when she saw Andrew sitting on the other side of the mahogany table with his lawyer. He was dressed sharply in a navy Hugo Boss suit, with the face of the Breitling watch shining brightly against the cuffs of his white shirt. He didn't say a word, just smiled smugly at Jessica as she sat down next to Sarah.

'Nice to see you that you've finally graced us with your

presence Anoushka,' said the man in the chalk striped suit sitting next to Andrew. He was tanned and clean-shaven but with thick, curly white hair. He looked as though he should have been taking over Jeremy Paxman's place on Newsnight or playing Hamlet at the Donmar Warehouse. Even though he was sitting down doing nothing except doodling on a notepad, he exuded charisma.

'It's a pleasure to see you too, Maxwell. Keeping well,' Anoushka replied as she sat at the head of the table and opened her laptop.

'Doing well as always,' Maxwell said with a smile.

'Well now that we've got the pleasantries out of the way let's get down to the business. When is your client going to refrain from being such a arsehole and stop making such unreasonable demands?'

Whilst Jessica sat in what could only have been one of the most surreal moments of her life, Richard was sitting waiting for the arrival of Dr. Marcus. He'd spent so much time in this hospital that he was wondering if it'd be out of order if he asked for a wing to be named after him or at least give him free parking. The amount that he'd spent on parking fees was outrageous and he wondered how parents like Liam, who were just keeping their heads above water financially, coped when they had a child in hospital for months. Even with the return of his oldest daughter and her children, Richard could openly admit that this had been the worse summer of his life and for all he knew this could be the last summer of his life. He'd been through every emotion possible. He'd fought and tried to remain positive when all he wanted to do was go to bed and wait for that beautiful angel of death to take him away. He'd convinced himself at one point that his death would be the greatest gift that he could give his family, especially when he found himself suffering from the side-effects of the treatment that was supposed to help him. He was glad that Felicia wasn't with him. She'd wanted to phone the university and tell them that she wouldn't be able to make the faculty meeting that morning but Richard had persuaded her to go. It would be easier to deal with the news on his own without having the pressure of having to comfort his wife if the news wasn't good.

'Richard, how are you feeling? You look like you've put on a bit of weight.'

'I put on six pounds and then I lost it again. I'm blaming the shark cartilage.'

'You didn't?' Dr. Marcus said, his face a mixture of surprise and shock.

'No, but if my grandson had his way I would have been and if it didn't cost so much money I would have given it a try.'

'Well, I'm glad that you didn't try it. Don't get me wrong, I don't think that modern day medicine is the answer for everything, there's so much that we don't know and I've got no issues with experimental treatments or alternative therapy but there are some things that I draw the line at. Anyway, back to you.'

Richard took a deep breath.

'It's good news.'

'What? What's good news?'

'I know that the chemo and radiotherapy has been aggressive but there has been a significant reduction in the tumours.'

'Are you serious?'

'Yes, I'm serious. Your MRI scans are quite remarkable really.' Dr. Marcus spun his computer monitor round to show Richard. 'If you look here.' The doctor indicated around a dark grey area on the screen with his pen 'In comparison to these scans from four months ago, even to a layman, you can see the change.'

'But what does that mean? Am I in remission?'

'As much as I'd like to I'm very reluctant to say that you're in remission. I don't want to give you false hope, as I told you in the very beginning, pancreatic cancer is…'

'I know what you said. The outlook isn't good. Only 18% live for a year after diagnosis. Only 4% live for five years and 3% live for 10 years or more. I can repeat those numbers in my sleep.'

'Look Richard, you're in a better position than most. You have stage 2 cancer and there are no signs that it has spread into your lymph nodes or any of the surrounding tissues of the pancreas.'

'So, what now? What are my options?'

'Surgery. And I'm not going to lie to you. Unless there's a chance that we can remove the tumours entirely there's not much point, especially if we take into account factors such as…'

'I know, my age. I'm not exactly a young man even though I can still play for Chelsea,' Richard said with a slight smile.

'QPR maybe. Look, I'm not saying that you should rule it out. Even though the tumours have reduced they're still measuring 3.6cm in diameter, which is still quite large but not inoperable, however there's no guarantee that this will cure you.'

'I understand.'

'And if you decide to have surgery and you get through it, you'll still have to undergo 6 more months of chemo.'

'So what do I do now? I mean, I want to beat this. Not just for me but for my family. What would you do?'

'I can't tell you what to do, Richard.'

'I'm not asking you to tell me what to do. I'm just asking what would you do if it was you?'

'This is completely against the rules, you know.'

'You supporting Manchester United when you've told me that you were born in Reading is against the rules doc,' Richard said. 'So go on, I won't tell.'

Dr. Marcus looked down at the photograph of his two sons on his desk. They were only three and seven-years-old and he couldn't imagine not being there to play football with them in the garden or just hold them at night. 'I'd try everything. Sometimes you have to take a risk.'

FIFTY-TWO

'THAT WAS brilliant,' Carter said, almost jumping up from the sofa as though he'd just received an electric shock.

'Do you really think so? I wasn't too sure about how I sounded with the last song,' Lucinda said as she fiddled with the microphone stand. 'The show is in just two weeks. I don't think that I'm ready?'

'Stop panicking. You sounded good to me,' Dave the guitarist said, whilst Luke on piano and Sebastian on the bass guitar nodded their agreements.

'Yep. Carter was definitely right about closing the song without us. I may even have been moved to a tear or two,' said George who was still holding onto his drumsticks as he sat on the floor. 'You need to tell your mum that she has nothing to worry about. You haven't lost it. In fact I think you sound better then you did before.'

'Mom, honestly that was amazing. Absolutely amazing,' Katelyn said as she struggled to get up from the battered sofa, considering that she was squeezed in between her brother, Carter and Luke. Lucinda didn't have the energy to smile. It had been a long day. In fact, it had been a long couple of weeks, especially as her dad was now recovering in hospital after his surgery. The decision he had made didn't surprise her in the slightest but the fear she felt that her dad might not leave the hospital alive had shaken her very core. Thankfully the operation appeared to have been successful, now she prayed that he was fit enough to recover from the savage invasion of his body. She'd literally done a whole circuit of London today. She'd been down to the South Bank to be interviewed by Lorraine and then had to return back to Notting Hill where *Allure's* photographer was waiting. As soon as they were done, she'd jumped into her car, picked the twins up from school and driven straight to St Thomas' hospital to see her dad for an hour before speeding down to New Cross. She was convinced that in a few weeks time there would be at least six speeding tickets through her door. As she'd driven down the Old Kent Road and literally flew over the flyover, Reece pointed out that they'd never actually seen their mother perform live. They'd obviously heard her singing around the house and watched old videos of her and their aunts but they'd never seen her standing in a room with a microphone in her hand, singing with her entire soul. Seeing her children sitting in the studio waiting for her to sing filled her with nerves that she hadn't experienced. She had uprooted their lives so much that there was no way she could let them down now.

'Right, why don't we give *Stripped Back* a go?' Carter said as he picked up his own acoustic guitar. It was the very first song that they had worked on together but she was unsure about singing it now. It was written when she was at her most vulnerable and like all of the LeSoeur women she was very good of painting a picture of strong warrior whilst her insides shook as though a Jack Hammer was attacking her. 'Come on,' Carter said as he saw the brief look of vulnerability pass in Lucinda's eyes.

'Fine. I suppose it won't kill me,' Lucinda said as she pulled up the stool and adjusted her microphone stand as Carter begun to strum the opening chords. When Lucinda finished you could have heard a pin drop, even the sounds of the passing traffic couldn't penetrate the glassy silence, until the room broke out in rampant applause.

'Mom, I have no idea why you were worried. That was beautiful,' Katelyn said as she sprang out of her seat and straight into her mums' arms.

'Oh, thank you angel.'

'Well, I don't care what you say, you're definitely ready to show them that you're back,' Carter said with a wide grin.

As they drove to Greenwich, Lucinda couldn't stop the smile that seemed permanently etched on her face since she had left the studio. It came both from the joy of knowing that she was doing what she was born to do and from knowing that her children were proud of her. As she pulled into the driveway, she could see that her mum was already home, her car parked neatly on the drive.

'Gran,' both of the twins shouted in unison as soon as they threw the door open whilst Lucinda straddled behind them carrying the bags of Indian takeaway that they'd picked up. 'I'll be down in a minute,' Felicia's voice echoed down the stairs.

'I'm just on the phone to Noah.'

'We'll be in the kitchen,' Lucinda shouted back. She stopped at the door of the *good* living room and watched the piano standing silently by the window. Lucinda couldn't help feeling emotional; after all this was where it had all started.

'Oh, you brought food. You didn't have to do that,' Felicia said as she walked into the kitchen to find Lucinda unpacking the takeaway.

'Seeing as dad is in the hospital I didn't think you'd feel like cooking and I thought it'd be nice if we spent the night with you to keep you company,' Lucinda said as she handed Reece the plates.

'I would have been fine, but thank you. Your dad said to tell you thanks again for his dinner.'

'Grandad couldn't eat that hospital food. They said it was mac'n'cheese but that was the whitest mac'n'cheese I'd ever seen. In fact, I don't think that there was any macaroni or cheese in it,' Reece said as he sat down at the table.

Even though the children talked animatedly with their grandmother over dinner, Lucinda couldn't shake off the feeling that something wasn't quite right with her mother. It could have just been that this was the first time in years that she'd been in this great big house on her own. That wasn't to say Felicia had played the role of the good little housewife. There had been more times then she could remember when she'd disappeared for spa weekends with her sister or gone on holiday with her girlfriends but whenever Richard had gone away she'd always had Emma to keep her company. Now that she was gone all Felicia had was Ares the dog, which had been moping around the house ever since Richard had gone into hospital over a week ago.

'I should really sort out the bedrooms for them. I haven't done a thing since your dad went into hospital and with work…'

'Mum, don't worry about it. I'll go upstairs and sort the rooms out and these two can clean up,' Lucinda said as she got up to leave the kitchen.

'You know where everything is?' Felicia asked.

'Mum, I used to live here, of course I do.' As Lucinda brought their overnight bags upstairs into the room she paused briefly on the stairs to look at the family photos on the wall. She would never have imagined when she left home all those years ago that her parent's walls would be covered with photographs of her own children at various stages of their lives. Lucinda touched the glass of a recent edition to the gallery. She didn't remember being there when the picture was taken. It showed all of the grandchildren: Lena, Katelyn, Reece, Theo, Issy and even baby Sam with their grandparents who were smiling broadly. There were no signs on Richard's face that he was even ill as pure joy radiated from him. It must have been one of the frequent days that the twins had just turned up on their grandparent's doorstep. Lucinda didn't remember ever giving them that much freedom when they lived in New York. As she walked up the stairs to the bedroom it didn't escape her attention that there were hardly any pictures of her as part of the family.

'Play it again,' Felicia said as she stared wide-eyed at the TV screen. Reece had hooked up his MacBook air to the television and was enjoying the stunned look on his grandmother's face.

'Didn't I tell you gran?' Katelyn said as she stood in the middle of the room still in her school uniform, though both her and her brother had long since discarded their ties, holding the remote control in her hand as she turned up the volume.

Lucinda stood up straight in Emma's old bedroom as she heard her own voice drifting up the stairs. She left the room and went down the stairs, stopping midway down to lean over the banister in the way she used to do when she was eight years old and tried to creep down the stairs after she'd been told repeatedly to go to bed. From the open door she could see her mother sitting on the edge of the sofa with her hands over her face as Lucinda's voice sang the song she'd performed with Carter only a couple of hours before.

'Oh Lou,' Felicia said when Lucinda walked into the room. 'Oh my baby girl.'

* * * *

'Do you know that I never saw you girls perform. I mean, I saw you on the television but I never went to watch you,' Felicia said as she sat with Lucinda in the now empty living room. The twins had disappeared upstairs after seeing their grandmother's eyes wet with tears.

'I always thought it was just because you wanted to stay with Emma,' Lucinda said as she blew across her cup of hot honey and lemon with a dash of her dad's whisky, whilst

Felicia sat with a large brandy in her hand. After seeing Lucinda perform she'd disappeared into her bedroom for half an hour and cried over so many different things.

'That's what I told myself in the beginning. Someone needed to be at home but once she got older I couldn't use that as an excuse.'

'Why didn't you ever come? I mean dad was there and even uncle Stephen would come and watch us perform, even though I suspect he was acting more as our unofficial bodyguard.'

'I just never wanted it for you. Not that life. I wanted you girls to be secure not to subject yourself to someone else's opinion of how you should be.'

'Mum, that's just an excuse. Come on. You knew what I always wanted. I wasn't like Bea telling you at seven years old that I wanted to be a lawyer or Jessica telling you one week that she wanted to be a stuntman and the following week that she wanted to be a nurse. I knew I wanted to sing, that I had to sing. I didn't want anything else.'

'I thought you'd grow out of it but it didn't happen and Jessica always wanted to do everything that you did and then Beatrice. The worse thing was that no matter how much she said that she was just helping you out I could tell that she loved it.'

'And so you hated me for it,' Lucinda said bluntly.

'No. I never hated you for it. I could never hate you.'

'But mum, you're not getting it. It felt that way. Look, I'm not stupid I know that you never planned to have me no matter how many times dad told me I was a love child.'

'That didn't mean I loved you any less. You're my child,'

Felicia said softly. 'Look, I won't lie. Getting pregnant when I did wasn't part of my plan and I thought about…but I couldn't do that. No matter how much my head told me that it was the right thing to do, my heart wouldn't let me do it.'

Lucinda said nothing as she sipped her tea. It may not have been what she wanted to hear but it was the first time she'd ever spoken so openly with her mother.

'I envied you,' Felicia said.

'Why? If you knew the mess that I've made of things mum, you wouldn't be saying that.'

'We all have our ups and down but it's true. You're not supposed to be jealous of your daughters but when I saw you growing up so strongly and with such a passion for life I envied you. You were always such a fighter and everything you put your mind to you achieved. You were so determined and independent.'

'But mum, where do you think that I got that from? I got that from you. You did everything. You worked, you played with us, you cooked with us and you always told us that we could do anything we wanted. You gave us that passion. You were the one who told us that our power came from the ability to choose.'

'I did that?' Felicia asked not quite believing it.

'Of course you did, mum. If you hadn't been the woman you are, I'd never have turned into the woman that I was meant to be.'

'You always had a way with words,' Felicia said with a laugh.

'Who do you think I get that from?'

'Well, I'm glad you got something from me. Your singing talent definitely comes from your dad's side of the family. Do you know that was the first time that I really listened to your voice? I mean, I've heard you and your sisters sing but I never actually listened before. You have such a beautiful voice. I have such a beautiful daughter.'

'Oh God, you're going to make me cry. Mum, will you come?'

'To what?'

'My show. Will you come and watch me? If you're worried about dad, I'm sure uncle Stephen wouldn't mind staying with him, or even Reece could stay.'

'You know what, baby, just try and keep me away.'

FIFTY-THREE

IT HAD been the longest week of her life. Jessica could think of a million and one things that she would rather have been doing instead of making the journey to the Royal Courts of Justice every day. Beatrice had often told her that it was one of her favourite buildings in London but Jessica couldn't appreciate its beauty as she walked into the grand and opulent hall with its marbled floors and ancient oak panelling on the walls, not when each step she took meant she was one step closer to her life possibly changing forever.

'Are you ready?' Anoushka asked as she took the coffee cup from Jessica's hand and dumped it in the bin behind her.

'I think so. I want it to be over but then again I don't. I mean everything could change forever once I walk through those doors,' Jessica said as she stared ahead at the dark wooden door of court 14 in front of her. 'What do you think the judge will do?'

'Honestly, I haven't got a fucking clue,' Anoushka replied. 'I wish I did but I don't. This is the point that I normally tell my clients to start praying to whatever God they believe in and if they don't believe, well, I suppose there's always animal sacrifice or if that doesn't work good old fashioned cash in a brown envelope.' Both women immediately went quiet as Andrew and his lawyer walked through the double doors at the end of the corridor. Jessica looked quickly away as she could see the grin on Andrew's face even from where she was sitting.

The court door swung open and a petite blonde woman in her early fifties stepped out, her black gown almost swallowing her.

'The judge is ready for you now,' she said to Anoushka before shouting, 'All parties in Horncastle and LeSoeur to court 14 now please.'

Jessica felt herself holding her breath whilst Anoushka sat next to her with her perfectly manicured hands folded in front of her on the table. She sat as still as a statue. Jessica allowed herself to breathe out as she felt Sarah gently squeeze her hand. They were all nervous, as no one had a clue as to what Justice O'Byrne was going to say as he sat up on the bench and waited for his laptop to load up with his judgement.

'This is an application that's both vexatious and vindictive,' the judge began in a deep, baritone voice that betrayed his slender size. Jessica could feel the corners of her mouth turning upwards whilst Andrew's smile was beginning to turn into a firm grimace.

'There is no merit to this application,' the judge continued. 'I feel nothing but sympathy for Ms. LeSoeur. I do accept everything that has been said about her financial assets but quite frankly Mr. Horncastle you're not entitled to anything that Ms. LeSoeur has built. I rule that you have absolutely no entitlement to her agency, or her home. How you even believed that you were entitled to a share of her royalties that have been received as income from the sale and licence of Euterpe songs, products, and so forth is, to be quite frank, beyond me.

Accordingly, I shall order that the wife will pay to the husband on or after decree nisi a lump sum of £740,000 that being 50% of the balance within their joint savings account. This then means that he'll exit the marriage with property and funds of £745,855. Thus, in my judgment, the sharing principle, on the assumption that such may arguably be applicable here, is subsumed within her needs and indeed in the total figure with which he exits the marriage. That is my ruling. Ms. McMillan and Mr. Fields.' Both Anoushka and Maxwell stood up from their seats.

'If you'd care to wait for a short while my clerk will hand you my full judgement. You should have received it earlier, but let's just say that there were some technical difficulties. Ms. LeSoeur.' For the first time that morning, Justice O'Byrne turned his attention towards Jessica, the furrows in his face settling down to reveal a man that despite the demanding and fearful tone of his voice was naturally gentle in nature. 'A divorce is distressing enough as it is without it being played out within the full glare of the media and that's something that I hope Mr. Horncastle will have the good grace to reflect on and the decency to apologise for. If Mr. Horncastle considers that my adjudication to be unfairly low, then I will simply say this to you Mr. Horncastle.' This time there was no sympathy in his voice as he directed his gaze towards Andrew who was silently simmering with anger. 'As it was your decision to pursue this application for ancillary relief proceedings it was for you to make a rational and logical case for the award that was sought. You put forward an excessive, indeed exorbitant, *claim* therefore what you have received is only fair. You have behaved disgracefully and have sought to destroy Ms. LeSoeur's reputation by the slanderous allegations that you have made against her character. As I said before, an apology from you should be forthcoming.' Anoushka poked Jessica in her elbow as Justice O'Byrne rose from his seat and left the court.

'Is that it? Is that really it?' Jessica asked after the judge had left the courtroom.

'Well once we get the decree nisi and another six weeks for the decree absolute to come through then you'll officially be a free woman but yes it's definitely over,' Anoushka said as she indicated for Sarah to pack up the numerous lever arch files that had sat in front of them like a shield for the past week. From the other side of the courtroom, Jessica could barely make out the hushed angry tones of Andrew as he spoke to his lawyer.

'Thank you. Thank you so much,' Jessica said as she grabbed Anoushka in a hug and squeezed tightly.

'You're most welcome,' Anoushka replied as she hugged her back. She let go when she spotted Maxwell walking towards the court doors.

'I hope you won't be crying into your Bordeaux tonight,

Maxwell,' Anoushka said.

Maxwell shook his head, clearly humoured. He walked over towards Anoushka, leaned towards her ear and whispered, 'Only if you're buying my dear and you're wearing Le Perla.' Anoushka could barely contain her smug smile as she picked up her bag.

'Right you, let's get you out of here,' Anoushka said after the clerk arrived and handed her a copy of the thick 25 page document that contained the full judgement. As they approached the main door of the court Andrew appeared from the side and discarded the cigarette that he had in his hand. He didn't approach Jessica but stepped towards Anoushka, leaned in towards her and said one word.

'Bitch.'

'Oh darling, tell me something that I don't know,' Anoushka replied as she grabbed Jessica's hand, pushed past Andrew and made her way down the steps.

* * * *

'Andrew looks like someone has just taken a big shit on his Porsche. Like Biff in Back to the Future'

'Lou,' Jessica said clearly surprised to see Lucinda standing at the bottom of the stairs as Andrew walked quickly past them and hailed down a black cab.

'Oh, wow. Another LeSoeur,' Anoushka said. 'I love the coat.'

'Thank you,' Lucinda replied as she smoothed down the lapel of her Max Mara coat. 'I think that it's old enough for me to get away with calling it vintage. Well, my divorce was rather boring in comparison to yours. Congratulations.'

'I didn't think you'd be here,' Jessica said as she hugged her sister and waved goodbye to Anoushka and Sarah.

'Bea called me last night and told me that you were receiving the judgement this morning. So, I figured that the least that I could do was support you. I got into the public gallery just in time to hear the judge ripping Andrew a new one. If I had my way I wouldn't have given him a penny.'

'I couldn't really argue with the joint account. I'm just glad that it's over and I've kept my house and the business. I don't know what I would have done if I hadn't...'

'Stop it. Don't even think about it. It's over. Anyway, I did have another reason for coming here this morning.'

Jessica looked at Lucinda and wondered what it could possibly be. Despite the apologies and the promises that they would try and move forward there hadn't been that much progress beyond a few texts and a short phone call here and there.

'Will you come with me to the Loose Women show? I have to be there in...' Lucinda lifted the sleeve of her coat and looked at her watch. 'Thirty minutes.'

'You're going to be on Loose Women?'

'Yes, Sal has been brilliant and I'm on there today as a guest panellist. I'd completely understand if you said no, I know that you have to work...'

'No. I'd love to come. If you're sure you want me there.'

'Of course I do,' Lucinda said as she grabbed Jessica's hand.

'What do you want to do? Walk? The studios are only

across the Waterloo Bridge,' Jessica asked.

'You're having a laugh aren't you? Have you seen my heels?' Lucinda said as she lifted up her right foot and revealed the familiar red sole. 'Five inches darling. I'm not walking anywhere and when we get into the taxi you can read this.' Lucinda reached into her bag and pulled out a copy of the latest issue of Allure magazine. It wasn't due out for another week but a copy had been couriered to her that morning. Jessica ran her fingers across the cover, which featured a stunning picture of Lucinda with the heading 'Comeback Queen.'

'You look gorgeous.'

'Stop it. I told them to airbrush me to death. Come on let's go,' Lucinda said as opened the door of a taxi.

As they sat next to each other there was silence as Jessica read the article. The silence was only broken by her audible gasp as the taxi pulled into the gates of the television studios.

'It wasn't supposed to make you cry,' Lucinda said as she paid the taxi driver and they waited for the security guard to phone them through.

'I just never knew. Oh Lou, I'm so sorry for everything.' Jessica said as she pulled a tissue out of her pocket.

'Jess, there's no me without you. It's as simple as that,' Lucinda said as she linked arms with her sister and they walked towards the studio doors where a runner was waiting for them.

'Oh my God. I thought you were going to be late,' Emma said as she ran into the makeup room to greet Lucinda, leaving

Sal talking to the production manager.

'When am I ever late?' Lucinda replied as she sat almost motionless as the makeup artist finished her makeup.

'I know, I know but I was calling and then...oh Jess.' Emma said as she noticed Jessica sitting quietly behind Lucinda. 'What are you doing here? I've been trying to call you. Bea texted me and told me about the hearing. I thought you were in a pub getting pissed somewhere.'

Emma clapped her hands to her mouth when she realised what she'd said. 'Shit, sorry sis. I didn't mean.'

'Please, don't worry about it. Seriously. Lou asked me to come so here I am,' Jessica said.

'Cool, it's a shame that Bea isn't here but I've told her to watch.'

'We're ready for you now,' a young production assistant said before speaking into her headset.

'Good luck sis,' Emma and Jessica shouted as they left the dressing room and made their way to the studio.

Lucinda closed her eyes and silently said a prayer. She would be performing *Stripped back* live for the first time without the safe walls of the New Cross studio that she'd initially thought was a crack house, or before her usual audience of Katelyn and Reece. 'Ok. I'm ready,' Lucinda said as she got up from the make-up chair and walked towards the studio.

'You definitely have to come back,' Andrea Mclean said as she gave Lucinda a hug at the end of the show. 'You were simply brilliant.'

'Thank you, I'd love to come back. Thanks for having me,' Lucinda replied, feeling exhilarated by the whole experience.

As she walked out of the studio building, Lucinda felt the full force of her younger sister as she hugged her. 'You were bloody fantastic. I knew you would be. Wasn't she brilliant, Sal?' Emma said.

'You most definitely were,' Sal said as he squeezed into between the sisters and hugged Lucinda tightly.

'She should have her own show. Sal, Jess, we've got to find a way to get Lou her own show. I've already been receiving calls from fuck knows who. Who knows where this could go,' Emma said talking at a hundred miles an hour. Jessica simply rolled her eyes as she continued her conversation on the phone, more than used to Emma's manic disposition when she was over excited.

'Right, that's sorted,' Jessica said as she put her phone into her bag.

'What's sorted?' asked Lucinda.

'I've just booked us a table at Maze and Bea is going to meet us there. Sal, you're more than welcome to come.'

'Nah, I think I'll leave you girls to it,' Sal said as he grinned. 'I love you all but I can only imagine what it's going to be like once you lot get together.' He kissed them all and left.

'You need to read this,' Jessica said as she handed the magazine to Emma. 'And you better take these too.' Emma looked at Jessica oddly as she took the pack of tissues from her hand.

'Fucking hell. I can't go in there looking like this,' Emma said as she stood in the restaurant foyer watching her reflection in the black compact mirror. 'Why did you have to say all of those things Lulu? Why couldn't you have just done an article saying how fabulous you were and that you survive on a diet of brown rice and green juice? Selfish cow.'

'Sorry sis,' Lucinda said as she took the mirror away from Emma and took out the small sponge and started to cover up the traces of mascara that had run down her face.

'So you should be,' Emma said with a smile.

'That bastard has just sent me the rudest message,' Beatrice said as she entered the foyer and immediately hugged Jessica. 'I just texted Andrew back and told him to go and fuck himself and that I'm applying for a restraining order. Jess, promise me, if you ever, and I mean ever, decide to get married again, get a pre-nup.'

'I have absolutely no intention of getting married again,' Jessica replied.

'We need champagne,' Jessica said to the waiter before they had even sat down at the table. Beatrice, Lucinda and Emma all looked up at her from their seats. 'Don't look at me like that. I'm not drinking. I'll just have sparkling water and a virgin mojito.'

'Oh sis, you have to read this,' Emma said as she handed the magazine, that was now well read and already opened at the article on Lucinda, to Beatrice. It didn't take too long for Beatrice to start sniffing away as she read Lucinda's words.

'See, do you see what you've done?' Jessica said as she

handed Beatrice a tissue.

'Thank you. All, I've got is bloody baby wipes in my bag,' Beatrice said as she gratefully took the tissues.

'I've got something to say,' Jessica said halfway during their afternoon of champagne, virgin cocktails and lobster and king prawn dumplings.

'Do you have to?' Beatrice asked as she put down the spoon containing her chocolate profiterole. 'Because I'm telling you that I'm quite pissed and may not appreciate the sentiment of your words.'

Lucinda fell into Beatrice's arm laughing. 'I can always say a few words if you fancy a good cry again.'

'Hell no,' said Beatrice.

'Right, I promise that I won't be long. If someone had told me at the beginning of the year that we'd all be sitting here, together, well I wouldn't have believed them. We've all been through so much,' Jessica said.

'It has been a bit shit,' Emma interrupted.

'Yes, you're right it has been a bit shit but we're here together now and I never thought that we'd have that again and I just wanted to say that I love you all and I'm so blessed to have you all as my sisters.'

'Oh crap. I need a drink before I start crying again,' Beatrice said as she reached for her glass of champagne.' She immediately put her glass down as Emma let out a scream, which caused a waiter to stop in his tracks and for other diners to turn their heads.

'What the hell Ems,' Lucinda said as Emma leaned over the table and handed over her iPhone to Lucinda.

'How on earth did you manage…?' Lucinda said as she read the email again, not quite believing what she was reading.

'It doesn't matter. All that matters is that I did it. I got you Ronnie Scott's,' said Emma.

FIFTY-FOUR

'SO, HOW does it feel to finally be home?' Owen said as he placed the last of the cardboard boxes on the floor.

'It feels, I don't know. I really don't know,' Lucinda replied suddenly feeling overwhelmed by the fact that after nearly six months she was now walking into her own house. Madeline had left the house absolutely spotless and had even gone so far as to hire painters and decorators. The front door gleamed after being sanded down and painted in a glossy lilac and all of the rooms had been repainted to give the house a fresh, clean, welcoming feel.

'Hey come on,' Owen said as he put his arms around her. 'This is a good thing. Look how far you've come and being back here is a sign of that.'

'You're right,' Lucinda said as she put her arms around Owen's neck and kissed him. 'Where are the twins?' Owen asked. He'd only met them a few times and didn't think they'd react warmly to finding him kissing their mother in their living room.

'Don't panic. They won't be home for ages yet,' Lucinda

replied as she kissed him again. 'You know, I still can't believe all of this is happening to me,' she said.

'Well you should do. We're allowed to have good things in our life, Lou. You're definitely a good thing in my life. I don't even regret how we met.'

'As I recall, you were shouting at me in the street.'

'It wasn't really shouting. It was more like an enthusiastic conversation.' Lucinda laughed and leaned into him to kiss him again but stopped when she heard her name being called.

'Who's that?' Owen asked as he stepped out into the corridor where the front door was still open.

'It sounds like my dad,' Lucinda replied.

'Lulu, why have you got the front door wide open?' Richard said as he walked into the corridor.

'Will, you stop rushing about,' Felicia said as she emerged behind him. 'You're still recovering you know. Oh hello,' Felicia said as she spotted Owen in the corridor.

'Mum, dad what are you doing here?'

'Your father insisted that I bring him,' Felicia said as she hugged her daughter.

'Well, you're not letting me go to the show tomorrow so I thought I'd pop in and see how you're doing,' Richard said, without taking his eyes off Owen. 'But you seem to be doing ok.'

'Hello Mr. LeSoeur. I'm Owen, Lou's erm…'

'You're probably a bit old to be calling yourself her boyfriend, so what is it partner, significant other?' Richard said as he shook Owen's hand.

'Richard. For Pete's sake, I'm Felicia. It's nice to meet you finally,' Felicia said as she shook his hand also. 'Just ignore him. I think that he's got cabin fever.'

'So would you if you were cooped up in hospital for three weeks and then you were stuck at home,' Richard said as he walked along the corridor, running his hands against the wall and inspected the paintwork on the ceiling.

'Lulu, tells us that you own a restaurant,' Richard said.

'Yes, I do,' Owen replied as he followed Richard. 'If you're planning on staying for a short while, perhaps you'd like to come for a late lunch.'

Felicia shook her head as she watched Richard and Owen walk away. 'He's been driving me mad all week.'

'Well, it can't be much fun for him being stuck at home all day.'

'I know all that but he's acting like he's cured but who knows what could happen. I just don't want him pushing it. He's still not fully recovered from the surgery.'

'Mum, you wouldn't be happy if he was just sitting at home feeling sorry for himself. You know what dad's like, he wants to feel part of the world.'

'I know and I shouldn't complain when I think about the alternative. But anyway, let's not dwell. He seems nice, your friend.'

'Oh, Owen. Yeah he is nice. He's really nice. I've been really lucky with everything.'

'You're blessed child. You'll have to invite him round for Sunday dinner.'

'I don't think he's ready for that. Not all of us all at once.'

'Well, you may just have to. I can't see you hosting a

dinner party anytime soon,' Felicia said as she looked around the chaos of the room. There was furniture that hadn't yet been arranged and boxes that had yet to be unpacked. Lucinda could have stayed in the rental house for a few more weeks but as soon as Madeline had handed back her keys with a caveat that the decorators needed just one more day, Lucinda had gone straight there. Walking into her own house was the final piece in the convoluted puzzle that had been her life.

'Oh mum, I've got something to show you. I wanted you to be the first person to see it. Just wait there,' Lucinda said as she left the room and ran up the stairs to her bedroom. Felicia did what she was told; she could hear Richard and Owen talking in the next room. She laughed. Owen didn't know what he'd let himself in for. As she waited she spotted an open box filled with framed photographs. She picked up one that she'd never seen before. Lucinda, Jessica, Beatrice and Emma had been captured. The love between them radiated from the picture that the waiter had helpfully taken of them that day Jessica had walked away from her old life.

'Can I have this?' Felicia asked when Lucinda walked into the room. Lucinda looked down at the photo in her mother's hand.

'Of course you can,' Lucinda replied as she took the photo out of her hand and replaced it with a book.

Bon Jè, ' Felicia exclaimed as she looked down at the book in her hand. 'A Seat in My Kitchen by Lucinda LeSoeur.' She read out loud as she began to flick through the pages.

'It's just a proof copy but I wanted you to be the first to read it,' Lucinda said as she kissed her mother.

'I'm so proud of you,' Felicia said as she hugged her daughter. 'I really couldn't be prouder.'

* * * *

'Mom, you need to relax. Do some yoga or something,' Katelyn said as she watched her mother pace around her bedroom. 'You're doing my head in.'

'Auntie Lou, do you want me to call my mum?' Lena asked as she sat next to Katelyn on the bed.

'No. Don't be silly. I'm fine. I'm fine.'

'You've been to the toilet like five times already.'

'I could be making a big mistake. A really big mistake. What if I'm terrible?'

'Please, that's not going to happen. Mom, you're not going to be terrible,' Katelyn said. 'Come on, there's nothing to panic about. What is it you always say? "There's nothing to panic about, as soon as it's over it just becomes a memory."'

'Well what if no one turns up?'

'Oh for the love of God,' Lena said. 'It's sold out. You've been sold out for weeks. There's no way that no one is not going to show up.'

'I always hated being on stage without your mum and Auntie Bea,' Lucinda said as she sat down on the bed between her niece and daughter. 'No matter how I was feeling on the night, I always knew that when I turned to my left Jessica would be there and when I turned to my right, Bea would be there. This time it's going to be just me.'

'Mom, stop worrying. You've done it before and people

would come and see you if you were just reading out the train announcements at Charing Cross Station.'

'Ok, I'll stop worrying,' Lucinda said with a laugh. 'Right, let's do a last check that we've got everything and then we'll just wait for cab.'

'No way, are they here already?' Lena said as they heard the front door bell.

'I'll get it,' Reece shouted out from the bottom of the stairs. Lucinda busied herself with allocating her bags and outfits and makeup bags when she heard a familiar voice that made her want to smile from the inside.

'Lou, where are you honey?' Harrie's voice boomed as she made her way up the stairs.

'Harrie,' Lou screamed as she ran towards the staircase.

'Surprise,' Harrie screamed as the two women ran into other's arms. 'Jesus Christ, I can't breathe,' Harrie said when they finally let go of each other.

'What are you doing here? You said there was no way that you could come.'

'Like anything was going to stop me. I wanted to surprise you. Did you really think that your best friend wasn't going to be here for your big comeback?'

'Oh Harrie. You have no idea how happy I am to see you and your bump,' Lucinda said as she placed her hand on Harrie's stomach and gently rubbed it.

'Do you know that you're the only person that I let do that? I've missed you so much,' Harrie said. 'So how are you feeling? Are you ready?'

'No, she's on the verge of a breakdown,' Katelyn said as she went to get her own hug from Harrie.

'Well, it's a good thing that I'm here,' Harrie said. 'So, how's my favourite goddaughter?'

'I'm good. I've missed you,' Katelyn said 'Oh, this is my cousin, Lena.'

'Wow, you look so much like your mother,' Harrie said as she kissed Lena on the cheek. 'Right, how long have we got to go?'

'About forty minutes,' Katelyn replied.

'That's enough time for me to jump in the shower and for your mother to get a shot of vodka down her throat,' said Harrie.

* * * *

'I still can't believe that she's doing this.' Beatrice said as she walked into the famous Ronnie Scotts jazz club. The place was already packed and there was a buzz of excitement and anticipation in the air. It had taken Beatrice and Jessica a while to reach the VIP area as they had stopped to take selfies and sign autographs for Euterpe fans.

'Do you ever miss it?' Beatrice asked.

'Honestly?' Jessica replied as she looked at the stage where Lucinda's band was setting up. 'I do. I miss it all the time. I miss the buzz of being up on the stage and singing and knowing that everyone out there is for you. There's nothing like it.'

'Oh my God, me too. I told Jake that I didn't miss the travelling, and hotel rooms and mindless interviews or being in a recording studio singing the same line over and over but I do miss the stage. God, I think that I might even be jealous,' Beatrice said as she sat down in the red velvet chair.

'Thank God you're here. You should have seen the queue outside,' Felicia said as she arrived at the booth with Rachel, her sister-in-law.

'Mum, you made it. Hi auntie Rachel,' Jessica said. 'You both look fantastic.'

'Do you really think so? I didn't think that your sister would forgive me if I didn't make the effort.'

'This takes me back,' Rachel said as she hugged her nieces. 'Your uncle proposed to me here. He was drunk as a skunk and he couldn't remember anything the following morning but this is where he did it. Oh my God, look at you two,' Rachel said when Lena and Katelyn appeared. They were both dressed up and looked so much older. 'They look just like their mothers.'

'I think I was Lena's age when Lou came up for the name for the group.' Beatrice said.

'God we were so young,' Jessica replied as she looked proudly at her daughter.

'Euterpe! I thought it was the most ridiculous name ever.'

'I had no idea what it meant and when I asked Lou she said, "I want us to be unique. I want us to be remembered." I told her no one will know what it means, no one will remember us.'

'It means Giver of Delight.'

Everyone turned their heads to the direction of the voice.

'Hey, you made it,' Katelyn said. 'Wow, you actually own a

suit and shoes.'

'Of course I made it,' Carter replied as he shoved Katelyn playfully. 'Sorry, but I had a bit of an obsession with Greek mythology when I was younger. Euterpe was one of the muses. The muse of music. Hi. I'm Carter.'

'So, you're Carter. I'm Jessica,' Jessica said as she shook his hand.

'No wonder Lulu was spending so much time at the studio. He's quite fit,' Beatrice whispered into Jessica's ear. 'Hi, I'm Beatrice,' she said, shaking his hand.

'You wouldn't believe the traffic out there,' Emma said as she pushed through the crowd. 'I can't believe you lot got here before me. I need a drink.'

Carter turned around to face Emma and there was no mistaking the look that passed between them as if Eros had passed through at that exact moment.

'Oh,' Emma said, feeling for the first time in her life slightly lost for words as she felt a slight twinge of electricity pass through her as she shook Carter's hand. 'You must be Emma,' he said.

'I am, I'm Emma,' she said.

'Why don't I go and organise some drinks for you ladies,' Carter said, still holding onto Emma's hand.

'Looks like I arrived just in time then. Hi everyone,' Sal said as he slapped Carter on the back. 'Come on then, seeing that you're buying.' Sal said as he pushed Carter away.

'That's Carter?' Emma said as she watched them walk away. Both Jessica and Beatrice nodded.

'And he's single,' Katelyn added as she smiled at her aunt

Emma. 'I mean really, really single auntie Emma. Like no attachments - no women who just want to be friends. Nothing'

'Alright, thank you very much young lady,' Emma said as she turned her head and caught Carter looking back at her.

There was still another twenty minutes to go and the place was now full putting to rest any beliefs Lucinda had that no one would turn up. Owen had arrived not fully realising how it'd feel to be subjected to seven LeSoeur women at the same time. 'Wow, there are a lot of you,' he said as he stepped towards the table.

'Don't let them scare you,' Emma said as she introduced him to everyone. It didn't take long for Owen to find himself subjected to a full-scale interrogation by Jessica and Beatrice whilst Felicia and Rachel sat back bemused.

'Our Lou always seems to land on her feet doesn't she?' Rachel said to Felicia. 'If I was thirty years younger I'd have him myself.'

'Jesus Christ,' Felicia said as she took a glass of champagne from the waiter who had arrived at their table, feeling relieved that Owen would have the sanctuary of male company as Sal and Carter returned to the table.

'Hey everybody,' Harrie said, as she threw herself down onto a spare chair feeling slightly flustered after her own battle through the crowd. She began to fan herself frantically with a drinks menu. 'Lou's ready but she's slightly nervous. I don't know why, she could do this standing on her head.'

'I should go and see her. She was fine when I spoke to her earlier,' said Owen.

'No disrespect but I was thinking it'd be a good idea if you guys went to see her,' Harrie said as she turned towards Jessica, Beatrice and Emma.

'You know what,' Emma said to Jessica and Beatrice. 'Maybe you two should go. It's only right.'

'Bloody hell, you're not planning on dancing in those things,' Beatrice said as she entered the small dressing room.

'God no. I plan to walk on that stage, grab the mike and not move for an hour and a half,' Lucinda said as she stood up. 'How do I look? Because If I look anything like I'm feeling that's not a good thing.'

'You look fantastic. But let me just fix this,' Beatrice said as she untwisted the strap on Lucinda's dress. Jessica looked around the dressing room.

'God this takes me back,' Jessica said as she perched herself on the dressing table. 'But it's a lot better than that poor excuse for a dressing room that we had to get ready in when we performed at the Spectre Grand.'

'There was nothing grand about that place.' Beatrice shuddered at the memory of being forced to get dressed in a freezing cold toilet and having to apply their makeup in the corridor with a flickering light whilst Lucinda had sat with her back to the toilet door to stop people from going in.

'I'm so glad that you're here.' Lucinda said.

'Where else would we be?' Jessica said as she grabbed each of her sister's hands.

THE SISTERS

The club erupted as soon as Lucinda stepped out onto the stage. Felicia had never heard anything like it and had found herself standing up and screaming Lucinda's name with everyone else. Lucinda looked out from the stage and blew a kiss to where her family were standing. She even managed to spot Henry, Brandon and Darren who enthusiastically waved back feeling quite honoured that not only had Lucinda remembered them but she'd also added them to the VIP guest list. She had to stop herself from laughing when she saw the look on Darren's face when he realised that he was standing only 2 feet away from Jessica.

'Good evening everyone. Before I start, I just want to thank you all from the bottom of my heart. I wouldn't be here if it wasn't for your love and support and I definitely wouldn't be here if it wasn't for my family and I would never ever have stepped onto his stage if it wasn't for my sisters, which is why I'm dedicating this first song to them.'

'Grandad, it's starting,' Reece said as he turned up the volume on the TV. Even at the last minute, Felicia was reluctant to leave Richard alone in the house until Reece had offered to stay with his grandad and Jake had called to say that he would make it a boy's night. Stephen had arrived just in time with boxes of pizza and beer. For those who couldn't get a ticket, Sal had come up with the idea of streaming Lucinda's comeback gig on her website, for a fee of course. So, once again, Reece had hooked up his laptop to the television and brought Ronnie Scott's into Richard and Felicia's living room. Richard leaned forward in his chair unable to stop the smile and the joy that he felt at seeing his daughter back on the stage where she belonged. Even Beatrice's twins were transfixed as they sat with Jake on the sofa and watched their aunt perform. There was no mistaking the presence that Lucinda had on stage and that she was born for this.

'I've got one request to make,' Lucinda said to the crowd as she finished her encore performance of Stripped Back.

'Oh no,' Beatrice said as she instinctively knew what was going to happen next.

'She wouldn't dare,' Jessica said. 'I haven't sung in years.'

'The last thing that I sung was "Twinkle, Twinkle Little Star" to Sam this morning.'

'I know how much you all loved Euterpe,' Lucinda continued. 'And I'm sure that you'd love it as much as I would if my sisters Jessica and Beatrice, joined me on stage.' The crowd erupted into a frenzy as the spotlight found Jessica and Beatrice. Despite their initial hesitation, neither of them could resist the lure of the stage or the cheers of the crowd.

'Don't for one minute expect me to dance,' Beatrice said as she took the microphone from one of the sound crew and took her place to Lucinda's right.

'I wouldn't dream of it,' Lucinda said with a smile. 'Are you ready?' she asked as she turned to Jessica who was on her left.

'No, but what the hell,' Jessica replied as she looked out into the crowd and heard the opening bars of their first number one 'Electrify.'

'It's mummy,' Issy shouted when Beatrice appeared on the stage waving at the crowd and begun to sing the opening line of Electrify.

'I've never ever seen them perform live together. Look at them. They're amazing. My wife is amazing,' Jake said proudly as the twins got up and started dancing in the middle of the room. Richard couldn't say a word; the immense swelling of pride stopping him from speaking and covering up the pain that he was feeling from the surgery. It was only when the sisters finished singing and hugged each other on stage before giving in to the crowd's chants for another song that he was able to speak.

'They fixed it.'

THE END

ACKNOWLEDGMENTS

Now, before I go any further, mum, I'm putting this in black and white. No, this book is not about you and no you're not in it. But seriously, mum and dad thank you for everything and for always being supportive of my dreams and for giving me all of your library cards when I was younger.

Gaynor and Lavinia. Yes, you two. You're both priceless and I honestly have no idea where I would be without your continued encouragement.

I have the most amazing, funny and beautiful aunts. Roslyn (*The Children of Cherry Tree Farm, have a lot to answer for*), Glenis and Elma. Thank you for being amazing and your continued support. *(This is turning into an Oscar speech. Cue music)* I couldn't get away without mentioning my two brothers, Gavin and Jason, who provided me with much needed entertainment when I procrastinated. Thank you for being geeks just like me.

Thanks again to you and to all of my friends and family.

The Sisters wouldn't have seen the light of day if it weren't for my editor, Keidi Keating. She really is a book angel. I can't thank you enough. Final thanks to Dalim and Polgarus Studios for making my book complete.

Thank you very much for buying and reading *The Sisters*. I sincerely hope that you enjoyed reading it as much I enjoyed writing it.

ABOUT THE AUTHOR

Nadine Matheson was born and still lives in London. She is a lawyer and now a writer. *The Sisters* is her first book, however, there's a lot more to come.

You can visit her at
www.nadinematheson.com
and send a tweet to
@nadinematheson

Printed in Great Britain
by Amazon